Blue Streets and Avenues

A. Claire

978-0-6485543-4-9

Cover Art by Xenia Sorokina

Edited by Katie Livingston

Typset by Katie Livingston

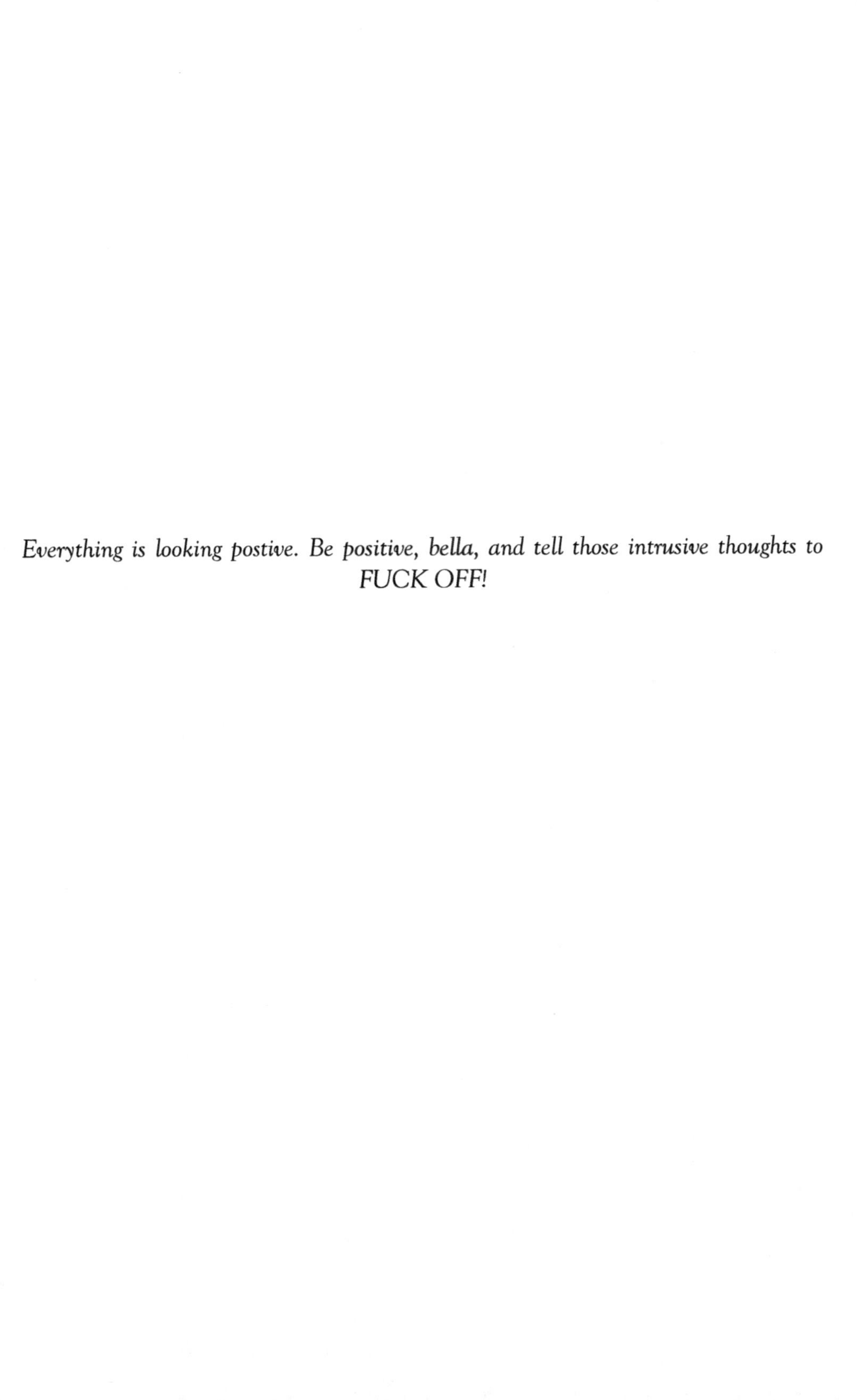

Everything is looking postive. Be positive, bella, and tell those intrusive thoughts to
FUCK OFF!

Chapter One

RAYNE

Boston was so cold in January. I personally thought it was warmer in December this year, or maybe it was the leftover Christmas spirit people let loose around the city at night. Whatever it was, I was a Grinch around the time of giving, because I honestly had nobody to give to.

I moved to New England just a year ago, and my mom and dad couldn't have been more proud of me, that is, if they were. They hated the idea, and I never got along with my drunk of a father and workaholic of a mother. The two of them seemed to be doing just fine back in Florida without me, I hadn't received a call since my birthday; even that was a great reminder that I was a failure in their eyes.

I was twenty-two years old, dead set on living my own life and busking on platform three at South Station, I got by. I lived in a crappy rundown apartment just east of the station, it was only a thirty-minute walk, but I won't lie; Boston at night was pretty scary, and I would rather a nice warm bed in a welcoming home than where I lived now.

Every morning since May last year, I'd lugged my guitar strap over my shoulder, pulled along my mic and speaker and made my way down to South Station. I bought the same type of bagel, making sure that it had cream cheese on it, then stepped down the tall cement stairs leading to platform three. I then set up right against the side of it, threw my cap upon the pavement, plugged my guitar in and hoped to make some cash.

South Station was always bustling, and the type of people I saw every day depended on what time I decided to get out of bed. I tried to make it to my spot before ten in the morning, my voice was croaky and harsh around that time, and I was able to sing low tune blues without much effort. I saw men in suits in the morning, holding their

Boston Bugles with one hand, their suitcases with the other. Women done-up top to bottom in pretty work dresses, cell phones to their ears. Even though I sang in the morning, they never really made the effort to listen – that's the problem with people these days, they're so focused on their phones.

In the mornings, I got my typical grouchy passers-by, the ones who turned their noses up and scoffed to see a young woman playing guitar and asking for change. They probably thought I was homeless, which I could have been many times before if not for that one kind soul who'd come along by, who appreciated good music and decided to give me a twenty-dollar note, or a ten.

But, that didn't happen most days, the last time someone ever popped a ten in my hat was a month ago.

The afternoon was a better time for my money making, I had a lot of younger people who hung out with their friends and nodded to me as they passed, some threw loose change in my hat, and I was definitely appreciative of whatever nice comments I was given, especially if it was from a cute girl.

By night time, it would get too cold, and people were more dead set on jumping on their trains and getting home before they froze to death.

I'd gotten used to it, and dressed comfortably for these cold winter days, even if it was the same pair of black skinny leg jeans, a worn out t-shirt, whatever sweater I had lying around, and my dad's old red aviator jacket. It was a much bigger size than I was – I was rather tall, but he was rather big and I found myself having to pull the sleeves up as I strummed my guitar strings. Sometimes, it was quiet and not one person would speak, my voice would echo along the tracks and I felt truly lonely.

It was hard to not get lost in my own songs, I would try and change my music up a little day by day, but every night I ended my busking shift with a song that all depended on what my heart felt, and usually it ached.

True, I was lonely and frightened for most of my stay in Boston. I had only a few friends: those I'd met at bars at night, girls I had one-night stands with.

But, no true friend to call my own, not one that I could hang with and have a conversation with. It got pretty sad down here on platform three.

Today, I found myself at South Station later than usual, mid-afternoon when it began to rain. Platform three was undercover-well, most of it- so I dried myself off and made sure that my guitar was tuned correctly, even if that meant checking constantly before I started a new song.

It was busy when I finished a cover of 'For You' by Angus and Julia Stone, and many youths around my spot had turned their heads to listen. Even over the roaring trains that puffed into their terminals, I continued to sing.

I was never one to make eye contact with anyone when I sang, only sometimes to those who popped money in my hat, a sign of thanks, I never focused on those around me.

But I was glad I changed that today.

I took a moment to breathe between the second verse and chorus, to fix the mess of my long black hair, pulling it all to the left, baring my undercut.

My fingers had begun to ache, the cold three o'clock breeze chilled my already shaky playing digits.

On the corner of my left eye, a flurry of red caught my attention, just slightly.

I was curious, and I could multitask.

A few feet away to my left stood a girl. She had to be about my age and wore a vibrant long red coat, nothing like I'd seen before. She was focused on her cell phone, but as I sang the chorus, in her direction, she turned her attention to me.

I instantly focused on her eyes, beautiful green orbs that fluttered my way. Her hair was a dark brown, medium length and only a little messy. On her head she wore a black cap, like the reporters used to wear back in the forties, my dad had one laying around the house.

She caught me staring, and I felt frozen on the spot, unable to tear my tired eyes away from hers. She smiled gently, scanned me for a moment, then fiddled with her phone again.

I brought my voice to the chorus, turning my head to face a couple who stood before me; a short man and a woman who smiled and dropped a few coins into my hat. I nodded once, but had to fight the urge to turn my head left again, to stare.

I waited till I reached the chorus again, my voice strained as I pushed my limits, okay maybe I was trying to show off just a little, to a gorgeous girl like that? How couldn't I.

I peeked with my left eye, and she had shifted, she leant against the same wall of the stairwell as I, with a brown knee-length boot kicked up behind her.

I had a moment to myself, I worried that she'd look my way and think I was being rather creepy by singing and making eye contact, she probably thought I was begging for money. I whipped my view away just as she began to turn her attention my way again. I didn't want that, even if this was just momentarily.

I felt my head falter for a moment, as the train down on the right roared this way. It screeched over my music, the strums of my guitar and the pulling of my lungs. I eased my head away from the peircing horn of the train, and watched as the waiting passengers around me began to fluster. Most, but a small number quickly handed my hat a few dollars and I did not stop singing once – I couldn't stop mid song to say thank you, and I thought that might be a little rude of me.

The rain began to harden from outside, some of the snow blew in and chilled my legs, my boots were already wet and muggy. I shivered, but my suffering was soon to come to an end. From the corner of my eye yet again I saw the girl in the red coat step my way.

She faltered around me for a moment, not too close though not too far. I could see her face clearly now, and she was gorgeous. A slightly tanned woman with distinct freckles across her nose and sprinkled along her upper cheeks. I lowered my voice to the end of the chorus, had it been five minutes already? I thought as I tapped my guitar's body instead of the song's classic drum set bass. The train haltered, as I finished my song, and I smiled like a complete idiot when she passed me a ten-dollar note. I hoped my hand was clean when I opened my right palm for her. The brunette kept making quick glances to the train and then back to me, as she placed the note nicely into my hand and nodded, like a thank you. *Please*, I felt like saying. *I should be the one thanking you!*

But, I only returned a nod myself, and watched her board the train towards West Boston. It emptied rather quick around my standing place, the train down west was usually packed, but I took a few glances, to see her find a seat on the carriage.

The rain was at its peak now, a cold shower that I could hear over the bustling of feet.

Though I felt much warmer where I stood, remembering those green eyes.

Chapter Two

RAYNE

I had to admit, that little interaction earlier in the afternoon left me quite giddy. I don't really understand why, but the more I thought about it the less I cared about my anxious feelings, all I know is it that made me happy in that very short moment.

I think I watched that train ride off down west, until it became a speck of black and fissured from my vision. I held that ten-dollar note in my hand, and I squeezed it quite tightly.

Who would have thought the day I was late to my spot in South Station, I would experience something like that, some gorgeous brunette taking the time to give me her hard-earned cash. I felt a little selfish.

As more passengers began to flock around me, I realised I'd been standing there in silence for a good ten minutes. The clock upstairs on the main floor began to chime, notifying us that it'd struck five in the afternoon, I only had a few more hours before I would leave.

My guitar was freezing in my hands and the strings would sting whenever I strummed them. I had to buy some sort of gloves before I got back to my apartment, or all that would be left of Rayne Holmes and her solo busking career would be two frozen solid hands next to a ragged snapback hat.

I sniffled, slipped the note into the pocket of my jeans and cleared my throat.

Again, as I sang my next song, a slower tune, I went back to making no eye contact with those around me. Instead, I closed my eyes and secretly hoped that young woman would be back tomorrow, maybe for just a moment. I could feel my mind wander off, into an abyss of worries and future endeavours, something I was quite used to.

I always forgot to think about the present and lived in either the past or the future.

I was never quite happy with what or where I was, or who I turned out to be.

At least a good night's sleep, a warm cigarette and a beer would numb those thoughts for just a few hours.

When I decided to clean up on platform three, I had about forty dollars all up from the days busk. It was pretty good, and my daily haul was always wavering between twenty and fifty, it was a confidence boost, on most days.

I packed up my things, just as it began to softly snow outside, I contemplated sitting the faint storm out, so I wouldn't get a cold, but I really wanted out of this station, at night it always ended up smelling like day-old piss.

After I'd shoved my equipment into my duffel bag, and thrown my guitar over my shoulder once again, I rummaged through my pockets for a cigarette. It was an awful habit, but it kept me warm on these chilly nights. Man, was my guitar always this heavy? I thought when I roamed back towards the north of South Station. I grimaced and lifted it higher over my shoulder, I needed to buy a new strap for the instrument, when I had a few more bucks to spare.

The walk to my apartment was quiet and, apart from the ice-cold snowflakes that stuck to my hair and clothes, actually pretty peaceful, my cigarette didn't even go out, it was my kind of day.

Just one block from my current housing, there was this little convenience store that I'd bought my necessities from. Y'know, the basic stuff, tissues, snacks, beer and toilet paper, that's all you needed to live, right?

The glass door made its usual bell ring as I entered, and from my left at the counter, stood Carla. She was in her late forties, short and pretty grubby, always chewing on a piece of jerky, hair always a mess.

'Hey,' I sighed, then proceeded to brush the snow from my jacket.

'Hey to you too!' Carla snapped. 'Don't go brushin' that shit all over my store floor.'

I grouched her way, she was always being so goddamn passive aggressive. I think from my year of coming in and out of this place, she's only truly gotten angry at me about one thing, and that was the fact I had a knack of rubbing my boots against her welcome mat.

But Carla had been good to me, she'd given me discounts when I never even asked for them, told me she had been on the same page as I, living alone in Boston with two shit parents; so a discount on two minute noodles was necessary for my survival.

It was nice to hear someone else's story; her negativity never really lifted my spirits that much but I was appreciative of her support, if that's what you'd call it.

'Jesus, sorry,' I laughed shortly. I took a step back and opened my arms. 'I come in peace.'

Carla scoffed my way, she rolled her eyes and mumbled something under her breath, but I took no notice to what she had said.

'How was your day, kiddo?' she asked, voice croaky with a heavy Boston accent. 'You seem less miserable than usual.'

I chuckled as I grabbed a few packs of instant ramen from the shelves, saltines and whatever candy was cheapest. I'd been living on instant noodles for five months now, and I missed the warm feeling of a home-cooked meal. I mean, sometimes I found myself at McDonalds for a late dinner, and I tried my absolute best to not look like a homeless person.

'Is that so?' I asked, sarcastically. 'I made some pretty good cash today.'

I shrugged my shoulders as I spoke and roamed to the back of this tiny corner store, giving the beer a quick scan. From the counter, Carla huffed yet another laugh. 'Straight to the beer then.'

I smirked and grabbed a four pack of Zoom Bourbon, a mixture of cola and whisky, it went down with my awful cooking skills, or maybe it just made swallowing whatever I'd cooked easier.

I made my way back towards Carla, and she quickly glanced to my haul, piled up in my shivering arms. She was judging, as per usual.

'A nice selection, and I'm guessing you want cigarettes too,' she asked, turning to face the back wall, where the cigarettes were held.

I thought for a moment, it was a disgusting habit but it was honestly the only thing I found myself doing when I took a break from singing, I wasn't a chain smoker, more a casual. Either way, it was a shitty habit to have.

'Yeah,' I mumbled. 'Whatever is cheapest.'

As she rambled through the cupboards, I salvaged the cash I had. I pulled the ten-dollar note from my pocket, and as I leant forward to drop it on the counter, I paused.

Another thought fell over my mind in that store, I don't know if it was just overthinking or another feeling of uninvited guilt, but I had a pretty good idea that the girl who had given me this note, would rather me spend it on my rent, or on a good meal.

Not on cigarettes.

I rubbed the back of my neck, grimacing when I pocketed it back. 'Actually, I'll pass on the smokes.'

Carla turned with a grouch, and I grinned sheepishly. 'Sorry.'

She scanned through my items, and with the Zoom Bourbon it all came to about twelve bucks, not bad at all, I still had a few dollars to pop in the rent jar back at my apartment.

Carla sighed and handed me the grocery bag, a bright green plastic monstrosity of a thing with *Thank you!* written all over it. I think if Carla had her way, she'd be handing bags with *Fuck off!* written on them instead.

'Alright, kid,' she eyed the door. 'Go home.'

'Yeah, yeah,' I sighed, content on leaving and getting somewhere warm. 'I'll see you soon.'

'I hope not.'

'Ha ha.'

My sarcastic tone brought a smile to her lips, she waved me off again.

After the short walk home, passing houses with children playing in the snowstorm, fathers coming home from work and greeting their wives with a kiss at the door, faint laughs from inside houses. I felt that awful feeling of loneliness once again. I too missed the early childhood memories of my father coming home, before he became the biggest asshat of the century.

By seven, I was lugging myself up the stairs to my apartment. I passed the door of my landowner, another angry Boston resident, who lived with her anxious wreck of a brother. She was pretty harsh, I wonder what was going on in her life to be so negative all the time, but I made sure to have my monthly pay ready early, and kept away from her wrath.

Ah, I thought as I reached my door, right down at the end of the cold hallway of the building.

Home sweet home.

I shoved my key in the lock, jiggled it a little and turned, receiving a blow of musky old apartment smell. For what I paid, it wasn't so bad.

A three room apartment, one bedroom, a bathroom and kitchen. The colour was terrible, everything had a shade of black and brown, miserable.

But it had heating, that's all I cared about right now.

I closed the door behind me, ignoring the sound of the next-door neighbour and his wife arguing, and turned on the lights.

I took a deep breath, and finally dropped my duffel bag, it emitted a large thump on cue. Next was my guitar, I slid that off and placed it neatly across the TV unit, out of everything I owned, it was the most precious.

No guitar, no money.

After I'd dragged my tired feet to my kitchen, I stripped from my big bulky jacket, and laid that across the ragged couch. With all that weight of my shoulders, I could finally relax these sore muscles of mine.

I didn't go to gym here in Boston, but I tried hard to keep my body at a peak prime of tone. Back in Florida I used to kickbox with my friend Cole, and that gave my stomach a hardened shell, and my arms the strength they needed to lift a duffel bag with all that equipment. A few sit ups here and there worked pretty well.

I tensed my neck, trying my hardest to release a nice crack of my bones. Man, this weather did nothing but leave my body exhausted. I couldn't stay up past ten these nights, either that or I fell asleep on the couch watching whatever junk played on TV.

I yawned heavily, kicked my boots off and opened a bottle of Zoom Bourbon with my belt buckle.

As I sculled, I took a moment to savour the taste in my mouth, the rush of alcohol as it hit my many senses. I listened to the sirens outside my windows, the dreary groan of the fridge and the pipes surrounding the apartment complex.

When I dropped the bottle from my lips, I sighed loudly, it definitely did hit the spot, even if it failed to fill an empty void deep inside my chest.

Before I slept that night, I showered and skimmed through a photo album that I'd brought from Florida. I kept it close to my bed and always focused on one photo in particular. I think everyone tends to look back on prime times of their lives, try to relive that moment inside their minds, or in dreams. For me, looking at this particular photo of my family left a sour taste in my mouth, but on some days I yearned to be back home in Florida, if I knew I was welcome there.

I grumbled to myself, and reached for my jeans on the floor. Again, my fingers wrapped around that ten-dollar note, and I placed it into my nightstand drawer, alongside a bunch of other notes for my end of month pay.

As I slept that night, my mind began to wander again. I tried my absolute hardest to focus on anything else but whatever worried me, and found it quite easy to relax at the thought of seeing her again tomorrow.

Her, as in green eyes, the girl who hadn't left my train of thought since late this afternoon. Man, what was I? A teenager again? Unable to get one pretty girl off my mind, when we made contact for less than a few minutes?

I groaned loudly and threw myself under my itchy blanket, I definitely needed sleep.

Chapter Three

RAYNE

I didn't have a cell phone, so I relied on my body clock to wake me up in the morning. My negativity surrounding technology came as a blessing, I wasn't used to all that negative crap on social media. However, my parents called the apartment landline, it was so awkward whenever the owner would come knocking at my door, handing me this grotty small house phone.

I opened my eyes at the crack of dawn, very unlike me. I was used to waking up multiple times every morning, I'd dream I was up and walking to South Station, grabbing my bagel and setting up in my spot, then find out I was dreaming the whole goddamn time.

But, this morning was different.

I lay there, in the morning cold, covered by my itchy blanket and with my head against my flat pillow. Yet my eyes were wide awake, peering up at my blotchy ceiling. On my bedside table, the wall clock digits struck six in the morning, and I felt a groan escape my parted lips.

Well, I was awake now. No use laying here, time to get productive.

I chuckled to my thoughts as I rose; what a joke, me being productive? I sulked out of bed, dragging my tired body into the bathroom. If being productive meant, hurry to the same station for a year now, play a series of the same songs and eat the same bagel twice a day, if I was lucky. Then I was destined to be the most productive person in the world.

I yawned as I changed, three loud dinosaur sounding stretches, and a quick sneeze.

Yeah, it was still freezing in here.

My bathroom had a loose pipe somewhere, or my window had a crack in it, because the cold breeze got in so easily that it drove me absolutely mental on these chilly mornings.

I leant over my sink, and quickly washed my face with lukewarm water, swearing to myself as the chill went down my spine.

I would catch the 6:45am commuters if I was quick about it, they were usually tired and groggy but would appreciate a nice song to ease their spirits – and would hopefully show that appreciation if they popped whatever change they had lying around into my hat.

In ten minutes, I was dressed top to bottom in the warmest clothes I had, and my dad's jacket topped it off. I forgot to buy gloves yesterday, and I would probably pay for that stupid mistake. My hands were already shaking as I grabbed my guitar and my duffel bag, hauling them over my shoulders.

Thursdays in Boston the city was busier, and I could make out multiple fresh footprints in the two inches of snow as I walked down my street. I don't remember the last time I had gotten up this early before. The wind was picking up, trees shivering beside me as I walked, dead leaves crunched under my boots.

My breath was visible in the morning cold, and I blew into my hands to keep them toasty. From beside me, the same houses I passed last night were just waking up under the sun. Some already up and shovelling the new snow from their driveways, some starting their cars up and some hand in hand with their kids, if my parents made me go to school this early, I would have learnt swear words at a pretty young age.

South Station was busy, as per usual. Though Murphy's Bakery was pretty quiet at this time of morning, and I spotted the older woman working on a fresh new batch of baked delights. My stomach grumbled, reminding me I hadn't eaten in hours. I patted it, quietening its angry growls.

Mrs. Murphy caught my attention, and she too glanced at the time, shocked at my early appearance. She was in her sixties and wore the same old green Rasta cap and red coat as she always wore, even in summer.

The old bag wasn't all there, but she meant no harm.

'Kid, up early?' she asked, voice harsh and slow.

I shrugged my shoulders again, smiling once. 'Yeah, surprised myself too.'

She grinned, and I could notice her eyes, bloodshot. She worked alone here at this little bakery in South Station, I felt bad for her. I wonder if she was lonely.

'Well, here you go kid.' She handed me my normal order, a plain bagel with cream cheese.

'Ah, thanks.' I smiled, handed her the correct change and then turned on my heels.

'You sing a song for me today, alright?' Mrs Murphy croaked. I'd already crunched down into my bagel, but I shared a quick glance, to nod and smile once more. 'Sure thing.'

I made my way down platform three's stairwell, trying my hardest not to bump anyone with my bulky items. I could already spot familiar faces from my time in this area, those who left the terminal for work or school, then returned back that night.

They recognised me too, but only a handful made it clear they noticed the connection.

I set up my gear once more, turned the power of my speaker and mic on, and threw my hat to my feet.

What song would I start with today, I wondered? I bit my bottom lip and chewed it as I thought, tuning my guitars whacked out strings. My notes echoed down the platform, and some turned their heads, I was used to it.

I began the chords to Kimbra's 'Two Way Street.' It was a chill song for a morning like this, and I didn't have to strain my voice as much. Unless, a pretty brunette was to come by and stand near me. I felt my ears redden from the thought, and grimaced down at my feet through lyrics. I thought maybe I'd wake up and stop thinking of that cute freckled face, oh boy was I wrong.

I gained attention from a few girls beside me, they whispered that they knew the song, their lips moved with mine and I couldn't help but smile.

I adored moments like that, when I felt my music had lightened someone's mood, even for just a second. Sometimes I cared more about those small things, than money and fame. But, we were all human and with no money, there was no life.

I leant against the back wall, the microphone picked up my voice well and I felt like showing off a bit – hey, we could all get a little cocky right?

It turns out I'd timed my cockiness perfectly this Thursday morning.

Two minutes into the song and I thought a guitar riff might be the best thing for my audience, even if it was a bunch of high school girls and working folk. My acoustic skills had been worked on for a decade, and I could focus on other things while my fingers did the work.

I watched as the westbound train made its way into the station, stopping at a screeching halt. The Boston trains were so loud and rusted, surely they'd fall apart sooner or later.

I focused on whoever walked off each carriage, some glanced my way and raised their eyebrows, others walked right past. I didn't care, I was lost in my riff and I was trying my hardest not to let my voice waver awkwardly.

And as I began to sing, there she was.

Luck was never on my side, but I was pretty happy with this timing.

She was walking towards the platform exit, which was the stairwell I set up against, and I waited for her to notice that I was the same singing girl she'd tipped just yesterday.

I focused on her coming this way, and the closer she got the more I realised she looked a little troubled. She was on her phone, holding it close to her right ear and she spoke rather vastly into it.

I felt my chest drop; maybe she wouldn't notice me today, and all that thinking about luck was bogus.

'Well, is she alright?' I heard her say. 'Is there anything I can do, at all?'

I finished my chorus, and strummed a little softer on my guitar, I didn't want to bother her serious conversation as she passed me. Even over the chatter, I heard her voice clearly, it was sweet.

The crowd she was in was huge; a big bunch of people that wanted to get out faster than whoever stood in front of them. I saw some cash being thrown into my hat, but I was too focused on her to notice anybody else..

When she was just a few feet away from me, her head turned my way. I didn't know what to do, so I just stared, it was all I had.

But, she smiled. The right side of her lip curled into a cute smirk, acknowledging me through the bustling crowd she had gotten herself caught in.

It was all I wanted that morning.

Okay, so I snuck a few more looks when she turned to the stairwell, and I saw her do the same, her ear still pressed against her phone. I felt like waving, but thought that might push it a little, so I just returned a lopsided grin.

As my song came to an end, she was gone. Around me, some clapped and dropped coins into my hat, I thanked them with the same smile, I couldn't tear it from my face.

Alright, I had to cool off. My cockiness was passing pretty fast, and I could feel my anxiety rush over my body.

What if I'd looked stupid in front of her? I knew if she'd come in from the west, she'd be taking the same train to go back.

I'd be seeing more of emerald eyes than I'd thought.

I played it cool, I think I did.

With her on my mind all day, my mood was lifted pretty highly. I found myself singing much more energetically than usual, busting out a few songs I'd keep hidden away for the weekends, when drunk adults would dance around my hat and pat me on the back, tell me I was wonderful and pass me a note. A month ago, a bunch of tipsy girls sat next to my stand and passed coins to me like I was some living jukebox.

I was totally okay with requests, to be honest, all that was going through my head during the afternoon was a scenario that maybe Emerald Eyes would ask for a song-

and to be honest I was hoping that emerald eyes would ask for a song. I surprised some of the elderly during pensioner hours; they would hobble near me, and I would purposely cover a song from the forties and fifties, it was quite adorable to see how they'd react.

I thought of myself as a people person, but around pretty girls, a bustling babbling buffoon.

I was on my feet for the majority of the day, usually I sat down and strummed a few low keys when I was tired, but I definitely did not want to miss the chance to see her again, how foolish of me.

I never, ever reacted this way to a girl before, but there was something oddly addictive to the thought of her smile, those eyes.

I crouched down in an attempt to warm myself up, by mid-afternoon it was super cold, my fingers were shaking and I had to take a break to grab an cheap coffee from the machine at the end of the platform. I took a sip and instantly regretted it, it tasted fucking awful.

My break consisted of that shit coffee, and a cigarette. It would have been the bane of my day, if it wasn't for the constant anxiety that I'd miss her if she came back. I sat next to my bag and leant my head back for a moment. My guitar had to be retuned for the fiftieth time, and I had to stretch before I became a living icicle.

When I stood up, someone got way too close to my personal space. He was standing awfully close for my likings, and I grimaced. He was middle aged, clad in a long maroon coat, dark pants and a fedora to top it off.

A cop.

'Oh, my apologies,' he said in a gruff voice.

I didn't particularly like it when the police stood in front of me, I'd only gotten into trouble with them back in Florida, when I'd stolen a packet of gum from the convenience store – man, I was grounded for three months after that.

'What can I do for you, officer?' I asked, a little too sternly. 'I'm not doing anything wrong am I?'

He laughed, and finally lifted his head. He was middle aged, maybe in his fifties, but had a very gaunt face, like he'd smoked four-thousand cigarettes in a day.

'Nah, kiddo,' he chuckled. 'Just need to check I.D.'

I swallowed nervously, relief washed over me just for a moment, but I scrambled to my bag to find my wallet. 'Alright.'

They did this a few times, to check if I was over twenty-one, if I was allowed to be on the streets busking. I sniffled and tried to bare my right sleeve, patterned in tattoos I'd gotten back home, maybe that would be enough for him to leave.

Alas, he did not.

I sighed and grabbed my grimy wallet, and flipped through the cards. When I'd found my old Florida I.D., I passed it to him with a grouch. Thankfully, he stepped back and examined it closely.

'Ah, from Florida,' he examined. 'What are you doing all the way in Boston?'

Man, I felt like kicking this guy in the shin, and telling him to back off. But I wasn't in the mood to be arrested. I looked around for a moment, some people glanced my way, how embarrassing.

'I'm just living on my own,' I admitted. 'I like to sing.'

I tried to be short, but he curled his lips into a playful smirk, then handed me my card. 'Alright.'

I pocketed my wallet, and picked my guitar up once more, hoping that would be another sign for him to go away.

'Sorry to bother you, ma'am,' he tipped his hat my way. 'I'm Detective Rodgers.'

I pursed my lips and cleared my throat, a little anxious.

'I'm not here for any trouble,' he smiled shortly. 'But I just had to do my job today, a lot of you kids are getting into the wrong stuff these days.'

I shrugged to him, 'Not me, Sir.'

He stepped back, then smiled once more. 'Alright, well...'

I waited for him to finish, and pulled my sleeve down again, my arm was getting the worst case of goosebumps. His voice was hoarse too, I felt like taking his cigarettes from him, wherever they were hidden inside that huge trench coat of his.

'You take it easy, now,' he said, then turned to make his way down platform three. I watched him from under my long locks of hair, he paused. Great.

'Also,' he lifted a finger and pointed it to my guitar, I was waiting for another question to do with my current living status, how much money I was making, what power source was I using, blah, blah, blah. 'Could I make a request?' Detective Rodgers asked.

Oh.

I felt flustered and stood with a silly look. I straightened myself up, then held the hilt of my guitar tightly. 'Sure...'

He grinned, and brushed the back of his neck with his big hands. 'It's pretty old, I'm not too sure if you'd know it.'

I chuckled back, 'Try me.'

He huffed and gave me a competitive look, a twist of his small lips.

'Alright,' he grinned. 'Undecided. Ella Fitzgerald, I bet you have no idea who that is, you're way too young. Heck, even I'm too young for her stuff.'

'Done,' I smirked, I began to strum my guitar.

He was right, this song was from the goddamn late 1930's, but I knew the track from my grandfather's old records. He had great taste that old man, too bad he passed away just two years ago.

As Detective Rodgers stood there, I began to sing and he was pleasantly surprised. His eyebrows were raised, and he nodded in approval. I took another look at his face, and located two huge scars running down his neck, man that would have hurt.

Of course, my voice was nothing like a woman from the thirties, so I had to modernise this song the best way I could.

It was an upbeat tune, and I could feel my voice strain at some of the higher chords, but nothing to worry about.

So today I bonded with a Detective, that was good karma right?

When I'd finished my song, he clapped loudly, and others did too. Most claps were probably because he was a cop, they had to, it was the law.

I chuckled weakly and he handed me a twenty-dollar note, but I honestly couldn't take it, not from a cop.

'No, it's okay,' I smiled, denying his money. 'It's alright.'

'Kid,' he said cocking his head to one side and nodding once. 'C'mon now, take it. You deserve it with a voice like that.'

I clenched my teeth together, I really didn't feel right taking money from an officer. I rubbed the back of my neck awkwardly and took the note into my own hand. 'Jeeze, thanks sir.'

Detective Rodgers left with one more genuine smile, he pocketed his hands deep into his coat, and wandered off towards the next platform, almost dazed, like he was stuck in some memory.

I cleared my throat once, still trying to piece together exactly what had just happened.

I sang a song from the thirties after being questioned by an officer, who gave me a twenty-dollar note.

Right. Completely normal day-to-day activity.

I sighed into my hands and pocketed the note. The wind kicked up again and received an unwelcome reaction from many who stood around me, I began to hear the conversations rise.

'I heard it's going to be a chiller tomorrow, negative everything!'

'It's going to be so goddamn, cold tomorrow.'

'I hate this weather; I absolutely hate it.'

'I'm seriously considering not leaving my bed for work tomorrow, not with the weather forecast.'

I rubbed my arms and glanced towards the LCD screen above platform three's entrance, and these people weren't kidding, it was going to be absolutely freezing tomorrow. But Fridays were my best days, and I made most of my cash at the end of the week.

I'd be fine.

At five-thirty, I spotted Emerald Eyes again, as I sang another low-key monotone song. The west train had stopped on que, her ride home.

She was with a friend, a tall redhead with a grunge attire, she was cool looking and wore a long black coat, a part of me hoped she wasn't her girlfriend.

As they passed me, the redhead widened her eyes, pointed at me and laughed.

'Oh, man! Is that Red?' she asked loudly. Beside her, Emerald Eyes her went absolutely red in the face, and she literally threw her cackling friend onto the nearest train carriage.

Red?

I blinked towards them, clearly I heard the whole thing, and Emerald Eyes was totally aware. She smiled to me again, very rushed, but still adorable, then turned to face her friend as the doors closed.

I think they were arguing, but the redhead had pulled Emerald Eyes into a headlock and teased her a little. She took the brunette's hat off her head, and wore it with a smirk.

Hey, at least it wasn't a kiss.

Chapter Four

RAYNE

On Friday morning, all I could think was; *fuck*.

It was the coldest morning I had experienced her in Boston, and all the clothing stores were downtown, nowhere near South Station.

I needed gloves so goddamn bad that I contemplated not even leaving my apartment that day. But I did. Of course I did after seeing Emerald Eyes blush like that. Maybe she would come say hello today.

Or maybe I should make the first step? Something told me I'd make a complete fool of myself.

I slept in today, so I probably missed her early in the morning.

I didn't think that'd sadden me as much as it did, and I hadn't even met her yet.

South Station was still busy at eleven, I would have expected at least half of the normal amount of people, given the weather.

But, life went on unfortunately and people had jobs to do, places to go.

My teeth were chattering when I reached my spot, I kicked a few pieces of trash aside and placed my bag down. I think there was actual icicles dripping from my nose, I wiped them off grumpily.

I yawned loudly, and watched a cloud of mist fly from my open mouth, I felt my body wobble.

Okay, maybe today wasn't such a good idea, I didn't even think I could sing a line of a chorus without rolling into the foetal position to shiver and shake.

The trains kept coming and going, and I sat down against my duffel bag, I should have brought a blanket, but then I'm sure I'd look more homeless than usual.

Today would consist of guitar solos, I don't think my voice was up to the challenge, and I'd rather keep myself warm, ugh but that meant money.

I sighed and cracked my knuckles, I forgot my bagel this morning too.

The day was ruined.

I played a few songs, I didn't even bother to set up my mic, not yet. I had a few people give me the thumbs up when they walked by, and I grinned sheepishly their way, before my chattering teeth took over and I hissed at the winters breeze. Yeah, I should have stayed in bed this morning.

I examined the west train roll up, and I had a habit of getting my hopes up whenever it arrived. I secretly hoped Emerald Eyes would show up, jump off one of those carriages and be wearing that iconic red coat of hers. But after three arrivals, every twenty minutes, I was starting to lose that little hope.

So what? She probably had much better things to do. A smart looking girl like her would be at home right now, probably cuddled up to some lucky guy with a smug look upon his face, probably had that stupid hairstyle with the quiff at the front. I grouched and crossed my arms over my guitar, crossed legged on the subway floor. I was a grump today; I really should have stayed in bed.

'Aren't you freezing?'

I glanced up quickly to the sweet voice, and instantly froze, but not from the cold.

Emerald Eyes asked her question as she walked by me, a little slower so I could answer. I blinked pretty harshly, wondering if this was a trick of my imagination. She stopped in her tracks, her hands pocketed in her coat. I focused on her eyes and could see how tired she seemed. A soft spot in me hoped she was getting enough sleep, she was gorgeous and I already wanted the best for her.

I could tell my mouth was parted, like a kid. And I scurried to my feet, quickly.

'Uh!' I stammered. 'Yeah! It's pretty bad.'

I rubbed the back of my neck awkwardly, and she looked me in the eye. 'Did you think I was a statue?'

Oh great, what a good joke Rayne.

Emerald Eyes laughed cutely and I felt my blood boil, the butterflies were going absolutely bonkers in my stomach.

'You definitely made me look.' She paused, held her hands together and lifted her finger, eyebrows raised. 'I-I mean as in, I thought you were frozen!'

'Yeah!'

'Uh-huh!'

We stood in silence, a quick few seconds before she waved her gloved fingers and sped off.

'Have a good day!' she called.

'Y-you too!' I replied, my voice chattered, from nervousness or the cold, I had no clue.

I watched her disappear up the stairs again and found myself contemplating rushing after her to continue talking. I was frozen on the spot, but I could feel a silly smile pull at my lips.

I was being constantly surprised these past three days, being caught off guard had its perks, even if it ended up being a little awkward.

A little awkward was cute, right?

Well, Emerald Eyes wasn't finished surprising me.

At half past four, she appeared on the corner of my eye again, while I stood and fumbled with my cigarette pack. She just had to catch me as I was putting one to my lips and taking a suck.

She held a coffee cup in her hands, and she walked slowly to my side. Again, I felt my body react unexpectedly, and I stammered on the spot.

'Hey,' she said gently. 'I thought you might like something warm, I mean, you don't have to take it, I know my mom always told me not to take things from strangers.'

It was cute, how she rambled on like that.

She never looked me in the eye when she spoke, I wonder if I was scary, I know my brown eyes were pretty dark and gloomy at times.

'I work at the café just outside the station,' she started, nodding a little. 'I just felt really bad you were out here all alone, freezing your butt off.'

I felt my cheeks blush, she really thought of me? I took the cigarette from my mouth and stepped a little closer, flipping my guitar so it pressed against my back.

'Oh, wow,' I chuckled. 'Thank you, this means a lot to me.'

It honestly did. I don't think I've ever had someone genuinely think of me that way, and we didn't even know each other's names.

I took the polystyrene cup from her hands, and was careful not to burn her with the end of my cigarette, her hands barely brushed against mine, and the contact left a static shock all over my body. Emerald Eyes nodded again, and fixed her cap, I could finally see every aspect of her face, and boy was she gorgeous, it was hard not to stare, especially if she was centimetres away from me.

'Thank you, uh...' I paused.

She gasped a little, rubbed her hands together and laughed nervously at herself. 'Oh goodness, I'm sorry!'

Again, I felt like blurting that she had nothing to be sorry about. She flashed me a smirk and passed her right hand out to me, batting her eyelashes sweetly.

'I'm Juniper,' she said. 'And you are?'

I found the perfect chance to tease her a little; it was cruel, but I meant no harm. 'Apparently I'm someone called 'Red", I think.'

Juniper's freckles were more prominent when she blushed, and she covered her face with an embarrassed chuckle.

'Oh, God,' she groaned. 'Ignore my friend, she's ridiculous.'

I was already warm from her generous drink, but hearing her name for the first time, and that beautiful laugh of hers left my heart racing faster than usual.

'Hey, I don't mind it,' I admitted. 'I'm Rayne, but Red's okay too.'

Juniper looked at me, a gentle look that hit me right in the chest. She seemed to be thinking of one thousand things in her mind, the way her eyes nervously darted to my feet and then my eyes. I glanced around us for a moment, then nodded.

'Thank you, really...' I paused, lifting the warm beverage. 'For this, I appreciate it, Juniper.'

Her name rolled off my tongue quite nicely and I found myself blushing again, maybe if I flicked my hair aside she'd think it was just me playing cool.

'You're welcome, Red,' she stifled a giggle. 'Ah, I'm so sorry for that nickname! I had no idea how to describe the girl who sat at South Station and sang such a gorgeous voice.'

The compliment got me, and I laughed over her words, shaking my head in denial. She stepped forward a little, and pushed my shoulder, the contact left my head uneasy.

'I'm serious! You have a wonderful voice, and your jacket...' Juniper paused and pointed at it. 'That was the only other thing that stood out about you, I mean! I'm not saying nothing else about you stands out, it's just such a vibrant red a-and...'

'It's okay! I honestly don't mind it,' I interrupted her, a smile on my lips. She was honestly saying all the right things; she was warming me up, right to my ears.

Juniper breathed in, and I watched her step back a little. My heartstrings began to tug, this was goodbye already?

'Okay, well I better get back to work,' Juniper mumbled sweetly. 'Before my boss goes ape.'

I nodded and kept my eyes on hers, she faltered under my gaze and fumbled a little.

'You know! You shouldn't smoke, Red,' she pointed to my cigarette, and playfully winked. 'It's awful for you.'

I felt the blood rush from my face, and the anxiety take hold of the reigns. I'd stuffed up, I knew I should have stopped smoking months ago. Though her wink had the butterflies battling in my stomach, I frowned playfully to her, and opened my mouth to explain. 'Ah, yeah!'

Good one Rayne.

Juniper lifted her right hand again and waved with her fingers.

'I'll make you a proposition!' she called over the train's roars. I blinked and waited for her to finish, my heart holding onto every word that left her mouth.

'I'll bring you a coffee every day I work, and you stop smoking.' She stopped in her tracks, 'deal?'

I raised my hand and smiled again, 'Sure, deal.'

Juniper seemed pretty content with my answer, and left.

I knew I looked stupid, standing there. I had to pinch myself, once, twice.

Okay, that definitely happened, and we definitely made contact. Of course, it was hard to make direct eye contact with her, but I really wished I had.

I stepped back, glanced up once more to make sure I was alone, and then chucked the cigarette to the floor. I examined the cup for a moment, before bringing it to my lips. The brew was sweet, just how I liked it, with a hint of caramel and vanilla. It fell down my throat and soothed every cold ache, wow.

I held tight to my beverage, and couldn't hide the smile any longer. I'd finally met Emerald Eyes, and I was a little glad I didn't have to be the one to search for her, she sought me out and that meant a hell of a lot.

I stomped the cigarette down with a smirk, there wasn't a use for those anymore, just the thought of Juniper warmed me to the brim.

Chapter Five

RAYNE

I made a deal with Juniper, and I was going to keep it.

And she kept her side of the bargain too.

When she finished work that night, we shared another small conversation, even if it was just hello and goodbye.

She was in a rush to catch her train, and I didn't want to hold her up, even if it was saddening to watch her leave.

I know it was weird, but I didn't have the heart to throw away her coffee cup, I held it in my hands as I walked home and every trashcan I walked by, I just couldn't muster the strength. It meant so much to me, that I didn't really know how to react.

Should I be upset? Or over the moon? Had I been so isolated that I'd forgotten what it was like to feel this way?

Or was I overthinking, allowing that anxiety to swallow me up again, getting my hopes up.

A cigarette would calm the jitters, I knew that, but I also hated the feeling of being guilty. Even if it was to a girl I'd just met.

I scrunched my loose pack in my pocket and threw that away instead.

I'd be lying if I said I slept well that night, I tossed and turned and lay thinking for hours. I worried about what time Juniper would turn up, I didn't even know what days she worked, maybe it would have been smart to ask.

By about five in the morning, I finally fell asleep, listening to the raging snowstorm outside my window. I could feel the chill in my dreams, even when I tried focusing on Juniper's smile.

I worried about the weekend, for the first time in a year.

I reached South Station at around twelve on Saturday, I blamed nobody but myself.

The cold had subsided a little, and I could finally sing again.

I sang a series of tunes: from modern versions of olden day songs, to acoustic versions of pop songs the radio constantly played.

Juniper arrived at two o'clock, and handed me yet another warm beverage. She complimented my voice once more and smiled at me. All I could manage was a wave, and she was off.

On Sunday afternoon, Juniper looked a little flustered when she gave me a coffee, and a paper bag. I was a confused, but blushed insanely hard when I saw a couple of cookies wrapped neatly in a napkin. I wanted to hug her, but I only thanked her.

'Juniper,' I laughed. 'That's sweet of you.'

She shook her head and waved it off like it was nothing. 'Oh, it's okay. Red.'

The nickname got me again, and I held the coffee really tight in my hand. The lid popped right off, scorching my right hand with slithers of hot coffee.

Juniper gasped first, and I yelped in surprise.

'Oh, jeeze,' I groaned.

'Ouch, Red,' she eased her eyes as I crouched to place it next to my mic stand. 'You okay?'

I laughed nervously, and began to wipe the hot liquid from my hands on my jeans, I'd smell like coffee for a while but that wasn't bad.

'I'm ace,' I grumbled under my breath and tried my absolute hardest to look as calm and cool as I could while I attempted to fix the lid, the paper bag hanging from my lips. 'Absolutely, ace.'

I could see her boots shuffle a little from where I sat, but I was levelled to her face once she joined me down on the ground. 'Here, before you end up burning yourself more.'

I paused when she grabbed the cup and fixed it quite easily, wiping it down with her sleeve.

'Oh, no.' I panicked softly. 'Don't do that!'

I felt so awful to see the sleeve of her red coat splotched with brown, and I scanned her face to find the same feeling.

She didn't mind at all; her smile hadn't left her lips.

'Relax, Red,' she said. 'I've had plenty of coffee spilt on me in the past, this is nothing different. I mean you should have seen the guy who spilled a whole black latte on me, it was unbelievable.'

Juniper explained this story, about some middle-aged guy with a grumpy look upon his face. He'd come right to the counter of the café she worked at, slammed his cup down and ignored the scorching liquid that went absolutely everywhere, and all over Juniper's hands.

She was so vivid when she described the past, I sat back and watched her as she explained, every tiny detail.

I found myself staring again, at how her eyes spoke alongside her mouth, the fullness of her lips and how they curled in the corners when she smiled.

'I felt like writing a paper on that asshole,' She growled. 'Headline it: Coffee and the Beast.'

I laughed, a genuine chuckle that she seemed very enthralled to hear. She was just so animated when she spoke, and I wanted to hear more of her voice.

Juniper smiled and showed me her hands, 'The guy even scarred me, Red!'

After she had taken her glove off, she showed me the back of her right hand. And she was right, there above her index finger knuckle, was a flurry of tiny bumped lines.

I grimaced at the sight of them, just the thought of someone hurting Juniper left me swallowing a hot lump of anger.

Instead I focused on how long and elegant her fingers were, the way her nails were shaped, I forgot to catch myself when I leant forward and took hold of her hand with mine.

'Aw, man he did too,' I groaned. 'What a dick.'

I was genuinely upset, and I brought her hand close to the middle of my face, examining the skin with my two tired eyes.

When I looked up, Juniper had gone quiet. Her hand in mine was still, and I instantly realised what I'd done.

'Oh!' I spluttered, letting her hand go. 'Shit, sorry!'

'It's alright!' Juniper nervously giggled, the winter chill evident by her warm breath. 'You seemed pretty interested in my hand–I mean! Uh.'

She rose quickly and waved her fingers again, I saw her face contort into an embarrassed grin while she fixed her hair under her cap.

'I'll see you later!' she blurted. 'Bye, Red!'

Juniper was much faster today, and I didn't even get to say goodbye.

'I hope so,' I mumbled under my breath.

§

I didn't know Monday would be the last time I saw Juniper for a week.

But I had an awful feeling when I saw her smile half-heartedly to me that morning. I focused on her as I sang a slower song by Eyes the Behaviour.

I was halfway through the second chorus when she walked by me, and waved once.

I could see how Juniper's eyes shifted under my glare, her eyebrows concerned, but not for me. She was troubled, that much was clear. The way she walked was less enthusiastic as I'd seen these past days, she was carrying a heavy load on her shoulders, that I just wanted to reach and take from her. If only I'd known what exactly was wrong.

For the rest of the day, I kept my eyes out for Juniper. I hoped she'd come running with another coffee, maybe another story to keep my mind busy, but she never came.

It was a little amusing to hear how my songs went from happy go lucky acoustic modern songs, to slow depressing tunes, it all depended on my mood, and right now I felt pretty damn awful.

I caught another glimpse of her at the end of the night, when Boston was preparing for yet another cold winter storm. Juniper passed my spot, acknowledged me with a short glance, then left on the west train.

I was worried, about a girl I'd met a few days ago.

Tuesday was cold, and I sang nothing but what my heart felt.

Wednesday was cold, and I was lonely.

Thursday was cold, and went by very slowly, I think I forgot to blink because I was hoping Juniper would come by.

Friday was cold, so cold that my G string on my guitar reached a limit of tightness, and broke. It sliced my pinkie finger then wobbled at the end of my instrument.

I didn't react to it, I listened to the awful sound it made, and ignored the stinging of a fresh wound. It cost me twenty bucks to buy a new pack of strings.

My heart was screaming over every other pain aspect of my body, I felt pretty useless.

On Saturday, I wanted to stay in bed. I was just on the edge of agreeing, but I felt the need to get up and go. I know it was childish of me, to stand in the same spot hoping for a girl to come my way.

So, Saturday I was angry, and upset.

Angry with myself, angry with the thoughts that rushed through my bustling mind. Angry at how I allowed my heart win this battle yet again,

I hated the feeling of being forgotten, if that was what Juniper had done. I wouldn't know. But I wasn't angry at her, at least I didn't think I was.

By Sunday I had made about a hundred bucks from my week's makings, that was very low, considering I'd made a lot more the week before.

I sat down against a cold tile stairwell, and kicked my feet over each other. My boots were tearing at the back, I cussed when I saw this. If I kept this up, I'd end up homeless by March.

January was coming to an end, and I hadn't even noticed.

I lost myself Sunday night, in my own voice, my songs. I shortened my microphone stand, sat there for hours, and only focused on me.

The trains ran pretty late on Sunday nights, and people came to and from each side of Boston, connecting in the middle right here at South Station.

There was a drug deal happening on my right at eleven at night, a fist fight on platform two across the tracks. A pack of laughing men acting like absolute hyenas to my left.

A typical Sunday night, when I decided to be a depressed puddle of goo and sit here singing to myself.

This reminded me of back home, during high school when I was a bit of a loner. The kids in my senior year were all total idiots, and Cole was my only friend at the time. He didn't like to admit it, or show it off, but he was a great singer. A warm-hearted guy like him? Of course he was.

Cole meant no harm to anybody, but if anyone hurt those he loved, he'd be on that like a kid in a candy store.

We hung out for a fair amount of time, before I made the decision to leave and come here to Boston. He was all for it, and told me where to find him if I ever came back.

I missed him a lot, and I found myself wondering what he was getting up to these days.

By twelve, it was freezing, but I had no motivation to move. I'd sing here all night if I had to, even if I only made a couple of bucks.

A flurry of red caught my attention, on my left again.

I sniffled and continued to strum my guitar, and noticed Juniper as she slid to a sit on the cold concrete floor, just a few feet away from where I sat.

She had her arms crossed, her hair a little messy, and a red nose. She'd been crying, I could see that from here. I kept staring while I sang, and waited for her to finally look my way.

Juniper looked absolutely exhausted, and failed to give me a full smile. It was a tired, small twitch of her lips.

I didn't want to get up and ask if she was alright, I think she was happy where she sat for now.

So, I tried to cheer her up. I looked her way, and sang into my mic, a loving song that could lift her spirits. As I started the chords, I was a little worried she'd take it the wrong way, but I'd sang plenty of love songs in this spot, I'm sure she wouldn't bat an eye.

As I sang, my fingers felt like ice across my strings, I swallowed deeply and concentrated on Juniper's face, as she leant her head back and looked my way.

There was a moment shared between us, I'm not too sure if I understood it completely, but she and I kept our eyes locked.

From where I sat, I made out the warn out look on her face, the tired way her eyes blinked. I felt the need to embrace her, tell her everything would be okay.

C'mon Rayne, get up and do something!

I couldn't. I sat and continued to sing, but I never looked away once, Juniper did the same.

I took a breath, aware of the words that left my parted mouth, they were sweet, soft and loving which we're dedicated to her.

Juniper's lips twitched into a smile again, and I smirked back a bit.

Did it work? Did my sap song lift her spirits just a little?

The cold breeze left me shivering, and I saw her do the same, rubbing her arms slowly. I hadn't found myself in a situation like this in a very long time, but there was no way I would let it go.

I finished my song early, and stood up. My bones were aching when I took my guitar off my shoulders, and my walk to her was slow.

I placed my guitar next to her, and stood still for a moment. Juniper glanced up once, not ready to make the same eye contact we had made prior, and sniffled.

I wasn't ready to speak either, so I pulled my dad's jacket off, and crouched to her side. I'd been wearing it for hours, so I hoped it was warm.

God, I was afraid to touch her, out of fear that she'd crumble right there. she was in a very sensitive state of mind.

But, Juniper allowed me to wrap my jacket around her shoulders, even if I had to lean in close to do so. I didn't have time to sit back in awe of how cute it looked on her, how big it was over that thin body of hers.

Our fingers brushed once, when she adjusted my jacket a little better.

I glanced around us, to examine a few passengers shiver from the cold, tap away on their smart phones. Nobody was expecting anything from me at this time of the day, I could focus on Juniper all I wanted, without the fear of being watched.

'Hey, Red...' Juniper croaked, voice weak.

I sat on her right, and cleared my throat, 'Hi.'

Juniper looked to me, and I glanced back. We were still and quiet, until she shuffled a little closer and sighed. 'I had a bad week, a really, really bad week.'

I figured as much, she wasn't herself at all. 'Did you want to talk about it?'

Juniper shrugged, eyes dazed. She focused on her hands, twirling them and rubbing fingers together. Another moment of silence, and I waited.

'Honestly...?' she began, looking up at my face once more. Her eyes were bloodshot, but she was still so beautiful. 'I'd love to just sit here and listen to you sing.'

I stared at her gently, sympathy rising in my chest. I wish I could know what was going on in Juniper's life, maybe someone was giving her trouble, and I could give them trouble back. She waited for my response, holding my jacket close to her shivering body, I was fine, just sitting next to her was making me warm.

'Sure.' I mumbled. 'Of course, I can.'

I pulled my guitar back over my shoulder, by being so close the neck of it touched her lap. I cleared my throat again, but she didn't seem to mind if my hand was close to hers. I didn't mind either.

I resumed playing the same song as before, focusing on the strings and my fingers. I was calm and content sitting with my legs straight in front of me, right here with Juniper, even when her head touched my shoulder.

She needed someone, and I was here.

I think she cried a little, over my voice I could hear the little hicks coming from her throat, but I didn't know how to react. But it pained me to know she was shedding tears.

I swayed her a little with my shoulder, hoping shed chuckle and flash me that smile again. Juniper glanced at me a few times, when she knew it was safe to do so, when I was concentrating on my chords.

By two in the morning, she had nestled deeper into my shoulder, and I hadn't stopped playing for her. The last Westbound train for the night was approaching, and I think it was my job to get her home safely. I stopped singing, halted my strumming, and nodded towards the train.

'You better get going, Juniper,' I said. 'You should get some sleep.'

Juniper looked to the train too, then her watch on her left wrist. Her eyes fluttered tiredly, and slowly she sighed. 'Yeah, you're right Red.'

I was, but I wished it was earlier in the night, so I could sit here with her a little longer.

I stood up with her and flung my guitar over my back. I took another look at her face, and she'd cleared up a little. No more signs of tears, just exhaustion. I wanted to reach out and hold her, tell her everything was alright, I know I wished for that some days, from anyone really.

Juniper began taking my jacket off, and I threw my hands out to catch hers. 'No, you wear that.'

She paused and locked eyes with me, and I smiled shortly. 'You can give it back another time.'

It meant I'd see her again for sure.

Juniper finally smiled, a pretty smirk that left my heart leaping. 'Aw, Red...'

I patted her back once, and pointed behind her. 'Get going.'

The train barked its horn, and Juniper jumped in her boots. I think she was contemplating something, before she waved once and nodded. 'I owe you, Red.'

I returned a laugh, and left my hand up in goodbye.

Juniper stepped on the train carriage, and I had a wave of anxieties rush over me. Was she going to be alright? Did she have a safe way home after she got off at her station?

I pulled a worried face, and Juniper saw it.

She waved from inside, before the doors closed. I didn't drop my hand until her train was long gone, I swallowed deeply.

I didn't think I was much help when I walked home that night. I think I could have done a much better job, I could have offered to take Juniper home, or find that extra sweater I kept in my duffel bag for her.

I stopped in my tracks and lifted my head to the night's sky, then groaned loudly. My voice echoed down the street, and I could hear some neighbourhood dogs react to it. I rubbed my hair in roughly, itching the back of my neck in frustration.

What a week.

Chapter Six

RAYNE

On Monday morning, I spent a good hour sorting through my cash in my bed. After successfully pulling myself from a warm cocoon of itchy blankets, I sniffled and placed my rent in a pile. Man, there goes a good three hundred bucks, to an angry landowner.

I pouted when I stuffed the last fifty in my pocket, it'd buy me lunch and a new pair of gloves today. I thought I'd rather go do something other than sit in my usual spot at South Station, something different. I think after last night's endeavours, I needed a break from singing, just for a day.

I paused in my tracks, and took a deep breath. I could still smell Juniper's perfume on my shoulder, I was so exhausted when I got home that I'd fallen asleep in my clothes, I hadn't even taken my boots off. I cleared my throat and rubbed at my face, hoping that silly blush would vanish fast.

Okay, I spent a good majority of the morning worrying about Juniper again.

I wondered what had happened, I really wish I'd known.

It was pretty funny, that this girl had just popped out of nowhere, and become my train of thought. But honestly? I didn't mind it at all.

I took a quick shower, dried my hair so it wouldn't become ice by the time I stepped outside, then tussled up my mullet.

Fuck it, I thought as I changed into a fresh pair of black jeans and a grey sweatshirt. I was going to go check up on her, see if she was alright.

I was tough, at least I thought I was. But the walk through South Station to the little alleyway of shops just outside of it, left my knees wobbling nervously.

It was one in the afternoon when I began scanning each store I walked past, there was a barber shop, a children's toy store, a couple of Asian restaurants, and then a busy café right at the end. The weather wasn't that bad today, the sky was blue with minimal clouds, but the sun was out and it made everything awfully slippery.

I nearly lost my footing at one point, and I caught some attention.

Stupid Rayne.

When I'd caught myself, I mustered the strength to take a peek inside the café. A sign out the front said City Café, cute.

I could see myself in the glass door reflection, a tall woman scanning every worker in the store as they bustled and called out coffee orders, man it was packed!

I had to step back a few times for a bunch of people, who grouched at me, sipped their coffees and continued on towards the station. One man nearly whacked right into me, his body was turned towards the café, waving shakily to someone inside.

'I'll see you l-later then!' he called. 'Thanks for the tips!'

He was super lanky with a short head of hair, and he wore a bright red varsity jacket. His voice was a croaky mess of anxiety. It wasn't as cold out today, and he looked pretty cool in his college attire. I stepped out of his way and he nervously thanked me, pocketing his hands when he rushed off.

Odd.

'Yes sir, I assure you it's decaf,' came a voice I instantly recognised. 'If you're awake tonight, sue me.'

I chuckled as Juniper walked my way, her attire was adorable. No red coat today, just a pair of black jeans and a plain white t-shirt, but she still rocked it well. I waited for her to turn and bump into me, but I didn't move out of the way.

I caught her waist with my hands when she finally turned my way, and her eyes lit up, honestly it was so nice to see her smile again. 'Red!'

'Hey,' I grinned. 'You're smiling again; I'd started to think you'd forgotten how.'

Juniper gasped and hit me across the stomach playfully, 'Blasphemy!'

I chuckled and took a step back, just touching her waist had left my fingers trembling, I quickly pocketed them.

'So, are you alright?' I asked over the noise. 'I uh...'

She saw me hesitate and I cleared my throat harshly, 'I was pretty worried.'

I didn't like to lie, and I was never good at it, only when it was necessary. Juniper crossed her arms and hummed to herself, she scanned our surrounding then sighed. 'I think I'm alright.'

She did look better, after a night's rest her eyes had become less glazy and much sharper, her freckles were even cuter up close.

Juniper held her hands together and nodded, she glanced into the store once more and I had the feeling she needed to get back to work.

'I'll let you go,' I muttered. 'I just wanted to see if you were okay.'

I shuffled on the spot, taking in a deep breath. Juniper was quiet for a moment, and I was worried I'd done something wrong. She breathed in and bit the side of her lip.

'I am now,' she admitted. I watched her eyes widen into a flurry of realization, 'Oh! I mean, I'm okay after that good night's rest, plus I started pretty late today, so–'

I couldn't help but laugh, and she grouched to me softly. Harmless teasing, I think she knew.

'Hey, I finish in half an hour. And I owe you, Red,' Juniper said. 'Stick around and I'll buy you lunch?'

My heart leapt for joy, like a date? A real date with a cute girl?

'Uh…' I felt my voice crack.

'Hello?' Juniper teased. 'Earth to Red?'

I snapped out of it quickly, and held my hands out. 'Oh! Yeah! Sure, that'd be awesome, I mean you don't have to pay for me. I can pay for myself.'

I wondered how silly I looked to the people around us, we didn't speak that loud but my body language must have let the world know I was nervous as all hell. I cleared my throat once again, and straightened up.

'I mean, yeah,' I smiled. 'Yeah, I'll wait.'

Juniper got right back to work after that, and I stood against the wall facing the store. Trying my absolute hardest to look cool, I wasn't that good at it.

She smiled my way whenever she could, whenever she handed beverages and lunch to those who sat in the dining area outside. Hey, this would be an awesome experience. I could finally sit and talk to her, know more about her, learn about Juniper's life.

I think I checked the clock above her store a lot more than usual that afternoon.

When the time came, I found myself sitting inside with Juniper, facing her across a plain wooden square table, where our feet touched underneath its small shape.

She told me that the calzone was the best thing to order here, and her boss was a mean Slavic cook. I could hear his thick Slavic-Boston accent whenever the swinging door to the kitchen swayed, and Juniper would shiver, a little embarrassed.

So I ordered that, and a caramel latte. I reminded her as she ran to pop the order to the front desk, that I would be paying and she wouldn't, but she rolled her eyes and agreed sarcastically.

'Sure you are, Red,' she said.

When we'd finally settled down in our seats, Juniper was the first to begin talking. She leant on her elbows and examined my face, then smiled.

'So!' she began. 'An aspiring singer, a guitarist with a beautiful voice.'

I leant back and grimaced playfully. 'Hey, now.'

'A quiet soul who sings at South Station, with her trusty microphone and hat.'

She sounded like a reporter, a really adorable reporter.

I wasn't ready to bring up last night's fiasco just yet, she was too interested in me, and it was a little selfish, but I liked the attention.

'What are you, Juniper?' I joked. 'A reporter?'

'A journalist in training.' She replied. 'Thank you very much.'

I raised my eyebrows and took a sip of my coffee, the barista who had made it wasn't Juniper, so it didn't taste as good.

'So you study?' I asked another question. Juniper sighed loudly and took a scull of her own coffee, lifting the cup high. 'Guilty.' I grinned as she rolled her eyes. 'Another one of America's students, struggling to maintain,' she said.

'You seem to be doing quite well.' I replied.

She poked her tongue out a tiny bit, denying my words. 'No way.'

'Where are you currently at?' I questioned, glancing to her face. She took a deep breath then exhaled, fiddling with her hands again.

'I'm at Boston University,' she said. Huh, that wasn't too far from South Station, that made a lot of sense. That campus was ginormous, and a few big names came from there. I'd only stumbled across it a few times, when I first came to Boston.

So Juniper studied journalism, worked here at City Café, and was just the same as I in a sense, struggling for money.

'I'm so tired from juggling all this stuff.' Juniper groaned. 'Study, work, study, work. It's a never-ending trial of skills.'

She was opening up to me, and I really liked that. I made sure to hang onto every word that left her mouth, I was interested in her stories just as much as I was a week ago. Her sarcastic manner was a cherry on top.

'I should probably cut down on work though,' she leant in to say this, and I moved in to hear. 'I don't want to drop out of college.'

Juniper's eyes glanced over mine, and she smiled. 'Just don't want my boss to hear that, he'd go off his head.'

'Hear what, little one?' came the deepest voice I'd heard in a long time.

Juniper jumped in her seat again, and gave me the biggest pair of frightened eyes I'd seen. I held my lips together, trying my absolute hardest not to smile as her boss placed a big hand on her shoulder from behind. He was a tall man, clad in a rough fur-collared coat. He smiled big and wide, his head shaved to a number one cut.

Juniper turned and groaned at the man, 'Jesus! Vadim.'

Odd name, never heard anything like it. He laughed and placed my food in front of me, then continued to tease Juniper. 'You are whispering about me!'

'No! I'm not!' she growled. 'I'm having a private conversation, something you don't seem to understand whenever I have friends around.'

Friend, that made me smile.

Vadim raised his hands and waved his fingers, 'Oh, my apologies little Juniper.'

She gave him a sour look, that the thirty-year-old tried to imitate as he walked away. Juniper groaned and looked back my way, I hadn't spoken a word, but my food smelt incredible.

Oh man, when was the last time I came out for lunch, and actually eaten something fresh? I couldn't remember. 'Man, I can't recall the last time I was out.'

I blurted my thoughts, and pulled my sleeves up. Juniper's eyes darted to mine and then to my right arm, a big grin on her face.

'Oh wow, Red!' she gasped, grabbing at my hand. 'Look at all that.'

She meant my tattoos, some of my parting gifts from Cole back home in Florida. We'd go to the tattoo parlour every month and add something to our bodies, he chose a small design for the back of his left shoulder, and I went all out on my right arm.

They were quaint designs, nothing too big and flashy. Just a couple of foxes, a stag and a vibrant black and white forest surrounding it.

This time, I let Juniper take my hand and bring my arm close to her, two of her right digits sliding to and from my wrist to my elbow. I lifted my glass with my free hand, hoping the warm drink would stop my goose-bumps rising from her touch. 'These are unbelievable, where did you get them done?'

I froze and grimaced into my glass, ah great, I hoped I wouldn't have to speak about back home, I guess it was inevitable.

'Back home,' I said. 'In Florida.'

'You're from Florida?' Juniper scoffed. 'What the heck are you doing here in Boston, freezing your butt off?'

Suddenly my food didn't look as appetising as a few minutes ago, I didn't like unfolding the past. But when I glanced at Juniper, she seemed genuinely curious. I took another deep breath and pulled my arm back to my side.

'I uh,' I shrugged. 'It's a really long story.'

She leant forward again, itching the back of her neck. 'Uh-huh.'

'Like,' I eased my head. 'A really, long story.'

Juniper didn't budge, she had her eyebrows raised, in anticipation. 'Mm?'

Yep, there was no hiding my past from Juniper..

I sighed and took a bite of my food, trying my best to savour the taste. She waited patiently, but I think she wanted to shake the information out of me, her reporter side going crazy.

I wasn't one to open up the big dusty book of Rayne Holmes for anyone, I don't remember the last person I opened up to.

I made Juniper an exception.

I began at elementary, told her what my parents did for a living and what my family consisted of. After I spoke to her about my time at junior high, I explained the change in my father's personality, and my mother's depression. Juniper's eyes had softened when high school came into the picture, I told her in depth of the friends I had made, Cole and the others. She was both amused and sympathetic when I described stealing that packet of gum and being grounded, she said it was cute. When I spoke, I focused on Juniper's eyes, but I too could hear myself talk, and the way I described my life left me with an empty feeling in my chest.

I would be lying if I said it wasn't a comforting feeling, letting out some stress to another pair of listening ears.

I showed her the tiny scar under my left eyebrow from a fight I had with a bunch of girls in school, and Juniper couldn't help but throw her hand out and brush her index finger along the length. I felt like a puppy, being pet.

My food was finished by the time I reached the end of my story, and I tried my absolute hardest to rush the depressing details in the easiest way. I hated the way it sounded coming from my mouth;

'I packed my bags, left my home with barely any cash and scrounged around Boston for a week before I actually had somewhere to live.'

As of expected, Juniper's eyes were eased sympathetically, and she nibbled at the side of her lip again.

'Wow, Red...' she croaked. I liked the way her voice faltered sometimes. 'You've been through some hard times, that's for sure.'

'Ah, it's nothing!' I chuckled, I wanted the emotional stuff to pack its bags and leave, so I could lighten the mood again. 'I'm okay.'

Juniper opened her mouth to reply, but paused and dropped her hands to her lap. I blinked and lifted my lukewarm coffee to my lips, I'd forgotten to take a break from talking. She looked around again, she had a habit of doing that, I wondered why. She then brushed a few loose strands of brown hair behind her ear, and sighed. 'Are you?'

Ouch, that hit me right in the chest. I felt a warm lump form in my throat, and make its way down to my heart, kicking and shoving it around like a big bully. I placed my glass down, and rubbed my arm nervously. Wow, I hadn't been asked that in a while, I forgot what it felt like.

'Huh,' I muttered, leaning back in my seat. 'Well...'

She began to fiddle with a napkin, ripping the sides of it with her nails. I chuckled to myself, and shrugged.

'Y'know, I'll get back to you on that,' I said. 'But I think things are starting to look pretty okay.'

I was looking in her direction when I'd said that, and she noticed my sweet remark. Before she could reply, I patted my hands across the table, making the cutlery wobble.

'But, enough about me.' I said. 'What about you, Juniper?'

Juniper laughed and adjusted her cap, I watched her take it off to ride a hand through that beautiful hair of hers. 'My life is boring!'

'Oh, C'mon.'

'Seriously, Red! It's nothing compared to yours.'

'Stop that, tell me,' I crossed my arms and gave her a sly smile. 'I wanna learn about the journalist in training.'

'Oh, please,' Juniper snorted, then mumbled something under her breath about what I'd said. She pursed her lips and stretched her arms upwards, I found it hard to not catch a glimpse of her thin stomach.

'Fine,' she teased. 'Buckle up.'

Just like a week ago, Juniper described her early life with confidence. She'd lived in Massachusetts all her life, grew up in Somerville with her dad and a younger sister, Nat. Now she lived on campus, alone.

Juniper had been a busy bee since a young age, she was dead set on being a reporter, and described the way she'd interview children in the playground with a plastic microphone and a clipboard. She'd been suspended from high school when she took the presidential role a little too seriously, blasting the Principle for his lies about cutting funds. And she worked hard to get into Boston University.

I'd never gotten to that point in my life, but I think Boston University was pretty high in the scholar lists.

Smart, sarcastic and adorable. Juniper was pretty damn perfect in my eyes.

I waited to hear a saddening story, but she hadn't reached that point in her story yet. I hoped she wouldn't have anything upsetting to share, but wishful thinking was weak.

'My Mom left when Nat was born.' Juniper paused, collected her thoughts and sighed. 'Nat has forever blamed herself, the kid is so young, she shouldn't be blaming herself for anything.'

I grimaced and fiddled with my pinkie finger, brushing the cut from the other day. It stung when I touched it, I probably should have put a band aid on it.

'I hope she doesn't turn out like me,' Juniper blurted. I locked eyes with her, curious. And she saw that expression, hers turned to a saddened frown. 'I'm constantly in over my head, and getting myself into trouble' Juniper sighed. 'I want

Nat to be the complete opposite, but it seems trouble finds her these days.'

I didn't understand what she meant, but I could see a lot of sibling love.

I'd been an only child, so I didn't know what that felt like, and I didn't think telling Juniper that was my parents mistake would be a good idea, even if I'd been told it one hundred times.

I cleared my throat and finished my drink, the glass was cold in my hands.

'Hey, we all gotta be a bit like that,' I started. 'Y'know, getting into trouble.'

I smiled to her, and she waited for more.

'As long as you're getting into trouble for a good reason,' I joked, lightening the mood.

Juniper chuckled and shrugged her shoulders, she scrunched the napkin she'd been ripping away at, and threw it into her empty glass.

The breeze was warmer than usual outside, as it blew into the café from its big open glass windows. It carried the many scents of winter flowers, fresh baked bread and for once it didn't leave a chill down my back.

Juniper enjoyed it, I watched her close her eyes and take a deep breath. I was instantly brought back by her beauty in that moment, I wasn't one to find the positive first before the negative, but I think I'd started to now that I'd met Juniper.

'I hope this doesn't sound too odd,' she suddenly said, her hands tight around her empty glass. I hummed in reply, cocking my head to the side.

Juniper smiled sheepishly and leant forward on her hands, 'I'm glad I met you, Red.'

I felt my ears redden, and my heart race like a greyhound at full speed. Oh man, I hoped my face wasn't a mess right now.

'I'm glad I met you too,' I returned, I couldn't make eye contact with her though, I'd crumble under that emerald gaze.

'Aw, you're not as hard as I thought you were when I first met you,' Juniper joked. 'You're a big softy.'

'Hey now!' I grouched playfully. 'I'm a tough cookie.'

'Super tough…' she teased, eyes batting towards me. 'You're as red as a tomato.'

I growled and rubbed my face quickly, ignoring her laugh. She sure was good at making me heat up like a furnace, and I think she knew too.

'Red, would it be okay to write about you in my paper?' Juniper asked. 'If that's okay, I really don't mind if you say no. I mean, having your story given to a professor you don't even know, how odd would that be?'

'Sure,' I said. I didn't even think before I said it, and she was quite right. It was a little weird to think about some middle-aged teacher reading about a girl from Florida, as she busked at South Station to make a living. But I wanted to be as nice as I could to Juniper, she'd lifted my spirits very high.

Juniper flashed me another clean smile, but it faded when someone popped up beside our table, over the big window.

'Juni!' he called. 'Funny I'd see you here.'

I examined his face, a chiselled profile with a thinning beard and goatee. He wore a cap on his head, backwards like those college frat boys. He was tall, not as tall as me. And he had big blue eyes, that he battered Juniper's way.

'Funny you'd see me at my workplace?' Juniper retorted. 'Wow, Reedy. I'm so surprised too!'

Damn, she was good.

Reedy grinned and leant close to her face, peering into her eyes. 'Pfft, you're so cruel.'

The way he got close to her, pulled at my heartstrings, I worried that he was someone close to her, maybe her boyfriend. But she seemed honestly annoyed by his presence, and sighed when he laughed and patted another guy next to him. I instantly recognised the same boy as before, lanky and nervous.

'I heard you gave Christopher here some tips.' Reedy head locked the guy. 'About self-confidence.'

'Something you seem to have way too much of, Rob,' Juniper groaned.

I smirked at her reply, catching Reedy off guard. He turned his attention my way and smiled;

'Oh! Hey you're that singer.' He patted Christopher against the chest when he spoke. 'South Station, right?'

I nodded and glanced to his nervous friend, he kept glancing to Juniper and back at me, a worried look upon his face. I was curious, how could one guy be such a wreck?

'You have a great voice, darling,' Reedy chuckled. I felt my brow furrow from his pet name, it was definitely not needed, and pretty uncomfortable.

'Thanks,' I sternly said.

He paused, and waited a few seconds for a bigger appreciative comment, which he wasn't going to get. Reedy chuckled again, and turned to Juniper once more.

'How's Nat holding up from last week?' he asked, his voice lowered.

I saw Juniper tense up, lips curl into a frustrated twist. I think he'd hit a pretty big nerve, something that even I didn't know about.

Juniper's green eyes shot the angriest look Reedy's way, and he noticed it fast. He widened his own eyes a bit, and fumbled with his hat.

'Oh, uh,' He stammered. 'I mean; I'll see you later.'

He pushed Christopher back, and gave me a quick smile before they were off down the street. Reedy kept looking back, before he blasted into conversation with the nervous boy next to him.

It fell silent between the two of us, I saw Juniper chew at her bottom lip angrily, and I worried that she'd start bleeding any second.

'Hey...' I mumbled. 'Juniper?'

'Yeah, Red?'

'Everything okay?'

'Everything is fine.'

She stood and grabbed at her red coat, which hung off her seat. She rummaged into her pockets, pulled her wallet out and winked to me. 'I got my wallet first, which means I'm paying.'

I didn't know what to do, play along with her or ask her for more answers? about her sudden sadness that was so evident just moments ago.

Juniper didn't receive an answer from me, I was struggling to say anything, too much on my mind. 'Okay, give me a moment.' she mumbled. 'Fucking, Reedy.'

I heard her whisper under her breath as she stomped towards Vadim. Once she'd paid and returned to the table, she was still grumbling.

Even as she put her coat on, and left the café with me, she was still talking to herself. I caught her hand in mine when she began to walk off, I didn't think the tug was that strong until she was twisted and pressed against my chest.

'Oh, shit,' I laughed weakly, then stood back to give her space. 'Sorry.'

'It's alright.' Juniper sighed. 'Sorry about that, Red. I just...'

She looked to the ground, and kicked a lonely branch aside. 'I'm sorry, Reedy doesn't think before he speaks, I know he means no harm but he's such an idiot sometimes.'

I let her rant, vent and throw her anger over the guy towards me. She told me how they'd met a few months ago, through the café, and he'd always bothered her since.

Juniper paused and groaned a little, then smacked her forehead with her palm. 'Shoot! I forgot your jacket too.'

I shrugged and grinned. 'Doesn't matter.'

She sighed and grabbed her mobile, passing it to me. I hadn't touched a cell phone in a year. What was that? A tablet of some sorts? It was huge.

'Your number?' she sweetly asked. 'So maybe I can come by and drop it off.'

I stood still and pulled a silly grin, 'I actually don't have a phone.'

'You don't?'

'No, sorry...'

Juniper giggled and pushed me against my stomach, 'You're so cute.'

I didn't know how having no phone made me cute, but I still took the compliment.

I itched the side of my nose and faltered around her, again, saying goodbye sucked.

Juniper pocketed her phone, then opened her arms. 'Well how about it? New friends, a hug to close the deal.'

I was waiting for this moment, when I'd be able to have Juniper close to me, I felt too bashful to even move. 'Uh.'

I think Juniper was used to my reactions to any kind of contact, and threw herself into my arms. I swallowed as her arms wrapped around my back, fingers pressing into my spine, her head against my collar. We fit like a puzzle, Juniper and I.

I touched her waist with my hands, fingers shaky. The last time I held a person in my arms, let alone a woman, was a while ago, and it was nothing like this. But they never lasted long.

Juniper let me go and gave me a heads up on when she'd be working next, so I could visit her. She usually worked early mornings and then had class later in the afternoon back at her university, but it all depended on Vadim's orders. I was still a little taken back by the hug, and she gave me a moment to reply. 'I'll see you soon,' I said.

'I hope!' she returned sweetly.

I always heard people complain about Mondays. How they were awful, a day right after a weekend? Yuck. Garfield even complained in his comic strips.

But my Monday, at least this week, was everything I'd hoped for.

Chapter Seven

RAYNE

As expected, my mood on Tuesday consisted of nothing but joy. I woke up early, had a fresh shower, finally went to the store and bought some gloves, and set up at South Station yet again.

The weather wasn't bad today either, just like yesterday it felt a little warmer than usual. I could smell Mrs. Murphy's bagels from down here, and God I felt like running up and eating a whole fresh batch of them.

My cravings had gone pretty haywire after the nicotine began to vanish from my body, I felt pretty twitchy. I thought of buying an E-cigarette, something to imitate the smoking pattern, but a part of me knew Juniper would lecture me.

Which would probably be really adorable, but not worth the drama.

I breathed in tightly as I stood in my spot, thinking twice before I started to play my chords. I felt like I hadn't sung in ages, like the muscles in my throat hadn't been tugged, forced so my voice echoed much louder than usual.

So, I'd change that today. I was allowed to show off, once a month, that was the deal.

I grinned to my thoughts, then started my cover of London Grammars 'Strong.'

A powerful song, that went from a total zero to a hundred in just a series of guitar strums. I'd often have this song stuck in my head back home, and pissed dad off a lot when I'd practice singing in my room. I think the nicest thing he'd ever said was;

'Rayne! You have a beautiful voice,' he had said. 'But shut the fuck up!'

I caught the attention of a lot of people today, and I wasn't really one to have a crowd. The first time I'd ever had three or four people sit by me and watch, was the end of last year, around Christmas time.

I think they were trying to be generous, try to convince St. Nick that they hadn't been total assholes earlier in the year.

I could feel eyes on me, and I would be lying if I didn't have a moment of panic. I didn't like it when people stared, but I think that was out of the question regarding my current job. I was here to entertain these souls, whether they'd be lonely or full of life, I wanted to make memories in South Station.

More memories with Juniper.

I caught myself when I began to blush, and I lost my rhythm for just a moment, before I jumped back into it.

Be careful Rayne, I thought. *Don't get too ahead of yourself, you technically just met her yesterday, give or take.*

I closed my eyes when I sang, and I received a wolf whistle from platform four as I hit the chorus. I could hear a bunch of boys banter and call out to me, but I ignored it.

When I sang, I either was aware of what was going on around me, or I did my absolute best to drift off, lose myself in the lyrics, the chords.

I peeked once, and spotted a few bystanders, flip their mobiles out and begin to record me. Eugh, that made me uncomfortable.

Oh, he just took a photo, now I feel even more awkward.

Okay, that guy definitely took a twenty-dollar note out of his pocket, looked my way, then put it back. And that girl whispered into her friend's ear, pointed at me and then giggled.

Now I was feeling the pressure, as another pair of eyes glanced to me. It wasn't negative, no, nobody laughed at my face and called me awful, nobody made it obvious they were uncomfortable, I think I was the only uncomfortable one.

I focused on my left hand, my fingers with the strings of my guitar. Pushing now, I felt my skin rub against the tightened chords. I had another two minutes of this song, I should shorten it, maybe pretend to make a mistake and apologise.

Why was I so nervous today? I think only one more thing could drive me over the complete edge, and she appeared just like magic.

Juniper, seemed giddy when she stepped in front of me. I continued to sing, even when she pulled that gigantic phone out in front of her, and managed to get herself and I in clear shot of a photo. I thought it was a photo, until she turned to face me then back;

'And here she is!' she announced. 'Red!'

I saw my face retort into a confused grimace, head cocking and eyes peering her and the cameras way. Juniper giggled again and stepped back, I worried she'd trip over my stuff. She waved her left hand dramatically, headlining me.

'The singer from Florida.'

Ah, she was being a reporter, again.

Juniper turned to face me, and I locked eyes with her, giving her a playful grouch.

'How do you feel, making all the ladies swoon?' she teased. 'What do you gain from it?'

Not that anyone else could really hear her words over my voice, I wanted to pinch her, she was making me red. And boy, did she know it.

I sang on, my expression telling her to watch it or she'd be chased across platform three.

It was a cute thought, racing her and catching her in my arms, maybe she'd even squeal in delight by the way my hands tickled her.

Fuck.

I whipped my view from her camera, my fingers trembled by the image replaying in my mind. I took a quick glance to those around us, some chuckled in Juniper's direction, recorded her, recording me. Others, well, they didn't really care that much for the whole situation.

She continued to wave her phone around our faces, and although I could smell her perfume again, feel her movement all around me, I made sure to finish my song.

I received a few claps, but the girl in front of me continued her antics. 'So?'

I blinked and lowered my guitar, leaning close, over her right shoulder. 'Huh?'

'What do you gain from making the ladies swoon?' she repeated. 'You gotta tell me now.'

I laughed nervously and thanked a few who popped spare change into my hat, Juniper smirked to me but I wasn't prepared to answer a question like that.

She wasn't going to give up, no way.

'Red!' she pouted. 'C'mon!'

I sighed and turned my mic off; everyone was going back to their businesses anyway. I took a moment to appreciate Juniper's attire; she wasn't wearing her trusty red coat today, instead, she wore my jacket.

It made me smile, how didn't I notice it before? Probably because Juniper had a knack of catching me off guard, and I became Rayne the sap whenever she was around.

'Hello, Juniper,' I grumbled to her camera. 'Here you stand, bothering me.'

I was joking, and she knew. But she still reacted like I'd yelled one thousand profanities at her in one go, she frowned playfully. 'Mean.'

I took a close look at myself in her camera, and fixed my hair up, I'd play along for now.

'Well, you have gotta tell me...' I asked, examining my sharp jawline. 'Did I make you swoon?'

Got her.

Juniper blushed then turned to face me, sliding her phone into the back pocket of her jeans. 'Hey!'

I flinched when she propped her hands to her hips, twisting her lips into a pout.

'You can't ask the reporter questions, Red.' She simply said. 'There are rules.'

'Oh? is that right?

'Yeah! Lots of rules, you're breaking the biggest one!'

'And what's that?'

'You're attempting to charm the reporter in charge!'

I laughed at her response, and finally gave her the benefit of the doubt. 'Alright, alright. You win.'

Juniper looked proud to hear that.

I yawned and stretched, cracking my knuckles before I crossed my arms and thought aloud.

'Well...' I mumbled. 'I never realised that. Making the girls swoon?'

I grinned and shrugged my shoulders; 'Sorry, don't notice it.'

'You're kidding me.' I heard her chuckle. 'Red, you're blind.'

I didn't know how to exactly take her words; but she gave me a sly smile then grappled at my jacket. 'Here.'

She slipped out of its big shape, I noticed her falter with her actions, like she would miss it. Juniper took a deep breath and handed the jacket to me. 'I thought I'd drop this off before I got going.'

'Where are you off too?' I asked, just a little saddened to see her go. I took the clothing from her hands, popping it on my duffel bag.

The brunette rubbed her arms, now she stood in a knitted grey sweater, and a pair of tight black jeans, that complimented the shape of her legs pretty damn well.

I took my eyes away from them and cleared my throat, itching the bridge of my nose. Play it cool Rayne.

'I'm off to see Nat,' Juniper explained, she pointed her thumb towards platform four behind her. 'Off to Somerville.'

I hummed to myself, and nodded. 'You got off work?'

Juniper pressed her hands together, almost blessing whatever deities ruled above. 'Yes, thank the Gods.'

I grinned to her, adjusting my guitar over my shoulder. It felt heavier, maybe I was just tired. Juniper sighed and lifted her hands, taking hold of my elbows. I froze.

'I wish you had a phone, Red!' she said. 'So I could call you and nag you, I've taken a liking to doing that.'

I shook my head and pocketed my hands. 'I don't mind it. Wouldn't call it nagging though.'

Juniper eased her green eyes and couldn't hide the smirk, 'Oh, someone definitely woke up on the charmer side of the bed this morning...'

'Pfft, not in that itchy bed.'

I heard her laugh, and it warmed me to the brim. Juniper's laugh was definitely becoming my favourite thing about her, second were those eyes, then her nose, okay, maybe her lips.

'Hey.' She let my elbows go, and patted my left arm. 'I'll see you soon, but if you do ever get a phone...'

She fumbled with her back pocket again, pulling out a marker. I gave her a confused grin, she just kept surprising me.

'Oh please, don't be so shocked,' she bit the lid off. 'I'm a journalist. Of course I have tools on me at all times.'

Juniper lifted my left sleeve, and leant down to scribble across my forearm. Her writing was rough, but still had a uniqueness to it. I smiled at her as she wrote, though she didn't catch my grin until she looked up from writing. Juniper paused and held my arm a little longer, and I huffed a laugh.

'A journalist in training,' I corrected.

'This just in,' she paused and widened her eyes. 'Red's actually a major dork.'

'Oh, Ha-ha.' I grouched. 'Juniper, you're so funny.'

She laughed and quickly gave my arm a hug, squeezing once. 'I'm just kidding.'

I knew that, but I got a hug out of it, maybe I should play around more often.

With her arms around one of mine, she glanced to her watch, groaning. 'Shit, I gotta go.'

We parted with haste, she had only a few minutes to rush upstairs and manoeuvre to platform four. I was alright with the quick goodbye, because I'd be seeing her in only a few moments.

I kept my eyes out, and caught her as she stepped down. From all the way here, she still looked unbelievably cute.

We caught glances, and she waved with her fingers again. I'd be lying if it wasn't a sad moment for me, it panged my heart to hear her train come, knowing quite well she'd disappear behind that hunk of long metal and cords.

Can you fear losing someone you'd just met? Did that exist?

I thought someone became a huge part of you after months of moulding and shaping. How come it was so different with Juniper? I had thousands of questions to ask her, that I thought of in the shower, in bed, while I cooked a boring dinner of ramen noodles and Zoom Bourbon.

I caught Juniper's tease once more, she pointed to her left arm, then at me, then lifted her phone to her ear. I rolled my eyes and lifted my hand, a thumbs up her way. She really wanted me to get a phone.

How could I say no to that face?

Carla erupted into laughter as I explained my story, of meeting Juniper and being a babbling idiot whenever she was around. The adult patted the store counter with a snort then threw a hand to catch my shoulder. 'Oh God.'

I grouched, and she took a hold of herself, breathed in, looked me in the eye again, then erupted into a flurry of laughter once more.

'You have the hots for this one, kid,' she chuckled. 'You are so young.'

'Shut up, I am not,' I denied her words. 'Just show me what phones you have.'

Carla let me go and finally took a breath, she crouched and rummaged behind the counter. 'Well, you're a few years late to join the smartphone bandwagon.'

That was true, the last phone I had was a really crappy old flip phone, it wasn't that bad, it did its job.

'Okay, well,' Carla sighed, hinting she was still amused. 'The cheapest I have, is this.'

She lifted the box and handed it to me. I examined the sealed object, and the image of the phone plastered on every fucking side of it. 'Jesus.'

'No, just call me Carla,' she snorted. 'It's sixty bucks, yes or no?'

I grimaced, that was expensive for a piece of technology, at least I thought so. I rubbed my left arm, itching the place where Juniper had written her number. Yeah, I wanted this; of course to keep in contact with her, but maybe I'd even reconnect with Cole, and say hey to mom and dad.

'Yeah, alright,' I said, grabbing my wallet. 'I'll get it.'

Carla nodded, then pointed to a pamphlet next to the box, with a whole bunch of gibberish I couldn't understand.

'Now you gotta buy credit and a sim card, so you can actually use the phone and call your girlfriend.'

'Are you serious? And shut up.'

'Yes.'

'Fuck.'

Another twenty bucks, banged the price up to eighty dollars. I let Carla set the phone up for me, while she snickered about how old-school I was, and that she was more street savvy then me. I had to stand there and learn how to use a smartphone from a forty-five-year-old.

The appliance wasn't so bad looking, a nice size, definitely not as big as Juniper's phone, hers was huge.

In twenty minutes, I'd learnt how to call and find the text box, and I stood still as

I tapped Juniper's number into the contacts application.

'This is hard,' I grimaced. 'Stupid.'

'Yeah but you're still doing it,' Carla chuckled. 'Such a sap.'

I wanted to yell and scream, throw the phone on the floor and stab it with a piece of Carla's jerky. It was nothing like my old flip phone.

'It'll take some getting used to,' she admitted. 'But you'll be fine, just don't drop it.'

I sighed and glanced outside, it began to snow softly. Carla huffed too; 'Yeah and don't drop it in water either.'

'What about sand?'

'Smartass.'

I thanked her quietly while she finished my transaction, before I left she gave me her own personal number, and now I could be the one to tease her. The woman cared about me, even if she called me out on being her most despised customer.

'Get out of here,' Carla snapped. 'Go text that June girl.'

'Juniper, her name is Juniper.'

'Do you even know her last name?'

I paused and gritted my teeth, rolling my eyes, 'No.'

'Ha!'

'Man, I don't even know what your last name is,' I replied. 'So shut it.'

'Hey!' Carla growled, shaking her fist my way. 'I'll ban you from the store you little shit.'

I chuckled and grabbed my bags, raising a hand. 'Thanks for the help.'

The adult waved me off, mumbling; 'Yeah, yeah. Get a haircut.'

I didn't text Juniper until I got home and set the phone against my coffee table. When I mustered up the strength, I tapped very slowly on its ridiculously sensitive screen, and made a whole bunch of mistakes.

He7y Juniper, Its Red';o

I tried to erase the monstrosity that was my text message, but I pressed send instead.

Shit.

I waited for a few minutes, in odd anticipation. I was really hoping I got the right number down, and found myself checking the digits on my arm, to the digits in my phone. I sat back, hands between my knees, and stretched. Aw man, I probably looked super lame, what twenty-two-year-old doesn't know how to use a smartphone these days?

Rayne Holmes, of course.

The phone emitted an awful vibration, and my heart jumped from the sound of it, rubbing against the wooden table. I grabbed it in my hands, unlocked it with a stupid pin number that it came with, and turned instantly red.

Wow Red, cute and dorky even through text message. You're on a roll, girl!

Juniper's message had just the amount of sarcasm I liked about her, another vibration.

You got a phone! Now I can bug you. You've made an error!

I grinned and typed very slowly, so I wouldn't make any actual errors. My smile never left my lips as I fiddled with my new phone, nobody had that effect on me.

Bug me all you like, but now you have an excuse to let me know you're alright.

Only a few mistakes this time, I was getting used to it. And just knowing I had ways of conversation with Juniper at the tips of my fingers, filled the empty hole in my chest a little.

We texted for another hour or so, she told me she was staying in Somerville, and that her sister had fallen ill with something, a bug maybe. And she would feel like quote; 'The biggest asshole in the universe.' If she left her sister sick and alone with her father, who was pretty bad at taking care of a sick child.

I called Juniper sweet, and something told me she was flustered miles away, tapping away furiously at her phone. It was evident in her awfully fast reply;

Stop it! None of that, Red. You're not allowed, you're banned from saying anything nice.

I leaned across my couch, kicking my boots off.

You're kidding me, that's impossible.

Wow, have a look at that! No errors at all.

Juniper informed me she was getting sleepy, and that she was sitting in front of the TV with Nat watching documentaries about 'fast food ruining the youth of America.'

I mentioned that it was a nice image to think about, a big sister caring for her little sister as they bonded over late night TV.

And Juniper was the one to call me sweet.

My heart fluttered when she sent me a picture, cuddled up to her little sister on the couch, who'd fallen asleep, enshrouded in blankets. I couldn't see her face very well, but I could see Juniper's perfectly.

She gave the camera half a smirk, her green eyes tired and exhausted. I think I stared at it for a good five minutes before finally saying goodnight.

That night, I lay in bed.

My eyes drooped, my tense body relaxed. My new phone was charging, and lit up to inform me that it was the first of February.

I hadn't even thought about the weeks that went by, how time was running faster than the speed of light. When I was with Juniper time seemed to stop.

Chapter Eight

RAYNE

The next morning, after doing a few push ups in the comfort of my own apartment bedroom, I sealed my rent money tight in an envelope and slipped my rent under the landowner's door . Whenever I did this, I always had a moment of panic at the thought of it vanishing. I couldn't make four hundred bucks in a day, no way in hell.

I paused at her door, and glanced left, then right. I fell to my knees, and tried to peer under the doors gap, hoping to see my envelope full of blood sweat and tears, safe.

Instead, I saw a pair of shoes, then felt the bump of a doorframe against my head. I groaned and leant back quickly, just as my angry landowner stepped forward.

'What are you doing?' she asked, voice shrill. 'Snooping?'

I rubbed the dent on my head and lifted myself from the floor. She was such a grumpy bum, Mrs. Long, more like...uh.

I couldn't think of anything.

I glanced up at her eyes, thin because of her Asian descent. She had a choppy hairstyle, and blemishes on her pale face. I wasn't a fan of her, at all.

'Sorry!' I nervously chuckled. 'I just wanted to check if my pay–'

'Yeah, I got it,' she interrupted. 'Anything else?'

I paused and grimaced her way, shaking my hands. 'Nope.'

'Then goodbye!' she slammed the wooden door right in my face, my nose barely brushed the paint. I stood still for a moment, feeling the anger rise up in my chest. I flipped her off in secrecy, with both hands. A mischievous part of me hoped she'd see me giving her the double bird dance through her peek hole.

'Yeah, happy first of February... asshole,' I whispered quietly, her witch ears probably heard it.

I wonder what it'd be like to have an actual nice landowner, you know, the little hobbling old ladies that made sure young adults were fed and warm. I crossed my arms as I walked downstairs into the lobby, the grimace hadn't left my face, and my forehead was red from that bump.

I had days where I wanted someone to completely look after me, make me a dinner and rub my shoulders. I caught the blissful thoughts when they came by, taking hold of them and cherishing the idea.

I'm sure Juniper would do a great job at that, I bet she made really good soup. She'd panic when the pot would boil over, spill over the sides. I imagined her yelping and grabbing at my hand; pointing at the stove and screaming. 'Red! I can't control it! I'm a reporter, not a cook!'

I chuckled at the thought, a tiny exhale from my nose. She still hadn't packed her imaginary bags and left my train of thought, nope, not at all.

I was totally fine with it, having her on my mind.

I yawned loudly and brought my phone out of my pocket, I still wasn't used to this machinery. I grouched and unlocked the screen, taking one more quick glance at the photo Juniper had sent me last night. I stopped in my tracks, feeling the snow under my feet. I think today I'd do the honours of texting her again, she seemed like an early riser.

I simply said good morning, nothing else, no spelling errors.

As I walked towards South Station, I kept my phone tight in my hand. Thousands of thoughts rushing through my busy mind, a normal routine for me. Back in Florida, my mind used to be so packed with anxiety, that I would find it so hard to leave my room. Every positive thought that came to my mind, was erased and a big fat negative sticker was slammed over it.

I didn't like to think I had anxiety, or depression. But it was pretty clear, to myself at least.

I sighed and held the strap of my guitar tight to my chest, I wore my dad's jacket again, it smelt a lot like Juniper, like she'd doused it in her perfume.

Before I started to panic about the fact I might have actually smelt really bad, and Juniper had been so desperate that she used a whole bottle of expensive liquid to perish the sin from its every fibre, I took a quick turn into Carla's shop street.

I would be lying if I didn't quickly smell myself, under the jackets sweet scent. Nah, I smelt fine. I think.

'Hey,' I asked Carla, she was busy reading a trashy magazine, but glanced up with tired eyes.

'What.'

I leaned over the counter and grouched. 'Do I smell?'

She shot me a glare, then hit me with the paper. 'Why are you asking me? Smell yourself!'

I gawked and leant back, sniffing my shirt underneath. 'I don't know! I'm just asking.'

'I'm not your mom.'

'Thank God.'

Carla went to hit me again, but I flinched and threw my hands up. She glanced above my eyes, and chuckled loudly. 'The hell happened there?'

She pointed to her forehead, and nodded towards my own. I sighed and explained the situation back at my apartment, of course she laughed, but she also took a quick look at it. Aw, she cared.

'You're gonna have a sore head all day,' she scolded. 'How dumb are you?'

I was grabbing a packet of crisps as she spoke, but I shrugged my shoulders. 'Oh well, one more bruise for my battered body.'

I reached into the fridge, took hold of some orange juice and shivered from the chill.

'Did you hear the news, kid?' Carla asked. 'You're not going to like it.'

I heard her tone change from her usual nagging self, to something completely different. I stepped towards the counter again, right when she slammed the newspaper down, facing me. I chuckled weakly and threw her a confused look;

'I swear, if this is another celebrity I don't care about I will honestly...' I paused.

There, on the front page was the headline; 'A Cleaner Station.'

I peered towards the text, and instantly regretted doing so. Carla's index finger pointed at one sentence in particular.

'Those who set up for entertainment purposes at stations all around Boston, must hold a busking licence. This costs a total of six hundred dollars, and allows the entertainer to perform. This action will be effective by the 18th of February, any who do not hold a licence will be arrested or persecuted.'

I cussed loudly to her words, and took the paper in my hands, reading the same line over and over, hoping to find a fault, a typo. But it was the real deal, I was going to have to scrounge up six hundred bucks in two weeks.

'Are you serious?' I moaned. 'Are you fucking, serious?'

My day was ruined, even when I felt my phone vibrate in my pocket, my day was absolutely ruined.

I was going to end up on the streets, there was no way I could make that money that fast. Only if I had the same person give me fifty bucks every day, and I was used to only making a twenty if I was lucky.

'I don't know what to tell ya, kid,' Carla spoke, softly. 'You better get cracking.'

I looked at her face, and she pulled a saddened look.

'You can do it, right?'

I wanted to tell her no, throw my things on the floor and go on a three-hour rant about how Boston was a piece of shit state. This law had to be coming in, because of the drug dealers that swarmed every station, pretended to be what they weren't to get away with their deals. I clenched both fists at my side, and took a deep breath.

'I don't know.' I answered sternly.

Carla didn't speak. She could see I was furious beyond the need for nice words; they wouldn't help, I don't even think Juniper could help me in this state of mind.

I rummaged through my pockets and held whatever loose change in my hands, I think I'd be living on dust for these two weeks, no more spending. If I wanted to make that six hundred dollars, I'd have to work from six to twelve every day until I could get my licence, and it had to be before the 18th.

'I blame the Fire Jackals, personally,' Carla scoffed. 'They're popping up all over Boston, probably recruited so many kids at stations.'

I peered her way again, shaking my head. 'Who are the Fire Jackals?'

I sounded pretty unenthusiastic, rude and snarky. I caught myself before I fell deeper into the depths of anger.

Carla took a deep breath and patted the counter with both hands, I thought I saw her tap the wood quickly. 'They're a clan, bunch of little shits running around the state causing trouble.'

I hadn't heard of them, and Carla was speaking about the group like it was a bunch of Nazi's. Did I really let stuff like this rush over my head?

'They're trouble, been all over the news, murders, kidnapping, you name it.'

I shivered, that sounded awful. And now they were going to be the reason of my unemployment. I hated them. 'Jesus.'

'Yep, they're everywhere,' Carla added. 'You never know whose part of the gang, that's what's scary about it.'

I grimaced and handed her the paper, she took it back and shrugged. 'I'd keep your eyes out.'

'I'm not scared of a bunch of assholes,' I snapped. 'If I see any, I'll kick them in the face.'

'Oh! That's the spirit,' Carla laughed. 'Tough puppy, I think you're still teething.'

She grabbed at her mouth and teased me, but my mood was already spoiled. I shrugged my shoulders and handed her my food, I didn't need them anymore, not after that pile of great news.

I breathed in deeply, scanned the convenience store, then rubbed my forehead angrily.

'Damn, this is really shit,' I grumbled. 'Really, bad.'

'I know, kid,' Carla replied. I didn't want to look at her just yet, in case I started to cry. 'You just get out there and sing your little heart out.'

I waited for a snarky reply, to add to my list of shit. But she never said anything rude, I think she felt the energy around us waver from giddy to goddamn plain depressing.

I stepped outside into the cold, and my body shivered from head to toe. The door of the store behind me chimed, twice, and it made me even sadder.

I was lost.

I swallowed and rubbed my hands together, my plan for the day was to rush to the station, sing nonstop, put a lot of effort into my voice and hope for the best.

Something told me my luck had run out.

I didn't stand around, I got to South Station, felt like kicking the very wall I set up against. My microphone and stand finally at the ready, I took a breath.

The first of February fell on a Wednesday, Juniper would usually be working, but she was still in Somerville. Her text message id received back at Carla's was a simple message, telling me she had to take Nat to the doctors, and she couldn't speak much.

Another reason to be a grumpy Rayne.

How selfish of me.

By one in the afternoon, I'd made ten dollars.

By three, fifteen dollars.

By six, I had twenty dollars.

And by eight, I was very close to throwing my guitar into the train tracks.

My songs were also angry, powerful songs. I could feel my throat disagreeing with me, and my head fumbled whenever I sang a little higher than I should have.

I gained a lot of attention, just not a lot of money.

This wouldn't bother me, no, not usually.

But knowing I was on a tight budget, left me scared and worried about my place in Boston. Just the thought of going back to Florida, left my body aching.

I'd be a laughing stock of the family.

"Oh remember when Rayne went to Boston and failed?"

"Rayne, you made a fool of yourself."

"Rayne, we're so disappointed in you."

My parents would say the exact same things, and constantly remind me I was a total moron for leaving.

No way, I didn't want to go back to the way I was before I left Florida, a big messy pile of anxiety and deprived feelings.

The tight feeling in my chest was still lingering, constantly on the edge of wanting to scream or cry, push and shove someone, rip the very organ from your body.

I took a seat, pulling at the strings of my boots.

What an awful start of the month.

I thought maybe Juniper could help, and I took my phone from my jacket pocket, to see she'd already messaged me a couple of times.

It warmed my aching heart for a moment, as I read her text.

Hey, you should come over, to my dorm. She had written. I want to talk to you about something.

Okay, so this wasn't normal for me. I hadn't been invited anywhere in a long time, and it was Juniper asking me. I paused then and there, and let it sink in.

She had come home, and I didn't even notice her step off a train. Maybe she was upset at me, and that's what she wanted to talk about.

Oh god, the anxiety.

I rubbed my chest and replied; *Sure, directions?*

Juniper was quick to respond, but there was an oddness in her messages. The feeling that something lacked, I was already so quick to judge, that I contemplated asking her what the matter was.

But I thought it'd be better to wait, maybe this would be good for me and I could get all this anxiety off my chest.

She lived on campus, which was Boston University. That was just five stops away from South Station, five slow stops.

When I'd bought my train ticket for five bucks, I stood and waited for the train to come pulling around the corner. Mindless worries filling my ears, voices becoming distant from the cries of anxiety in my head.

I rubbed the sore spot upon my forehead, it stung with every prod, just above my right eyebrow. I was so lost in the emotion that filled my chest, the past and future were constantly battling, and I was so tired.

So, so tired.

The train ride wasn't bad, again, I hadn't been on a train in a year now.

I'd been surrounded by them every day, but it was a weird sensation being on one.

I sat quietly, held my gear and wondered, glancing outside to Boston's city night sky. If this was any other day, I would be giddy as a girl, knowing I was going to see Juniper, and her dorm room.

But the more I thought about seeing her, the guiltier I felt for being in this mood.

I jumped off the train at Yawkey Station, I didn't even smile at the name, because c'mon, what sort of name was 'Yawkey'?

I jumped on the nearest bus heading further west, and held tight to the railing when it moved. The last thing I wanted was to drop my stuff.

The walk to Boston University's Housing was about ten minutes from the bus stop, if I didn't dawdle. Juniper told me she'd rather take the bus around this time, because walking at night frightened her.

Honestly? If anyone got in my face tonight, I wouldn't know how to react.

It wouldn't be pretty.

And, at eight-thirty, I stood outside the housing complex. Two gigantic towers of brick and steel, fenced off to the public, aka, me.

I breathed in tightly, and glanced to the nearest apartment window, trying to guess which room Juniper lived in. She seemed like a girl who hated heights, one who wouldn't sit back let someone pressure her into jumping from any high distance.

A strong girl.

I texted her, to let her know I'd arrived. The wait wasn't long, and she buzzed me into level two, her dorm number was 152.

Walking into a university campus was super awkward, some students stood in the hallway I walked down, a bunch of jock boys who made it quite obvious they were staring, stopped their game of Frisbee. It was hard to believe that these guys were probably the same age as me, even older by the looks of it. One had more hair on his face than a monkey.

I paused at Juniper's door, took one more long breath and knocked softly.

I heard a jingle of glasses inside her room, evident scurrying. Once the door was open, she smiled wide. 'Red!'

Okay, that cheered me up a little.

She stood before me in a plain grey t-shirt, and wore shorts, that once again; did a great job of showing off her legs.

Make eye contact, Rayne. I reminded myself.

'How are you?' she asked, then stood aside so I could walk into her room, jeeze it was big.

I didn't reply to her, as she closed the door behind the both of us, I scanned the interior. For a college housing dorm, there was a heck of space, a tiny kitchenette and bathroom, the rest worked out as a living room and bedroom in one.

Juniper definitely wanted to be a journalist, plastered all over her walls were newspaper cuttings, magazine photos and sketches, notes, I have never seen so many sticky notes in one place before. She had a few band posters, I knew the names well, old school stuff. I'd keep that in mind, maybe sing a song for her one day.

Her bed was messy, and at the foot of it, against the left wall was her desk. A beauty of furniture, a large dark brown oak piece of work that was filled with books and papers, some teetering over each other.

'Ah, ignore the mess,' Juniper chirped from behind me. 'I'm not usually this messy.'

'I like it,' I admitted, quietly. 'It's got Juniper written all over it.'

She chuckled and stepped by me, I made sure my eyes were above her waist.

I watched her, as she leaned over her desk and sighed gently. I was curious now, and placed my bags aside, somewhere out of harm's way.

'So...' I started. 'Everything okay?'

Juniper stepped towards me, and I smelt a familiar scent on her. Alcohol.

'Yeah, do you want a drink?' she asked, taking hold of my hands. I looked her closely in the eye, and saw the same dazed look tipsy people had. Ah, shit.

'Juniper?' I chuckled awkwardly. 'You been drinking?'

Juniper twisted her lips into a pout, and drastically let go of my hands. 'Ugh, yes. Only because I'm stressed and annoyed with everything at the moment, Red.'

She walked to her kitchen, and I saw her rummage through her fridge. 'I got dropped off by dad today, after taking Nat to the fucking doctors.'

Oh, hearing her swear was pretty new to me, and her tone had lowered to something more, angry. Juniper successfully found a bottle of whisky, and pointed it towards me. 'And that, is why I'm drinking.'

I was confused, and gave her a look full of curiosity. Her reasoning behind being tipsy, wasn't clear at all.

'Okay, that doesn't really help me understand,' I said, Juniper glanced to me as she drank. She swallowed, pulled a face and shivered. 'Ugh, this is awful.'

I wanted to storm up and grab the goddamn bottle from her hands, I didn't like seeing people drink away their problems, it reminded me too much of dad, and then of me.

Juniper leant over her kitchen table, and sniffled. 'I need to talk to you about something, I haven't been honest with you.'

I didn't like the sound of it, and I wished I'd never come tonight. She looked me in the eye, and I froze up, her half lulled green orbs were tired, sad, again; she'd been crying.

'Okay.' I began, nervous. 'What's up?'

Juniper straightened up, glanced to her surroundings, and then held back a sob.

'I haven't been honest with you, about Nat,' she croaked.

Fear and sadness struck me pretty fast, Juniper's whole personality fell.

She stepped towards me, arms crossed, slightly dizzy. 'About last week? When I... When I was the way I was, at the station.'

Ah, yeah I was still a little confused about that night. And she never really explained the reasoning behind that moment. I didn't want to bring it up at lunch the day after, she seemed too happy to be crushed down again.

I chewed the inside of my bottom lip, and examined her walk the line between the kitchen counter and the spot in front of me. She seemed to be contemplating, wondering if she should open up, and I needed her to spit it out, before I got frustrated. 'Juniper.'

'I know!' she whined, throwing her hands out. 'I...'

She held her face with her hands, inhaling then exhaling a shaky breath of air. 'Nat was hit by a car last week.'

I felt my heart drop, and I could see Juniper collect herself a little.

'Some assholes, hit her in broad daylight, and left her,' she explained, her mood darkened. 'I remember getting a call from dad, telling me I had to hurry to Somerville.'

Juniper slumped to her bed, and sat on the edge of it, her eyes wandered again. 'And when I came, she was in the ER.' Juniper paused and chuckled sarcastically. 'She'd been hit at such a force that she was knocked out cold, but alive.'

I wanted to reach out and hold her again, she was so close to breaking down, I too could feel my chest ache. Juniper breathed in again, and laughed into her hands, a broken, heartache of a giggle.

'She woke up, two hours after I'd arrived,' she looked me in the eye, and forced a hurt smile. 'And she said, "Juniper, I can't feel my legs." My little sister couldn't feel her legs.'

She couldn't finish her sentence without it turning into a sob, her eyes welled up with tears. The moment I stepped forward, she got up and stormed into the kitchen once again. I watched her scull the rest of the whisky, before she turned and pointed furiously at me.

'And you know what?' she called. 'She showed signs of improvement, the doc's said she was temporarily paralysed, and that our insurance would cover it, no big deal!'

I swallowed when she clenched the empty bottle tight in her hands, she was getting drunker and drunker by the second.

'After that night at the station, I began to think of the positive,' she huffed. 'I was positive everything was going to be okay, and that we'd dodged a bullet in the Bridges family.'

Bridges, her last name. I pursed my lips, and she then rushed forward to the end of her room. She tugged at her sliding cupboard door, and revealed a whole new section of newspaper cut-outs, pictures of people, cars and numberplates.

I watched Juniper Bridges crumble and fall that night, and she didn't hold back.

'Some fucking asshole,' she repeated. 'Hit my sister, and the goddamn doctors, told us she'd be alright.'

She turned to face me, and lifted the bottle to point at me; 'But! They didn't fucking do their jobs correctly, and now she's progressively getting worse, because one of the goddamn disks in her spine has moved.'

I felt my back ache at the thought, the poor kid.

Juniper lost herself again, she leant forward and held onto the nearest support, the edge of her couch. 'B—Because of some asshole, my sister is getting worse and worse...' she swallowed loudly, collecting her loud breaths. 'We can't afford the surgery, and I'm stuck wondering when she'll wake up paralysed from head to toe.'

She turned to face her cupboard, then took another shaky breath. 'I just found out today, that all this shit was inevitable.'

Juniper's words began to slur, and she cursed at her lack of vocabulary. 'I'm going to make sure that guy, or girl, pays for what they did.'

She threw her hands at the collection of papers, and I finally began to move closer. She was frustrated and started to scan the photos of each car stuck there, whispering to herself. I had to be careful now, she was in a state of absolute panic.

'I'm going to catch this piece of shit, and sue him for every buck he has,' She yelled, voice quivering. 'A hit and run, I can break the case if I snoop enough, and then I'll catch him on his ass.'

Juniper straightened up again with a groan. She pulled a shaky hand through her hair, and sniffled loudly.

'Red, I need to find the person that did this.' She looked at me, I was only a few feet from her now. I didn't speak, no, not yet.

Juniper rubbed her eyes and stepped back, losing her footing once or twice. I jumped when she threw the glass bottle in her hand, straight into her cupboard door. It shattered into a thousand pieces, excess whisky dripping down laminated articles. I could spot one name in particular, the same gang Carla had told me about; those 'Fire Jackals.'

'You hear that?!' she cried, 'I'll catch you, asshole!'

Worried now, I grabbed her waist with my hands, but she broke free of my grip. 'Don't!'

Juniper was over her head now, she sobbed loudly and dropped to her knees, throwing tiny bits of glass forward. 'The same night,' her chest heaved, and she whimpered. 'The same night it happened, there was a Fire Jackals meeting being held around Somerville.'

The tone in her voice had become very slurred, she scrunched the carpet below her, and breathed heavily. 'Natalie was just... she was just walking, who would do something like that?'

Juniper looked at me, and my heart broke. I had learnt many things about Juniper Bridges in such a short span of time, but I never wanted to see this side of her, I only wanted what was best, and for no pain to come her way.

Reality sucked.

'Juniper...' I mumbled, gently. 'Hey...'

She shook her head again, and pushed my hands away once more. 'Red, don't!'

I didn't know what she wanted me to do, I was as lost as I was coming here, but now my problems didn't matter, I wanted her to be alright.

'You'll help me right?' she sniffled. 'You'll help me find the person who did this!'

She looked me in the eye, sharply. 'What do you think?'

I eased my head, and rubbed the back of my neck quite awkwardly. 'Honestly?'

'Yeah, honestly...'

'I don't know, Juniper.'

'What do you mean, you don't know?'

'I think you're going to get hurt, if you try anything else.'

Juniper rose angrily, and pointed a finger right into my chest. I froze under her touch, she looked so hurt. But it was true, if it was the Fire Jackal's, she'd be walking into a minefield.

'Red!' Juniper whined. 'You don't think I can do it, do you?'

'I... Uh.' I lost my words, and she scoffed sarcastically.

'You're meant to be on my side!' she ranted. 'Why won't you help me?'

I shook my head and listened to her drunk cries, she pushed me a little, taking all that frustration out, unfortunately I was in her way.

'Hey!' I argued. 'I just don't want you getting hurt.'

'I'm not the one hurting!' she looked at me and let more tears fall. 'I need to save her.'

She breathed in loudly and broke down again, her body shivered and her hands trembled. I could spot the tears falling, dripping onto her lap. 'I feel sick.'

Well, I saw that coming. Who knows how much booze she'd inhaled before I got here, and finishing whisky that fast was never a good idea.

She struggled to her feet and passed me, holding herself up with a groan. I rushed after her, knowing quite well what was coming next, she hunched over the toilet, and lost the battle against all that alcohol.

I'd been in the same place as Juniper, many times before. Yet I'd been alone during those times, and honestly, I wished someone was behind me like I was now.

I crouched quietly behind my new friend, and held her hair in my hands. She sobbed as she lurched, coughing and spluttering. I wasn't bothered by it, the sounds made me flinch, but more so her cries.

'Oh, Red.' She groaned. 'Red...'

I shushed her sweetly as she collected her breathing, she fell back into my arms and I held her close. I dragged myself and she against the nearest wall, and brought her close to my chest. Juniper sobbed loudly, clutching to my arms. 'I'm going to lose her!' she cried. 'I'm going to lose her.'

I shushed her as she repeated her words, cooing her to calm down, that everything was going to be alright.

'You're not going to lose her...' I mumbled sweetly, 'Juniper, everything's going to be okay.'

I felt a bit guilty saying this, because I honestly didn't know the extent of Natalie Bridges' pain. But if I could numb her sister's aches for the time being, I would do everything I could.

Juniper breathed hollowly, her anxiety taking hold of her. I continued to calm her down, my cheek against her forehead, rocking, back and forth.

She cried for another ten minutes, but I never let her go. No, I wouldn't want this happening to me. My chest was tight, full of its own anxiety. I forgot all about the busking licence, the money, all that didn't matter to me right now.

Juniper was exhausted, once her body had calmed down, and her cries had ceased. I held her in one long embrace, and I was glad to feel her fingertips press into the back of my neck.

'Red...' she croaked.

I shushed her once more, I knew what came next, all the apologies. She needed to rest, and take some sort of painkiller.

'C'mon,' I simply said. 'Let's get you to bed.'

She was tipsy even when I picked her up, her mood changed from sulking to giddy laughs. 'You, are so goddamn strong,' she said as I lifted her into my arms, she was light as a feather, and I had no trouble walking to her bed.

I glanced at Juniper's face, and she grinned, pressing her forehead to my chin. 'Super Red.'

I couldn't hide a smirk; I think this was the part that amused me the most. 'That's me.'

After laying her down upon her messy bed, slowly and safely, I grabbed her a glass of water. Then spent a few moments rummaging through drawers to try and find some sort of pain medication. Whenever I got wasted back in Florida, Cole would give me one super strong pain killer, and I'd wake up the next morning with nothing but a headache and a dry mouth.

That guy was a magician, I tell you.

I found something, it wasn't as strong as I'd hoped, but it was still something. A single pill.

I sat on the sidelines of her bed, and handed her the glass, the pill I gave her was dissolvable, the worst types .

Juniper drank the whole thing, washing the awful taste in her mouth away, she furrowed her brow and held the liquid in her mouth a bit, before swallowing and poking her tongue out. 'Ugh, gross...'

'It'll feel gross for a bit,' I replied. 'Just get some rest, alright?'

I took the glass from her hands and paused to scan her face. She laid there, a smile on her lips, she'd remember everything in the morning, but for now, the innocence could stick around.

'Hey...' she whispered sweetly.

I placed the glass down, and nodded once. 'Hm?'

Juniper's hands reached for me, and I nervously took them with mine. Her green eyes were still slick with tears, but she was cheerful again.

Her right hand escaped my grasp, and she brushed her fingers across my forehead when I leant a little closer to her reach.

'Did you hit your head?' she chuckled, 'You are such a dork...'

I told her the story, of my evil landowner, and she watched my mouth move with a sleepy smile. I grumbled and touched the bump, hissing at the pain. 'She's evil, I tell you.'

Juniper hummed to herself, and pulled my arm down towards her, before she leant up to press her lips against the sore spot above my eyebrow.

Again, my body froze, but I savoured the moment and closed my eyes. She kept her lips there for a few seconds, before exhaustion took the rails and left her dropping back down against her pillows.

'There,' she mumbled, turning her head to rest. 'Now you'll be alright.'

I was more than alright; I was over the goddamn moon. I smiled to her, a short line. And she blinked tiredly, prodding my cheek with the fingers of her right hand. 'Loser...'

I chuckled and tucked her in, and in a few short minutes, Juniper had passed out.

I watched over her, just until I knew she was somewhere other than here. Somewhere full of happiness, a healthy sister and where you couldn't cry.

She kept her hand tightly around mine, and that told me she didn't want me gone from this spot. I let the event sink in, itching the bridge of my nose. So, that's what Reedy had asked about, she must have told him.

Hey, I'd be angry too, if some guy went around spreading the news of my sister's car accident.

Nat came to mind next, and I remembered the photo Juniper had sent me, that poor kid was in for a ride of hurt, and I had to do something to help, alongside comforting her big sister.

Bad things really did happen to those who definitely didn't deserve it.

I spent the next hour cleaning up Juniper's shattered bottles and aftermath of her drunken rage, and she slept soundly, without a worry.

I locked her dorm door, turned the light off, and took the couch. I think I'd give her space, so she would have time to piece together what had happened, tomorrow morning.

Chapter Nine

RAYNE

I had a pretty weird dream that night. I dreamt that I was underwater, swimming deeper and deeper into a dark depth. It started off peaceful, but my eyes adjusted to the light and I could feel the air begin to vanish from my lungs. I was drowning, and I began to panic.

I pulled and tried to submerge from the depths, and when I felt a pressure on my head, being forced deeper, I realised that this was indeed not a dream, and reality.

My eyes split open quickly and I could see only white, porcelain. I yelled, my voice bubbling. Okay, there was no way this was happening.

I pushed back against the force, and broke free of the tight hold, gasping loudly for air. Water poured from my mouth and my lungs screeched for sweet salvation. My eyes adjusted for a moment, until I was shoved back under.

My adrenal glands acted up, and I threw my head back harshly, hitting whoever had their hold on me. I heard a growl and a yelp when I'd lifted myself from the water, and I wasn't going to sit by and be attacked any longer.

'What the fuck!' I yelled, wiping down my face.

'Oh, I'm not finished with you, love!'

I was grabbed against the collar, and pushed into a solid object behind me. In my line of sight, a figure cleared into view, a tall woman with messy red hair had her grip on me, and God was it a tight grip.

'Hey!' I yelped when she lifted me off the ground, she was strong. 'What are you doing?!'

My vision was clearing up with every second, and I think I was back in Juniper's bathroom, from the familiar interior. I struggled against this grip, and tried my hardest to kick off.

'Get the hell off me!' I roared, lifting my right fist. I smacked her across the face, and she reacted harshly, stepping back with a gawk my way.

'Oh, no you fuckin' didn't,' she snapped, her accent was thick, Irish. And I think I was the first to recognize that it was Juniper's friend from a few weeks ago, but why was she beating me up?

I coughed when a fist hit my stomach, a strong punch that hitched the absolute wind from my lungs. I could really use some help, I thought, Juniper should be here any second.

'What did you do to her?!' the redhead asked as I spluttered below her feet. 'You better not have drugged her, or I swear to fuckin' God I'll make a bag out of that pretty face of yours.'

I tried to answer her question, but the wind was still forming in my empty ribs. She gave me no chance, and lifted her right leg, kicking me right in the bladder.

'Fuck!' I yelled loudly, that definitely got some attention, as Juniper rushed in, eyes wide.

'Arty!' she cried. 'What the hell are you doing?!'

Arty spat down at me and turned, arms wide. 'Oh! You're alright!'

Juniper glanced at me, then back at her friend with a shocked expression, eyebrows creased.

'Uh, yeah?! I'm fine.' she argued. 'But why are you beating Red up?!'

Arty paused and looked my way, I was still crouched below her feet, with a desperate feeling looming over me. I really hoped she wouldn't hit me again; the pain was unbearable.

She froze for a moment, then clicked her fingers. 'Ohh!'

Arty laughed loudly and wiped the sweat from her forehead, 'Lord, here I was thinking she'd snuck into your dorm.'

This was anything but funny, but she stood with a huge grin across her face. My hair was soaking wet, and hung like a rag over my shoulders, I swallowed loudly and looked to Juniper, for some sort of guidance, I was really, fucking, confused.

'Arty! Oh my goodness,' Juniper scolded, rushing to my side. 'Are you serious?!'

'Hey! I didn't know it was the guitarist, love!'

'You didn't stop to check who she was before you went throwing her into a fucking torture chamber?'

Juniper's arms took mine, but I lifted my hands in denial. 'G-give me a minute,' I gasped.

Arty sighed, groaned and stepped forward. 'Oh, well I'm sorry! You should be careful next time, you gave me a key!'

'So?!' Juniper yelped. 'What does that have anything to do with this?'

Arty gave us both an over exaggerated shrug of her shoulders, wiping the water from her hands. 'I saw you, you looked unconscious, and then a dark stranger on your couch?' she pointed at me, and I glared back. 'It was just a bit odd! I panicked.'

Juniper laughed sarcastically, her hands rubbing my shoulders. 'You think?'

There was a quiet moment between all three of us, I swallowed loudly once again, my breath recovering. Arty tapped her foot against the bathroom floor, and rolled her eyes.

'Okay, I wasn't going to kill her,' she pouted. 'I hadn't even gotten to the good stuff yet.'

I didn't want to know what that stuff was.

Juniper groaned from the bottom of her throat, voice cracking when she and Arty continued to argue. The brunette told her she'd been hungover, that she had a bad night prior. And although Arty took her by the shoulders and asked if she was alright, Juniper was focused more on the aching girl on her bathroom floor, me.

'Arty, just,' Juniper paused and pulled her hair back, frustrated. 'Just help me.'

They both lifted my wet body from the floor, and god it hurt when I straightened up. I groaned loudly, and cussed to Arty. She tried to hide a smirk, and patted me across the back. 'You're alright, lovey.'

I was the one being put to bed now, Arty stood back as Juniper checked for any sort of bleeding. She lifted my wet shirt, examining my stomach. If this was a different situation, I'd be totally okay with it. I saw the redhead roll her eyes and pull a pocketknife from the back of her jeans; 'Hadn't even used Stella yet.'

Juniper grouched and flashed her a greased look. 'Put that away.'

Okay, now I was annoyed, and I pushed Juniper's hands from my stomach. 'I'm fine.'

They both glanced to me, Juniper's eyes concerned, Arty's amused.

'See?' she said, hands out. 'Red's fine.'

I coughed a little, and Juniper bit her bottom lip nervously.

'No hard feelings,' Arty chuckled. 'Right love?'

'Yeah,' I eased, lifting my body from the bed. 'You better stay away from me, or I'll drop you.'

Arty gasped and pointed at me, then to Juniper. 'Oh! Did you hear that? A challenge.'

'No,' Juniper growled, to both of us. 'Stop it, both of you now.'

I clenched my teeth, ready to snap. But Juniper's fingers touched mine, and I was instantly calmed.

I took a closer look at Arty, she crossed her muscled arms across her torso, grinning my way. She was strong, so strong that even I fell to the floor like a shivering baby.

She wore a tight sweater, and three-quarter track pants, like she'd been at gym all night. We were both sopping wet from our hustle just moments ago, but she didn't seem to mind it.

Juniper shook her head, turned to Arty and lifted a finger. 'Don't, do that again.'

'Aw, I love it when you get all mature,' the other replied.

I took a quick glance at Juniper's face, and she was not amused, at all. 'Arty.'

'Alright!' Arty sighed, like a pre-teen. 'I'm sorry, Red.'

I didn't like her using Juniper's nickname. 'Rayne.'

Arty rolled her eyes yet again, 'Right, Rayne.'

I sniffled and tore my eyes from her, and glanced outside. It was storming, early morning and groggy as all hell. Yet another day was going down the drain, I now had less than two weeks to make all that money. Juniper rose off the bed, and it creaked sadly when she did. 'What are you doing here, anyway?'

Arty poked her tongue out, raising her hands. 'I wanted to say hello.'

'At five in the morning.'

'Yes.'

'After beating up my friend.'

'Yes.'

'You were out fighting last night, weren't you?'

'Yes.'

Juniper scolded Arty, she shook her head and took a step back. 'You needed a place to sleep.'

'Correct, love.'

'Well you can't stay here,' Juniper pouted, she glanced my way and huffed. 'No way.'

Arty chuckled and raised an arm around the smaller girl's shoulders, shaking her gently. 'Oh c'mon, you love cuddlin' up to old Arty.'

Juniper grimaced and ignored the flirtatious tone in Arty's voice, instead she pointed to the couch. 'You can sleep there.'

I rubbed at my stomach, the pain still struck gold. I was a bit bothered by Arty's personality, how easy it was to get close to Juniper, and that comment, I hoped it was just sleeping they were doing. Juniper was finally given the chance to wake up properly, and I kept my eyes on her. She stood still, crossed her arms, looked towards the cupboard door filled with news and then turned to face me.

Yeah, she'd remembered last night.

I was wide awake after all that. Who wouldn't be? I was afraid to close my eyes around the redhead, who laid across the couch and whistled to herself.

The room was dimly lit; Juniper had obviously turned the bedside table light on after hearing the commotion from her bathroom. Its brightness burnt my eyes, and I felt an awful headache come on. I had a lot of time to think last night, while Juniper slept. I couldn't get the image of her tear ridden face from my head, it pained me.

She was still set on this plan of hers, to find more information about a deadly club and maybe find the person responsible for Nat's injury. I was never one to pry for information, but a journalist and reporter like Juniper Bridges? Saying no was out of the question.

Juniper sat beside me, and we said nothing to each other.

Until she leant across my left arm, head nestling into the crook of my neck. 'I'm sorry, Red.'

She had mumbled, quietly and sadly. I fiddled with my shirt, it was freezing cold against my skin. 'Don't say sorry,' I returned sternly, then twisted my body so my legs hung over the side of her bed. She was forced to move from me, but I could feel her eyes on my back.

'I don't want you getting hurt,' I admitted. 'And this plan of yours...'

She waited, with bated breath. I sighed and itched the back of my neck, my hair was just beginning to dry. 'It's crazy.'

'I know,' Juniper mumbled. 'But I can't sit idly by, and watch Nat suffer, Red.'

I rose to my feet, and pulled my shirt over my head. This was the first time I'd unchanged in front of Juniper, but we were both women, I'm sure she'd be alright with it. Arty whistled playfully, and I shot her a glare. 'Hey.'

'Yah, yah,' she chuckled. 'I'll look away.'

'You better.'

'Watch your mouth, Red.'

Arty used the nickname to fire me up, and it worked pretty damn well. I tensed up, then grumbled something under my breath. With my partially dry shirt, I wiped down my face and neck, it was an old shirt anyway, and I was so exhausted I didn't even care anymore.

I sat back down, and breathed in tightly, trying my best to ignore the sharp pain in my gut.

My shoulders dropped, and I flipped my loose bra strap back the way it should have been. 'Nat's going to be okay.'

I mumbled this quietly, I wasn't sure Arty knew. When I looked, Juniper diverted her eyes from my chest to the bedsheets below, clearing her throat. 'I hope...'

I nodded slowly, and rubbed at both my arms. 'We'll talk more later.'

I leant back beside her, not too close, but not too far. I guess I had full access to her bed, and it felt really nice to be against soft sheets and fluffy pillows. I felt my eyes strain, but Juniper was still on the edge of saying something, and keeping her mouth shut.

I turned my head her way, and sighed. 'I know Juniper.'

She slumped beside me, propping her upper torso up with her elbow. I swallowed and blinked tiredly. 'I know you're still hurting about earlier.'

I took the words right out of her mouth, from the pained expression on her face afterwards.

'I don't know, Red,' she muttered. 'I just, I wasn't thinking straight. And when I'm upset about something, I'm really…ugh.'

She fell closer beside me, and bumped her nose against my left shoulder. 'I'm just, lost…'

It left my heart aching to hear those words escape Juniper's lips. But the next left me surprised.

'And you have a habit, of just making things much easier to deal with…' she paused and fiddled with her hands.

'You've come into my life at a very disturbing time, but I honestly couldn't thank you enough.'

Her words were close to whispers, and I heard every single one crystal clear, she was close enough for me to hear her every breath.

'Yeah…' I replied. 'I should be thanking you.'

I could hear my voice falter; exhaustion was wavering over me again. A wild night, had become even wilder. Juniper didn't ask for me to explain, but she lifted her hand, and brushed the loose strands of hair from my face. The contact was comforting, and I hoped she'd continue.

'Somethings bothering you, Rayne.'

My eyes shot open, and my expression tensed. I hadn't heard my name escape her lips once since we'd met. It was a very, unfamiliar setting between the both of us.

'I mean… you don't have to tell me; I don't want you stressing out,' Juniper fumbled again, 'I'm sorry, I'm being too, uh, too forward.'

I was still taken back by the use of my real name, I'd always been 'Red.' Since now. I was exhausted, but I was so afraid to close my eyes. Juniper focused on me, her eyes scanning my face. I froze up when her fingertips touched my shoulder, she sighed once and slumped down again, her head close to mine. 'We can talk more later, you're right…'

Man, I hoped she couldn't hear my heart, I could feel it pumping back and forth. I watched the skin above my bra prickle by her touch, goose bumps rising.

'I'm sorry I pushed you, Red,' Juniper mumbled into my ear. I relaxed to the sound of her voice, replying with a faint croak from my throat. I was so close to drifting, as much as I wanted to stay awake and talk, I couldn't help the tiredness.

'They don't make people like you anymore,' she chuckled softly. 'You're a keeper.'

My smile pinched at my lips, and I returned a tired laugh. 'Yeah, I'm pretty great.'

Juniper giggled and brought her body closer to mine, warming me up entirely. 'And a little cocky…'

'Maybe just a bit…' I tiredly replied. 'I bet you can't help… but swoon.'

Juniper laughed through a shaky breath of air, she breathed in to speak, and I leant in close to hear. 'That'd just make your day wouldn't it?'

I was tired, and she was aware of this, and I could probably get away with some harmless flirting, I mean I was, right then and there. And it was nice, for her to play along.

'You bet…' I mumbled, lips becoming dry. 'I make all the journalists…swoon.'

She laughed again, and clutched closer to my shoulder. I think we both shivered from the contact, and blamed it on the cold weather. Juniper mumbled something, left my body, turned the light off and threw the blankets over both of us.

I expected her to turn and fall asleep in her own space, but she returned to my side and snaked her left arm over my bare stomach.

It was dark now, almost pitch black if it wasn't for the early morning lights peering in from Juniper's blinds. I turned my head to face her, and she glanced back. I could feel her eyelashes flutter against my skin, and I smiled, crookedly. Even in the darkness, I could make out those adorable freckles of hers, that I wished I could kiss then and there.

I know, our friendship was still a few weeks fresh, but I'd gotten awfully close to her in such a short time, and we both had this connected feeling, like we'd shared something with each other, by just a few distant glances.

I think, for a moment, I caught Juniper's eyes look to my lips, it could have been exhaustion playing with my mind.

But I liked the idea anyway.

She smiled once, nestled deeper into my shoulder, and closed her eyes. 'Sleep well, Red.'

I nodded, I couldn't find any strength to use my vocal chords. Instead, I pressed my head to hers, and finally submitted to slumber.

Outside, the sky rumbled angrily, reminding me that this moment wouldn't last.

So I cherished it, as best as I could.

Chapter Ten

RAYNE

I would usually wake up to the sound of car horns, sirens and the rattling of dirty pipes. My fridge would make this terrible humming sound that would clinker and shake every thirty minutes, and for the first two weeks of living in Boston, I was convinced that my apartment was haunted. My bed was rock hard and itchy, pillows flat and chunky, blankets rough and dry.

But, oh.

I had missed the feeling of waking up in a soft bed, with clean sheets and fresh pillows. I wasn't used to it, and I wasn't used to the feeling of another girl holding onto me so tightly, the way Juniper was.

The wind actually woke me up today, it hadn't stopped storming and I had an awful gut feeling I would get sick if I left the coop. A snowstorm in would be the reason for no money today, kudos to you Boston.

I sniffled and glanced to Juniper, who'd gotten closer to me since before. I could feel her hand against my stomach still, fingers warm on my skin. She'd lifted her leg over mine, twisted our feet into a tight bundle.

I was comfortable, here with her.

I was still afraid to touch her, to the extent that she was touching me. I guess my courage faltered in situations like this, but it didn't mean I couldn't try.

I blinked and shifted by body, just slightly, Juniper reacted with a mumble, a croaky break in her tone as she pressed her head against my collarbone. I lifted my hands above my head, stretching them towards the ceiling. My bones crackled and released, and I sighed pleasurably, nothing better.

Juniper woke, well I thought she did.

She leant up, and glanced at me. We shared a mutual look, until I realised she was just as asleep as she was a moment ago.

She rubbed her eyes, mumbled something I couldn't understand, then fell against my torso. I caught her tightly, my arms around her back.

'Oy.' I whispered. 'Juniper?'

She mumbled back, a high questionable squeak, as she laid on top of me. I could feel her chest press against mine, and I instantly turned red.

I took a moment to glance at the time, her alarm clock was flashing at eight in the morning, ugh, I could sleep until three in the afternoon if I really wanted to.

Juniper inhaled again, I could feel it against my right breast, then she mumbled again, in realisation.

I chuckled nervously when she lifted her head, took one look at my chest, widened her eyes then glanced up at me.

'Hello.' I laughed weakly.

'Oh! Uh!' she threw herself off me, rolled to the side and nearly stumbled to the floor. 'Red!'

Juniper was up fast, her hair tangled in her hands, flustered and babbling on about how sorry she was. 'I'm so sorry! Wow, I uh,' she eased her eyes and rubbed her neck. 'I must have rolled over you, I didn't notice. I'm really sorry, wow. Did it get hot in here?'

I smirked a little, c'mon it was amusing to see her in this adorable state.

Juniper hopped a bit on the spot, and pointed to the bathroom. 'I'm gonna go shower!'

'Alright,' I replied, trying my hardest not to imagine her doing so.

Juniper grinned lopsidedly, and rushed off, I think I heard her groan in embarrassment from afar.

I laid there, listening to the showers rush, and rubbed my eyes as I rose.

Arty was still asleep, I didn't know how she slept, her whole body was falling from the couch, legs sprawled out. For a moment I wondered how she'd react to being dragged into the bathroom and almost drowned.

I itched the back of my neck, and listened out for the thunder in the sky. It was booming, awfully close. I grimaced, thinking about my job, that could easily be destroyed in the next coming week.

There was so much going on now, and I know it wouldn't be the right thing to do, but...

I had to keep this from Juniper.

For now, I had to focus on what mattered most here, and that was a young girl's life in jeopardy. Losing Nat would drive Juniper absolutely insane, and I couldn't bare that at all, nobody could.

Arty finally lost her balance, and slipped to the floor, grumbling profanities. I remembered our fiasco last night and huffed. She said she needed a place to stay, was she homeless? Or in the same boat as I?

Either way, Juniper gave her sanctuary here in her dorm room, she was too nice for her own wellbeing. I wonder how long they'd known each other, what was their story?

Yeah, I was worried.

I felt my bare stomach, Juniper's touch still lingering. It gave me butterflies, left me flustered. I exhaled loudly, my hair needed a good brush, and I needed to find a shirt.

I took a moment to stare around Juniper's room again, getting a better look at what I might have missed before. I'd looked right past a bookshelf, close to the couch Arty now slumped against, stacked top to bottom with mixed literature. I recognised a few titles, funnily enough they were all murder mysteries or bittersweet love stories.

Juniper Bridges might be as sappy as I was.

I'd been sitting there for a good twenty minutes, waking up slowly. Was this the way to act after you'd nearly died?

Arty answered that question for me, she chuckled when she awoke, flipping me a thumbs up. 'I'm glad nobody died last night.'

Her voice was hoarse and low, she still hadn't fully woken up. 'Juniper would never forgive me.'

'Huh,' I sarcastically grumbled, rising to stretch. 'Never thought it'd be that easy to make the decision, to end someone's life.'

Arty raised her arms and shrugged, 'Eh, you were a threat.'

'I was not.'

'In my eyes you were.'

'Well, now you know I'm not.'

'Do I?'

I glanced to Arty, and she wiggled her eyebrows rudely. 'You're still fresh. I'll be keeping my eye on you around Juniper.'

I wanted to throw myself at the redhead, and start a fist fight, but I found a good time to ask. 'What's the deal with you two?' I questioned. 'Dating? Dated?'

Arty heaved a laugh, then waved me off. 'No, no at all.'

Phew.

'She and I have known each other for a few years,' Arty yawned. 'I got kicked out of this very school.'

She seemed amused when she explained, telling me that she had gotten into a knife fight with a group of boys, and Boston University didn't want any of that.

Juniper had met her through class, warned the girl that she'd get booted from the program. But Arty was stubborn, she had said, and ended up being expelled the week after.

'Not that I cared,' Arty sniggered. 'I'd rather do something better with my life, than study.'

I'd grabbed my duffel bag while she spoke, at least the tension between us was slightly easing, but I wasn't going to hold my breath to it.

People don't become friends right after attempted murder.

'Juniper drives herself into the ground, love,' Arty mumbled, her voice was serious now. I made eye contact, sternly. Arty sniffed and shrugged again, leaning back down against the couch. 'She's stronger than you think.'

'I never took her for a weak person,' I answered. 'She's proven her strength, many times.'

I rummaged into my bag, and pulled a spare shirt from the bottom, sniffed it and then threw it over my bared chest.

'Oh, is that so?' Arty asked, snarky. 'She'll bite, darlin.'

I didn't see what was bad about that, and turned to give her a confused smirk. Arty's expression was serious, and I stopped in my tracks.

'She won't stand by for anything, if it gets in her way,' Arty shook her head. 'Just remember that, so you can get her out of trouble.'

'She told me trouble found her younger sister.'

'Oh, it finds Juniper too, love.'

I couldn't help but spot the angry tone, directed towards me, and I got quite defensive. 'What's your issue?'

Arty pursed her lips and itched her head a bit, a smug smile on her lips. 'Oh, nothing, just don't want some street singer trying to get into her pants.'

I felt my face flush, and I threw my index finger in her direction. 'That's not true.'

Her face retorted into a sarcastic grouch; 'Please.'

I clenched my teeth and heard Juniper shut the water off, I faltered on the spot before I flipped my finger Arty's way again.

'If this is your way of asking me to take care of her,' I began. 'Then you have nothing to worry about, love.'

I bit back with a sarcastic tone, and Arty looked a little impressed, she crossed her arms, raised her eyebrows and nodded. 'Well, alright then. That's what I like to hear.'

I rolled my eyes and zipped my bag up, but she wasn't finished just yet.

'Just don't make it so bloody obvious, that you're staring at her arse.'

I was so embarrassed I pulled myself towards her, angered by her smug smirk. She stood perfectly still, while I fought back the tempting idea of head-butting her right there and then.

Arty and I glared for a few seconds, before she blew in my face and left me flinching. 'You're good, love.'

I was brought back by her words, and softened my glare. Maybe, just maybe she wasn't that bad of a person. I would have to find out in the long run, to really change my views on her.

'Yeah,' I mumbled, stepping back. 'Thanks.'

We went silent after that moment, Arty rummaged through Juniper's cupboards, and helped herself to cereal, man, I was hungry too. But I wasn't at that level of comfort yet, it would be rude.

Juniper was fresh and clean by nine, I didn't really understand why it took her a whole forty minutes to shower and prepare for the day ahead, she could look brilliant in a garbage bag.

She dressed warmly, a pair of blue jeans and a black sweatshirt, patterned like a varsity, with three red strikes down her back.

Looking cool, Juniper Bridges.

She glanced to me, then to Arty, 'Already eating all my food?'

Arty grinned and raised her spoon, milk dripping over the curves, 'You know it, lovey.'

Juniper rummaged through her desk, pulling her laptop from under a pile of papers. I watched her roll her sleeves up, tug her hair behind her ear and concentrate on turning it on.

Ah, she looked good doing anything. And I was driving myself nuts, examining every single tiny detail about her.

Before she began typing, she turned to look my way, and I smiled like a complete dork.

'Hey, you can have a shower too, Red,' she smiled. 'I don't mind.'

I rubbed my neck, itched the back of my ear and didn't hide the fact I was nervous. 'Yes.'

'Yes?'

'Uh.' I paused. '....yes.'

Juniper blinked, chuckled and nodded towards the bathrooms direction. 'Off you go then.'

I dawdled and pointed to her laptop; 'What are you doing?'

She took a deep breath, and mumbled to herself.

'I'm searching for something,' Juniper muttered, face still. 'I posted a blog last week, about the whole thing.'

I was a little taken back, Juniper made a blog to search for her sisters hit and runner? Something told me that wasn't very smart of her, and that it caused more problems. I bit my tongue and stepped closer to her, glaring at the screen over her shoulder. I was taller than her, so she didn't mind when I leant in close to see, I could smell how clean she was, the sweet scent of mint lingered all over her.

'An anonymous source…' she croaked. 'Has given me some information on that Fire Jackals meeting, that was held around town.'

She glanced to me, her nose barely brushing my jaw. I grimaced, and showed her that look. 'Sounds dangerous.'

'I trust them.'

'You trust someone on the internet?' I asked, sarcastic. 'Aren't you a little bit afraid?'

Juniper's eyes wandered ahead, then she smiled and shrugged her shoulders. 'That's why I've got you, right, Red?'

Dammit! She wasn't allowed to do that! Turn it around and make something sweet.

I eased my eyes to her, and she grinned cheekily.

I sighed, leant in again and examined the map of Somerville on her laptop screen, she'd circled an area up north. 'And what is this?'

Juniper knew she'd won, and clapped her hands. 'This, is the potential place. Where I can find out more clues about Nat's accident.'

'And you want to go there?'

'Yeah, today.'

I diverted my eyes to the weather outside, giving her a grouch, 'Really?'

Juniper looked too, at how snow was literally piling up on her windowsill. She thought aloud, then leant back to catch Arty's attention.

'You'll drive me right, Arty?'

I glanced to the tall woman, she chewed loudly as her eyes fluttered. 'What? Yeah sure, whatever, lovey.'

I wanted to headlock that Irish moron and strangle her, she was the one putting Juniper in danger now.

Juniper continued to type, and ignored my stubborn face. I didn't really think that driving in a snowstorm was the best, but I also knew that arguing with Juniper was inevitable.

'Go shower,' she turned and prodded my stomach. 'And then we can get going, it'll be an adventure!'

Juniper chuckled and clicked her fingers, 'We can headline it, The Adventures of Bridges and…'

I was totally okay with people knowing my last name, but now, I wanted to call my dad up and yell at him, for having the last name Holmes.

'H...' I clenched my teeth and sighed. 'Holmes.'

I have never heard Juniper laugh so hard in all my time of knowing her, she had to hold herself up with my shoulders, tickling me whenever she could.

'Oh my god!' she clutched her ribs. 'No way, Red! There is no way this is for real!'

I rolled my eyes playfully, I wasn't winning any of these battles that's for sure. I looked to Arty for guidance, but she'd lost herself in her bowl of cereal, I think she forgot we existed. Of course, hearing Juniper's laughter was music to my ears, but she was being cheeky, and I had to fight back somehow.

'You're a monster,' I joked. 'An absolute, terror.'

Juniper wiggled her eyebrows and grabbed my waist, I froze under her touch and she leant forward; 'No shit, Sherlock.'

And, there it was.

I groaned and pulled myself from her laughing fit, messing her hair up with my hand. 'Get out of here.'

It was a moment I'd never forget, something so simple as a shared joke, added another piece to my sore heart.

Juniper smiled one last time, but when she took one look at her computer, her smile dissolved into something more, concentrated.

All jokes aside, she was ready to put herself in a dangerous situation, all for another human being.

I couldn't complain, I was about to do the same.

I'd never been to Somerville before, it was a quaint town with picket fences and tall houses in some directions, and then huge, tall buildings in the other. I asked Juniper if she lived close, and she said she'd point out her street when we drove by.

Arty was a smoker, and I think the smell was making me nauseated. I hadn't picked up a cigarette in three weeks, and I couldn't stand the stench of burning tobacco. She drove messily in this storm, window partially open so she could vent out the car, I think if she hadn't done that, I would have exploded in the backseat.

Arty offered me a cigarette at one point, and Juniper was the first to deny it, for me. She and I made eye contact, before she apologised and turned back in her seat.

The drive to this location was even rougher, and all I could see through hazy storm fog was industrial buildings and crops.

'This is great,' Arty grumbled. 'Lovely place, me arse.'

Juniper diverted Arty's view to the road, reminding her she didn't want to die today.

'So, what are you two even going to do in there?' Arty asked. 'Just snoop around an abandoned building, hoping to find the fucker that hit Nat?'

'Basically,' Juniper answered, I saw her readjust her paperboy cap. 'Clues.'

'This isn't NCIS, lovey,' Arty said, I agreed with her there, maybe she'd talk some sense into Juniper. 'But it'll be pretty fun.'

Nope. I was wrong again.

We finally arrived at this shack of a looking building. I grimaced from inside the car, it was gigantic and old, broken and had signs written all over it.

'See?' I muttered. 'Says right there, "Do Not Enter." And what are we going to do?'

Juniper turned from the passenger seat, and gave me a giddy grin, 'We're gonna enter!'

Arty sat back and yawned, patting the brunette across the head. 'Don't get killed.'

'Oh stop it you two,' Juniper scolded, she pulled at Arty's ear. 'I should be saying the same to you.'

I wanted to know what she meant, I hardly knew anything about Arty's background, it was murky and unclear.

'Be careful, you idiot,' Arty smirked. 'And you, lovey.'

She pointed to me and grouched, 'If I see one scratch on Juniper, I'll break your hip.'

'You're not coming?' I asked, a little afraid of the third member vanishing.

Arty patted her dashboard, then shook her head. 'Gotta watch the car, cops could be coming around anytime.'

I unbuckled my seatbelt, and watched Juniper throw herself out of the car. She seemed a little too eager, dangerously eager.

'Watch her back,' Arty said to me. 'Please.'

Her words were sincere, enough for my good heart to take into consideration. I nodded once, and stepped out into the blistering cold.

I groaned from the ice, and eased my eyes to find Juniper, who waited for me at the front of Arty's car.

'You okay?' she called over the wind.

I couldn't say yes, but I shouldn't say no either.

I stepped to her side and took a deep breath, 'Kinda.'

I turned to face the building, and shivered at the thought of a huge clan of murderous assholes meeting up for drinks and pizza, or whatever they did.

Juniper's hand took mine, long cold fingers intertwining with the webs of my left palm. I glanced to her face, and caught her anxious look. So I squeezed her hand to assure her everything was alright, and I was here.

'Okay,' she whimpered. 'Let's take a look, Red.'

Chapter Eleven

RAYNE

Juniper and I had to find an alternative to the front door, I think she actually thought the door would be unlocked, and stood there kicking at it with her foot for a good three minutes.

We found a way in through the back, even if it was dark and dusty, and Juniper groaned in agony at the smell of dirt and sewerage.

Inside was as expected, cold, dusty, rotting at every side and an awful shade of brown. The building was falling apart, but when we took the stairs going down, it progressively got sturdier. Juniper commented on all of this, very quietly. I stuck behind her, always turning to see if someone was there, I didn't like this one bit but I didn't want to dawdle either.

'So…' I began.

Juniper hummed in reply, she held her phone in front, using it as a flashlight in this dark murky place. I sniffled and eased my eyes as a leak drippled down my neck, I rubbed it awkwardly.

'Any idea where this meeting was held?' I asked. 'Are we even sure it's this place?'

'No.'

'No?'

'Nope. I just hope it is.'

Now Juniper Bridges was adorable, don't get me wrong. But situations like this? Dangerous teetering buildings probably filled with bugs and asbestos in the walls? She was silly, very silly.

I kept quiet, and gently touched her waist whenever she paused in her tracks and thought twice about walking forward. Every time she halted, a part of me hoped she'd realised the danger. But I'd find a grouch on my face when she continued forward, her footsteps quiet.

We came to a long dirty hallway, with four broken doors on each side, and I had every horror movie scene flash before my eyes.

I was never, ever, good with horror movies.

'Ooh...' Juniper lowly laughed. 'Spooky.'

I tried to be tough, my hands clenched into tight fists and I did my absolute best to wash the image of Silent Hill from my mind. Juniper had no issue searching each room, flashing her flashlight for information, hoping to find a wad of papers or a notebook, while I feared a frightening ghost coming right at us.

'Let's just keep moving,' I pressured, voice a bit higher than usual. 'Okay?'

Juniper turned to me, with a sly smile. 'Red, you're scared?'

I rolled my eyes and brushed itched my nose. 'Absolutely not.'

'You so are,' Juniper grinned and continued to move, and I stuck close. 'You scaredy cat.'

I wanted to grab her hand and tell her that this was crazy and dangerous and we'd get into trouble, but it was also a little exciting, even I could admit that.

I mean, here we were, alone in an abandoned building.

'For our second date, this was a beautiful place to pick,' Juniper joked. 'Don't you think?'

I had already lost all functionality when she mentioned the word 'date,' and I felt my heart stutter for just a small moment.

Juniper turned, aware of her tease. And I, cleared my throat a little. 'Right.'

She chuckled and rushed forward, towards two huge copper doors at the end of the hall. I instantly felt the anxiety bubble in my stomach, and I touched it in means to calm it down. The door was padlocked shut, with awful graffiti splashed all over its rough texture. Juniper had no problems touching it, tracing the paint with her fingers.

'This has to be it,' Juniper mumbled, a little concerned. 'It has to be, there is no way this couldn't be it.'

Well, a part of me wanted to agree and disagree, it was a little odd to see a door plastered at the end of a trashed hallway. I took a quick glance around us, and sighed deeply.

'Juniper, are you sure you want to.'

'Yes!' she interrupted, turning to grab my arms. 'Red, c'mon!'

I took her hands abruptly, then squeezed them tightly. 'Juniper...'

She hugged me quickly, closely. 'It's going to be fine, stop worrying.'

I didn't have the chance to hold her back, because she'd already turned and begun tinkering with the lock.

'I did a little research...' she paused, lifting the block of metal to check its keyhole. 'About pick locking...'

I pursed my lips and remembered a few nights in Florida, when I was a teenager, before I'd met Cole. I was with a few bad kids, and we'd sit in a local diner for hours, while they showed me the tricks and tips to do wrong.

I hoped Juniper would unlock it somehow, but she was getting frustrated and grumbled under her breath. I held the air in my mouth, fumbling on the spot, before I groaned and slipped beside her.

'Here.' I sighed. 'Give me a pen.'

'What?'

'Pen, trust me.'

And she did, handing me her trusty ballpoint pen. I took a moment to examine the ink, she must use the thing all the time, because it hardly had anything left in it.

I scrounged the dusty floor below me, picking up the nearest nail.

'Hope you've had a tetanus shot...' Juniper mumbled from behind me.

I huffed a laugh and continued to tamper with the lock, every lock I'd ever picked in the past made it quite easy to break. I struggled for a moment, until I heard that godforsaken click. Juniper was impressed and grabbed my shoulders, patting them roughly.

'Wow, Red!' she whispered highly. 'You're so cool.'

I shook my head and pulled the lock from its hilt, passed her pen then stood shakily. 'No, that wasn't cool.'

Juniper blew my words off, and grabbed the doors handle.

'Such a good person,' she teased. 'Never doing wrong.'

I laughed back, oh man she had a lot to learn about me if she thought I was the best person in the world, I'd been pretty awful in the past when it came to rule breaking.

We stepped inside cautiously, Juniper ahead of me. She couldn't suppress a gasp of awe, and I couldn't suppress a nervous croak from my throat.

Inside, was huge. A big open great hall with tables, scattered chairs, broken glass, the whole deal. I felt the crackling below my feet, and glanced down, easing my eyes at the bloody sharp edge of a mirror.

'Ugh,' I grumbled. 'This is not good.'

Juniper was too busy rushing around, grabbing any sort of paper left behind, anything that would drive her to find more answers. Above us, hung wires, coloured streamers and broken roof. Leftover knives and weapons, bullet shells.

No, this wasn't good.

'Juniper,' I said again, calling over the eerie quietness. 'We have to go.'

She was too busy rummaging through a few boxes, her eyes concentrated and serious. She cussed whenever she got her hopes up, and threw some sort of dirty rag behind her. I listened to her rant on about how the possibilities of finding out clues was high, that there had to be something here or shed have no lead, that it only made sense because of the timing and area. Nat was hit closer to the city, but every car coming from this spot in Somerville had to go in one direction.

Juniper rose up and grabbed her hat from her head, scrunching it tightly in her hands. 'I have to find something.'

I sighed and helped her search, getting splintered fingers and sore feet as I scanned around this broken room. Juniper recommended that we check upstairs, the tiny rooms that surrounded the interior. And I plainly said 'Fuck no.'

She gave me the face, the puppy dog face that always worked, the charm. I groaned and followed her up the steel stairs, our footsteps echoed all around, it was that quiet.

Once we were upstairs, there was a whole other room, much smaller. I rubbed my hands together, the temperature in this whole place was below freezing, and my breath was like steam when I exhaled.

Juniper rushed to the desk at the end of the room first, and smacked her hands down hard. I jumped, she'd found something alright.

'See!' she yelped. 'Right here!'

I couldn't see anything from where I stood, so I stepped to her side, she was still tapping a big sign on the desk, a symbol of sorts.

A circle of red, with the face of a black jackal, and three flames above its sharp head.

'Proof right here.' Juniper smugly said. 'They were definitely here.'

I gave her a look, and raised my eyebrows. 'Yeah, I kinda got that impression from the blood and knives all over the floor.'

Juniper shook her head and opened the drawers of the desk, scrambling through them.

'No, see,' She started. 'Places like this are always being broken into, cops are always finding homeless and teenagers, but they've only caught a few members of the Fire Jackals.'

I saw her pause and bite at her bottom lip nervously. 'This is a big deal.'

I personally wasn't sure how Juniper knew exactly that the clan was behind Nat's accident, but she was pretty damn determined.

I started to believe too.

'Okay, well.' I mumbled. 'They just mark places everywhere they go?'

'Yes, to pretty much say "Fuck you, we've been here and you didn't catch us."'

'Weird.'

Juniper halted and looked me in the eye. 'No, not weird. Cowardly.'

I returned a confused glance, and she grimaced.

'They're a bunch of morons, hiding,' she snapped, hands tight on the tables edge. 'They run and hide.'

'Sounds like an awful game of hide and seek.'

Juniper tried her hardest to keep a straight face, but pursed her lips to me with a grouch. 'Red.'

I grinned awkwardly. 'Sorry.'

The tables turned there, she was usually the one to crack out of place jokes.

Juniper rummaged for another ten minutes, I kept my eye out for any dangers, being the mature one, I guess. I finally had a moment to breathe, until Juniper called me from the room next door. I panicked and found myself rushing in, expecting to find Juniper Bridges hurt or mangled.

Instead I saw the biggest grin on her face.

She leant against the back wall, and held a ragged piece of paper in her hand. When I reached her side, she threw it into my face, pointing at the bottom. I eased my eyes, and took her hand to hold still. 'What? What is this?'

'It's some idiot making a huge mistake!' she giggled. 'Oh my god, how dumb can you be?'

At first I thought she meant me, and I felt my heart fall. 'Sorry...'

Juniper was fast to turn back around, she gasped and took my side, shaking her head. 'No! not you Red, look.'

She stood beside me, and we both glanced over the sheet once more, I could see the same printed Fire Jackals mark, and a bunch of encrypted coded words, looked like gibberish to me.

'Um...' I muttered.

'Look, if you read it like this,' she held it still when she spoke. 'It makes no sense.'

Yes, she was right there.

Juniper began twisting and turning the paper, pushing edges into creases, until it was folded oddly. She flashed it back in my face, and smirked. 'But if you follow the lines, that the idiot previously folded. You get, this.'

I scanned the newly formed paper, and was awfully impressed.

There, much clearer now in a bolded font, was a date and location. 'Wow, nice job, Juniper.'

Juniper gleefully clapped her hands and examined it once more, 'This must be their next event.'

'Which we are definitely not going to, aren't we?'

'We are definitely, going.'

I was quick to judge, and opened my mouth to fight back, if it wasn't for the voices I heard from below us. Juniper and I made quick eye contact, both frozen.

'Look, I'm not going to go on about it,' came a male voice. 'But someone's been in here, the padlock was ripped clean.'

'You are going on about it, fuck,' said another.

I could hear them from the atrium downstairs, rustling through the same stuff Juniper was prior.

'Red...' she whispered, we still hadn't moved. I shushed her, and slowly reached for her hand.

'Look, can we just hurry up and find Pebble's spare key? I can't believe that dickhead forgot to grab it before he went speeding around in that shitstorm of a car.'

I felt Juniper's grip on me tighten, and I felt the anxiety rush over me.

Oh no, it couldn't be.

'Yeah, that's what I'm worried about!' came the first voice. 'It doesn't seem right, that he'd be so careless, he could get into serious shit with the big boss.'

I heard their footsteps begin ascending, and I reacted very fast.

I grabbed Juniper close to the wall beside the doorway, pushing my body against hers. 'Don't. Say. Anything.'

Her hands took my shoulders, and I could feel her swallow nervously. We stood still, it'd been the closest we'd ever been, but what a waste, the situation was terrible.

I could feel her heart thump against my chest, especially when she heard the footsteps enter the room we had just been in.

'Just, look around.' Louder voices now, I heard the clunk of a hard metal object hit the table. 'It can't have gone too far.'

Juniper's voice began to hitch, and I took her mouth with my left hand, pressing my forehead against hers, eyes wide and serious.

She frightfully stared back.

I gestured a hush with my lips, giving her a nod of assurance, even though I was just as scared.

'What did he do anyway?'

'I don't know, hit some kid on the way back.'

Once he spoke, Juniper's hands clutched my shoulders, and I saw her eyes close tightly. Yeah, she'd heard the words just as clearly as I.

I nuzzled the bridge of her nose with mine, trying to comfort her as best as I could.

This news proved it, and I'm pretty sure Juniper wasn't ready to hear the news.

'Idiot panicked, forgot that he'd left his spare key here, for his friend or something.'

'And he couldn't come here on his own?'

'No, that'd be stupid.'

'Why? This, this is stupid.'

'Because, you know how important he is to big boss.'

'He's a little shit.'

I felt Juniper's hands tremble, and fall to my sides, if I hadn't been pressed tightly against her, I think she might have fallen.

I too, could feel the dreadful emotion take hold of my chest, drain my blood and leave my ears ringing.

I had never met Nat, but hearing the truth, left revenge in my veins.

I loosened my grip on Juniper's mouth, and she swallowed again, exhaling as quietly as she could, I saw her breath clearly in the cold.

'Hey, check the other room can you?'

'Fine.'

My heart began to thump loudly in my ears, I didn't know what to do, how to react. He was getting closer to the door, and if he just looked to the right, he'd catch us in seconds.

I pushed into Juniper more, and she held me tight, head buried in my neck.

If she and I were to die then and there, I would hope her death was painless, even if that meant a back full of bullets.

I concentrated on the sounds of his footsteps, big hard boots. And the closer he got, the more afraid I became.

I saw the barrel of his shotgun before I saw a hand, he sniffled and peered left, a tall brute of a man. I didn't take my eyes off his figure, and prayed.

'Hey wait, got it,' came the other. 'Under the desk.'

I felt the sickening release of anxiety wash from my face, as he turned completely left, and stalked back.

'Great, can we leave now?' he growled. 'It's freezing.'

'Yeah, yeah. I'll give Pebbles the key this weekend.'

'Oh yeah, can't wait for that, should be a good night.'

'Poker, girls, booze and fighting,' the first male laughed. 'That's the Fire Jackal way.'

'Don't let the boss hear that.'

They erupted into laughter as they left, stomping down the stairs, calling out profanities about the weather and the job they were given.

Juniper and I waited, until we heard the voices vanish, we were safe. I pulled her close when her hands clung at my back. Her body was shivering, as was mine.

'Oh god,' she whimpered. 'Shit.'

I nodded, and kept her in my grip. I could finally breathe again, but my heart hadn't stopped beating fast. This was the danger I was warning her about, if he'd just looked left he would have seen us. That was the most luck bestowed on me in years, when it came to a life risking situation.

Juniper sniffled and pulled back, letting her head fall against the wall behind her.

I held her waist, and we both stood there, breathing like we'd run a marathon. Juniper swallowed loudly, sighed and grappled at my face.

I froze under her touch, as she began to cry. 'Oh god, Red.'

Her tone was frightened, shaky and full of breaks. Juniper's body arched and her head fell, hitting my collar. And it took me a moment to realise that I too, was crying.

Once she had felt my tears, she looked at me with a smile, a sympathetic grin. I smiled back through a heave, shaking my head.

'You're so silly,' I gently sobbed. 'You are such a silly, silly girl.'

Juniper fell into my embrace, and I held her tighter than ever. She nodded, admitting it.

'I know...' she said.

As we made a quick haste out of the building, we didn't speak once. I had a moment to think about Arty, hoping she hadn't been caught in the gang members line of sight. Juniper, I'm not too sure if anything else was on her mind, only the news we had heard. She had this dazed look in her eyes, like she'd found out too much.

I knew, later on? That dazed look would become a determined one, to find 'Pebbles'.

It sounded silly, a gang name such as 'Pebbles', but we never joked about it, this was serious. And I think I'd reached my limit.

I paused before we left the building, the gang members had left the front unlocked. Juniper sniffled and turned to my halt, confused. 'What?'

'No more.' I said sternly. 'No way, are you going to that event.'

She opened her mouth to argue, but I stepped forward.

'Juniper!' I raised my voice. 'This is ridiculous, you're going to get yourself killed!'

She scanned my face, and furrowed her brow. 'No, I wont.'

'Yes!' I yelled now, and she flinched. 'You are! You cant just go around doing this kind of stuff, you're going to end up hurt, and I wont be there to help you!'

'You don't have to help me then!'

I was the one who flinched next, she raised her voice just as high as mine.

'You just don't get it do you!?' Juniper yelled, her voice cracked again. 'You don't understand anything that's happening here!'

I wanted to grab her shoulders and shake the idea of going this weekend from her brain.

'I do!' I answered back, turning to brush my hands through my hair, I was frustrated.

'No!' she stepped closer, hands at her sides. 'You don't. and you wont, because Nat isn't your sister, and she isn't dying!'

'So you're going to get yourself killed, for your sister?'

'What kind of dumb question is that?'

'A serious question, if you go this weekend, you'll be getting yourself into trouble.'

'I'm going, and I wont get killed, I'm not stupid.'

I laughed sarcastically, throwing my hands outwards. 'You don't think this was stupid?'

Juniper's face retorted, into something quite hurt. I wasn't finished yet, I needed the sense pushed into her, she wasn't letting it.

'Juniper, this was a dumb idea, and yes, we found out some crucial information,' I paused and swallowed. 'But now we know who did it, we know these guys were behind Nat's accident.'

She wouldn't look me in the eye, she only crossed her arms and bit back fresh tears. I felt like an asshole, I really did.

'Now we have to focus on getting her that surgery.'

'Well we won't!' Juniper finally screamed. I felt the blood drain from my face, as she glared at me.

'I'm going to find him, I'll find him and make him pay, she won't make it, I'm not that stupid to see that!'

I couldn't believe my ears, she wasn't giving up, and now she was telling me Nat had no chance? Juniper breathed in loudly, and I felt the guilt wash over me.

'Juniper....' I muttered.

'Don't, Rayne.'

I think my heart was torn out, hearing my name again. Juniper took her anger out on the entrance doors, kicking them with a loud yell. And I watched her disappear into the storm, stomping towards Arty's car.

The redhead stepped out, and looked my way, her shoulders heaving in confusion.

Man, I was going to get into even more trouble now.

Chapter Twelve

RAYNE

The second of February, an awful day, really.

I'd woken up next to a gorgeous girl, driven all the way to Somerville with her raging red-haired best friend, then snuck into an abandoned building to find clues, like this was fucking crime scene investigators.

I never expected to have a near death experience, or, whatever you wanted to call that situation. I'd never been so scared, for Juniper too. Alright, maybe I feared for Juniper's life more than my own in that moment, to see her eyes widen like that, struck with sincere fear, it left my heart aching.

Now, I sat in the back seat of Arty's car, feeling pretty damn upset with myself.

I was only trying to tell her the truth, tell her she was getting in over her head. This was becoming too serious, something two girls couldn't fix. It had to be handed off to someone in a much bigger field. We didn't have guns, or armour, or any sort of protection, we only had ourselves, it wasn't enough.

Juniper Bridges was stubborn; I'd seen it many times now. Yet she had good intentions.

She was never around to make someone suffer, she never wanted to see another cry. When 'tough' singer and guitarist Rayne Holmes cried?

Juniper didn't like it, that was also clear from the way she held me, I felt better by that comfort.

Arty hadn't said anything to me yet, and that was very unusual, but I could see her grouch at me through the rear-view mirror, with Juniper in the passenger seat next to her.

The brunette had her elbow propped up against the window, watching the rain finally pass by us. This storm was one of the worst, but calmed once we hit the city.

Arty mumbled to Juniper, and they spoke about Nat for a little, but I stayed completely quiet. Juniper got into depth about the condition of her sister's health, what could happen, how much it would cost, and the digits were higher than I expected.

Arty cussed and hit the steering wheel with her tough hands, chewing gum loudly. 'Shit.'

From both of them, ideas were thrown back and forth about how to make the money. Arty thought she could cage fight, make the money in some odd tournament I'd never heard of. But Juniper literally laughed in her face at the idea, a smug sarcastic chuckle that Arty shrugged to, she knew it was a bad idea as well.

Juniper thought selling some stuff laying around the house would help, her dad recommended a few more jobs she could take, but that would mean leaving school. When that topic was brought up, I saw Juniper grimace and lean against the window once more, she brushed a hand through her hair, then glanced to me through the side mirrors reflection.

I tried to smile, but it only ended up becoming a straight line.

Juniper looked away.

Arty suggested checking up on Nat before we headed back to Boston, Juniper considered it but denied the offer, because her sister would be at the doctors with her father. I wished I could meet the girl, and see what Juniper's childhood home had looked like.

Arty was biting her tongue, I think she wanted to explode at me, and I wasn't ready for it. She kept giving me these side glances, like she'd reach behind her seat and grab me by the throat.

She'd told me not to hurt Juniper, threatened me if the girl had even one scratch on her face. But I couldn't help but feel a bit hurt myself, Juniper was just being stubborn, clearly Arty could see that too.

It took only twenty minutes to get back to Juniper's apartment complex, and I swallowed sadly when she left the car first, not even bothering to wait for me to catch up.

Once she was a few feet away, Arty turned furiously to me, and I rose a hand. 'Hey! Before you go ape-shit.'

'I'm going to go more than ape-shit, love!' she snapped. 'What the hell happened in there?!'

I groaned and unbuckled my seatbelt, as I reached for the door handle, Arty quickly locked it. I let out an exaggerated sigh.

'Look!' I started. 'Juniper's over her head, she's going to get seriously hurt this weekend.'

'Those fuckers, hit Nat,' Arty simply said, eyes peering at me. 'I don't think she cares.'

'I do!' I yelled over the end of her sentence.

Arty breathed in tightly. I shrugged my shoulders, and shook my head.

'Jesus, what is with you two and heading right into danger?' I asked, confused. 'This is a fucking gang; they're not playing around!'

'So we get a few cuts and bruises,' Arty said. 'It won't break her spirt. And she won't wait for you, if you're not coming.'

'So, what am I supposed to do about a wild idea like this?' I snapped. 'Wonder if I'll see her on Sunday? Alive?'

Arty paused then, I was hoping she saw through my anger, hoping she'd turn around and say I was right.

'Hey, I'm worried too,' she grumbled. 'But Juniper, when she's dead set on something, she'll do it.'

I just couldn't understand the concept behind it all, I was missing something, I had to be. Arty sighed and rubbed her temples.

'Rayne, she loves Nat more than anything,' she mumbled, her tone was calmer, the calmest I'd heard. 'She'd run into a minefield for that girl, and think nothing about it, at all.'

I crossed my arms, clenching my teeth together. 'I know.'

'If you know, then also know she won't give up. Juniper's going on Saturday, and I'll be there too.'

I felt a little better when Arty said that, she'd be able to protect Juniper without a doubt. Arty glanced outside to spot the brunette, waiting aside the gate. I turned my glance away, rubbing my neck awkwardly.

'I know you don't want her to get hurt, lovey,' Arty cracked her knuckles, eyes on mine again. 'But sometimes, you gotta risk a lot to save someone you love, right?'

The words sounded odd coming from her mouth, and I never took Arty for a kindred soul. I sniffled and shrugged again, 'I guess.'

'Juniper's going to win this,' Arty assured. 'And we have to help her, and Nat.'

The pressure, suddenly felt less like pressure and more like a duty. Juniper Bridges needed not only Arty, but I'm sure she needed me too. The redhead turned to me once more, and hit me across the knee harshly, I yelped angrily. 'Hey!'

'Look, shit,' Arty paused and tensed her neck. 'I used to be with them.'

'With who?'

'Are you serious, love?'

'Oh you're not...oh c'mon!'

'I am. Juniper knows, that's also why she's so positive about getting the information she needs.'

Great, I was in the presence of an ex-Fire Jackal.

I raised my finger, giving her a stern glance. 'You've seriously killed people?'

Arty paused and lifted her eyes to the roof of the car, almost trying to remember. 'Nah, just hit a couple guys here and there.'

'Jesus.'

'Hey, that's not the point!' Arty growled. 'Juniper's got a direct link to these shitheads, and finding out where their next meeting is? Bloody ace!'

I was at a loss for words, and chewed on the inside of my cheek. Arty waited for an answer, but all she received was a nervous grumble.

'I left because of reasons,' Arty explained. 'But, they see me? they're going to let me in, no issues. But I can't go asking who 'Pebbles' is, I'll look sus.'

'After you left?' I asked. 'Why'd you leave anyway?'

She shook her hands wildly, 'That doesn't matter,

I wanted to fight back and say it did matter, but she'd interrupted me again.

'Yes, they'll be confused at the start,' Arty said. 'But as long as I'm not seen by the big lugs, guys in charge, then everything will be fine. I'll go in there, sneak you two in and you guys scope out. Find the address book upstairs, search for Pebbles and you'll find out who that fucker really is.'

Arty crossed her arms, proud of her plan. 'Nobody refers to each other by their real names, you'd fit in quite well, Red.'

I rolled my eyes and let the idea sink in, even if it drove my mind absolutely astray.

'And why can't we go to the police about this?' I blatantly asked.

Arty smirked and chuckled. 'You want a bloodbath? They'll go raiding through Boston after being caught out.'

It was true, the police couldn't know, as much as I'd like them to. There was just too much of a cost, for this particular night. Given the area it was in, smack bang on the outskirts of the city.

I finally sighed, and itched my knee, it still stung from Arty's smack.

'Look, I'll come...' I mumbled. 'I care too much for her, and if she got hurt? I'd never forgive myself.'

'She'd want you to forgive yourself though, lovey,' Arty replied. 'She knows the risks.'

I grouched and waited for her to unlock the door, and once she had, I left the car with another sigh.

If I thought that was the worst part, walking towards a grumpy Juniper Bridges had to top the list. She saw me finally exit the car, and turned to move on.

Hey, at least she waited.

The walk was quiet, the ride in the elevator? Even quieter.

I hated the feeling of standing in these machines, really hated it. I glanced to Juniper, and she had her eyes set on the door, she never turned to look my way.

I'd already thought of a thousand ways to apologise by the time we reached her dorm, and swallowed an awful feeling when she'd opened her door.

My guitar was still in its place, bags and all.

Juniper stalked to her desk, threw her coat over the chair, then moved to her cupboard of clues. She sniffled as she unwrapped the cryptic note we'd found earlier, sticking it on a spare place. I stood pretty awkwardly, rubbing my arms from the rooms chill.

It was hard to imagine I was cuddling up to this girl just hours ago, I honestly felt like holding her even more after all this.

I could feel the tension, and I wondered if it was even worth standing here and fighting. Fighting to tell her I was sorry for a reason I might not even have to be sorry about, how was I meant to fix things?

I sighed softly and grappled at my guitar strap, the rustling of my movement catching her attention. I think I'd go home today, not even bother with the money making, I was too tired to even talk, let alone sing.

'Red?' her voice was low, concerned.

'Yeah,' I mumbled back, pulling the weight of my duffel bag over my shoulder.

Once I looked her way, Juniper had her arms crossed, but her eyebrows were still creased, furrowed. I waited, and swallowed the awful feeling in my chest. 'You're going?'

I nodded to her question, I had to go, I wasn't in the right place.

We stood still, no eye contact was made, nothing. I could hear the students in the dorm over, laughing loudly, some ran down the hall and called out to each other, but in dorm 152, nothing but silence.

I breathed in and nodded again, turning to leave. 'I'll see you on Saturday.'

'Rayne...'

There she goes again, with my name.

I felt my shoulders drop, it bothered me. 'I like it when you call me Red, Juniper.'

She was behind me now, her arms wrapping around my stomach, forehead against my back. I concentrated on my breathing, the colour of her door, anything else but the hurt.

'You've shown me something today...' Juniper started. 'Something that, I can't watch you do anymore.'

I let her turn me, to face her, but I still looked anywhere but her eyes. I was worried for what she'd say, worried I'd stuffed things up.

'Hey...' she cooed. 'Look at me.'

I didn't want to, I really couldn't without breaking. 'I...can't.'

'Then... Just listen to me,' she mumbled, hands at her sides. 'You're so focused on worrying about me, that you're forgetting about yourself.'

I guess that was true, I mean, I hated the idea of dying at twenty-two. But the more I thought about it, the more I realised I couldn't stand the idea of her leaving or getting hurt.

I focused on her desk again, swallowing back my sadness. 'Mm.'

'Please,' She begged softly. 'Don't forget to think of yourself, I don't want you to break. I can't stand the thought of you...'

Juniper paused and sniffled. 'I just, can't stand the thought of you breaking apart. It's been such a short amount of time, but this has brought us together, and I just...'

I saw her desk blur; my vision had become wet. I hated the human body, I hated the feeling of tears.

'Please,' Juniper pushed her head to my collar, then, again. 'Please, don't.'

I was still confused, just a little. I knew she wanted me to take care of myself, I'd been told that many times, I just never really did it, ever.

I'd always thought loving myself was selfish.

Blame it on my childhood, parents, life in Florida, but whatever it was; I wore my heart on my sleeve. I craved the feeling of being wanted, being adored. For someone to calm my stressed shoulders, for someone to look me in the eye and tell me everything would be okay.

I did this, to Juniper, because I knew it was needed, I knew it wasn't easily found. I hadn't realised until then, in that moment.

I'd fallen in love with Juniper Bridges.

I still couldn't speak, but I leant down to kiss her on the head, to assure her, I might be alright.

I left Juniper's apartment feeling guilty that afternoon.

Instead of taking the bus, I walked across the streets of Boston. I didn't focus on what was ahead, or what was behind. I just kept walking.

I saw faces blur by me, some looked my way, but I didn't know where to go, or what I wanted to do anymore.

I know, it sounded so unlike me, to be so torn over something so little.

But it wasn't, it wasn't little at all.

Juniper was right, I'd only had a few relationships in the past, back home. All girls, and I spent the majority of each worrying if I was right for them, if they were right for me. And, both ended up cheating on me.

Relationships were very, very complicated.

But Juniper, ah. Juniper Bridges was something completely different.

Boston girls, they're much nicer.

Maybe it's the situations we'd gotten ourselves in, all this 'drama' surrounding our haste meeting. I didn't know what it was, yet I had faith, only if it was a small amount.

We cared immensely for each other, that was clear. I'd seen it in her eyes, hopefully she saw it in mine too.

Now, more than ever, did I wish for a normal life.

I sniffled and stopped at a corner of shops, the storm had subsided and all that remained were awfully shovelled pavements. I adjusted my guitar, and scanned each window, hoping to find some sort of hiring sign.

I wasn't going to make the money for a busking licence, there was no way, not at this rate.

It sucked to think that way, but reality had gotten in the way, as well as a gang.

I stepped by a mechanic, loud noises emitting from every tool being used. I recognised one boy in particular, shaky and tall, lanky.

Christopher.

He was working on the radio system in one awful looking van, his left leg hanging from the side of its open door. I never took him for the mechanic type, from the way he scattered around like a bug. It took him a moment to realise I was a few feet away, but when he caught my eye, he nervously smiled.

What the heck, I thought, and made my way to say hello.

Christopher was around the same height as me, but had this awful bend in his stance. He waved awkwardly and slammed the door shut, jumping at his own action.

'H-Hey there!' he grinned. 'Rayne, right?'

'Yeah,' I answered, grinning to him weakly. 'Christopher?'

'Yep, that's me,' he laughed nervously, and examined his surroundings. 'You caught me at a bad time.'

'How come?'

'Ah, just a lot of work to do.'

'Least you're making money.'

Christopher blinked at me, confused. 'You haven't got a job?'

I chuckled weakly, and explained my situation, but just the busking issue, nothing more. I didn't want to end up crying in front of a somewhat stranger. Christopher pocketed his hands into his varsity, humming to himself, a thought.

'Well, I could always ask around.' He offered. 'My dad knows a bunch of people, I-I'm sure I could see, y'know...if you could get some time somewhere.'

I was shocked by his words, and nodded enthusiastically. 'Honestly? That'd be great.'

His eyes were jolting left and right, back and forth. He was a nervous one alright.

'S-sure, I'll talk to someone when I can.'

'Hey! It's the busker girl!' Reedy interrupted, throwing himself from the third car garage. Christopher flinched, and gave me a nervous grimace. *It's okay buddy*, I felt like saying, *I don't like him either*.

Reedy stepped to Christopher' side, and gave me a winning grin, that I felt like smacking.

'I overhear you need work?' he asked, nodding to my guitar.

I grimaced and nodded, 'Yeah, you heard correctly.'

Reedy wrapped his arms around Christopher' shoulder, shaking the lanky boy a bit. 'Dude, she could totally help us with that job.'

Christopher glared back, his expression becoming confused. I was too, and had to question.

'That job?'

Reedy patted his hands together and excitedly took my arm, I grouched.

'Yeah! This guy I know.' He started, lowering his voice. 'A super big millionaire, not even joking. Six grand each to deliver some goods to a client.'

I didn't like the sound of it at all.

'Goods?'

'Yeah, goods! I think like, electronics or something, Christopher' dad knows him.'

I looked to the lanky boy for guidance, and he nodded softly. 'Y-yeah.'

'So, this guy is openly giving six grand to you two,' I asked, a little suspicious.

'Yeah, no kidding. Talk to Michael over there, he's done a job with the guy before,' Reedy pointed to a buff man working on a car's engine, he didn't look too flashy.

I eased my eyes and thought for a moment, six grand? That could pay for my busking licence, and months' rent, I could get right back on track.

Y'know, I could even help pay for Nat's surgery, yeah I should put that first.

Before I caught myself worrying, Reedy clapped his hands. 'So?'

'Dude, you can't blame me when I say it's a bit weird.'

'Nah, I totally get you. I was suspicious too, but then I met the guy and he's serious.'

I wasn't used to taking a stranger's word, but Reedy grinned with excitement, like a typical boy about to get a paycheck. I guess I was down to trying, maybe it was honestly a simple task of delivering goods.

'I'll keep it in mind, when's the job?'

Reedy grabbed his cell phone with a pondering hum, he scanned it for a moment, then nodded. 'Sunday, this Sunday night coming.' He said.

Great I thought, right after my Fire Jackal adventure.

I shrugged once more and looked to Christopher, he'd been staring down at his feet ever since, chewing nervously on gum.

'I'll think about it, and get back to you,' I muttered, grabbing my phone from my pocket. 'Here.'

Reedy took it quickly and tapped away. 'Awesome, here's my digits.'

He took a few minutes, before handing me my phone with a smile. 'Dude, think about it, six grand.'

'It does sound nice, thanks for the heads up.'

'Nah, no worries. I was like you once,' he paused and collected himself, rubbing the back of his neck. 'Jobless, I mean.'

I hated hearing that, it sucked.

It fell a bit awkward between us three, and I shuffled on the spot. 'Okay, I'll text you.'

'Yeah!' Reedy grinned, grabbing his dirty oil rag from his belt. 'I hope you can join us, it'll be awesome.'

Awesome, wasn't the word. More like, odd and risky. But I'd gotten used to that.

I bid farewell to Christopher, and he could only give me a distance glance, a short twitch of his lips and a wave.

I continued on east, looking forward to taking a nap when I got home.

Chapter Thirteen

RAYNE

As expected, I didn't sleep very well last night.

My mind was awake, my ears ringing. I did try, as soon as I had finished roaming the streets of lonely Boston's city, I crashed to bed. I'd been lying there for hours, but I couldn't think straight. I wondered how Juniper was, what she was doing or how she was feeling. I caught myself falling deeper into a spiralling conclusion that I had ruined everything, that we were empty.

I'd be empty again.

I was afraid to be empty, or be engulfed with the feeling. It was a feeling of constant disappointment, that pang at the bottom of your chest, the feeling that you've done wrong; when you could have done nothing at all.

I wanted what was best for Juniper, and those around me. Cole and I had similar arguments, he told me I'd needed to step back and think before I'd helped those around me, he told me people take advantage of that.

Why would people take advantage of helping?

I'm sure we all did it, somewhere down the tracks of our childhoods maybe, but adulthood?

Who would even stop and think to hurt another, if they aren't hurting you?

Even that, if they aren't throwing you into a fire, what excuse do you have to hurt another being?

I pondered on these thoughts, until I fell asleep just as the sun started rising.

An irritating sound woke me up, a sudden vibration that bothered me to all ends. I'd just closed my eyes a second ago, didn't I?

After taking a moment to figure out what the sound was, I scrambled across my bed for my phone. Hands sliding to and from under pillows, my feet, and legs.

I found it by my thigh, and didn't even bother checking before I answered it, half asleep and grumpy.

'Hello?' my voice was hoarse.

'Hey, Red,' Juniper replied, softer.

I froze in my spot, and itched my bare stomach, I had a habit of sleeping in my boxer shorts.

I breathed in deeply, my eyes adjusting to the morning light. I think I grumbled something to her in reply, a low groan from the bottom of my tired throat. I laid back down, closed my eyes and waited for her reply.

I was happy to hear her voice; it was a relief to know she wasn't entirely over mine. Doing my best to ignore the exhaustion taking over, leaving my mind astray and fuzzy, I spoke again.

'You okay?' I asked.

'Yeah, I just wanted to see how you were doing, I didn't think you'd answer.'

It was harder to push the wavering feeling from my eyes, I was so tired and my words were slurred. She'd caught me at a bad time.

'Silly,' I mumbled, the pillow under my head felt less like cardboard when I was this out of it. Juniper chuckled, only lightly, but it made me even tireder.

'I wanted to see you today, think I could pop around?'

Her words were like static in my ears, and it took me a total of three seconds to let it process.

'Yeah, yeah, yeah.' I repeated. 'Yeah... yeah that's fine.'

I started mumbling afterwards, I think it was a mixture of directions and numbers, but Juniper replied with a faint. 'Uh, what Red?'

I squeezed my eyes tightly, and peered at the roof.

'Uh, sorry.' I groggily spoke. 'Sorry.'

She told me it was fine, and that I had to repeat my address, which I did, thankfully it was correct. I realised her words were much slower after that, like she was talking to a sick patient, comforting.

'Alright, I'll come around noon. Is that okay?' Juniper asked.

I replied with another muffled moan, and she hummed back playfully.

'I'll see you soon,' she said.

My phone dropped from my ear, it fell to the floor and I finally closed my eyes, completely enshrouding my mind into a calm darkness.

Even the rattling pipes couldn't wake me now.

The first knock, I ignored.

Second, twitched my eyes.

Third, woke me up in a grouch.

When someone's knocking at your door, with such haste, I react the same way. In Florida, dad used to always have packages delivered to the door, and I would sprint from my bed in a quick flash so I wouldn't miss the stupid postman.

I was living in that memory today, and rushed to the door with only my boxer shorts on and a loose sports bra around my chest.

Another knock left my frustration toppling over, who the goddamn hell was tapping on my door at this time of day.

Which time of day? I wasn't aware.

I took a quick glance outside when I stomped by the window, grabbing the door handle with a grunt. I pulled it, ready to blast at whoever thought it'd be funny to come around and disturb me, my teeth clenched, ready to pounce.

Oh.

Juniper lowered her hand from the doorframe, a confused expression drawn over that cute freckled face.

I stood there, in my sleep attire, with the stupidest look on my face. Juniper cocked her head a little, and I finally realised.

'Oh! Ah, shit,' I groaned, pulling the door open for her. Juniper watched me itch my head, rub my neck and glance around, I didn't even clean.

'You totally forgot didn't you?' she joked. 'Red...'

'I didn't forget!' I muttered back. 'I was asleep when you called, and I just totally blanked out.'

I rambled on when I closed the door, my rushed apologies just falling from my dumb mouth. I groaned and squeezed my eyes tight again, rubbing my sinuses.

'Sorry, Juniper,' I sighed. 'I fell right back asleep; our conversation was like a dream.'

Juniper took a quick turn to see my shitty rundown apartment, then smiled my way. It wasn't a big smile, but it was still something.

'I know,' she replied, setting her bag against the foot of my couch. 'You sounded very tired, are you okay?'

I took a quick glance at her attire, the weather had apparently been warmer, because she only wore a long sleeved white shirt and black jeans. I blinked and watched her eyes divert to my stomach, a chuckle leaving her lips.

'You've dressed appropriately for our date again, I see,' she teased. 'Looking great, Red.'

I lost my words, but groaned loudly.

At least things were a bit, calmer between us. But there was definitely a conversation brewing, I didn't know when it would be ready to spill.

'Yeah, yeah,' I said. 'Let me go change.'

'You don't have to; I don't mind the view.' She giggled, my face turned red.

'Hey,' I warned, covering my boxers quickly. 'Man...'

Juniper shook her head playfully, and took another look around the room we both stood in. I felt embarrassed instantly;

'Yeah,' I eased, gritting my teeth. 'I didn't get to clean, not that it'd make a difference. This apartment isn't the best.'

'I think it's fine,' she replied, touching the fabric of the couch. 'It's normal.'

'Normal.'

'Mm, normal.'

Our lack of conversation was pretty awkward, and I sighed deeply. We needed to have that unsettled talk now, or never.

I took her hand and lead her to my room, and she didn't deny the touch at all.

My room wasn't a mess, because I had nothing but my guitar and bed in there, my bedside table and the bathroom to its right.

Juniper sat down against my bed, and waited for me to sit too, but I stood. I was nervous, and I didn't know how to react to anything, I was still so tired and I just wanted to sleep. I opened a few of my drawers, to grab another pair of jeans and a shirt, to cover my bareness.

'Juniper.'

'Red.'

I paused, goose-bumps on my neck. That was a good sign, right?

Juniper was back to calling me 'Red.'

I cleared my throat, I wasn't going to get my hopes up just yet. The memory from yesterday was repeating itself, yelling and anger, even the tears, on constant replay.

'We should finish our talk,' I mumbled. 'I think.'

'Okay,' Juniper simply said. 'Let's do it then.'

I couldn't hold back a mean smile, and turned to face her, 'Do it?'

She got flustered, and lifted her foot to kick my leg. 'Well, yeah you know what I mean, I meant like, do it. Do the deed, uh.'

I blew her off, and flinched when I was tugged by the shirt from behind. I fell beside her, my back pressing into the hard mattress.

Juniper smiled to me, and laid beside me. 'You're a jerk.'

'I know,' I replied, softly.

With the silence, the warmth and Juniper's presence, my exhaustion was back in action. I sniffled and set my hands by my side, feeling her left pinkie finger brush against my own. I twisted my digit around hers, and held it close.

She didn't speak, I didn't either.

We just laid there in silence, let whatever emotions had us by the neck, drift off into nothingness. I gradually got closer to her side, until our hands intertwined. Juniper looked at me, and I could only smile weakly back.

I loved her, a lot.

I hadn't found one flaw about her appearance, the way her eyes looked, beautiful green. I felt awfully bashful whenever I focused on her lips, the temptation was getting harder and harder to maintain and keep hold of.

I liked the way she smelled, the way her freckles aligned and decorated her gorgeous face with uniqueness.

I really had nothing to dislike about her.

Juniper seemed taken aback by my gaze, and squeezed my hand with hers. I could see the blush forming around her cheeks, my own heart began its rhythmic beating.

'Hey, Red...?' she asked. I could hear her voice tremble. 'I meant what I said...'

She halted, and glanced back to the ceiling, I kept my head in the same position, at her. She twisted her lips, and brushed the bottom against her upper teeth.

'I really, really cannot stress enough...' she sighed. 'I need you to know, the thought of you breaking leaves my heart aching.'

Juniper swallowed, she lifted our hands up and simply dropped them once again. 'I dunno, I mean we've only known each other for what? Nearly a month now?'

I nodded a bit, my eyes focusing on hers, she looked my way again and sighed.

'With the way things have been going?' she spoke calmly. 'It feels like, months.'

I felt my heart tighten, and my fingers react with a small twitch. I'd wanted to say the same thing, since we'd had our first conversation at the café. Since I'd watched her eyes glaze over mine like I meant something, like she cared for what I had to say, respect and appreciation.

There was chemistry between us, there was no denying it. I was always under the impression Juniper wasn't looking for anyone, let alone a girl.

But I caught small things, her teasing, flirtatious smiles and her tendency to brush those long fingers against my stomach.

She was comfortable around me, there was trust built that wasn't ready to be broken.

When all your trust is packaged tightly and handed to someone, you expect them to cherish and keep it safe. I wasn't used to that, trust wasn't easily handed over by me, and I was surprised by it myself.

I'd wrapped my trust into a red box, tied it with a bow and handed it to Juniper Bridges with a rose.

'You're funny, charming and brave,' Juniper admitted, squeezing my hand again. 'And you're just, different.'

I hoped she meant that in a good way.

Juniper's voice became a hoarse croak, and she shrugged her shoulders.

'I'm not used to people like you,' she said. 'Used to people, sticking around and making me feel, well, wanted...'

I was so glad to hear this, hear that she was thankful for my presence, thankful for me being myself. I shuffled a little closer to her, my heart was absolutely thumping by this point.

'And I just really, want this whole Fire Jackals thing to be over,' she sounded determined again. 'So I can help Nat, I know the police wouldn't do this much work for one little girl.'

Hearing her speak so vividly left my head swirling, I tried to remain cool, but my breath began hitching.

'So, having you do all this for me...' she murmured. 'Putting yourself before me, because you care so much...'

Her eyes diverted and began examining the awful patterned shapes on the ceiling, that I'd sat and counted when I couldn't sleep. Juniper's face calmed, and she smiled to herself, like she'd realised something.

I hoped it was that realisation.

'It means a lot,' Juniper turned her attention to me, and nodded once. 'A lot.'

'I know,' I replied, eyes on her lips. 'I know, Juniper.'

She seemed to get frustrated, and she lifted her upper torso. 'But you don't, Red.'

I blinked when she said this, I honestly thought I was on the same page. Juniper sighed, and took my hand again, slipping her fingers through mine once more.

'I mean, I just...' she was losing her words. 'I know what you're like. I know you'd rather do good than bad, but you sometimes forget yourself in the process.'

I saw her bite her bottom lip, breathe steadily. 'I'm sorry, I keep lecturing you, and I know you're doing right.'

Juniper let her voice drop, and she hit me gently against the chest. 'You're so stubborn sometimes.'

'As are you...' I replied, as nicely as possible.

She chuckled and left her hand against my collar, the motion caught me off guard and I froze. Juniper kept her look there, and blinked.

'Just know, I couldn't ask for a better person to be around,' her eyes were on mine now. 'And whatever you're thinking, about me...'

I held onto her words, and waited for the words she held back. Though she averted her look once more, and started to fumble. 'Red, I just.'

Her fingers were at my shoulder now, nails gently digging in. The movement had my stomach reeling with excitement, butterflies erupting from one thousand cocoons.

I just, couldn't push the feeling away.

Quickly and as gracefully as I could, I lifted my upper body and took her chin with my left index finger. She started to speak as I turned her attention, but instantly lost her words once my lips touched hers.

Juniper froze against me, and I shut my eyes as tightly as I could, my hands close to her neck now. Police sirens from further up the street had begun to echo this way, busy city cars, the wind.

But I heard nothing but my own stuttering heartbeat, with my lips against hers.

Juniper instantly kissed me back, and took a deep breath. I'd already melted once, but after her returned gesture, I'd begun to reform and dissolve once more.

I'd wanted to do this many times, even before I left her dorm yesterday, but I was glad I'd prolonged the moment.

My lips were the first to part, and put pressure against hers, she allowed herself to be dominated by the move and touched my tongue with her own.

I couldn't fathom, I was lost in this kiss from the beginning, as much as I was lost in her eyes weeks ago. I'd felt multiple emotions wash over me, happiness and heartache, lust and greed. It was truly something, that I'd never experienced before.

Juniper took hold of my shoulders, and straddled herself onto my lap. Now I was the one being dominated by her confidence. I broke off and took a breath, before she kissed me once more. I'd started to understand now; I think Juniper was craving this too.

My hands trailed up her back, and I could feel the tension escape from her tight muscles. The moment turned from sweet, to heated quite fast.

I knew humans were attracted to the idea of sex and love, they thrived on the feeling of pleasure and compassionate attention, wanted to take it and hold it whenever they could. I had fought the urges of sex for months now, but they'd begun to topple over themselves.

Juniper croaked through our kiss, enjoying it. Even if it was just a hitched breath, I took it as a compliment and touched her shoulder blades, massaging the tension.

Her hands were tight around my neck, fingers at the back of my head, I didn't even want to pull away, even to breathe.

Her lips were soft, and whenever her tongue touched the tip of mine, the static that hit my abdomen was unbelievable. As per usual, I couldn't understand the moment, if it was what my heart wanted or what my sexual needs desired. I wasn't sure if it was the right place, the right time, had I let lust overcome me? Had we allowed it to overcome us?

I got too careless, and touched the bottom of her shirt. Juniper froze against my touch; her hands took my shoulders.

When she'd broken off, I longed to grab back, anything to keep that rush going, but Juniper kept me down.

'R-Red,' She whimpered. 'Um...'

I examined her face, red and flustered. She hadn't opened her eyes yet, but eased her head to clear her throat. 'Red, we can't.'

Oh God, my heart fell.

'I mean, it's not that w-we can't,' She stammered, blinking softly 'I just, I...'

I wished she'd spit it out, but her voice quivered. 'I'm sorry.'

The rush of adrenalin was still there, yes. But Juniper had changed emotion quite quickly, and I was now concerned.

I let my hands fall to her waist, flat against her hips.

She probably didn't want to talk, so I embraced he tightly. 'It's alright.'

Juniper shook her head, kissed my right cheek deeply and shifted from my body. I watched her stand still, then rub the back of her neck. My own hands fell to my sides in shame, I felt stupid.

'I'll see you tomorrow afternoon, okay?'

'Okay...'

'Alright, I'll... uh.'

'Yeah...'

Juniper looked my way once more, and took a deep breath. 'It's not your fault, Red.'

I was expecting to hear my real name, but it was a nice itch of relief when she didn't, it meant things weren't entirely as bad as I thought.

She leant forward and kissed me across the forehead, before she let herself out.

The moment was over before it'd even started.

I sat there for a good twenty minutes, before I pieced together the beginning from the end. I scooped up the feelings I'd experienced, and swallowed them back up, my brain began to worry.

Juniper and I had touched lips, our tongues danced, and our hands had grappled at one another with such force and want.

But we weren't sure we'd wanted it at all.

Chapter Fourteen

RAYNE

Waves and waves of emotions had rolled over my body through the night, and continued on in the morning. Like a crashing sheet of water on a seabed, I was being dragged to and from states of complete misery and pure happiness.

Juniper's kiss lingered on my lips, her scent on my bedsheets and clothing.

If I concentrated enough, I could still feel her hands in my hair, around my neck. I dreamt of her, her smile and her body close to mine, I awoke hoping to find her next to me.

But she was never there, no.

I was caught in a tangle of webs, but I didn't struggle. I wanted to, but I thought maybe if I lay in those tight knots of heartache longer, I would only see the positive of what it was like to truly love someone.

Love, I never thought about it. I was never one to become attached, ever.

The girls I dated back in Florida, they were gorgeous girls who'd kissed me and told me I was perfect. But they never held me like Juniper did, nor did their kisses remain on repeat in my mind, over and over.

I knew there was bigger things to think of, today was the day we'd be sneaking into a clan meeting full of murderers and rapists, drug addicts and weapons dealers.

And all I could think of was my early grave, and Juniper's.

I was tempted to see Nick Rodgers, tell him of the location, our plans and our progress. But then Arty's words hit me and reminded me that leaking information to the federal force would only cause further issues.

Further issues that even Boston wouldn't be prepared for.

I chose my darkest clothes, and couldn't help but think of a spy movie spin off, bound to go wrong. I would have expected Juniper to jump for joy at this idea, of how she would be snooping around a state wide murderous group. But, I think she had finally realised the seriousness of the threat, something that I'd wished for a long time.

She was still determined though, that much was clear.

I hoped we would find Pebbles, and finally bring this whole messy situation to an end. No more sneaking around and trying to find clues, no more pain and crying, muddled feelings and big headaches.

Just simple answers, simple answers that we deserved.

I sat against my bed, in the same spot I had with Juniper, I tried to relive the moment. I pictured her against my lap, the half-lidded look in her eyes. My hands around her waist with her forehead against mine, our lips locked.

A pure blissful moment, that I hoped would repeat.

No, I couldn't think like this.

It was selfish, and there were serious issues at hand.

Love would have to wait, even if it felt fucking terrible.

Juniper, Arty and I met up outside the nearest Rocket Burger. Its gigantic red spaceship was easy to catch as I walked from the bus stop, it was sticking out of the top of its red and black building. It was a fast-food joint, and when I'd finally reached the other two waiting outside, Arty was scoffing down on a burger. The fiery redhead saw me first, and waved her sandwich like an idiot.

I saw Juniper turn, and my stomach did awful flips.

I was happy to see her, but I still couldn't get the image of her lips against mine out of my head.

Juniper wore black too, a turtleneck and jeans, way better looking than my plain black shirt and men's gym pants, I hated how the women's version looked, all tight and uncomfortable.

Arty, I guess didn't have to worry about wearing a dark set of clothes. She was only heading inside the Red Jackals meeting to open a passage for Juniper and I, a part of me had begun to worry that Arty wouldn't be allowed in.

I didn't even think there was a plan B to follow.

'Looking good, lovey,' Arty scoffed at me, chewing into her burger again.

She leant against the hood of her car, and her eyes wandered around my body.

'Very "special ops,"' she grabbed imaginary guns from her pockets, and pointed them to me.

I grimaced and pocketed my hands, then turned to Juniper.

There was a nervous energy around her, who couldn't blame her? This was probably the stupidest thing we could be doing, and would likely end in the worse possible way.

But there was information we needed, and we had to obtain it, or Nat would only get worse.

Juniper took a deep breath then turned to Arty, who chewed obnoxiously towards me, I chuckled weakly.

'Okay,' the brunette mumbled. 'So, what's our plan again?'

Arty blinked and shuffled on the spot, 'Uh.'

I saw her ponder, then shrug her shoulders. 'Beats me.'

'Arty!' Juniper groaned. 'C'mon.'

I saw Arty grimace then rustle through her pockets, she grabbed her car keys and jingled them.

'I take you two somewhere quiet where nobody can see you,' she began. 'Then make my own way down and get into this shithole of a party, then sneak you in.'

She looked to me, then to Juniper. 'Right?'

'Sounds about right.' I muttered, pocketing my hands. 'That is, if you get in.'

Arty laughed loudly, and pointed a finger towards my chest, leering.

'Trust me,' she grinned. 'I'll get in there.'

'Then we find a way upstairs,' Juniper began.

'Where they keep the black book, in most events...' Arty interrupted. 'Hopefully.'

'Hopefully?' I asked. 'You mean there's a chance this book, won't be upstairs?'

I glanced to Juniper, and she pursed her lips.

Juniper had previously scoped out the area before we made our final decision to go that day, and was positive that an upstairs vicinity was visible. Now we just had to hope that this 'black book of names' was up there.

It was like playing Russian roulette.

Arty looked a little nervous, but she wouldn't let the world see her fear.

'Hey!' she snapped, ignoring Juniper's gaze. 'We'll be fine. Now, c'mon'

Surprisingly, Juniper sat in the back seat with me. She smiled once to me, an assuring smile that let me know that she was alright, even though I felt I wasn't, I returned a small smirk.

'Okay,' Arty sighed as she closed her door, I glanced to her; just as she tightened her grip on the steering wheel. It fell quiet, before she turned her attention to us, eyes serious.

'This is going to be big,' she reminded us. 'Really, big.'

'I know,' Juniper answered, nodding to me. 'We know.'

Arty pondered for a moment, her mouth opening and closing on a set of words. I waited to hear her continue to warn us, but she turned her attention to me and grimaced.

'Don't die in there, you moron,' Arty sighed. 'And don't let Juniper down.'

'The thought of doing that never crossed my mind,' I replied.

Juniper from beside me chuckled, and leant forward to hold Arty's arm. 'Arty...'

'No, don't give me those eyes, lovey,' Arty eased her head and twisted her lips. 'Not that puppy look.'

'Everything will be okay,' Juniper continued. 'Even if we do get a little bruised and battered.'

I didn't like the accepting tone in her voice, she'd already accepted the fact she may be hurt. I couldn't promise anything; I couldn't say the typical hero line; 'I'll protect you.'

As much as I would like to, false hope wouldn't do any good right now.

The Fire Jackals event started at nine and went on all night into the early morning. I hoped we wouldn't have to stay long.

On the way there, Arty described her time in the clan. I was shocked to hear that she was forced to beat the living hell out of other people, even clan members who had stolen a pint of beer from the cooler. They did hard-core drugs, and named marijuana 'Sea' to make it easier to sell on the streets.

They ate like rabid animals and listened to stories of betrayal and murder, how they'd cut this man or punched the other.

Arty fell a little quiet when she told us about a man named Ego who'd abused and killed a girl prior to one meeting, and boasted on about it like he was a hero.

What a disgusting freak.

'I mean,' Arty paused at the red light. 'Don't be surprised to hear gunshots if I see that asshole tonight, loves.'

'You brought a gun?' I asked, a little surprised.

She patted her dashboard and opened the little compartment on the left, showing me her handgun. 'Of course,' she replied. 'I'm not stupid enough to go in there empty handed.'

'What about us?' I grimaced. 'What do we do if we get into trouble?'

'Now that's too dangerous,' Arty replied, but she grabbed another object. 'Here.'

I flinched when handed me her knife, blade sharp and ready.

'Oh man,' I eased.

'Now, now,' Arty interrupted, kicking the exhaust forward. 'Last resorts.'

I sighed and leant back, barely touching the tip of its sharp edge. I had never stabbed someone before, and I couldn't even imagine doing so.

Juniper's right hand touched my knee, fingers brushing the bone. I paused and glanced to her, but she had her sights outside, waiting desperately to see that damned building.

I swallowed and touched her fingers with my own, hers curled around mine. It was a short moment, but I could honestly feel every inch of anxiety in her. I wanted to lift her hand and kiss each digit, peck away the fear.

I held her hand tight, and waited for her to pull away.

She didn't.

We drove in the back way, so we wouldn't raise any suspicion. I could feel my very heart begin its ached beating, insisting I turn around and run, get out of there before it was too late.

Juniper kept her fingers around me, and squeezed my hand when we all drove closer to the building. It was huge, surrounded by junk and waste, and lit up eerily. I could hear the loud voices, clanging of bottles and gunfire coming from inside, I shivered.

'Okay,' Arty mumbled, parking close to the forest roadside. 'Now, over there we found a back door right?'

She pointed to the far left of the building. The street was empty and dark, I tried to make out any figures, but it looked pretty abandoned.

Juniper nodded and hummed, positive. 'Yeah. You just have to find a way inside now.'

Arty shut the engine off and groaned, her head hitting the back of the seat. 'The hard part.'

Juniper breathed in loudly, and exhaled even louder, a croaky whimper escaping her lips. She finally let my hand go, and reached for the door.

'Wait,' Arty grumbled. 'Wait, wait.'

We paused and waited for her to continue, and she unbuckled her seatbelt. I could see her eyes wander for a moment, over the building and figures walking inside. With all she told us before, I could only imagine the awful things running through her mind.

I used to loathe seeing Arty, but now I just wanted to give her a pat on the back and tell her she was doing great.

'I want you two, to be extra careful,' she said. 'So careful, that you never take your eyes off each other.'

I wanted to crack a joke, tell Arty I never took my eyes off Juniper, but now wasn't the right time. Juniper took her hat off her head, something she hardly did, and left it beside her. I watched her tense her neck and crack her knuckles, then smile to the redhead.

'Of course,' she touched Arty's hand, and rubbed her arm. 'We'll be okay.'

Arty strained her face into a nervous grouch, and nodded once. 'Black book.'

'Black book.'

'With a symbol on the bottom left corner.'

'And a red ribbon.'

'And! It's pretty old, like way old, you know how it has the,'

'Arty,' Juniper interrupted, squeezing her arm once more. 'We'll be okay.'

I wanted to butt in and tell them my concerns, but I was a nervous wreck right now, nothing I could say would change the anxious feeling surrounding all three of us.

'Alright, lovey,' Arty mumbled. 'I'll give you two, thirty minutes.'

I glanced to my watch and nodded.

'If you're not back at the door by then, I'll come find you,' She said. 'And if you're running well on time, meet me back at the car.'

I saw Juniper nod and leave the car first, Arty glanced to me and nodded too, and I just sat there for a moment, allowing the multiple feelings of fear rush over me.

I never ever thought I'd find myself in a situation like this, this was unreal! But it was happening, and I was never living in the now, always the past and future. Blame it on anxiety, but how can you blame me? the future was dark and grey, and when you focus on the negative, it's only natural to worry.

I took a deep breath before exiting the car, into the muggy woods. In my back pocket was Arty's knife, and I could feel its sharp edge cutting through the fabric.

We made our way quietly through the bush, Arty in front and Juniper behind me. We were hidden quite well, but I jumped whenever I heard a gunshot from inside, followed by a barrel of laughter. None of us spoke, just slipped our way through the darkness, and found the same door we marked earlier.

Arty sighed and stood Juniper and I aside each other, examining us quickly. She grabbed her gun from her back pocket, and fumbled to hand it to Juniper. 'You should take this.'

'No,' Juniper pushed the barrel of the gun back towards Arty, shaking her head. 'No, you take that.'

'Juniper.'

'Arty.'

'Ugh.'

I liked to see Arty fumble around our journalist, it was pretty hilarious even in a time like now. She pocketed her gun and lifted her head, grinning awkwardly. 'Wish me luck.'

We did, and kept an eye out on her from the corner of the wall we stood aside. Arty strutted rather energetically towards the front doors, where two members clad in red and black stood side by side. They glared at her when she got closer, and stepped forward.

I held my breath in anticipation.

Arty seemed to be talking with confidence, leaning forward and hitting each member playfully on the shoulder. They'd raised their guns earlier, but lowered them after a few minutes. The one on the right nodded to his comrade, and the other shrugged his shoulders.

Over the booming music and chatter from inside, I heard them agree to allow Arty in, mentioning a few things to her that I couldn't make out.

When she stepped in, Juniper and I rushed to the back door. I was a bundle of nerves, and hopped on the spot. I didn't know what was behind that door, maybe a few guys ready to beat the hell out of us, maybe they had machetes and guns at the ready.

'Man,' I mumbled to myself. 'Ah, man.'

'Red,' Juniper muttered. She stepped to me, and I shivered under her touch. 'We can do this.'

'I know...' I replied. 'I know.'

She rubbed my arms and smiled weakly, and I had another series of intimate images rush through my mind. I swallowed nervously and cleared my throat. We hadn't spoken about it yet, about yesterday.

But I had to focus, I couldn't be thinking about that now. Juniper gave me a reassuring look, and I exhaled again.

'Okay,' I turned my attention to the door. 'Now we wait.'

'Now we wait,' Juniper repeated.

We stood for a total of five minutes, in the muggy cold, sometimes the breeze was freezing, others were slightly warm that smelt like awful garbage and dirt.

'Not the most romantic place, huh?' I joked, trying to break the tension.

Juniper chuckled lightly. 'Not in the slightest.'

I wanted to reach out to her, take her in my arms and keep her close. But as soon as I mustered the strength to do so, a horrid sound emitted from the door. I stepped back and held my knife close, pulling Juniper aside me.

The door rattled a little, then opened quite slowly. I was filled with instant relief when Arty peeked through, constantly glancing back and forth.

'C'mon,' she mumbled. 'Inside, go.'

I rushed in with Juniper, into a dark and gloomy back room that was full of generators. I heard voices from above and shook in my shoes. Arty hit me across the back, pushing me forward.

'Get going,' she snapped, voice lowered. 'They're already concerned about my appearance.'

Juniper made her way forward first, towards two big stairwells against the back wall. Arty took the one on the left, and we spend up the right.

Even though it was unbelievably loud inside the building, gunshots that shook the rattling walls, gruff voices and awful music, Juniper and I still sneaked hastily.

I was half expecting a bunch of gang members to pop out of nowhere, from the walls, the floor, wherever I looked.

But it was eerily quiet and abandoned, too weird if you asked me.

Juniper paused before a wooden door, and swallowed loudly, we'd been rushing and now she needed to catch her breath. I touched her back softly and she mumbled softly.

'Alright...' she swallowed. 'You sure this is the one?'

We didn't have much time to ponder and check around, so I grabbed the handle of the door, opening it quietly. 'Red.'

I paused and nodded, Juniper froze and took a deep breath, collecting herself for the hundredth time. I needed to do something, to comfort her. I reached out and took her tightly by the shoulders, pulling her close to me.

Juniper kissed me, just gently, and she held around my neck.

It was short, and sweet, but also had a tang of sadness on the brim of its touch.

She touched my upper lip, and I gripped at her shoulders, my hands clutching close. I wished I could lose myself in her embrace again, but not here, not now.

Juniper's fingers shook, and when she broke off, she kept close; hands against my jaw.

Our breath was short, we always forgot to breathe when we locked lips.

'If we die,' she said. 'I wanted to make sure I'd have your lips on mine again.'

It was music to my ears, hearing those sweet words escape. We touched foreheads, and Juniper nodded once. 'If we get out of this, you owe me more kisses,' she said.

I laughed softly, and pressed my lips to her nose. 'We'll see.'

Again, I wondered if that was an action of pure fear, lust and comfort.

A goodbye kiss.

I wanted to feel more than that, I wanted to escape the constant plane of existence that Juniper and I had found ourselves on, filled with fear and worry.

I gave her one small look, hoping she could read my mind and all the feelings with it. Her green eyes were eased, gentle. We shared a moment, fighting back the urges of want and need.

Juniper let me go, and waited for me to turn, and once I had, I clenched my teeth.

Inside was dark, gloomy and smelled rancid. I covered my mouth and stepped in first, my right hand out to keep Juniper back.

I didn't want to see where the smell was emitting from.

I watched my feet as I walked, creaking into the wooden boards below. I kept a sharp eye out, above and both sides, this room was a square, solid.

In front of me was a few desks, and a door to its right, guessing by the height of the building, it leaded to another stairwell.

'C'mon,' I whispered, ushering her in. 'Let's just do this.'

I heard her do the same as me, sneak around and creak whenever she put pressure on the rickety boards below. I spotted some books before I even reached the desk, but the smell was getting worse and worse with every step. Juniper groaned from behind me, cussing.

'Jesus Christ,' she hissed. 'What the hell is that smell?'

I shrugged and leaned forward, hoping the book wasn't bugged with any bombs. Who knew with these guys. I remembered Arty's description of the original, and found the emblem on one black book, left, below. 'Here, Juniper.'

She stood by my side and grabbed her flashlight from her back pocket. I watched her flip through pages and pages, of a rusty old book that was piled up with a bunch of similar ones.

I took a few and glanced inside, each page was doused in a red ink, at least I thought it was ink.

'I can't find him,' Juniper sounded irritated. 'There's so many names here, I just can't.'

I helped her, and we both scanned each page slowly, my finger aligning with odd clan names.

'Seven, Olympus...' I mumbled. 'Sensation, Koe.'

Juniper cussed to herself again, and flipped the pages faster and faster. 'He's not here, Red!'

It was true, in five minutes we'd looked for Pebbles and found nobody by that name. I could sense the anger rising in Juniper's body, and I reached to touch her.

She groaned and flipped through the pages again, until she hit the last page and gasped.

'What?!' I asked loudly, covering my mouth afterwards. 'Did you find him?'

She shook her head, eyes wide. 'No.'

I leaned over her shoulder, and she weakly huffed to herself. 'Something better, I think.'

I saw what she meant, a simple car key, sticky taped inside a page. Above its rusty shape, was a name.

'Pebbles.' I muttered. 'That's...'

'The key,' Juniper said. 'To the car that hit my sister.'

It was a shocking discovery, and left me quite baffled.

'Who would leave this lying around? Don't they think that's a bit stupid?' I asked.

'No.' Juniper retorted. 'Because they don't expect us.'

She had a point, although Arty's showing up was a little suspicious, no member of the Fire Jackals had the faintest idea of our big plans in the making.

Juniper ripped the key from its page and pocketed it safely. 'Okay, let's go.'

It was too easy, I thought.

I wished I hadn't.

The door ahead of us opened with a creak, and was nearly kicked in as a brutish man stepped through. He growled angrily towards us, his hair patchy and ripped to shreds. He was big, but I could hardly take a closer look before he raised his shotgun towards the both of us.

'I knew I heard some fuckers in here!' he yelled. 'Hey!'

We ducked when he shot, the sound rattled my ears. He shot another three times, and I listened out for his reload. 'You fuckers are gonna get it, coming to the party uninvited.'

I hoped he was the only one, and raised to throw my hands up, panic overruling my thoughts. 'Hey!'

Juniper tugged at my jeans, and tried her absolute hardest to pull me down. He paused his reload and pointed his big gun to my chest, he was a few feet away but he had a ninety percent chance of killing me with one shot.

'Hey, dude,' I started, shakily. 'Sorry! We must have wandered in somehow.'

He chewed angrily, taking a quick glance around. 'Yeah?'

He was being sarcastic, and lifted the gun to me once more, keeping his distance. I reached for my back pocket, feeling the hilt of Arty's knife around my fingertips.

'I smell bullshit, girly,' he yelled. 'You two really shouldn't have come tonight.'

He licked his lips and laughed, he was insane, and had this crazed look in his pure blue eyes. But I also realised, he was drunk, very drunk.

'Look, I can give you some cash…' I bargained. 'How's that?'

He pondered for a moment, and watched Juniper rise next to my right side. He grinned and pointed to her.

'Can I have her too?' he spat roughly aside his feet. 'I like the way she looks; I have a thing for innocent looking girls.'

My blood was boiling from his words, and I clenched the knife tight around my right hand. I hadn't dealt with this before, bargaining with a killer.

He licked his lips once more and nodded his gun towards Juniper, 'You give me her, and were good.'

I wasn't ready to hand Juniper over, that was out of the question. I felt her hand take mine, and wrap around the knife. I glanced to her, giving her confused eyes, and she smiled back.

'Sure,' she giggled, playing dumb. 'I'll go with a hunk like you.'

Juniper took the knife close and flashed her most charming smile his way, he grinned back.

'That's what I like to hear,' he chuckled, stepping back.

I didn't.

My heart had begun to race when she stepped towards him, I tried my absolute hardest not to focus on the knife in her right hand, and instead watched as the thug placed his shotgun down against the table. I grimaced when his hands took her waist, Juniper eased her head away from his lips, and caught my look when his hands squeezed her backside.

'You know,' she said sweetly.

'What's that, sweetheart?'

'You should really ask for a girl's name, before you go and grab her like that...'

He was confused by her words and let her go, waiting for the rest of her sentence. But Juniper just smiled, and threw her right hand forward, embedding the knife in his stomach.

He let out the biggest yell I had heard, and stumbled back against the rotten desk chair. 'Fuck!'

Juniper stood back shakily, her eyes wide.

She realised what she had done, and rushed to my side, 'Go!'

She pushed me through the door, trailing behind me with haste. But I could hear our fat friend roar and grab his gun, scattering over the table to shoot.

The first shot missed; the wall beside me splintered and I eased my head as I ran. The next, well, he got a lucky shot.

I heard the typical locking of a new bullet, and the blast was much closer. Again, the wood crackled beside me, and Juniper cried out in pain. I gasped and turned, catching her as she fumbled forward. I could feel the heat and wetness emitting from her left side, and watched her writhe in agony.

'Go!' she screamed over the shots. 'Just go!'

I pulled her along with me, adrenalin taking the handlebars. We sped down the stairs, ignored the yelling from above and pushed through another set of doors.

Juniper was whimpering when we ran, her breath hitched and loud. I called to her, assured her we'd be okay. But again, I was giving off false hope.

I was caught around the neck by another pair of hands, and pushed into the nearest wall. Another male, lankier now threw a punch my way. I blocked it angrily, throwing myself at him as well.

He clearly wasn't aware I knew how to fight, and my foot made contact with his crotch. He whimpered loudly and stood still for a moment, before he coughed and fell to his feet.

I was pissed off now, and threw him back against the floor.

I was furious, but more towards the fat asshole we'd faced just moments ago. I punched, and kicked and continued until my hands bled. I was never one to let my rage overcome me, but boy did I find it hard then.

Juniper pulled me from his bleeding body, and groaned as she took me back.

'Red!' she cried. 'C'mon! we have to go; we have to go!'

Once I heard a closer yell from upstairs, I threw myself back. I kicked the back door open with a cough, my hands were aching.

I pulled Juniper through the forest, and heard the commotion from behind us, they'd track us if we didn't hurry up.

I could hear Juniper moan behind me, and I took a look back. She was clutching her side, as it bled. Her face was pulled in almost agony, and I felt awful.

'C'mon Juniper,' I coaxed. 'You can do it, the car's close!'

I was worried now, what if Arty had gotten into her own sort of trouble, and we were running to an empty vehicle?

I didn't want to think about it, I just needed to run.

If she wasn't there, I'd keep Juniper safe, we'd be fine.

I felt my heart leap with joy when I saw Arty's car, it was on, the engine roaring. The redhead lifted herself out of the window, and rushed us in. 'Hurry up!'

I pulled Juniper closer, and flinched as gunshots gradually got closer to our whereabouts. Juniper herself cried out when she reached the passenger door, I opened it for her, and threw her inside, as carefully as I could.

When she was safe, I rushed in as well.

'Go!' I screamed to Arty. 'Go, Go, GO!'

She swore loudly, some of the vilest things left her mouth as she turned her body and backed out quickly. I was panting, and Juniper was laying against her seat, clutching her side through hisses of pain.

'Oh god.' Arty yelped. 'What happened to her?!'

I reached over and lifted Juniper's sweater carefully, easing my eyes from the eight close gashes. She'd been hit by the shotgun ricochet , but I was glad it wasn't a full blow.

'Ricochet,' I yelled. 'Some idiot,'

Arty groaned over me, she'd turned the car fully and pressed her foot against the pedal. I was launched back when we raced down the street, Arty's car screeched and its exhaust sparked. Arty and I argued for a good few seconds, she blamed me for Juniper's pain, and I hit back at her with all the reasons that wasn't true.

It was only when l Juniper's phone rang that we shut up and took a breath. I glanced behind the car, and spotted only a few lights, but they lingered far away.

'Shut up!' Juniper groaned, her eyes lidded with exhaustion. 'Both of you, shut up!'

Arty hit the steering wheel with a cuss, and I turned to Juniper. She was fiddling with her phone, trying to bring it to her ear. When I reached to take it, she flipped my hand away, swallowing loudly before she answered it.

'Dad!' she kept her voice normal, no quivers. 'Everything okay?'

I couldn't believe this, here we were, speeding off down the freeway to escape a clan of murderers, and she was casually speaking to her father.

Juniper nodded to whatever he was saying, and clenched her teeth whenever the pain got severe.

'Okay!' she cleared her throat. 'I'll take care of her tonight, you just get that work done.'

I glanced to Arty, and she looked back, we shared that mutual concern.

'Me?' Juniper whimpered. 'Yeah! I-I'm fine.'

I saw her nod more, and finally bid farewell to her father. She was good at hiding the fact she'd been shot.

I kept a clear eye out behind us and buckled my seatbelt.

'We have to get her to the hospital' I ordered.

'No!' Juniper replied.

'No?!'

'Yes, no!' She looked me in the eye, and I swallowed. 'We can't, they'll be suspicious, and we can't have that, remember?'

I saw Arty look my way, and I groaned.

'It's fine,' Juniper swallowed. 'It's just a few cuts, I'll fix them up at home.'

'And I can't be seen at all for at least a bloody month,' Arty admitted. 'They'll skin me alive.'

I paused and realised, that Arty was probably the one in most danger now. She'd shown her face to the Fire Jackals and mysteriously vanished in the night.

She really gave a lot.

Juniper breathed heavily and took her side, lifting it to examine her wounds. I saw her eyes roll back a little, her nausea rising in her face.

'Oh God,' she shivered. 'Oh my God.'

I took her hand and held it close, and I quickly glanced at my right fist, three knuckles had been skinned open, and bled too.

I couldn't even feel the fire burning, but I knew once the adrenalin had stopped, I'd be in a world of hurt.

'We're going to Somerville,' Juniper said softly. 'I have to take care of N-Nat tonight.'

Arty nodded roughly. 'Okay, we'll get you patched up there.'

I squeezed Juniper's hand, and she looked my way, breathing hoarsely.

'Did they get a good look at your face?' Arty asked. 'Because we're all royally screwed if they did.'

I told her no, and that the whole entire place was so dark, even I couldn't see the second male.

But the first definitely saw our faces clear as day, though he was drunk beyond words. I actually had a reason to thank alcohol, it was the reason for his shitty aiming.

The reason Juniper was alive.

Arty slowed down once we were safe, but I always made sure to look behind the car, in case we had an army of Fire Jackals on our tail.

The drive to Juniper's home was quiet, but Juniper reminded us of her pain whenever she hitched a breath.

I never took my eyes off her, so she wouldn't pass out. And I could see Arty give quick glances here and there.

I was glad the night was over, but now we had a hell lot of aftermath to deal with.

'Okay,' Arty mumbled to herself. 'Here we are, love.'

Juniper nodded and groaned from the bumps on the road, she chewed at her bottom lip and looked towards the dark sky through her window.

I tore my eyes away from her for a moment, just to see how nice her house was. It was a house that stood out from the others. A single-storey, grey colonial home with a big black pitched roof. .

I couldn't sit here and marvel in its homely wonders, Juniper had begun to cry in pain again.

Arty was already at her door, and threw it open. She took a quick look at me; 'C'mon help me!'

I sped out, body sweaty from the rush of the whole situation.

Arty took Juniper out carefully, and lifted her up, whenever she cried out, I felt my heart drop. I wrapped my arm around her waist, and tried to push the pressure down on my own body, Arty did the same.

When we lifted her up the stairwell, she shushed us. 'Don't make a lot of noise, I don't want Nat waking up.'

Arty and I shared a look, and nodded gently.

'Right,' Arty muttered. 'Where's your spare key, love?'

Juniper directed her to the fuse box against the wall, and I held all her weight when Arty fumbled with the lock on it. Juniper leant against my chest and mumbled the code, and once Arty had it, she rushed to open the front door.

It was dark inside, too dark for me to really get a good look at Juniper's home. But as we walked in, Arty knew her way around clearly. She stepped forward then turned left, opening one door. The bathroom light flickered to life, and I helped Juniper in.

'Okay, grab me the antibacterial...' Arty said, quietly. 'And the cotton swabs, all that shit.'

I nodded and closed the door softly behind the three of us, we didn't need to make a scene. Juniper's father was working overnight, I wondered how he'd react to his daughter bleeding in pain on the bathroom floor.

Juniper struggled to take her sweater off, and Arty was already rummaging through medical supplies. I made it my job to help Juniper out of her clothing, lifting it carefully over her head.

I flinched from the cuts against her side, and hissed softly.

The splits weren't all bad, but two were gashing and bleeding constantly. They were deep, and needed stitches, I wasn't sure how to do that, I hoped Arty knew.

'You know how,'

'Yes.'

'How?'

'I've been fighting for years, Rayne.' Arty dabbed a few cotton buds in the red liquid, grabbing Juniper's arms. 'I know how to seal a wound.'

Juniper whimpered to herself, and cried out when Arty began cleaning. We both coaxed her, told her it was alright.

But shit, did it hurt to hear this.

I saw her struggle on the spot, kicking her legs a little whenever Arty dribbled more antibacterial on her skin, Juniper's eyes were tear ridden, tired.

'Man, are you two lucky,' Arty said. 'These aren't as bad.'

Juniper huffed sarcastically, and Arty chuckled back. 'Oh, I'm only teasing.'

In about twenty minutes, Juniper had ceased crying. Instead she watched Arty thread a needle through her skin, cringing whenever the point touched her.

'Nearly done,' Arty comforted her. 'Then you'll be much better, love.'

It was something I wasn't used to, seeing Arty put herself out into danger for someone other than herself. Here she was acting like a big sister, coaxing Juniper with sweet words.

It suited her, even if she hated to admit it.

Juniper swallowed loudly after she was cleaned up, the cuts still looked sore. I watched Arty cover the wounds with patches, they must have come from the hospital, because I didn't think stores sold them at all.

Juniper could stand, and that's all that mattered. She sighed deeply and held Arty close for a moment, thanking her. I cleaned up a little, washing the dried blood from my hands, I didn't want to remember my blind rage earlier, and hoped the water would wash away the memories too. I jumped from a vibration in my pocket, and as the others spoke to themselves, I checked my phone with a wet hand. An unknown number flashed before me, with a few words in capital letters. *Fire Jackal business, are you in or are you out?* I swallowed nervously, reading over and over it. The job I was offered was for a Fire Jackal? Did Christopher and Reedy know ? I had too many thoughts running through my head, but it made more and more sense. Big sum of money, delivering 'goods'. This was a drug deal. I shoved my phone back in my pocket, turning just as Juniper began to look my way. I couldn't think about that now.

'Alright, we should check up on Nat,' Juniper mumbled. 'She'll probably be up playing games, as per usual.'

She sounded humoured, and I saw Arty grin back. 'You shouldn't have bought her that console, silly.'

I listened to them speak as I cleaned my wounds, it stung when I doused the cuts in antibacterial, but it needed to be done.

I wouldn't want an infection, especially not on my hands.

Arty left the room quietly, and Juniper finally turned to me. I glanced at her through the bathroom mirror, and continued to wash my hands under warm water.

'You feeling a little better?' I asked. 'Didn't look good, scared me absolutely to death.'

She hobbled to me and leant against my back, sighing. 'It's going to hurt, but I'll be fine.'

I was scared, very scared. With a pounding head, images of blood and pain filled my mind, I wanted out, now.

'Red, your hands?' Juniper asked.

'They're okay,' I answered softly. 'I'm okay now, it's over.'

It wasn't over, no way. We never found out who Pebbles was, but we did find an item of his.

Now how the hell were we meant to find the car the key belonged to?

Juniper gently held me, making sure to put all her weight on her right side instead. 'You did good, Red.'

I smiled weakly, and turned to face her. Juniper looked exhausted, but she still returned a grin.

'You did great,' I returned. 'You stabbed a guy.'

'Don't remind me,' she eased her head and pressed her forehead against my chin. 'Let's forget that happened.'

I chuckled and noticed Arty, she popped her head in and raised her eyebrows.

'You two lovers want to hurry up?'

I blushed from the use of her words, and stood aside. 'Hey, were not–'

'Alright, are you ready to meet Nat?' Juniper asked me, interrupting my flustered words. I blinked and rubbed my hands, touching the band aids.

I wasn't sure, why I was so nervous to meet this girl.

I had only heard small things about Nat, her relationship with Juniper, what school she attended before the accident, her age, twelve.

She was still a kid, and she was bedridden.

Juniper saw this evident sadness in my expression, and slowly coiled her fingers around mine.

'C'mon…' she sweetly said, carefully pulling me forward. 'She'll love you, Red.'

I followed the two of them through the living room, and turned right down her hallway. Juniper's home was clean and had such a warm feeling surrounding it.

I wanted to stare at photos on the wall, but I couldn't take my eyes off Juniper's back, as she took me and Arty towards the back room.

I recognised a familiar scent that lingered in the air, of antiseptic and cleaning supplies, like a hospital. I felt my stomach churn, and my nerves began to play up.

I wasn't ready for this; I wasn't ready to see a child in pain. If Juniper Bridges' pain left my heart screaming in agony, what would Natalie Bridges' pain do to me?

I was about to find out, and I held my breath in anticipation

Chapter Fifteen

RAYNE

I held my breath when Juniper opened Nat's door, and continued to bite my tongue when I finally saw her. My heart dropped, my eyes widened and I could already feel my emotions wash over me. surrounding her bed, stood an IV bag, multiple machines all hooked up her way. I focused on those before her body, listening to the familiar sounds of a hospital room. The constant beeping, reminding us that she was sick.

Nat Bridges lay still, her eyes tightly shut, her face sick and gaunt.

Her brow was furrowed, and her arms lay beside her little torso. I saw the drip was connected to her wrist, but there were so many other chords underneath the bed, I wondered if they were for her spine. Mounted on the wallclosest to her body was a flat screen television, angled so she didn't have to bend herself.

She'd fallen asleep playing some sort of game, the controller lay across her belly. I swallowed deeply when I got closer forward, but I stood behind Arty and Juniper, I couldn't move as fast as them.

I couldn't take another step towards a sick child, who had no reason to deserve what she was given. I watched her writhe in pain, lift her head and exhale to the roof, I could hear the hoarse croak in her throat.

Nat Bridges looked a lot like Juniper, they had the same nose, same faint freckles. But she was pale, cold and clearly suffering from this awful pain. Juniper sat in the seat beside her bed, shuffling through her sister's medication. She groaned softly, and turned to face Arty and I.

'She forgot to take her medicine,' she chuckled weakly. 'She hates this one.'

Arty grinned and sat beside Nat's torso, but her smile faded quite fast. Arty looked as hurt as I, and she had to collect herself before continuing to speak.

'She's a little shit,' she joked. 'Forgetting to take her medication...'

Her words were a little louder now, so Nat could wake. When the kid finally opened her eyes, she was surprised to see the redhead, Juniper and of course, me.

'Hey,' Juniper coaxed, brushing her sister's hair from her face. 'How're you feeling?'

Nat's eyes scanned over all three of us once more, before she hissed in pain and cleared her throat, 'Alright.'

I felt the cool rush of sadness rush over my heart, I wanted to leave, sit somewhere in silence and let this all sink in.

How come the world was so cruel? Why did this horrible pain have to be inflected on a twelve-year-old?

Juniper and Nat spoke for a little, she took her medicine and glanced to Arty, who smirked and rustled her hair gently, 'Hey kid.'

'Arty, you're here too?' Nat eased her eyes, smiling shortly. 'What's going on?'

Juniper exchanged looks with us two, then shrugged her shoulders. 'Dads got work, so I'm here to look after you.'

'He's not coming home tonight?'

'No, tomorrow afternoon...'

Nat seemed pained by this news, and grimaced. 'Okay.'

'Samantha should be coming in the morning,' Juniper leant forward and held her sisters hand. 'Just to see how you're going.'

'More needles?' Nat grumbled. 'Great.'

I'd never heard of that name before, but I assumed it was Nat's at home doctor. I was a little glad she was at home, surrounded by her personal things instead of a cold hospital bed. I looked around her room, and noticed a few objects that even I would have liked as a kid.

Baseball cards, action figures and plush toys, even a few newspaper clippings, just like her sister.

'Nat,' Juniper mumbled. 'This is Rayne.'

I turned to my name, and locked eyes with the kid. She blinked tiredly towards me, and watched me smile awkwardly.

Juniper took my hand and lead me closer, but I wouldn't budge. I was frozen on the spot, stuck in this poor set of eyes.

'She's a good friend,' Juniper explained. 'Really cool.'

I nervously rubbed the back of my neck, and moved out of Arty's way. She'd given me her spot and waited for me to sit, when I stood still, she literally shoved me down. 'Uh, hey.'

Nat examined me for a moment, then glanced to Juniper. 'She's tall.'

Her sister chuckled, and I swallowed.

'Hi, Rayne,' Nat croaked, passing me her weak right hand. I was afraid to touch it; in case she'd break. But I had to do my best, I wrapped my fingers around her small palm and shook it gently.

'Hi, Nat,' I replied. 'How you holding up?'

'I've been better, but it's nice to see everyone.'

She paused to cough, and we all flinched from how awful it sounded. My heart stung, I rubbed the spot with my palm and glanced Juniper's way. She sympathetically smiled to her sister, massaged her shoulder and shushed her sick moans.

I couldn't believe this was even happening, that Juniper was able to sit there and watch her sister splutter like this. I felt awful, Juniper was stronger than I thought.

How many times had she sat there, to be with her sister, ponder over the thought of when Nat might not wake up?

I felt like a royal asshole when I remembered telling her off, telling her that she needed to think straight, and how ridiculous she was for trying so hard.

I'd told her to stop fighting, for something so important.

I chewed my bottom lip and held Nat's hand again, close to my lap. She swallowed loudly and grinned lopsidedly, she looked just like her sister.

'I'm okay,' she mumbled.

'Yeah...' I replied, trying to smile, but I wanted to cry.

Arty cleared her throat, and pointed to Nat's game. 'You been busy, love?'

'Yeah!' Nat giggled. 'Finally beat the big boss I told you about, he was super hard.'

It was nice to hear her laugh, and as Arty joked around with her, it left a bittersweet taste in my mouth to see her happy.

I had to stay strong now, not only for Juniper and Arty, but for Nat.

Out of all of us, I think she was the strongest.

'C'mon, Arty,' Juniper said, rising from her seat. 'Let's get the guest room ready for you, hm?'

'You're sleeping over?' Nat exclaimed, eyes wide with excitement.

Arty grinned and stepped by her side. 'You bet lovey, and then I'll go buy you ice-cream tomorrow and we can beat another few levels of that junk.'

She pointed to the game once more, and winked to Nat.

While they spoke, I felt Juniper's hands on my shoulders, they slid to my neck and her thumbs danced along my skin. It was relaxing, but there was a reasoning behind it.

She knew, she knew I was close to breaking.

Nat saw this interaction, and blinked softly. 'And you'll stay too?'

I stumbled with my words, and kept her hand tight in mine. I gave Juniper a glance, and she nodded sweetly.

I guess that was a yes.

'Yeah, I'll stay too...' I muttered. 'I'm no good at video games though.'

'Don't worry, Arty's pretty good,' Nat croaked. 'She'll beat us both.'

I chuckled weakly, and Arty patted me across the back once. Nat seemed pretty excited to have this company over, and tugged me when I rose to follow the other two.

'I'll be back,' Juniper said. 'Stay here with Nat, okay?'

I gave her a look, and she nodded once before following Arty out.

It fell quiet in Nat's room, and the bed creaked when I sat back down on it. She examined my face when I turned, and I could see the little red lines in her tired eyes. She was exhausted, and so skinny. It must have been hard to eat, to even sleep.

Nat smiled to me, a little grin, cheeky.

'You like my sister...' she giggled softly. 'Don't you?'

I blushed and itched the bridge of my nose, no use lying.

'That obvious, huh?' I asked. 'I thought I was pretty good at hiding it.'

Nat's hand twitched in mine, and I rubbed her digits with my own, comforting her.

'No way,' she teased. 'You're awful at hiding it...'

I chuckled and felt the tension lift from my spirits, instead I leant forward and winked.

'She's a real special sister,' I admitted. 'I've been keeping a good eye on her.'

Nat blinked tightly, and nodded once, 'Thank you, she does nothing but worry about me.'

She paused and glanced around her room, I could see the IV drip clearly now, whatever was being pumped into her, was leaving her exhausted.

'I love my sister...' Nat began; her voice was small. 'And she's hurting, because of me.'

'No,' I answered back plainly. 'Don't say that, Nat.'

'But it's true,' she fought back quietly. 'If I hadn't been sick, she'd be happier.'

I froze and couldn't believe my ears, this kid shouldn't be blaming herself for her sister's sadness. I shuffled a bit closer and pulled my sleeves up.

'Listen to me, Nat,' I said, looking deep into her sick eyes. 'Juniper loves you, so much. I've never seen her fight so hard for you, because she wants to. Not because she has to.'

Nat swallowed sadly, and her eyes had already begun to moisten. I didn't like making kids cry, but she needed to know this.

'This is not your fault, sweetheart,' I mumbled. 'It never has been, ever.'

'But the money... and my dad.'

'Yeah, but you need to understand...' I paused and squeezed her hand. 'They're doing this, because they love you, and they can't stand the thought of losing you.'

'I feel guilty, Rayne,' Nat replied.

'I know; I can understand that,' I said. 'But there's no need to feel guilty, we're all doing this for you because we care about you, trust me.'

The room fell silent, apart from the constant beeping of Nat's heartrate, and the bubble of liquid processing through the drip in her arm.

Nat's eyes wandered over mine, and her bottom lip quivered. 'Rayne?'

I nodded and leant forward, listening to her quiet whimpers. 'If I die, please look after Juniper for me.'

My heart dropped, and I heaved a sob. I couldn't hold back the tears, at all.

Those words struck me down, like a sword.

I lowered my head into her hands, kissing the back of her palm.

'Stop that,' I eased out. 'Don't you ever say that.'

'I'm sorry...' she muttered. 'I am.'

'You're not going to die, honey...' I croaked.

I could feel the moistness travel down my cheeks, and I bit back another harsh cry. I couldn't let this happen, I know I couldn't play God, but I didn't want Nat to die, at all, nobody did.

I thought of the job opportunity tomorrow, the money and what it could do in this situation. I didn't care about my busking anymore, that was nothing compared to a girl's life.

I knew I'd get into trouble; I could be killed.

I'd be surrounded by drugs and weapons; I may have to kill another foe. Rayne Holmes would be stepping into a trap, and pressured to do things she wouldn't want to do, things that left her stomach turning.

I was about to become a criminal, but I needed to become one, so I could save Nat.

'Listen to me,' I croaked, lifting my head to look her in the eyes. She looked upset that I was, and lifted her other hand.

Small fingers trailed my cheeks, she brushed my tears with her digits and breathed roughly. I swallowed and took both hands in mine, clinging them close.

'Listen, I'm going to do something for you,' I said lowly, I couldn't have Juniper hearing this. 'It's going to save you.'

Nat blinked tiredly, and I nodded.

'I'm going to do something really stupid,' I repeated. 'But you can't tell your sister.'

I didn't want Nat keepings things from Juniper, but this was out of the question. Not even Arty could know about my ideas.

I'd join the Fire Jackals, pretend to be a loyal member, and find that rat bastard

Pebble's. on my own. I'd go undercover, I'd be able to help and sue this guy with Juniper's help.

I could use the cash from this job, to help pay for Nat's surgery, and watch her recover. I wasn't worried about myself, I just needed her to be alright.

Yes, I was scared.

But determined.

'Okay...' Nat replied. 'I'll keep it a secret.'

I smiled weakly and squeezed her hands again, patting them once. 'You're going to be okay, and walking again.'

Nat seemed thrilled to hear it, she smiled again. 'You think?'

I brushed her hair from her eyes, just as Juniper did before. 'I don't think, I know.'

She giggled and it was so nice to hear, I smiled to her, wiping my own tears from my face. 'You're strong, Nat.'

I lifted my sleeve and pointed to my tattoo, I had to lay my arm above her face, so she could touch the designs.

'You see this one right here?' I pointed to the deer, and she nodded. 'I cried like a baby when I got that.'

Nat laughed again, and pushed her fingers into my flesh. 'You're a baby...'

'I am,' I pouted. 'Such a big baby, even Juniper thinks so.'

'What do I think?' Juniper asked as she stepped back in.

'That Rayne's a baby.' Nat joked. 'A big baby.'

Juniper chuckled and crossed her arms, she stood by my side and glanced over to her sister, pondering on the thought.

'She can be...' she teased, pulling at my hair gently. 'When she wants.'

All three of us laughed, but Juniper and I were invested in Nat's giggle. It really was beautiful to hear. I saw hope in her smile, fight.

I hoped she'd keep fighting, because I would be.

'Hey, can you do me another favour, Rayne?' Nat asked.

'Yeah, what's that?'

'Take my sister out on a date.'

Juniper and I flinched, and her hands dropped from my shoulders. 'Uh.'

'Please?' Nat chuckled. 'Juniper never goes out anymore, apart from work and school.'

I looked to Juniper, and she eased her head a bit. 'Natalie...'

'Please, Juniper?' Nat whimpered. 'You have to do this, for me.'

I saw the two sisters share a mutual glance, before Juniper sighed and took my shoulders again, massaging them. 'Fine... maybe this week.'

'Japanese!' Nat cheered, coughing a little. 'You should take Juniper to Japanese food, she's a real dork with chopsticks.'

'Hey, watch it!' Juniper laughed. 'You're so mean to your big sister.'

'We are so going to Japanese now,' I joked. 'I want to see proof of this dorkiness.'

Juniper pinched my shoulders, leaning against my back to groan. 'Stop that.'

Nat told me about a certain lunch where Juniper had dropped everything she picked up, and ranted on about how it wasn't fair and chopsticks needed to be banned from all restaurants.

Juniper was embarrassed, but Nat still apologised.

'Thanks, Rayne,' she mumbled after our conversation.

I smiled and let her hands go, and as I rose, I bent down to press my lips against her forehead.

'You're strong, kiddo,' I assured her. 'You're going to be fine, and we'll be here.'

Nat looked me in the eyes, and gave me a concerned grimace, but I winked once more.

She was worried about this big plan I had, this 'really stupid' thing I mentioned.

Juniper lingered around for a moment, and took my hand tight. I turned to face her, and she nodded.

'My rooms on the far right,' she said.

I blushed deeply.

'Uh,' I stammered. 'You'll be sleeping with me?'

She chuckled and pulled my ears a bit. 'We'll see; I'm going to stay here with Nat for a while.'

I turned to Nat, and gave her a smile. 'I'll see you in the morning, kid.'

'Goodnight, Rayne,' she waved those little hands. 'Thanks again.'

Leaving the room was tough, but Nat seemed to be energetic about my presence, and told Juniper how cool I was.

I'd finally met Natalie Bridges, and it wasn't as hard as I thought it would be.

Yes, I'd made the decision to join a murderous group, but I worried less knowing that I could be saving her life, helping the pain ease.

Juniper's room was exactly what I thought it would be like.

Comfortable, spaced and filled with books, just like her dorm room in Boston.

For the first five minutes I stood in there, I looked towards a bunch of photos, hung above her bed. They were from her childhood, and I couldn't believe how adorable young Juniper was.

She'd had that reporter hat for a long time it seemed, as she wore it with pride as a toddler, even if it fumbled over her eyes in this one photo.

I saw her gradually get older in her photos, surrounded by her family, I even saw photos of her beautiful mother, I couldn't hide my smile, Juniper was going to grow up to be stunning.

I paused and sighed gently, I could still feel my heart ache when I began to take my clothes off, Nat's sick face was permanently imbedded in my mind.

It served to be a boost of determination, I was eager to go out there and make money, so I could fix her, with help of course.

I felt guilty already, I couldn't tell Juniper about this job, no way. I knew there was a price to pay before I'd even accepted it, it could very well ruin the both of us.

Trust was built, and I might as well go toppling over it.

I hope Juniper knew I would never intentionally hurt her, she deserved the world, and that's why I wanted to help.

I lifted my shirt, pulling it over my head. After I'd gotten out of my jeans, I stretched. I was used to wearing a pair of bike shorts over my underwear, I hated wearing clothes to sleep.

I could feel my bones crackle, my tension was still there, and it bothered me.

What if Nat died? What would happen to her family, her father, Juniper...

I shuddered from the thought and began pondering, sitting on the end of Juniper's bed. I was still picturing the images, of what could be and what had been. A funeral, or a party.

Happiness, or sadness.

Life never worked out for everyone, but it had to, for Nat. She was innocent, only a child, halfway to her teenage years.

I clutched my heart again, rubbing the sore spot. Not only had I felt the uneasy sadness draw its swords on me, but I felt horrible for not seeing this sooner.

Juniper had every right to fight me, push me and tell me I had no idea.

I didn't.

I had no clue what it would be like to lose a sister, or anyone at that.

That's why I was so connected to Juniper, she was proof that people could be loving and caring. I needed her in my life, I couldn't bear a world without her.

Jeeze, that was selfish.

I bit my bottom lip and groaned loudly, I'd found myself staring at the floor and didn't even notice Juniper walking in after a good ten minutes. I watched her close the door behind her, softly and quietly. Before she spoke to me, she carefully lifted her shirt over her shoulders, hissing from the pain in her side.

'She's okay,' she said, 'Sleeping.'

I nodded and kept my eyes on her, she looked stressed, pent up, 'You alright?'

Juniper stood still, and shrugged her shoulders, 'Got lectured by my twelve-year-old sister.'

I smirked a little, 'Oh?'

'She wants me to relax,' Juniper rolled her eyes. 'Said she'd be fine, that she was fighting.'

Juniper began undoing her jeans, I didn't take my eyes away, but I was a little afraid she'd be offended.

'So, I'll try my hardest not to worry, for now,' she paused and laughed weakly. 'You must have talked some sense into her, pushed her to keep trying.'

I saw Juniper smile, and turn to face me. 'Thank you, for whatever you told her.'

I felt like shaking my head, and saying that I'd done nothing. But Juniper nodded once and stepped closer.

I cleared my throat and looked to my knees, tracing circles against my bone. She breathed in before she spoke, 'You can watch, Red.'

I blushed to her words, and glanced up slowly.

My heart fluttered, and my stomach tickled. Juniper smiled sheepishly, and slid her jeans down her legs, my throat had locked and I couldn't breathe for a moment.

It was late, nearly two in the morning, but time had stopped again, as I watched Juniper strip in front of me.

I caught her waist when she stepped between my legs, my hands gently against her waistband. She wrapped her arms around my neck, and stood still, stroking the tension from my spine. Her stomach was thin, and had only a few freckles here and there, but I felt the warmth emitting from her, and I longed to touch it.

I brushed my right fingers against her left side, tracing the wound covers. She was so close, and I felt so far.

'I know that was hard,' Juniper explained. 'Seeing Nat, the way she is.'

I didn't speak, not just yet.

'It took me days to even utter a word to her, I couldn't believe she was the way she was.'

Juniper's voice trailed off, and she returned to hug my head with her hands. I breathed in gently and looked up. She smiled sympathetically;

'You did great...' she said sweetly. 'You really did.'

I felt guilty, she shouldn't have praised me, I had been awfully selfish about the whole thing, at least I thought so.

'I'm sorry...' I mumbled. 'For how I've been acting.'

Juniper shushed me, but I shook my head.

'I should have thought before I accused you of doing wrong, you had all rights to...I only realised that now,' I paused and sadly grimaced. 'Now that I've seen Nat...'

'Red...' she mumbled. 'It's alright.'

'No,' I returned, I sniffled and leant forward, gently kissing her against the stomach. 'No, I need to say this.'

I felt my words melt in my mouth, my anxiety was on the edge, ready to jump and make me flip. I examined her wounds again, pecking another part of her stomach.

'Juniper, you're so strong,' I glanced up, her eyes had become half lidded again. 'I should have never doubted you, ever.'

I breathed in again, and pulled her a little closer by her waist, pressing my lips against her navel. Her stomach was rising and falling with her breathing, and the moment had become intimate.

'I wanted you,' I admitted. 'I wanted you for myself, and you were right to say no.'

Juniper's watched my mouth move, and her right hand fluttered by my shoulder. I bit my bottom lip and shook my head. 'Of course you couldn't concentrate on... that.'

I felt guilty again, and I cussed to myself.

'You have bigger things to worry about, and if I pressured you in any way...'

Juniper shushed me quietly, denying that. She brought her fingers to my chin, feathered touches.

The moment was different now, we were close, and I was lost in her eyes. Her fingers traced my lips, my nose and my cheeks. It felt so comfortable, relaxing.

She smiled lightly, and palmed each side of my face, itching behind my earlobes.

I couldn't believe how much this girl meant to me, I swallowed.

'I love you,' I croaked, pressing my forehead against her stomach. 'I love you, Juniper.'

The words just fell out, and I didn't hold them back at all.

But they were true, so goddamn true.

I'd never felt this way for anyone, not one soul had connected to mine the way Juniper's did.

I longed to feel her embrace every day, wake up next to her, never have to worry about her not being my own.

It'd been only a month, yes I understood that, but I'd fallen pretty hard, considering our situation.

Juniper brought my face up, and I expected a serious look, but she lost herself in my gaze again. This wasn't all lust, I saw something else, something I'd been reaching for all along.

'I love you too, Rayne,' she muttered sweetly. 'I do.'

My heart stammered inside my chest, and I thought it would burst.

I wanted to cry, hold her and tell her of all the times I wished to have her, wished to keep her close.

She felt the same way, that was clear to me now, Juniper and I were on the same page, and I was extremely shocked.

'Juniper...' I said. 'What if I'm not all you think?'

'Don't be silly,' she replied. 'Don't doubt yourself....'

It was hard not to, especially when someone as gorgeous as Juniper Bridges was confessing her

love for me.

I held her close, pressing my forehead to her belly, 'Juniper.'

'Rayne.'

I liked the way her voice sounded, she was sincere now.

'You're worth everything,' she said, holding my head close. 'More than you know.'

Her words hit me pretty close to home, and I closed my eyes tightly.

My anxiety was kicking in, doing its absolute best to make me stress about this meaningful conversation.

I wouldn't let it, no, I was going to overcome it, for her.

For me.

I kissed her stomach again, my hands wandered up her bare back, and below. We stood there, in silence, with my lips against her bare body for some time. Before Juniper took her position on my crotch once more.

I wanted to deny the touch, and mentioned her wound, but she shook her head and pushed me down.

We sealed our confessions with a deepened kiss.

Now this, this felt right.

In that moment, there was no second guessing and no worrying of what we wanted. Juniper and I knew what we longed for, and it was happening.

I closed my eyes quickly, touching my tongue with hers.

There was still room for lust, and it took hold of us both, quite quickly.

But it was a different kind of lust, no, this had more meaning.

Juniper's hands wandered down my body, to my stomach and back up to my chest. I felt my abdomen tremble, longing for more of her touch.

Our lips locked tightly. We craved each other, I could tell by the way our kisses had become heated and messy.

I pulled myself up and grabbed her close against my crotch. She mumbled from the contact and wrapped her arms around my neck once more, her hands drawn to my hair, tugging at it.

My lips wandered to her neck, tongue pressing against both sides, down to her collarbone. She sighed with pleasure, lifting her head to give me more access.

I could feel the tension lift from my body, comfort wash over my tired bones.

Being in such close contact with Juniper had my heart thumping, the taste of her skin was sweet.

I fumbled with her bra, trying hard to keep my lips against her neck at the same time as unlocking it. I heard her giggle gently, and proceed to undo it herself.

I was nervous, I couldn't lie. I really didn't want to stuff anything up, it would be a major embarrassment.

Plus, knowing Juniper, she'd tease me about it whenever she could.

Juniper kissed me again, her tongue wrapping around mine. The throbbing in my abdomen had become more and more pleasurable by the second, and I reacted with a muffled moan.

Her chest was bared, and I was a little afraid at first, but she lifted her upper torso and welcomed me with a smirk.

Juniper's fingers clawed at my back as I pressed my mouth to her chest, licking upwards. She was enjoying the sensation; I could tell by her whimpers.

I brought her down with me, gently laying her below. She clutched to my back when I returned to her chest, my free hand above her head, balancing myself.

When I bit, she tried her absolute hardest to supress a moan, her right hand reached over my back, and held tight around my neck.

'Fuck,' she groaned.

In a few minutes, she and I held close to each other, both naked and a little nervous.

We constantly made eye contact, and I assured her everything would be alright.

My eyes had become half lidded when she reached for my right hand, I swallowed and allowed her to straddle me again, the thumping of my heart continued.

Juniper breathed in sharply, pressing her forehead to mine. I savoured this moment, exhaling against her lips. My love was pouring out, emotions taking over.

I swallowed when she brought my hand between her legs.

The heat between us was becoming unreal.

Before I let my fingers ease inwards, I let my index touch her sweet spot, and she shivered under my touch.

'Rayne...' she chuckled nervously, she held around my neck and kissed me.

I chuckled back, enjoying the teasing.

When I touched her again, she got rough, and bit my bottom lip. I was brought aback by the action, and felt lust tug at my stomach.

I wanted her badly, so badly I acted fast.

We made close eye contact as I slipped my fingers inside her, just two, but it was enough to make her mouth part in anticipation.

Juniper's forehead touched mine, and I closed my eyes to concentrate. She rocked against my fingers, and I felt how wet she was.

I was worried about her wound, and made it my job to constantly check to see if she was straining it, but Juniper was so distracted, she kept pulling me back, frustrated.

'Stop,' she ordered, voice low and seductive. 'Fuck me.'

My heart did whirls at that command, and I grabbed her even closer, our chests made contact, and I smirked at her.

Juniper pushed me back down, and I let my head fall against her pillows. Her fingers dragged below my chest, and she began.

Seeing her on top of me, riding my fingers was something truly unbelievable.

She was gorgeous, her body moved in such a motion it left me in awe. The only source of light in the room was from the bedside table lamp, and the way its gleam illuminated her tanned skin was beautiful.

I could have laid there, and counted every cute freckle on her shoulders.

Juniper looked me in the eyes a few times, breathing heavily. I did the same, just watching this left me breathless.

It was so intimate, the way we gazed at each other.

Her hands touched at my stomach, sometimes she reached forward to my chest.

But I was lost, in the movement, even when she twisted and pulled, I couldn't take my eyes off hers.

Juniper began to moan, short gasps of air as she rocked back and forth.

I bit my bottom lip when she did, I groaned when she groaned.

Her pleasure, was my pleasure.

We indulged for minutes.

This was a moment of pure ecstasy, as she lifted her head and cried out quietly. I pressed my fingers deeper into her, and she began to tighten around my digits.

I heard my real name, multiple times, rough and lustful, giddy and wild. She was enjoying it, and I loved hearing her sigh in utmost pleasure.

I rose again, to crash into her lips. And she pulled me into her body once more, her moan evident through our locked mouths.

She was throbbing from my touch, and I knew she was close.

The moment arrived when she couldn't kiss me, but our lips were in such close proximity.

Juniper held my face in her hands, her mouth ajar against mine, bottom lip brushed against my upper. I felt her climax around my fingers, and she took hold of my lips with hers again.

I flinched to feel her nails dig into my back, scratching downwards, Junipers release was like music to my ears.

She laid herself down on me, and allowed me to take hold of her body again. So she could muffle her orgasm through our kiss, afraid to wake the others.

I saw her eyebrows crease, furrow and soften. She shook against me, and I held her tightly.

It was a moment that brought us even closer, something that tied the ribbon on top.

There was raw emotion wavering from the both of us, and I could see it in her eyes when she controlled her breathing.

I took my fingers back, but Juniper still sat against me. We stared at each other, panting, breathless.

I closed my eyes when she took my face in her hands again, her thumbs alongside my jawline. Her touch was feathered, sweet, and calmed my tired body.

Man, if this was what love felt like, when two people indulged in its very power, I was honestly ready to spend the rest of my life like this.

Juniper looked nervous, and I smiled softly, holding her hands to my face.

'You sounded wonderful,' I exhaled. 'Wonderful...'

She chuckled, and brought her lips to mine. I kissed her back, my hands along her waist again.

'I want to hear you, too.'

Her words were whispered, against my mouth. I felt my body shiver from the tone in her voice, husky and eager.

'Okay,' I swallowed. 'S-Sure.'

Alright, so I was already stressing when Juniper slid off me. I clenched my hands and felt her move lower, her hands ran along my toned stomach, and I tensed from the contact.

'Rayne...' she mumbled. 'Relax, baby.'

I covered my face, hearing that pet name had my head swirling, 'Shit.'

When her tongue touched me, I held my mouth with my hands, biting into my flesh to stifle my ragged breath.

I must have been Juniper's first woman, she was shy and constantly made eye contact with me from between my legs. She was always gentle, never rough, and she needed a constant reminder that I was okay.

I decided to hold her hand as her tongue moved, this aided her worries and she became rather confident after that.

Whenever I felt her exhale, I shivered from the coolness against my skin. I think I said 'fuck' a fair few times, my fingers eagerly wanting to clutch at her hair.

I concentrated on her free hand, as her digits drew circles against my hipbones. The motion was calming, and aroused me without any complications.

I felt my breath hitch in only a matter of minutes, and I tugged at her hand, tight around mine. My grip was rough, and she reacted the same, with her tongue.

'Juniper,' I whimpered, my voice higher than usual. She held me closer, her pace quickening, my tone was exciting her.

My heart pumped in my chest, I could hear it, my own hastened breaths.

The rest was a blur, and I felt my eyes glaze over during my own release.

I'd forgotten how great it felt, and clenched my teeth as I strained my voice, emitting a deep groan from the bottom of my throat.

The feeling washed over my whole entire body, and I shivered from Juniper's touch.

I became sensitive fast, and pulled her over me again.

I never liked kissing the person who'd just been between my legs, but tasting myself wasn't so bad when I lingered on Juniper's lips.

I held her shakily, and she clung back.

It was overwhelming, and I couldn't help but smile. The feeling of mutual love was nothing but amazing, and looking into each other's eyes while we acted upon it, left my heart racing.

I was happy.

Truly, happy.

When Juniper broke off my lips, she leant across my chest, her body along mine. I raised my left arm around her shoulders, and examined the ceiling, where our shadows had previously danced.

I could feel the exhaustion waver over me, but I wanted to express my gratitude, my feelings.

Juniper and I lay in silence, our breathing had settled, I could feel the rise and fall of her chest. I stroked her shoulder, keeping her close.

'Rayne?' she asked.

'Yeah?' I replied, I didn't mind her calling me that now, after that experience? She could call me anything.

Juniper moved her head, but I continued to watch the ceiling, until she took my chin with her fingers, pulling my attention her way.

'You alright?' she questioned. 'You seem a little, dazed.'

'Can you blame me?' I chuckled. 'I'm lightheaded.'

I smiled to her, and brushed a lock of lose hair behind her ear, she looked cute after making love.

'Why's that?' Juniper returned a grin, and cuddled closer to me.

I breathed in gently, and closed my eyes.

'It just felt…' I paused and shrugged. 'Right.'

Juniper glanced at me, so I smiled again. 'I sometimes forget to think of the positive, or I find myself stuck in the negative far too much…'

I sniffled gently, adjusting my head against hers. 'I forgot how nice it felt to know someone cared.'

I knew I was being pretty corny, but everything leaving my mouth was true.

I could feel her legs rub against mine, she inhaled deeply.

'And it's not just, because we…' I paused, blushed and chuckled. 'Did that.'

'I know, Red.'

'Yeah but,' I eased my head, so I could lock eyes with her. 'I can't express how grateful I am for you, how much it means to me, that you care.'

Juniper focused on my lips, and leant up to kiss me. I pressed my lips to her nose instead, and she playfully cringed.

'Hey…' she chuckled. 'You don't get to say all the nice words, Red.'

'How come?'

'Because, I need to thank you too, y'know?'

I brought her closer, and she nestled into the crook of my neck. I could already hear the early morning birds begin to sing, so I reached over and turned the bedside light off.

Juniper mumbled quietly, cuddling closer to me, 'You're perfect.'

I wanted to say no, shake my head and tell her she was perfect instead, but she continued.

'Perfect, caring and loyal,' she brushed her fingers against my collar, sliding to and from each bone.

'Stubborn,' she teased. 'But wonderful.'

I scoffed a little, tickling her shoulder. 'Your dream girl?'

Juniper leant up quickly, and I focused on her back as she leant over to grab the bundle of blankets at the end of her bed.

'Don't get too cocky now.' She laughed quietly, exhaustion evident in her croaky voice. I caught her when she dropped again, clearing my throat.

'But yes,' she mumbled, her lips against my jawline. 'My dream girl.'

Ah, her words left me melting a little inside. I could have jumped up, did a dance, pumped my fists high into the air. The feeling was mutual, and it was so refreshing to hear all these positives about me.

Juniper breathed steadily, the blankets warm over her shoulders. I was content with being here, with her.

'Juniper…' I mumbled. 'I love you.'

She chuckled again, her voice soft. 'I love you too.'

Of course, I wanted to ask if she really meant it.

Everybody worries about that, especially someone who wore their heart on their sleeve. But I felt her words, they tugged at my heartstrings in every positive way.

'Sleep…' she whispered. 'Red.'

I kissed her goodnight, and it took her a mere minute to drift off.

As per usual, I lay there for a moment or two, compiling all that had happened in a span of an hour. I thought about the way she looked at me, the way she shivered against my touch. I felt a little giddy myself, knowing I could make Juniper feel that way.

In my moment of clarity, fear slipped in.

My smile left my lips, and I remembered that text message I had received earlier.

I was about to give in to something absolutely hazardous, put myself into some pretty wild danger. But it was for Nat, for Juniper.

Things would work out, right?

Chapter Sixteen

JUNIPER

I wasn't used to waking up naked next to a woman.

It might have been on my to-do list, but I never expected it to be this soon. I wasn't complaining, not at all. The feeling of Rayne's arms around me when I awoke, was anything but awful.

It was great, more than just great, it was brilliant.

So, it took me a few minutes to piece together our past night. I stared at the ceiling, just as she was. When I'd met Rayne, only weeks ago, the thought of kissing her had replayed on my mind twenty-four seven.

Who can blame me? She was handsome, strong and had one hell of a voice.

But she cared, I hadn't felt that emotion in a long time, from any romantic partner.

Rayne had the tendency to forget about herself, which was very admirable in some aspects, but pretty unsafe in others.

She wanted to treat me with respect, and I would do the same for her.

I turned to face my sleeping beauty, she was lost in a dream, eyebrows furrowed.

Usually, when I awoke next to my one-night stand, I would get out of there as soon as possible. I wasn't the best girl to commit to a relationship.

Rayne was way different; I couldn't stand the thought of her leaving. I didn't like picturing other girls with her, men staring at her in displeasing ways.

It boiled my blood, I was attached already, maybe a little too attached.

I slipped her hair from her eyes, and she crinkled her nose in response, arms loosening around my naked body.

From the first time she'd held me, I couldn't believe the emotions that ran through me, it scared me. Although, the more I found myself close to Rayne, the less it scared me, and the more it excited me.

She was a stubborn one, probably a little aggravating at times, but who wasn't?

She was only stubborn whenever I put myself in danger, whenever she was faced with something she loathed.

I sighed and examined Rayne, from that chiselled profile, roman nose and full lips. To the mess of long black hair draped over her chest – covered in an excessive amount of red marks thanks to yours truly – to her strong arms and her toned stomach. Down to her shaped thighs and long legs, I'd be lying if I didn't say she was dreamy.

Before I lost myself in my ridiculous teenage girl antics, I brought myself back to reality.

I wasn't sure there was anyone in this world, that could put up with Juniper Bridges' journalistic antics. Especially when they involved going undercover to find the hit and runner of her younger sister. Rayne was different.

She never acted like she was just 'putting up' with me. She enjoyed my presence, as much as I enjoyed hers.

Two days prior, Rayne had kissed me, I'd panicked and left her home alone, without explaining anything.

The truth was, I felt guilty.

I felt guilty that I could have made love to her there and then, while my sister was sick at home.

Until Nat had looked me in the eye, told me she was aware I felt for Rayne, and told me to be happy, did I finally take it upon myself.

I was in the comfort of my own home, Nat was only a few doors away. I couldn't relax completely, but knowing I would be there for her if something were to happen, aided my worries.

And Rayne understood that, and that's one of that things that made her so special.

The thought of Nat left my heart aching, I had to get up and check on her as soon as I figured out where this damn pain was coming from.

Oh, right.

I eased my head to my left, and hissed at my side.

There, soiled in red was my bandages.

I'd successfully bled through the night, and caused an awful mess around my torso.

'Shit,' I whispered gently. 'Shit, shit, shit.'

Rayne croaked in reply, half asleep, her arms twitching.

I shushed her as I rose, holding the painful area with my palm. Now that my body had relaxed, it hit me awfully hard.

I tensed up and groaned, last night was a good idea at the time, riding Rayne all night was all I'd wanted, but now I was swimming in a pool of my own goddamn blood.

Okay, it wasn't that much blood, but still!

'Juniper,' she mumbled from beside me. I saw her eyes flutter, but I didn't want Rayne worrying this early in the morning, she'd lose her head.

I coaxed her with a soft shush, tucking her back into bed gently, 'Nothing to worry about.'

I used my most relaxing voice, and she began drifting.

'What time is it...?' she asked, lips parting slowly.

I twisted my body to focus on the time, and regretted doing so.

'Fuck!' I whimpered through clenched teeth, I felt the stinging sensation become a fiery burn. It travelled upwards, and jolted my mind. 'Oh, you son of a....'

Rayne stirred again, and I kept her down with both hands, leaning over to check the alarm clock.

'It's seven, Red,' I muttered, hoping she'd drift off again. 'Keep sleeping...'

She grumbled and touched my thighs with her fingers, but they dropped in exhaustion to her sides. I felt like pinching her ears and teasing her, asking why she was the one who was so tired after last night, when I'd done most of the work.

She'd absolutely fluster at the thought.

Okay, all jokes aside. I had to get up and get this wound clean, before I copped an infection.

I sniffled and paced myself, dragging my body to the other side of the bed. Rayne clung to me for a moment, but I slipped from her weak grasp.

I heard her wail 'no' playfully, a sob leaving her throat.

'I'll be back,' I chuckled. 'I'll be right back.'

She grunted again, and I fumbled through my drawers, being butt naked in this cold weather was asking to get sick, and that would suck big time.

The pain had become absolutely excruciating, to the point I wanted to cry. I clenched my teeth again, pulling myself into my bathroom.

To be honest, I hadn't even processed the thought that I had been shot just hours ago. Thankfully, the bullet missed me, but not completely.

I groaned when I pulled the bandages off, trying my absolute hardest not to faint from the ghastly sight. My right side was absolutely skinned, tiny lines full of puss and festered blood. The two that burned and ached stood prominent from the others, the skin of each sewn back together. They'd opened again, just slightly.

And I blamed only but myself, I got too carried away last night, lost in Rayne's smouldering eyes and long fingers.

I blushed and grimaced, grabbing the nearest handtowel.

Trust Juniper Bridges, to have sex when she was battered and bruised. I was so sexually connected to her last night, that I hadn't even noticed the pain.

Oh, but I was noticing it now.

I contemplated taking a shower and was pretty frightened by the idea of it. It would sting, so awfully, but it would do wonders for the infection.

I stood in my bathroom, wiping away the blood from my weeping cuts.

I lost myself in thought, grabbing hold of all that had happened in the past month. The majority being negative, and quite life threatening.

But what kind of reporter doesn't get into trouble to find the truth?

This involved my sister, and there was way I'd let some coward step all over her, or me. I'd spent countless hours and days worrying about money, Dad and Nat. Rayne had come to me in great times of disappointment, and I felt selfish for it.

I longed for her attention, and she gave it to me with no hesitation. In the long run I had fallen for her, her kind nature and mysterious past, she was like a big juicy story I couldn't put down.

I wasn't one to get attached, the last girl I had a fling with clung to me like I was God's gift to this world.

She was great, and had awesome confidence, but I just didn't see myself with her.

We met in my first year of college, and dated like it was normal. But here was the hitch, ever since I started dating, anyone at that; I never thought I deserved happiness.

I couldn't have sex with her, even when I realised I was only interested in women.

We hardly lasted two months.

I'd dated men in the past, tried to convince myself I was looking for love in all the right places.

But even during my nights with a man, I'd imagine a woman.

What was the point of hurting myself? I just dropped the bomb on dad a year ago, that I was a lesbian, and he pretty much looked me in the eye and said, 'Cool, do you want pizza for dinner?'

It made me laugh, and wonder why I even worried.

I told Rayne, that trouble seemed to find me. But in all honesty, I found the trouble.

I had to constantly be on the move, doing something with my spare time.

I never relaxed and people called me headstrong for that.

Juniper had a temper, Juniper was stubborn, Juniper pushed herself too much.

Just the thought of settling down and doing something for myself was too much, that was until I'd met Rayne.

I was being so corny that it made me roll my eyes some days.

But it was true, Rayne and I met, and I couldn't stop thinking about her.

She started off as a great friend, someone I could rely on simply by looking her in the eyes.

And then I found myself dreaming about her, wishing she'd come by work and say hello more, I had to stop and collect myself various times just in case I came across odd or, obsessive.

So when she confessed to me last night, I was honestly caught off guard.

I loved teasing her, she was adorable when she blushed and became flustered. I thought that would be all we'd get to, simple mindless flirting.

Before Nat got into her accident, and being the typical Bridges family member I am, I poured out my anger and frustration on a kind soul who mended that awful ache with just a smile, or an embrace.

I didn't realise how much pent up emotion I had stored in this body of mine, until Rayne allowed me to express them.

She constantly blamed herself for everything, and I could see that happening further in our relationship, which could be a problem.

Rayne was enjoyable to be around, and so easy to get along with. I wanted to hear more about her family in Florida, more stories from her past.

She was a little hard to express her own feelings and emotions, and that's why it meant so much to see her cry for me, hold me tight and tell me she cared about me.

This wasn't a normal relationship, but in all the right ways.

I didn't want to thank this whole 'Sister hit by a car, Fire Jackals' experience, I would never call this a blessing.

But meeting Rayne was definitely a bright light at the end of one, long dark tunnel.

She really was something.

Okay, as much as I wanted to stand there in my bathroom, daydreaming about the girl who was laying naked in my bed, my wound was irritating me, and I had to do something about it.

I inhaled deeply, then moved towards my shower.

I swore a bit, contemplated turning the water on, colder or hotter, whatever hurt less.

'Shit,' I groaned. 'Shit, shit.'

The water felt cool on my fingertips, slowly becoming scorching hot. Any other day, having an early morning shower was no problem at all

But having an open wound, ripping down the left of my torso? That was another story, a story I honestly couldn't be bothered indulging in.

I thought maybe to grab Rayne, have her hold me up in case I fell and broke a goddamn hip. But she was exhausted, she'd had less sleep than I had.

I hated burdening people, even with tiny things like asking for drinks at guest's homes, or if I could sit down.

I inhaled again, pep talking myself into the shower. When I finally mustered up the strength, I stepped in and instantly felt the scorch of stinging pain.

It was like, one thousand bees were stinging me at once, then throwing salt in the wound.

I didn't scream, or yell, but I grit my teeth and lowered my legs to a crouch, which just added to the throbbing mess.

It's all worth it.

I reminded myself.

It's all for Nat.

No pain was anything compared to what my twelve-year-old sister was dealing with.

I caught my mouth with my right hand, muffling my irritated moans.

Maybe I should have gone to the hospital, they'd have better tools for this kind of stuff.

But then the questioning, how I got it, who did it, where was I, and blah, blah, blah.

It was too much to deal with, I already had enough on my plate, as did Arty and Rayne.

Arty was getting herself into trouble as well, she was willing to get herself killed last night just so we could find that son of a bitch; Pebbles.

Which we didn't.

There were days where I just, wanted to sit in my room, sleep eat and cry.

But I just couldn't, not until Nat was okay.

I needed her to be okay, the thought of her vanishing leaves my heart aching.

I would find the person who did this, and I'd get sweet justice.

The shower helped, if you call hot water opening up fresh wounds helping.

They still stung, but once I'd patched them up with new bandages, it wasn't as hard to put a shirt on then before.

I dressed carefully, and stopped to examine myself in my mirror, brushing the faint love marks upon my neck and collarbone with my fingers.

I did this countless times, maybe to remind myself I was here, in the now. Whenever I stared at my own two eyes, I wondered.

What was I even doing?

I wasn't a cop, or a real reporter. I was a college student, who worked at a café in South Boston. I was twenty-two, had no combat training and here I was stabbing disgusting gang members in the stomach for touching my ass.

I flinched at that thought, that was another part of last night's shenanigans that hadn't completely sunk in.

I sniffled and grabbed hold of the hair dryer, flicking it on. I'd already lost myself in thought, why not go deeper?

I was willing to leave school for Nat, which meant a lot of debt.

I was willing to close the doors on Boston University and never look back, until she was well and ready to stand.

It used to bother me, the thought of failing.

But now, nothing really mattered, except for her wellbeing.

I was playing hero, and getting my loved ones into trouble.

Of course I felt guilty, but they stood by me, and that left me feeling strong.

So, I'd met a gorgeous busker at South Station, my sister was in an accident, I drank away my problems, fell in love with said gorgeous busker, snuck into a Fire Jackals meeting, stabbed a guy and left with only one clue, a key to a car that could be anywhere in Massachusetts.

Sign me up for the best reporter in the world.

Reporter in training. Rayne would say.

I found myself smiling, and finished drying my hair.

Nat was still alive, and I had Rayne and Arty by my side. We could get through this, all four of us, even dad too.

Yet, I didn't know why, but it was so hard to believe, only sometimes.

I had this gut feeling something awful was going to happen, and I wouldn't be able to fix it.

Just the thought left my stomach churning.

I turned the hair dryer off and leant over the sink a little, sighing deeply.

In my reflection, I saw Rayne walk in, only in her boxers, cussing at the bright bathroom light.

'Ugh,' she grumbled. 'Ouch.'

Just seeing her made my stomach whirl in excitement, even if she was stumbling into the bathroom half asleep.

'Morning,' I mumbled, drying the back of my neck. 'Sleep well?'

Rayne was clearly not a morning person, she stood still for a moment, looked at me, then slumped against my back.

She was being careful with my waist as she wrapped her arms around my stomach. Being so tall, she could fit me right against her chest, her chin resting upon my head.

I couldn't explain the feeling rushing through my body, but it was positive energy.

Last night Rayne and I expressed our love for each other in the most intimate way, but I'd forgotten just how intimate an embrace could be.

She closed her eyes, and inhaled, kissing the back of my head gently, 'Yeah.'

It was a short answer, but I took it anyway.

Slowly, I relaxed in her arms, wishing everything could stay this way, calm and content. I was afraid that our time together would be short.

Rayne's eyes peered at me in the mirror, a warm glazed look that left me smiling. She gave me half a grin, the right corner of her lip lifting into a smirk.

'Sorry about the...' she paused and looked at my neck, brushing my hair to examine the biggest mark there. 'Rough night.'

She couldn't finish her sentence without laughing, but then she blushed and groaned in embarrassment.

I shrugged and turned to face her, holding her elbows. 'I don't mind; you've got a fair few yourself.'

Rayne scoffed and rolled her eyes. 'I know,' she flicked me across the nose. 'Thanks for that.'

She lifted her finger, eyebrows raised. 'I also have...'

I watched her turn, and point at her bare back, which to my surprise had three long red scratch marks traveling downwards.

I caught my mouth and chuckled, 'Oh, shit.'

'Yeah!' she joked, voice cracking. 'What the hell is this?'

She tried examining them herself, but looked like a complete goof as she stretched her neck uncomfortably.

'Dang, they're long,' I giggled, my finger travelling down the length of the middle mark. 'I'm good!'

'Good?' Rayne joked, turning to grab my waist again. 'Is that seriously your answer?'

I took my eyes off her chest, and smiled sheepishly. 'One hundred percent.'

Rayne went silent for a second, the same smirk on her lips.

And I exhaled, focusing on those eyes of hers. We fell quiet, but in a good way.

I wanted to take a moment, to examine this girl in front of me, even brush the loose hair from her eyes.

Rayne was coaxed by the contact, and leant forward to press her forehead against mine. I felt her hands slip lower, and I was fine with where they touched.

'Hey,' she mumbled, warmly.

'Hello,' I replied, the tip of my nose pressed against hers.

Rayne shut her eyes, and her eyebrows creased in some sort of realisation, I wasn't sure what she had realised though.

But I felt pretty special when she pulled me closer to kiss me, directly after.

Hey, check that out, no morning breath.

It was funny, how much a kiss could brighten a mood. The electricity was instant when her lips touched mine, I wondered if that would ever disappear.

I don't think so.

'Okay,' Rayne mumbled when she broke off. 'Morning kiss done, now for a shower.'

I nodded and tickled behind her ear, 'Yeah, you totally smell.'

Rayne panicked, and lifted her right arm, sniffing, 'Seriously?'

'Oh my god, Red,' I joked, pushing her back. 'No you dork, I'm just joking!'

She grouched to me playfully, but her expression changed to something more, sincere.

Rayne took me by surprise, kissing my nose quickly, 'Thank you.'

'For what?' I asked, a little confused.

'You know,' she muttered. 'For just, being Juniper.'

Rayne was already so open with her words; it was a little overwhelming to be completely honest. But I liked this new trust she had, it was building tall towers.

'Well,' I paused to nod. 'Thank you, for being Rayne.'

I pressed my lips to hers, quickly, before nudging her forward. 'Go shower.'

Finally, she listened to me, and let me go.

So I continued fixing myself up for the day, while I tried to keep my eyes on myself as she slipped her boxers down those long legs, but the temptation was too strong, and I caught myself staring.

When I stepped into Nat's room, I was surprised to find Arty lying next to her, both of them awake playing that video game.

Arty up at nine am? On a Sunday? Was she going crazy?

'Hey you two,' I chuckled. 'You're both up early, this is a shock.'

Arty yawned loudly, threw her hand up and waved at me. 'Yah, I promised the kid I'd play didn't I?'

Nat smiled to me, and coughed a little. 'Yeah, Arty's pretty good, even in the morning.'

I shook my head as I checked Nat's temperature, my hand flat over her forehead.

She was warm, but not severely. I was waiting for the moment she'd be flaming, and I made sure my mobile was on me at all times, hospital on speed dial.

'Nat, Samantha's coming in half an hour,' I explained. 'You eaten anything?'

Nat shook her head, eyes still on the game, 'Nope, not hungry.'

Here we go again, I thought.

Nat had this tendency to argue with me, about eating. She never had a big appetite, but ever since the accident she'd lost so much weight it was unhealthy.

'Nat,' I said, tone serious. 'We're not going to go through this again.'

'Go through what?' she asked, stubborn.

I pursed my lips and saw Arty snigger, she was gaining an attitude.

'You have to eat,' I demanded, sitting by her torso. 'Or we'll both cop an earful from Samantha.'

'Who's Samantha? She sounds cute,' Arty chuckled.

I ignored her, and took the controller from Nat's hands. She whined when I did so.

'Juniper!' she groaned. 'C'mon.'

I was in big sister mode, and I wasn't going to sit idly by and see my sister starve herself.

'Please, Nat,' I gave her a serious look. 'What can I get you?'

She opened her mouth to fight back, but closed it when she finally realised my tone. Arty glanced to me, and yawned.

'You can get me...'

'Not you, Arty.'

'Aw.'

Nat sighed and touched my arm as I held her hand tightly. 'So?'

She grimaced and shrugged. 'Toast, I guess.'

'Toast?'

'Yeah, but it'll suck to eat.'

'You gotta have something in your stomach.'

'I guess.'

I examined her gaunt face and sniffled gently. She had to eat, even if it left her feeling sick, she had to gain back her weight.

'Toast, no problems,' I hummed.

I knew if Nat didn't eat, I'd hear it from Samantha, and Dad. Dad was much better at convincing her to do it. I think he coaxed her with a new video game, or candy.

Whatever it took, to keep our Natalie alive.

I wandered to the kitchen, hoping Dad had bought bread, or I'd have to argue with Nat about eating cereal.

Thankfully, he had bought a loaf. And I slipped two into the toaster.

While that cooked, I stared around my childhood kitchen, imagining all four of us.

Four of us, even my mother.

Nat was too young when she left us, but I grew up next to that woman, and never ever thought she'd leave.

She was in California now, with a new spouse and a step child.

We don't keep in contact, but I still have fond memories of her.

Dad and Mom fell apart, but I never really knew why. I think it had to do with his job, or something like that.

But they ended it on 'good terms.'

Dad missed her, I could see it.

Mom had been calling recently though, especially now that Nat was suffering. She helped with the bills, so I guess she cared enough.

I was being sour, and crossed my arms tightly.

Money, it's all we worried about in this family. Dad was overworking himself, and he'd come home this afternoon, eat something and fall asleep in the chair next to Nat's bed.

Then I had to get going, find the car that key belonged to.

A real needle in a haystack mission if you ask me.

The toast behind me popped, notifying me that it was ready to be buttered and handed over to a fussy twelve-year-old.

Rayne caught me by surprise when I turned, she grinned awkwardly and held the plate up against her chest.

'Oy,' she eased. 'Sorry, Juniper.'

'Red!' I chuckled. 'Scared me.'

'On edge still?' she asked, concerned.

I shrugged and pulled along with me, sighing. 'A little.'

She asked if it was my pain, my battered right side. It could have been that, but I think that was only a minor reason.

I had a lot on my mind.

'Maybe,' I replied.

Rayne opened Nat's door for me, nodding once. 'You'll be okay?'

She seemed very concerned now, and I pondered, 'You going somewhere?'

She was dressed, fully, even with her shoes on.

'Not yet,' Rayne mumbled. 'But I will, later on.'

I wanted to ask more questions about this sudden nervousness or was it awkwardness?

'Hey!' Nat waved to Rayne. 'You're up the latest.'

Rayne chuckled and shrugged her shoulders. 'Nah, I'm always up late.'

I had to remind Nat to eat as she spoke, and she chewed stubbornly, grimacing.

Rayne had told me not to worry, rubbed my shoulder and gave me a smile.

Maybe it was just my nerves playing up, she wouldn't keep something from me.

At half past ten, on the dot, Dr. Samantha arrived.

She was a French doctor, gorgeous and tall, with distinct features. Her black hair was cropped short and looked healthy, her skin was smooth, and her grey eyes complimented her whole persona. She was only twenty-six, and she looked ageless.

Ever since Nat's accident, she came over three times a week, to do blood tests and all that whatnot.

Nat despised needles, especially the ones she had injected into her back.

And I despised them too, seeing my sister receiving them so often.

Samantha held her bag of medical goodies by her side, and took me by the shoulder. 'Juniper.'

'Hi there,' I smiled. 'Nat seems a little positive today.'

Samantha glanced over my shoulder, her eyebrows raised. 'It could be the guests lingering around her bed.'

Her accent was deep, and lingered on the tip of her tongue.

I smiled and glanced to Rayne and Arty, they both watched my sister play her game, both pretty intrigued. Samantha let my shoulder go, and took a deep breath.

'I'll need to talk to you afterwards.'

Oh Jesus, my heart was already dropping.

'Oh,' I swallowed.

Samantha's eyes were serious, but she still tried to smile a little, reassure me everything was okay.

It definitely wasn't.

She stepped by me, because I couldn't move yet. The anxiety had taken hold of my body, that disgusting shivered feeling that loomed around the middle of your chest.

One word could break me.

'Hello Natalie,' Samantha said. 'How are you feeling?'

'Hey,' Nat's voice was shallow, she got nervous around the woman. 'I'm okay.'

I hoped so.

When I turned, Rayne had her eyes on me, but Arty had her eyes on Samantha. I think I saw her gawk a little, her eyebrows furrowed like she'd seen a puppy enter the room.

Samantha did her usual routine, check Nat's pulse and temperature, adjust the bed.

Arty stood aside Rayne, both at the foot of Nat's bed, both pretty awkward.

'Uh,' Arty muttered. 'We can go, if you need us out of the way, lovey.'

Samantha paused and turned to face the two, and the smiles got more forced. I think it was Arty's heavily accented catcall that left the French doctor confused.

'It is completely up to Natalie,' Samantha explained, her hands on her hips. 'Natalie?'

Nat blinked and shrugged her shoulders. 'I don't care, it's just gonna be a bunch of needles and shit.'

'Hey,' I snapped. 'Language.'

Samantha chuckled and placed her bag down, pulling out packets and packets of medical mumbo jumbo.

But I still had my eyes on Nat's, confused by her sudden swearword. She'd been hanging around Arty too much.

I looked to her next, and she shrugged her shoulders, 'Don't look at me!'

The three of us watched Samantha inject Nat with antibiotics, but she seemed distant, and it scared me.

There was only bad news if Samantha frowned, she was a serious woman but she was usually very perky.

Rayne took my hand, and I eased up, just a little.

Nat moaned in pain when she had to lift her upper body, Samantha held her up, and all three of us flinched at her suffering.

'Okay, Natalie this is going to sting a little,' Samantha coaxed gently. 'Just for a few seconds.'

I hated this part, I absolutely hated it. I turned to face the wall behind me, twisting both hands around Rayne's left arm.

I couldn't stand watching that long needle inject my sisters back, and she could never muffle her cry, no matter how hard she tried.

Arty panicked, and made a few jokes that left Nat laughing through the tears, but the pain was too loud.

'Nearly finished,' Samantha mumbled. 'Almost done.'

I bit back tears, trying to plan my day, where I would start looking for that damn car.

What kind of pain I would inflict on the person who did this to Nat? how would I sue them?

'Okay,' Samantha finally said. 'Done.'

I turned to see Nat huddled over Samantha's arms, head lowered. I'd watched this procedure since day one, and it hadn't got easier at all.

Rayne shuffled on the spot a bit, I could tell Nat's condition left her biting back tears as well.

'You've got to rest...' Samantha said, but she looked at me. 'No more video games.'

Nat whined, and allowed herself to be laid back against her pillows. I saw Samantha glance at me once more, and I nodded lightly.

'No more video games,' I repeated. 'Not until you rest.'

Nat groaned something to me, something along the lines of my betrayal. But she was already drifting off, she still wasn't used to the drowsiness.

Samantha tucked my sister in, sighing when she lifted herself from the bed.

I knew this was my time to talk with her, find out that horrible news.

'Rayne, Arty?' I asked.

They both glanced my way, Arty's eyes were eased, Rayne's concerned.

'I have to talk to Samantha, so,' I made it quite obvious, that they needed to leave the room.

'Oh,' Arty laughed awkwardly, grabbing Rayne's arm. 'Let's go find something to eat.'

Rayne gave me a look, and I sympathetically smiled, she'd be worrying as soon as the door closed.

'C'mon, love,' Arty grumbled, pulling her along. 'She's not going to vanish.'

'Oh, ha ha,' Rayne snapped back.

Once the door was closed, they continued to argue down the hall. I was half expecting a brawl to play out in my home.

Samantha was rustling through her bags, and I stood still, frozen, nervous.

Nat had fallen asleep on the corner of my eye, and she breathed steadily, I was thankful for morphine, it was all that helped the pain.

'Juniper,' Samantha began.

I felt my heart stutter, and I did too. 'Y□yes?'

She contemplated and let her eyes wander around the room, until she simply sighed and stepped towards me.

'Juniper, there's something I need to talk to you about,' Samantha said, she stopped a few metres from me.

I could feel the anxiety rise to my chest, my eyelids already moistening.

'Juniper, she hasn't improved,' Samantha tilted her head, examining my newfound sadness. 'And she can't hang on any longer, we have to get that surgery as soon as possible.'

'I know,' I answered. 'Trust me, I'm trying.'

'To do what?'

I flinched and shook my head, I couldn't spill here. 'I'm trying to make the money.'

Samantha knew the money issue was all that was stopping us from getting Nat this surgery, she too wished it wasn't so expensive.

'I've spoken to your father, and he's trying his absolute best with the bank.'

Like that would help, I thought like saying. The bank had already told us no, it wasn't possible and we'd be in the worst debt yet.

Dad was getting older, he was in his late fifties, when he passes away, I'd have that debt, and I wouldn't be able to put Nat into college.

Samantha was still talking, about the statistics and Nat's surgery and what would happen. But I had stopped listening a while ago, ever since she told me Nat was getting worse.

Samantha must have been used to this, seeing her patient's guardians lose their absolute heads when bad news was thrown at them. So, she took me by the shoulders, and calmed my stress.

'I know you're trying,' she said. 'You and your father are both trying.'

I couldn't look her in the eye.

'But if we do not get this surgery in the next two weeks...' she sighed. 'Natalie's chance of paralysis is eminent.'

I tried to remain calm, and nodded constantly.

'Okay?' Samantha asked. 'You understand this?'

'Yes.' I returned. 'I know.'

I glanced to Nat, and felt the fear take me by the throat. I had to get going, I had to find the person who had done this.

'We'll have the money,' I muttered. 'Don't you worry about that.'

I sounded quite determined, that even Samantha seemed confused. I kept my eyes on Nat, the rush of worry had quickly turned into sheer anger and revenge.

I wouldn't stand for it.

'I'm going to make sure, she's walking again,' I said.

Again, I was leading myself onto a dangerous path. And once again, I didn't care.

I knew Rayne would scold me for it, I was being hypocritical.

'Well,' Samantha interrupted my thoughts, she grabbed her things, eyebrows raising towards me. 'Do not get into any trouble, alright?'

I smiled, nodded, and gave her my best lie.

'Of course not,' I chuckled. 'I'll be careful.'

Chapter Seventeen

JUNIPER

I lied to Samantha, and I absolutely hated lying.

I wasn't going to be careful, at all. Not one little bit.

Later that day, around noon, I had to leave for work. My big Slavic boss was short staffed and I couldn't say no to a few extra bucks in my pocket, for Nat of course.

Before I left Somerville, I cleaned my wounds again, surprised by its healing.

It would definitely scar, but hey, at least I had a story to tell.

About how Juniper Bridges and Rayne Holmes bested the Fire Jackals and escaped their deadly clutches.

Rayne and I said our goodbyes at South Station, after taking the train in together.

We stood silently, watching the snowy city of Boston gradually become larger the closer we got. I knew Rayne was still processing the night prior, hey, I was too.

I had to hold her hand and constantly remind her everything was okay, kiss her on the cheek, smile, that kind of stuff.

I really did love her, a lot.

She took me by the shoulders before we parted, hugged me tightly against her tall self, then kissed me deeply, trying her absolute hardest to hide our locked lips from the public eye.

I honestly didn't care, I wanted people to see, I saw enough heterosexuals tongue fighting at work and at school.

Rayne seemed a little saddened to see me step away from her, holding our hands close together, fingers through the webs.

She gave me those puppy dog eyes, and that half lidded smile. I told her I'd text her, as soon as I could.

'Don't worry,' I said. 'It'll only be a little while.'

Rayne kissed me once more, and I found myself fumbling around my departure. Her eyesbecame saddened, and much larger.

'Augh!' I'd smacked her across the stomach playfully. 'Don't give me that look, Red! I won't be able to forgive myself!'

I did my best to tell myself otherwise, when I thought our embrace would be our last.

As expected, I walked into a bustling café, and my boss was losing his head.

'Juniper!' he called, thick accented. 'My love!'

He was stressed, and sweat poured down his forehead like a broken faucet. I flinched as he reached closer, taking my shoulders with his hands.

'I am so glad you are here!' he sighed. 'Place has been a wreck! How is sister?'

'She's fine,' I said sternly.

I hated talking about Nat's condition, it left a sour taste in my mouth, like she was going to up and vanish.

Vadim smiled, brushed the awkwardness off and waved his hands above his head. 'Off to work then, come, come.'

I followed him towards the back of the store, a usual process I knew. He slammed through the back doors, stepped into the office and groaned to see his brother dozing off against the desk.

'Yefim!' he roared, waking the younger brother with a gasp. 'Stop being such a lazy ass.'

I was used to this banter between the two, they were twins after all and constantly bickered. I remember hearing the two arguing about a girl, the next day was about their mother, then their uncle.

It was constant. And through my time working here at City Café, I learnt to ignore it.

Yefim was shorter than Vadim, but had a smoother face, like a baby. He was always exhausted, and wore a terrible suit.

He and his brother stood now, arguing about the nap, until they got real close, right to their foreheads.

Both ready to strike, Yefim growled from the bottom of this throat. Vadim returned a grouch, edging forward.

I'd seen this happen before too, and in just a moment they would be laughing.

'Brother!' Yefim chuckled, grinning.

Vadim exhaled loudly, and clapped his brother against the shoulder. 'You need to sleep better, brother.'

I rolled my eyes as they joked around, held their necks and play fought.

'Are you two done making out?' I joked. 'C'mon we're being scorched out there!'

The brothers both turned to me, and grinned, the similarities scared me.

'Of course!' Vadim laughed. 'Here, here.'

He rummaged through a bunch of wooden boxes to the left of the room, handing me a spare apron. It wasn't the cleanest, but it would do.

I smiled shortly as I took it, giving him a furrowed brow, 'Coming to save the day, am I?'

Yefim was next in line to splutter a giggle. 'Tiny girl always saves the day.'

'Tiny?!' I bit back. 'I'm not small!'

Vadim and Yefim glanced to each other, quickly, and shared a mutual inside joke. I was already blushing, and I was pouting.

'You looked like ladybug compared to tall friend.' Vadim sniggered, bringing his right hand upwards. My boss was also tall, and Rayne was probably close to his height.

'You were here,' he grinned, pointing very low to the floor, like unnaturally low.

'And girlfriend was here,' Yefim threw his hand into the air, way over his own height.

Firstly, I blushed at the term 'girlfriend.'

To the Bobrov brothers, clearly every girl who hung around Juniper Bridges was the typical 'Gal Pal.'

But the fact Rayne was technically my girlfriend now, left my stomach whirling with anticipation.

I wasn't used to that term, I hadn't for a while.

Secondly, I reacted to their inside joke, with a stern furrow of my brow and a mocking grin.

'Oh, ha ha!' I smirked. 'You guys are very funny.'

I waved my own fingers towards them, giving them a little attitude. 'How long did it take to figure out that one?'

Yefim grinned and patted his brother against the back. 'Only a few hours!'

'Hours?' Vadim snapped back. 'You mean minutes, we are professionals.'

'It was hours.'

'Minutes!'

Before I was caught in yet another Bobrov family feud, I snuck out with a quick roll of my eyes.

I couldn't stand hearing another Slavic cussing competition take form in front of me.

As I tied my apron around my waist, I scanned over the stores full house. People were coming in, speeding out, lining up on one side, and then the other.

It was a mess.

I stepped beside my co-worker, a lanky teenage male, one of Vadim's cousins most likely. He was struggling with a customers pay, his fingers shaking over the till.

Jeeze, I was gone for a few days, and the place was falling apart.

'Here,' I said. 'Let me take care of this, you start on the orders.'

He seemed relieved to hear that, and sped towards the machines to begin making a long list of caffeinated beverages.

In twenty minutes, give or take, the store calmed to a normal pace. And by about four-thirty, we were partially empty.

I liked this time of day, it gave me a minute or two to breathe, before being hassled by another middle-aged man with a bad case of the grumps.

I leant over the counter, my elbows pressing into the marble.

It was funny, I found myself daydreaming that Rayne would come walking through those glass doors, with that same nervous look on her face. Probably come up to me, stutter and compliment my attire, even if it was a grimy apron that hadn't been cleaned in almost a month.

I was surprised by the process of my thinking, especially when they revolved around her.

Usually I was very preoccupied with my workload thoughts, what paper was due at college, or even simple things like; what I was going to eat for dinner, what Nat would like for her birthday coming up.

It made me feel like a teenager again, thinking about some high school crush.

But then came the awful anxiety, as it told me to think of more important things, Nat and the Fire Jackals, the car I had to miraculously find.

I wasn't too great at balancing the good and bad thoughts.

I always ended up feeling guilty about something.

When I thought of Rayne in any sense, romantic or just in general, I would worry about Nat.

If I worried about Nat, I began to panic about money.

Money left me wondering about college, and my studies.

And before I knew it, I had one terrible headache.

Unfortunately, there was too much on Juniper's plate, and I wasn't hungry at all for any of it.

I sighed to myself, out of boredom I clicked the top of my pen, constantly repeating the action. I only stared towards those two glass doors, and nowhere else.

Behind me I could hear Vadim and Yefim argue, their voices muffled by the back door. To my right I could sense my co-workers mumbling to each other, cleaning the coffee machines when they conversed.

I kept to myself, my eyes peering into the closest object, which was the countertop.

We were getting so close, to finding out who really hit Nat.

The more I thought about it, the more my nerves played up and left a grumbling in my stomach. I really had no plan, no starting point to find the car here in Boston.

For all I know, the car could be in California.

Or worse, destroyed.

I shivered, I hadn't even processed the thought of the car being gone, what would I do then?

Before the anxiety completely took hold of my already nervous body, a familiar face stepped in, but it wasn't someone I was looking forward to.

'Juniper!' Reedy called, that smug grin on his face.

I controlled my frustration, and smiled weakly back, 'Robert.'

He pulled a face to my response, shaking his head. 'No, Reedy will do, I can't stand my name.'

I chuckled weakly, hey, he wasn't that bad.

I met both Reedy and Christopher just a few weeks ago during my shift, Christopher was still just as nervous as he came across these days, and Reedy was still the flirty jackass.

But both were tolerable, Christopher a lot more than his jock friend.

'How are you? I haven't seen you in a while,' Reedy rubbed his stubble, leaning over the counter to talk.

Thank God for the marble between us, or he'd seriously be in my space.

I pondered before I spoke, shrugging my shoulders, 'Been taking care of Nat.'

His eyes darkened, and he sadly frowned. 'Yeah, how is she doing? If you don't mind me asking.'

I hummed from my throat, and wavered my right hand, pen clicking again. 'She's doing, alright.'

Alright seemed to make Reedy grimace, he pocketed his hands and cocked his head a little.

'I'm sorry,' he muttered. 'I can't even fathom how much it must hurt, if anyone touched my little sister I'd beat their heads in.'

Reedy threw his fists towards me jokingly, but he was pretty sincere about the action.

I chuckled again, rubbing the back of my neck, 'Yeah.'

There it was again, the awkward silence that seemed to linger around Reedy and I.

He smiled to me, a sympathetic grin, but still, sweet.

If he wasn't such a flirty jerk, he wouldn't be a bad guy, maybe he just acted that way around Christopher.

'Do you want a coffee?' I asked, readjusting my apron. 'The usual?'

His usual was a tall mocha latte, I was tempted to put pepper in his drink on some days, the temptation was so satisfying.

But I didn't want to lose my job over a harmless prank.

Reedy grabbed his wallet, a thick black leather square, that had bills sprawling out from all sides.

The kid was loaded.

I only remember Christopher telling me his mother was a fashion designer for some top brand.

I wondered if he'd hand over the small sum of twenty thousand dollars.

It's all we had to owe the Hospital, even with the insurance we had to cover a large sum of it.

'Ah!' he growled. 'Only if you join me!'

I would have denied the invitation, like a bullet on any other day.

But the store was dead quiet, I could sit with him for a little, I was getting tired of standing anyway.

'Alright, Robert,' I playfully sighed. 'But only this one time.'

'Brilliant!' he cheered, flashing a smirk. 'I'll go sit down then, and we can talk.'

I wasn't so sure what he meant by 'talk', but I nodded back. 'Alright, alright.'

Reedy sat close to the windows, the exact same spot Rayne and I had a while back. It bothered me, just a little.

That place was sacred to me! It was technically our first date, that ended with a furious Juniper Bridges, towards the man sitting in Rayne's place right now.

I grimaced and turned to my co-worker, handing him Reedy's order.

I couldn't let something that silly bother me, maybe I just longed for Rayne's attention.

Typical, I was already getting too attached.

Before I handed him his drink, Reedy stood and leant in for a hug.

It was super uncomfortable but I did my best, patting his strong back gently. He chuckled when he let go, and I saw his eyes glance to my lips, just faintly.

'So!' he sat down quickly, clearing his throat. 'Tell me what's new!'

I inhaled as I sat, stretching my neck. 'What's new?'

'Yeah, y'know with college and all that.'

I shrugged my shoulders, trying to avoid the question. 'It's...uh.'

Reedy took a sip of his coffee, eyes and brows raised towards me. I contemplated even answering, but I sighed, I needed someone to talk to.

'It's not the so great right now,' I admitted, glancing outside. 'Things could be better.'

'With the whole, Nat thing?'

'That, and other things,' I answered. 'But yes, mainly Nat.'

Reedy asked me about her, and I told the truth. What she was doing, how she was coping, the pain and the injections. I didn't even realise I had spoken for a good ten minutes about my sister's awful pain, and Reedy's face fell with every hurtful detail.

He reached over to grab my hand, but I stiffened and clenched my fingers into my palm, avoiding his eyes.

'It's alright, she's going to get through this,' I mumbled, my voice cracking. 'Once I find the jackass who did it.'

I saw Reedy nod, he crossed his arms and shrugged. 'I honestly, just can't believe someone would do that.'

I saw his face contort into a terrible pain, like my story had genuinely hurt him. I knew Reedy was a sweet guy, when he wanted to be. But maybe this talk wasn't such a bad idea after all, he seemed so angered by it all.

'Do you have any leads? Maybe you could go to the police about it.' He grabbed a packet of sugar as he spoke, sifting it into his beverage. 'I mean; they sometimes take these situations super seriously.'

'Sometimes,' I repeated his words, and Reedy sadly sighed.

'Yeah, sometimes.'

We fell silent, until Reedy patted the table gently. 'I can't help thinking, it was to do with those assholes.'

He clenched his teeth, throwing the scrunched up sugar packet to his plate. I saw his eyebrows dip inwards, he was frustrated.

'Those Fire Jackal twerps,' he finished.

I was getting fired up, with all the information I had consumed in the past few weeks. From the anonymous sender of emails, telling me the location of their meetings, to the conversation Rayne and I overheard, and finally finding the key.

I knew it was hard to trust people, especially partially new faces like Reedy, but he seemed to know something, maybe more than I expected about this gang. Maybe he knew a few people in the group, maybe he'd dealt with them before.

'Robert,' I grouched. 'It was them, someone from that group hit Nat.'

His eyes widened, and he leant forward, trying to create some secretive barrier around the two of us.

'Seriously?' he asked, I think he was on the edge of his seat. 'How the heck do you know that?'

I bit my bottom lip, all the information clung at my tongue, wanting to escape my mouth. Reedy stared at my eyes, and I sighed.

He could be a great ally; he could help me.

Surely he knew someone.

'I made this blog, a few days after the accident,' I explained. 'To see if anyone had any clue, to what had happened.'

It was true, I got hardly any hits on that website, until I started getting anonymous answers.

'Some guy, or girl.' I corrected, fumbling with my hands. 'Sent me the location of the Fire Jackals meeting, that was held on the same night Nat was hit.'

Reedy blinked, his fingers clung around his coffee cup in anticipation. 'Jesus, seriously?'

I nodded, breathing in. 'So, Rayne and I went.'

His eyes flinched to her name, and he lifted his hand high above his head, 'Tall friend?'

I chuckled, agreeing, 'Yes, tall friend.'

Friend, good joke.

'We snuck around the place, somewhere on the outskirts of Somerville and found a whole bunch of stuff,' I paused and leant on my hand, elbow pressing into the table. 'We rummaged around for a bit, and I found a clue to their next meeting.'

'Wow, Juniper,' Reedy laughed and raised his hands again, hitting his knees. 'You're some sneaky snoop.'

I shushed him, glancing around to see if anyone had overheard him, or I.

'Sorry!' he whispered, holding his mouth.

'But we were nearly caught,' My tone became serious, and I leant a little closer to the gap between us. 'Two members, came barging in, talking about some guy named Pebbles.'

Reedy pressed himself backwards, crossing his arms. 'Pebbles?'

'Yeah, Pebbles,' I replied. 'The guy who hit my sister.'

Reedy's look turned serious too, and he grimaced with confusion 'How do you...'

'They were speaking about it,' I itched the bridge of my nose. 'Said they were looking for the key, to the car.'

Reedy pointed to his own car keys, aside his wallet to his right. I nodded grimly.

'Yeah, car keys,' I said. 'They found it, left, and Rayne and I were pretty shocked.'

'I can imagine.'

'So,' I paused and shrugged once more. 'We snuck into the meeting.'

'Wait, you what?' Reedy gave me a concerned look, and I flinched under his gaze.

'We...uh, snuck into the meeting?'

'Juniper!' he took hold of his forehead, rubbing it slowly. 'Are you serious? That's so dangerous.'

'But I got the key!' I snapped. 'We found nothing, but the key.'

I blurted this out, and lowered my voice halfway through my sentence. Reedy eased his eyes, he looked pretty intrigued now.

'Really? What brand of car?' he asked. 'Surely it has the name on it.'

I rummaged through my back pocket, and pulled the key out, it was attached to a lock with all my other personal items.

I handed the black key over to Reedy, and he examined it closely. 'Looks like a Ford, I mean the logos been scratched off...'

'I don't know where to even start, Rob,' I sighed sadly. 'I have the key, but god knows where the car is.'

'You find the car...' he paused and I nodded.

'I find the guy who hit my sister.' I muttered quietly. 'The car has to have some sort of identification, even the number plate I could find out who owned it previously.'

Reedy chuckled and handed the key back, eyebrows raised impressively.

'You are one super chick,' he flirted. 'This is some serious detective shit.'

I blushed from his compliment and waved my hands a little. 'I couldn't have done any of it without Rayne.'

Reedy's confident smile faltered, and he looked jealous. 'Ah, you two are close.'

'Very close,' I tried to make it obvious. 'She's done a lot.'

I fiddled with my apron, hiding my giddy smile. Rayne was a distraction, even when she wasn't around.

Reedy sculled the rest of his coffee, releasing a satisfying exhale.

'Well,' he said. 'I could ask around work, y'know, at the mechanics.'

'They'd know how to find a lone car?'

'Probably, we always pick up random abandoned cars here and there.'

I felt my heartbeat fasten, and my hopes begin to rise. 'Seriously? You think we could find it?'

Reedy grinned sweetly, 'Yeah, I mean it might take a little snooping around...'

He paused and flicked me across the nose, I flinched from his touch.

'But you seem to be really good at that already.'

'It comes with a price...' I admitted, chuckling sheepishly. 'A lot of damage.'

'Be careful, okay?' he mumbled, rummaging to grab his phone. 'Here, I'll message you if I find anything out.'

I took his phone gratefully, nodding. 'Please, that would be awesome.'

I shoved my number in quickly, and he returned a smile. 'Maybe ask around the police department, say the cars been stolen... make something up.'

I hadn't even thought about that, I was a pretty awful liar, but if it was going to save my sister, then I'd become the best damn liar there was.

Reedy was happy when I hugged him closely before he left. 'Thank you, this really means a lot.'

'It's fine, Juniper.' He returned. 'I want to find this asshole just as much as you.'

Honestly, it was nice to hear that.

I was glad I had people like Rayne and Arty, and now I had Reedy too.

He patted my shoulder and glanced to his watch, grumbling.

'I gotta get going, have some stuff to do tonight,' He grinned and rubbed his fingers together. 'Making lots of cash!'

He was like a school boy, wiggling those eyebrows at the idea of money.

'Ah,' I teased. 'So you can take lots of girls on dates, hey?'

He smirked and shrugged his shoulders, 'Well, maybe we could go out sometime?'

I laughed quickly, hitting him against the arm, 'Never going to happen, Reedy.'

He pouted, lifted his shoulders and sighed. 'Worth a try.'

We said our farewells, and he lifted his phone to me.

'I'll get calling now, see if I can find out anything about the car,' he explained.

'That would be so great! Please text me if you find anything out,' I said, then grabbed his arm before he left. 'I'll go talk to the police later on.'

'Yeah,' he smiled. 'Tell me how that goes, okay?'

Reedy wasn't kidding when he said he'd start looking, he was already dialling a number on his mobile as he walked away, talking vastly into it.

Who knew Reedy could actually be someone I could trust.

Rayne might have some issues with him, but even she could come around at some point.

I bundled up my apron, taking in all that had been discussed.

Was it safe to say I was feeling a little more positive now? That we might find the car sooner than I thought?

Funnily enough, the car was our key to everything, not the actual key itself.

Rayne texted me at around seven, to let me know she would be out tonight.

It was cute how she thought to tell me, and spelled every word correctly in her message.

Of course I worried about where she would be, what she would be doing.

But I trusted her, that she would do the right thing.

I on the other hand, stood outside Boston South Police Station, contemplating if telling the authorities of my process was even a good idea.

Of course, as soon as Nat was attacked we went to the cops about it. Dad was furious when they pretty much shrugged their shoulders and said, 'We can't trace an untraceable car.'

They told us the case would be ongoing, give us some financial help for Nat's condition. But when the authorities heard the word 'Fire Jackals' they shrivelled up and loosened their ties.

I never expected a group of morons to be such a big deal.

But now, with my experiences surrounding them? I kind of understood why the authorities were nervous around the topic.

These people weren't kidding around.

I was still upset, and hassled the police for any information regarding the Fire Jackals, they never gave me any information, and so began my quest to find out information myself.

Hence the blog, hence the anonymous messages.

Maybe, with all the information I had now, they could trace Pebbles, or anyone at that.

I breathed in tightly, it was freezing out and I would much rather be in Rayne's arms right now.

She was probably out busking somewhere, making her pay and singing with that lovely voice of hers.

I snapped out of it, I couldn't stand out here and get all starry eyed about my new girlfriend.

Alright, I'll just go in, see the guy in charge, tell him that I had some more information.

Just like Reedy, maybe they had some information too.

I needed to snoop, and be extra careful about it.

Really, careful.

Inside was warm, and smelled like coffee.

Go figure.

The interior was gigantic, with white walls and black tile floors. Behind a huge front desk, sat three policemen, all head into their work.

It was quiet in here, and only a few people sat around, on their smartphones, waiting.

For what? I had no clue.

I stood by the door, chewing my bottom lip. I wasn't sure about this, maybe it wasn't too late to turn around and run back to South Station.

I could do this whole Fire Jackals thing on my own!

I felt a smile tweak at my lips, but I grimaced straight after.

No way, I needed third party help.

I cleared my throat and stepped forward, avoiding all eyes. I could hear my footsteps echo, the sound of my hitched breath.

Ahead of me, all three policemen glanced up from their computers, the middle one was the eldest, and furrowed his grey brow my way.

'Can I help you, ma'am?' he asked. 'You seem to be lost.'

I grinned nervously, lifting myself on my tiptoes.

Now would have been the best time to act like a smart, mature twenty-two-year-old. But when I went to speak, all that came out was a nervous;

'Uh...Hi!'

My smile had become wider, and I fiddled with my fingers.

If I was going to be arrested, it would be because I looked guilty as all hell. I cleared my throat again, tensing my fists.

'I was wondering if I could uh,' I paused and smiled to the other two cops. 'Talk to someone?'

They all glanced at one another, confused and slightly amused. The eldest turned to me once more, his beady brown eyes peering into my own.

'What do you mean?' he chuckled. 'Someone? Who do you need to talk to?'

Oh shit, I didn't know how to answer that question.

I knew no names, nobody from this department, was there a lead detective, or a leader?

'I uh,' I eased my eyes, hoping for a miracle. 'Someone in charge?'

There it was, that awkward silence.

I waited for their answer, the cop on the right cleared his throat first.

'Well, Detective Rodgers just clocked off an hour ago,' he explained, I tried to hide my smirk. 'So, you're better off coming in tomorrow if you want to talk to him.'

I grimaced and sighed to myself, nodding.

'Oh' I muttered, a little upset. 'Well could I leave my number or something?'

The cop in the middle peered up at me, almost as if he remembered something quick, 'Oh, I know you.'

I eased my head and blinked, 'You do?'

That was a little worrisome, I definitely didn't remember him that's for sure.

He nodded once, 'Big sister of the girl in Somerville, I was there.'

I felt my chest tighten, and I grimaced, 'Oh.'

'Yeah, I remember now,' he rubbed his chin. 'Maybe you're better off going to the Police Department in Somerville,'

'No,' I snapped back, my voice a little loud. I was frustrated now. 'They didn't do anything, for my sister.'

The three of them looked saddened, but especially the eldest in the middle. He glanced to his waiting list, then towards the group of people sitting a few feet behind me.

'Look, kid,' he mumbled, voice low. 'I'm going to be brutally honest with you here.'

Please don't, I felt like saying.

'The chances of finding out who really did that awful deed...' he paused and grimaced. 'Is so slim.'

'So I've heard,' I answered back. 'But that doesn't mean it's a dead case. So that's why I'm here, maybe you guys can do a better job, if there's some outside help.'

'Outside help?' he asked, head cocked to the side.

Oh no, I said too much.

'Uh,' I stammered. 'Yes, outside help. Someone willing to go undercover, someone who has guts.'

'Are you suggesting the Boston Police force has no "guts"?' the cop on the left asked.

I crossed my arms, and shrugged my shoulders.

'Well, from what I've seen back in Somerville,' I paused and pouted. 'They gave up pretty easily, so yeah.'

I was treading on mines here, and I was waiting for the handcuffs to come out. Old cop in the middle chuckled weakly, trying to process my words.

'Listen, kid–'

'Juniper,' I interrupted. 'Juniper Bridges.'

'Juniper,' he corrected himself. 'Look, I'll book you in to see Detective Rodgers tomorrow afternoon. He's the best one to talk to, if you want to bring this issue further.'

I huffed a little, three men couldn't handle a girl like me?

'Fine,' I mumbled. 'Thanks.'

He nodded once and took my details down, even if it was just my number and name. I was booked in to see Detective Teddy Bear at three in the afternoon.

I wasn't sure how to react to that, how would some big detective be any different from the three that faced me now.

'Okay, get home safe now. Ma'am,' The cop in the middle smiled. 'Goodnight.'

'Yeah,' I said. 'Goodnight officers.'

I could feel every set of eyes on my back when I left, my walk was hastened to the door and I kept a stern look upon my face.

Even if I was disappointed, I couldn't make it obvious.

The days were going by so fast and Samantha's words were hovering above my head; that Nat didn't have that long, that she'd get worse and worse if I didn't find the jackass that did this to her.

I was angry at the world, the government, Boston, America, everything.

She was so young, so goddamn young and bedridden.

I needed the police's help, and if Detective Care Bear was going to be stubborn about it tomorrow, then hell, so would I.

On my lonely way back to Boston University, I felt the urge to hold Rayne, be close to her.

I texted her, that's all I could to at the moment, and she didn't reply as hastily as I wished she would.

I was falling deeper and deeper in love, and unfortunately the timing was complicated.

I had lots of things to worry about, and Rayne was a big piece.

Instead, I thought about what was going to be discussed tomorrow, how would I convince the police to lend me a hand in finding an unknown car.

There was still so much to know, and surely the authorities knew a decent amount.

I hoped.

Rayne texted me before I slept that night, a simple.

Goodnight Juniper, job was a little hectic tonight, but I'm alright. I love you.

It left me a little giddy, to see those three words.

They completely distracted me, and I replied with only the same.

I love you too.

Chapter Eighteen

JUNIPER

I could still remember my first night terror.

I was only thirteen, young and naïve.

Of course, watching horror movies before bed wasn't the best idea, and many of my awful dreams had been triggered by those very films.

One night it would be zombies, the other a big ghost.

They were harmless nightmares, that woke me with a pulsating heartbeat and widened eyes.

I still remember the reoccurring dream I had for a long period of time, it consisted of a notepad and pen, the size of towers, chasing me through a valley of jumbled words.

Every time a page flipped, the grumble it made still left me shivering.

I couldn't look at my notepad normally for about a week.

Though as I grew up, I was vulnerable to the world and what it really was.

The cloak of childhood innocence and recklessness that covered my eyes was slowly being pulled away. I was starting to see what society was like, the way people acted, good deeds, bad deeds.

When I reached my teenage years, I never feared ghosts and monsters, no, I feared what people could do, and what the world was going to become.

My nightmares consisted of my biggest fears, being left behind, lost, afraid.

They slowly became worse, they'd mixed with my anxiety and become night terrors that left my breath hitching, my head swirling.

They appeared during different times, when I had finals, or when I was under great stress. Sometimes they never showed at all.

But boy, did I hate them when they did.

Especially when Nat lingered inside them.

§

I slept pretty late Sunday night.

I had this major assignment due that I had forgotten all about, I was carried away with my Fire Jackals progress.

It was due Tuesday night, and I couldn't risk failure.

I could write a paper in hours, my typing speed was unnaturally fast and sometimes even I was frightened by the amount of words that I spat out.

What can I say? When I get carried away, I get carried away.

Especially if my papers consisted of current affairs and topics I was passionate about, whatever revolved around the truth and picking the liars out.

I wasn't a fan of liars, or those who hid the truth to benefit for themselves.

I would sit at my desk, in my hard computer chair and stare at my laptop screen for hours, not even blinking.

And before I knew it, it'll be four in the morning.

So, when I decided to follow that route on Sunday night, I found myself tossing and turning. My dream becoming a terror.

I could feel it, the way my head hammered, the way images flashed and fissured into view.

Like old TV images, flash, flash, flash.

I saw Nat, as she lay there struggling. I saw her cry, I saw her face manifest into my biggest fears, I saw her die, I saw her live.

She would look me in the eye, tell me she hated me, tell me she wished she could walk again.

And I would tell her I was sorry, tell her I loved her.

The dreams used to be so small, but now they consisted of my true nightmare.

Losing my sister.

I focused on what I imagined to be the car that had hit her, I saw every person I trusted in that driver's seat, everyone.

Even myself.

I knew my dreams showed me what I loathed, what I feared the most. But God, did they feel real.

I needed to wake up, I needed to.

There were horrible moments of lucid dreaming, when I woke up in my nightmare and felt relief, only to be dragged right back in.

I was stuck, and I began panicking.

Finally, the dark figure that appeared at every climax of my terror appeared.

I imagined it to be a tall humanoid slender dark figure, that was made entirely up of my anxiety and stress.

It was heavy as it climbed over my still body, it would peer down at me like it saw right through my soul.

Until it fell, right upon my chest.

And I woke with a startled breath of ragged air, eyes wide and moist from fresh tears.

Lifting my upper body, I grappled at the bed sheets, and viciously scanned my room for that horrifying figure.

My breath was short, my chest heaved back and forth and I could still feel that heavy weight upon my body.

This had to be one of the worst night terrors I had experienced in a long time.

I swallowed loudly, and ran a hand through my hair, my forehead had broken out in a sweat, and I shivered like a child.

To my left, nothing, to my right, nothing.

I was safe here in my cold, lonely dorm room.

I sighed, real relief washing over my body, and leaned back down.

What was I expecting? I was stressed, and constantly being reminded my sister was sick, close to death.

Reminded I didn't have the money to help her, reminded I was losing this battle just as she was.

I felt my throat tighten, my chest pang with familiar pain.

The roof was still, and had stopped spinning. When I turned my head to the right, my bedside table clock was exceptionally bright. It was mocking me.

I grimaced.

Five in the morning.

Wonderful.

I turned back to the ceiling, taking one easy breath. If I lay still enough, I could hear the beating of my heart, it calmed to a steady pace in only a few minutes. As soon as I brushed the awful thought of Nat vanishing forever.

No, I was close.

So close to finding out the truth, with all my friends help, Nat was going to be alright.

So would Dad, and even I.

I'd find the sucker who ran away, uncover the truth.

Determination flooded my body just as much as exhaustion, and my eyes drooped.

I was afraid to sleep, but just for a moment.
Afraid I would see all that I feared, once again.

§

The first thing I did, when I finally awoke at a normal hour. Was call my home.

Dad answered, his tired voice croaky and rough.

I always panic whenever he talks like that, I always assume somethings gone wrong.

'Dad?' I asked, biting my nails. 'Everything okay? I had a bad dream and...'

'Everything's fine here,' he replied. 'Nat's asleep, Samantha should be coming around to help her.'

I sighed relief, rubbing the back of my neck eagerly, 'Thank God.'

There was a pause between both of us, until Dad breathed in.

'Juniper?' he mumbled. 'Are you taking care of yourself?'

I chuckled and sat against my bed, shrugging my shoulders. 'I think so.'

'You think so?'

'Yes, I think so,' I pursed my lips. 'I'm not worried about myself, Dad.'

He laughed back, a big grumpy huff that I was used to hearing, 'Yes, that's the issue here.'

'There's no issue,' I answered back. 'Nat is more important now, we have to get that money.'

I knew I would choke up in a moment, knowing time was not on our side.

'Juniper...' he said, his tone full of disappointment.

'Don't,' I begged. 'Don't say anything, if you're giving up—'

'I'm not giving up,' he sounded angrier now. 'Don't say that.'

I pursed my lips again and listened to his lecture. On how Nat was his daughter, that he'd tear the sky down for her.

He was planning on taking another loan out from the bank, something to pay back that hefty hospital bill.

I saw hope in that, but I also saw a disastrous future.

'Dad, if you take another loan.'

'I know, Juniper.'

'You'll be in so much debt, and I know Nat is worth it. But if you lose your job and...'

'I know, Juniper.' He repeated. 'But my little girl needs it.'

I could just see us now, all three of us, on the street, homeless. I bit my bottom lip tight, as if it was going to burst.

'Shit.' I sniffed, catching my mouth before I sobbed aloud. 'Shit.'

No way, this couldn't happen.

I wouldn't let my dad lose his job, die lonely and poor.

And I wouldn't let my sister die either.

I had to get out there, ASAP and find more answers.

'I have to go Dad,' I muttered. 'I'll be out today; I have to do some things.'

Those things meant, snooping around the police department, maybe find a few files on the Fire Jackals.

I could already feel the stress.

'Alright, be safe,' My dad said. 'I'll speak to you soon, please don't do anything silly. I know Nat means the world to you, she means the world to me too, but do not get yourself into trouble.'

I paused before I hung up, I wanted to tell my dad everything, every last detail.

I couldn't. I was lying, I hated liars, and I was being one.

'Dad,' I croaked.

'Hm?'

I let my eyes wander, but I still bit my tongue. I needed to focus, tell myself that this was for the right cause.

'Nothing.,' I answered. 'I'll see you later.'

When I hung up, my phone instantly began to vibrate in my hands. I groaned and lifted it, but my irritation was lifted when I saw Rayne's name pop up.

I fumbled with answering, sliding right on the screen before shoving the device against my ear.

'Hey!' I spoke, flustered. 'Hey, Red.'

'Hey Juniper.'

'I've been so worried about you,' I admitted. 'Were you busking last night?'

Rayne paused before she spoke, a nervous laugh came from the other end.

'Well, no,' she admitted. 'A different job!'

I eased my head, and pushed myself off the bed, 'Another job?'

I sounded curious, maybe a little too curious.

'Yeah, it's alright though,' Rayne cleared her throat. 'I'll tell you all about it.'

'Go on.,' I said sternly.

Rayne was a busker, she sang and strummed that guitar better than anyone I knew. Why did she need another job so suddenly? And what exactly was she doing?

'Well, yeah I want to tell you somewhere nice,' Rayne sounded a little flustered. 'Nat wanted us to, y'know...'

I searched through my wardrobe as she stammered, she was moving awfully loudly on the other line. I hummed back, waiting for her answer.

'That date sounds pretty nice, right?'' Rayne laughed. 'How about it?'

'Wow, Red,' I joked. 'You're being awfully romantic...'

I leaned back, my spare hand on my hip. 'What have you done?'

'Nothing!' Rayne chuckled, God her laugh was brilliant. 'Nothing, I just thought we could have a nice night.'

I chewed my bottom lip, I could already feel that anxiety rushing into my chest. The only thing stopping me from feeling guilty, was the fact this whole date was Nat's idea, and it would make her happy.

'Alright.' I giggled. 'What time do you want me, Red?'

I heard her cough again, and laugh anxiously., 'I would like to take you, on a nice date, at six?'

'Six?' I smiled. 'Alright, and where?'

'Meet me at your house,' she said suddenly.

I paused and felt my eyebrows dip, 'My house? As in, Somerville?'

'Yeah, I'm probably going to be there in a few hours.' Rayne answered, going quiet after.

'Why?' I was genuinely confused.

'Arty's there.'

'She's what?'

'Well think about it, she hasn't really left.'

'She hasn't?'

'No, she's staying low, remember?' Rayne muttered. 'She's taken refuge at your house.'

I sighed loudly, I knew Arty didn't have her own apartment, and she had a habit of staying over at her friends.

My dad was friends with her, said she was a good laugh and had the liver of an Irish superhero.

She could take her alcohol pretty damn well, and Dad liked the company.

'Mm,' I chuckled weakly. 'She's such a mess.'

'So am I,' Rayne replied. 'We're all a bit scattered.'

I was concerned by that tone in her voice, a high leverage that slowly fell to an upset grumble. I took a pair of black jeans out, grabbing a navy button up, my red coat would suit this whole outfit pretty well.

'You're not scattered,'' I sighed. 'You're adorable, Red.'

She coaxed me from the other end, I could see her blushing from here. 'Aw, thanks Juniper.'

I could have stayed on the phone with her for hours, I very well felt like it.

'So, six at my place?' I asked, stretching gently.

'Yeah, Nat would probably like to see us,' she said. 'I've got my guitar on me, maybe I'll get there early and play a few songs for her.'

I smiled wide, leaning over my desk to examine my laptop, 'Oh, such a charmer.'

'Hey now...'

'You're going to charm my sister with your beautiful voice, huh?'

'Of course, I charmed you didn't I?' she sounded flirtatious, and it left my abdomen swirling pleasurably.

'Such a tease,' I sighed roughly. 'But alright, I'll see you then.'

'Great, I can drive Arty's car,' Rayne explained. 'And you help me find that Japanese place, okay?'

I grimaced, Japanese food.

Chopsticks.

Making a fool of myself, not being able to pick up a simple piece of goddamn fish.

'Okay, sounds perfect.'

I listened out for her laugh, and felt a blush tickle my cheeks.

I couldn't help but hear a pang of sadness in her voice, some sort of edginess that she couldn't hide.

Rayne was probably just as stressed as I was, and I had a knack of forgetting that.

'Red!' I called before she hung up, urgency in my voice.

'Yeah?'

I fumbled with my words, straightening up. 'I love you, be careful, with...' I shrugged my shoulders and grimaced. 'You know, whatever you do today.'

Saying I love you to someone still left my chest tightening, love was such a scary thing and I was frightened by its abilities.

It could lift me high into the sky, but also throw me down below.

Saying it to Rayne was easy, because I felt so strongly about her. I couldn't see myself with anybody else, but the future was cloudy, for everyone.

There was no perfect life, and that was always at the back of my brain.

Maybe it was because I was dealing with all this unordinary stuff, clans and guns, hospitals and money.

Ugh, it was all such a mess, Rayne was right, I was scattered too.

'I love you too!' Rayne replied sweetly. 'Of course, you be careful as well. Don't do too much snooping, alright?'

I held the phone tight to my ear, and nodded once, 'Yeah, I won't.'

Lying to my girlfriend, shit.

That was hard.

I swear, when this was all over, and I'd found the car, and Pebbles and all that junk.

She and I would move out as soon as possible together, kiss every morning and every night, wake up together.

I heard her mumble another goodbye, and I felt the same words fumble from my lips, softer.

When she was gone, my heart felt like molten hot lava, but it was uncomfortable.

I rubbed my sore spot gently, glancing to the time.

In two hours, I would be sitting in a police department talking to a detective about the Fire Jackals.

What was I going to expect?

Maybe he'd cower in fear with his tail between his legs at the very mention of them.

Or maybe he'd arrest me for toying with the police, give me a stern talking and have me on my way.

I crossed my arms, my phone by my computer's side.

I'd argued with stubborn men in my life, beaten them in arguments, put them back in their places.

I should be geared up for this, ready and prepared.

But there was something different, a detective? The law?

What was I even doing?

I groaned loudly, rubbing my face.

'Juniper Bridges! C'mon!"I sighed. 'You're smarter than this, you'll find the truth!'

I pumped my fists as I fell back against my bed, and wobbled for a moment before I lay still.

§

Just as I was yesterday, I was nervous and looked like I'd robbed a children's toy shop.

I sat with my hands between my knees, my lips pursed and my hat over my eyes. I'd been ushered into this big office, its interior was dark and mysterious, as was the man who stood a few feet away from his desk.

He held a cigarette in his lips and watched the busy street from his window. I saw his profile, chiselled yet warn out, scarred, and tampered with.

He glowed in this dark room.

I saw him shuffle a little, grab his hat upon his head and slowly pull it upwards.

'So, Miss Bridges,' he mumbled, voice hoarse. 'You'd like to talk, I've heard.'

I swallowed deeply, and cleared my throat, 'Y–yeah.'

'And, what would you like to discuss?' he asked.

I watched him step forward, pull the black computer chair at his desk back, and twist it.

'I know your sisters case; I hear news from all around Massachusetts,' he explained. 'It was an awful situation, and I'm sorry for the pain it has caused you.'

He was already closing our discussion, and I hadn't even said two words. I breathed in deeply and leant forward, my hands still tight together.

'Mr. Rodgers,' I began.

It was easier to say his name, now that I knew he wasn't a walking teddy bear.

He was a tall man with a pair of gorgeous bright hazel eyes. They were unreal, I don't think I'd seen a pair like them.

He scanned my face over, and I felt nervous under his glare. I couldn't speak! This was so confusing.

'I uh,' I stammered. 'I just wanted to discuss how we could find more...'

I paused and looked up, Detective Rodgers took a swig of his cigarette, eyes peering towards me. He wasn't dangerous, at least not to me. He was very intimidating, but I could see dimples whenever he twisted his lips.

I breathed in again, 'I want to find more answers, about who hit my sister.'

'Miss Bridges...'

'No, I need to find out more,' I interrupted, ballsy move Juniper.

He waited for me to continue, and I scanned his desk, papers everywhere, folders and tiny objects here and there.

He looked so busy. And I hated burdening others.

'I know they're involved,' I said. 'I know.'

'Ah yes,' Nick smiled shortly. 'You seem like a determined girl. Not one to sit idly by and lose a fight.'

I nodded, and he chuckled, pushing the tip of his cigarette into the ashtray by his drink.

'And who are "they?" may I ask?' he leaned forward as he spoke.

I chewed my bottom lip, and examined the file under his fingertips. I watched him pull it out before he greeted me, it must have had my sister's case inside it.

I looked him in the eye, a stern glare, 'The Fire Jackals.'

He smiled sheepishly, leaned back and sighed, 'Ah.'

'I know for sure, that it was them,' I admitted, my right hand escaped my legs, and touched the edge of the maple desk.

'How?' he asked, curious. 'It could have been anyone, how are you so sure?'

I held back now, pursing my lips.

This was dangerous, this could honestly jeopardise everything I had done, everything Arty and Rayne and I had done.

Detective Rodgers' expression turned calm, content and friendly. He sighed and leant forward again, clasping his hands together.

'Listen, kid,' he said, lowly. 'I know what you're doing, I've been in this business for a long time, and I know a determined face like that.'

He pointed to me, wiggling his finger playfully, 'You know something, that I do not.'

I felt my gut tighten, and I grimaced back, 'Uh.'

He smiled again, his eyebrows furrowing, 'You need my help.'

I nodded quickly, looking away from his friendly eyes.

'You've been getting into trouble, finding answers for yourself.'

'Well can you blame me?' I turned to him again as I spoke. 'The police in Somerville tensed up at the mention of the Fire Jackals!'

Detective Rodgers was taken aback by my sudden boost of energy, I raised my hands as I spoke.

'They've done nothing but pat us on the back and apologise.,' I said. 'Of course I had to get answers for myself, nobody else would.'

I let my voice fall, I was becoming overwhelmed. 'I didn't want to watch my sister suffer, I needed to find out more for her, so I could fix this whole mess. So I searched, for days, and snooped and did all I could.'

I was being horribly honest, and it scared me. I really hoped he wouldn't turn around and tell me to leave, tell me it was nothing I should get involved with, tell me there was no hope.

'Which brings us back to my question,' he said sternly. 'You know something, that I do not, yes?'

I looked him in the eye, and he winked. 'Am I correct, Miss Bridges?'

Slowly, I crossed my arms and pouted, 'And how do you know that?'

He laughed at my counter-question, and took a swig of his drink, smelt like whisky.

'Because,' he replied. 'Why else would you be here?'

There were thousands of replies that ran through my head, but only the honest answer flew from my mouth.

'I know the Fire Jackals were involved,' I started. 'Because I've been receiving anonymous answers.'

His brow furrowed again, and he grabbed a pen, flipping the file open.

I hesitated, and he lifted his free hand. 'This is all confidential, between you and me.'

I didn't know how to trust him, and he saw this in my expression.

'Trust me,' Detective Rodgers said. 'And I will help.'

I took a deep breath, and thought of Nat, how happy she would be if we found out the truth.

I saw us back home, playing together like nothing had happened.

In a few months, she'd be walking.

'Okay…' I said softly.

I prepared myself to explain, and he nodded once my way, 'Go on.'

So, I sat in Detective Rodgers's office, and described my past month in detail. I showed him my own notes, the clues I had found, locations and emails.

He was impressed by some of my answers, but also greatly concerned. But he never spoke, he never interrupted.

Firstly, I told him of my blog, and how I was receiving anonymous messages with clues and hints. I explained how Rayne and I trespassed an abandoned building, overheard two members discuss Pebbles and his connection to Nat, which brought me to the meeting we had snuck into.

His brow fell lower between the valley of his eyes, he scribbled when I spoke, glanced at my face whenever he could.

I finally told him about the car, how I had snuck the key, been shot in the process. That Pebbles real name wasn't in the book and that we'd escaped.

I didn't mention Arty, I didn't want her being arrested because of her past with the group. I hadn't even mentioned Rayne's real name, I just called her my friend.

I spoke of my father's money issues, the hospital bills and Nat's short time. He looked pained when I told him, vulnerable to its saddening emotion.

When I thought I had explained everything, Detective Rodgers took a deep breath, and fumbled with his empty glass.

It had been an hour, of me constantly talking, yet he hadn't said a word.

I was getting nervous, and the key trembled in my hand.

'Well,' he mumbled. 'You have definitely done some snooping.'

I smiled weakly, brushing my hair behind my ear.

'But this is dangerous,' he muttered. 'You have put yourself into danger, with one of the most notorious groups in this state.'

I was being scolded, and from a cop as well.

'Not only have you put yourself in danger, you've been hurt in the process.'

He pointed to my side, and I nodded, 'Yes.'

'You have trespassed into buildings, one being abandoned,' Detective Rodgers pulled something from his drawer, and I flinched. 'Which is highly illegal.'

I knew he was grabbing handcuffs, I blew it.

He continued to tell me of all the wrong I had done; all the laws I had broken.

All I could stare at was my own two feet, I couldn't look him in the eye.

The room fell awkwardly silent, and I listened out for the clocks ticking. I was nervous, and couldn't hold back my sudden urge to cry.

'I did it for her,' I sobbed, catching my mouth as I huffed. 'I did it for her, and my dad.'

Detective Rodgers didn't move.

'You could have been killed, Juniper,' he said my name softly, carefully. 'Kid, why did you do this alone?'

I glanced up, and he spotted my tears. In his clutches he held a bundle of tissues, not a pair of handcuffs.

I watched him hand them my way, with a sweet smile.

'I wasn't alone,' I shook my head, reaching out to grab them. 'I had my friends.'

It was true, I was never alone.

Though some days I wished I could have done it all solo, never gotten Arty into trouble, or Rayne.

But doing it alone would have been suicide, and they both cared so much for me, I think their help was unavoidable.

'Look, the only reason Somerville's department was so cowardly,' Detective Rodgers paused, and sighed.

'Is because the Fire Jackals could run riot, kill hundreds,' I answered for him, wiping my tears from my face.

I hated crying, made me look awfully weak, especially in front of a cop.

He nodded, 'Especially with a group like them, we've had so many issues.'

I asked him what issues, and he looked hesitant to reply.

'They're a nuisance,' he said. 'And to be honest, this isn't the first time we've heard of this so called, Pebbles.'

I widened my eyes towards him, and he grouched, 'Yes, we've heard of him too.'

'Do you have any idea who he is?' I asked quickly. 'If we find him, Nat would be able to get her surgery! But not only that, he's apparently close to the head of this whole clan, we'd be finding the leader in no time.'

'We,' He raised a finger, and turned it to himself. 'The Boston Police, not you.'

I wanted to fight back, but he shook his head. 'From today, you don't get involved.'

I panicked a little. 'But, there's no time, what if–'

'Juniper.'

'Detective Rodgers, surely you can understand why I'm panicking here.'

'I know.'

'Do you?'

'Your sister,' he answered. 'You're worried if you don't find Pebbles yourself, we won't.'

He took the words right out of my mouth, and I felt guilty for having no faith. I slumped in my seat a bit, and adjusted my cap.

'I'm sorry, Detective.' I said softly, sniffling.

'Nick,' he said, a smile on his lips. 'Call me Nick.'

I nodded once, rubbing the back of my neck uneasily. 'Okay... Nick.'

'Now,' he said. 'To locate a lost car.'

He lifted himself from his chair, and stepped towards a set of filing cabinets, 'That's a tough one.'

I grimaced, itching the bridge of my nose, 'No kidding.'

I was hoping he'd turn and bring this magical device out of his pocket, that could track down a lone car all over America.

Instead, Nick turned and crossed his arms. 'We've caught a member or two, here and there.'

He began to mumble to himself, a bunch of names I had never heard of. He rummaged through his cabinets, grumbling whenever he lifted the wrong one.

'We could contact these members, try to coax this "Pebbles" figure from them, ask for his location...'

I listened to him, not speaking a word.

'Then I could contact the pound, maybe someone has seen this car, that is, if it isn't already destroyed.'

'That was my worry as well,' I mumbled, 'Without that car, we're hopeless.'

'Not necessarily,' Nick replied. 'For a car to be destroyed, it has to be either abandoned, or illegally disposed of.'

He stepped from the cabinets and sat back down in his seat. I saw him rub his temples, and grab at his cigarettes for another.

'And we have cops popping up all over the state, a car being destroyed would cause a lot of ruckus.'

'So...'

'So what I'm saying is,' Nick smiled. 'If the car was taken somewhere to be destroyed, say, the pound...'

He leaned forward and flicked the lighter against his cigarette between his lips. 'Then they would have records, of whoever brought the car in. Cameras, locations...'

I felt my heart start its giddy whirl.

'You really think we can find this guy?' I asked. 'In such a short time?'

Nick gave me another grimace and took a suck from his cigarette, 'No promises, Kid.'

I was waiting for that, and leaned back, a little disappointed.

'But I won't give up, I'm breaking my own rules here,' he chuckled.

I saw him smile, but I was confused.

'Nick, you're not going to get into trouble are you?' I asked, worried.

He laughed and leant back, grinning, 'Me? Trouble?'

I waited for him to say yes, and then tell me he'd changed his mind about the whole thing. I could understand, why would he lose his job over someone like me.

'Of course I'll get into trouble,' Nick smirked. 'But this is the most fun I've had in a while, I want to catch this guy just as much as you, Miss Bridges.'

I smiled, weakly, but it was a true grin.

'It's a story alright...' I croaked. 'I never expected to find myself in a situation like this.'

'That's life,' Nick told me, his eyes wandered. 'Bad things happen to good people, in this case it's your younger sister.'

I swallowed back fresh tears, and clenched my teeth tightly, 'Yeah.'

'And you've been strong, stronger than most women your age,' Nick continued. 'The Fire Jackals are a threat, and with this clue, we could bring them down.'

'Together?' I asked.

He fumbled, and opened his mouth to fight back.

Nick could probably tell by now, that I was determined, I broke the rules and I was set on throwing myself into danger, to help the people I cared about.

He seemed the same.

Before he could respond, a knock at his door left us both jumping. I turned to see the door peer open, and another lanky cop pop his head from the doorframe.

'Mr Rodgers?' he asked. 'Your next appointment.'

Nick clicked his finger and nodded. 'Oh, right!'

I watched him stand in his seat, and I followed.

'Well, Miss Bridges,' he stepped towards me, and I nodded.

'Detective.'

He chuckled and took me by the shoulder, patting once. 'You have to promise me...'

I saw his eyes glare sideways, making sure nobody could hear what he was going to say next. I held my breath, and saw him smile again.

'Promise me you won't go looking for that car, I'll let you hold onto that key. If I find the car myself, we won't be needing it.'

I knew the key wasn't much help, the car could have been anywhere.

But this is what I wanted.

I needed a cop with ties, with more information.

I wished we had more time to speak, there were so many questions.

'Here,' he said, grabbing hold of his wallet. 'Take this, give me a call when you need anything, and do me a favour, go get that side of yours checked out...'

'Thanks again, and don't worry, its healing pretty fast,' I said him, and took the business card from his hands.

I wasn't lying about my side, with the right cream and warm water, I only had those two awful gashes to take care of. And every morning I awoke, I could move just that tiny bit more without the worry of stinging pain.

Nick smiled once more.

Now I had my most powerful ally.

This meeting went better than I thought.

'Thankyou,' I said, glancing up to his eyes. 'Thank you so much, Nick.'

He nodded again, and patted my shoulder roughly, 'You're welcome, kid. We'll find this guy, don't you worry.'

I was going to worry anyway, a cop telling me that couldn't change everything.

But it was reassuring to hear, that's for sure.

Nick Rodgers was the nicest man I'd met, and that was saying something. But I couldn't help feel a sense of mystery surrounding that strong persona of his.

He was brilliant at reading my emotion, but he had something on his chest too.

It could be why he wanted to help me, why he didn't just say no.

The Fire Jackals were bigger than I thought.

§

When was the last time I had a date? I couldn't remember.

I think the last time I remotely had a date, was with my old college girlfriend, who played on her phone for the majority of its duration.

Let's just say, afterwards I was pretty sour when she leaned in for a kiss.

But that didn't matter now, all I could think of on the way home, was Rayne's gorgeous face, her flustered smile and cheesy jokes.

I took the train back to Somerville, but with a sense of stress on my shoulders.

I was going to be late, it was half past five already.

I didn't expect my talk with Nick to be so long, I was honestly expecting him to turn me down and say get out.

But he didn't, and for once, I felt pretty calm.

That being said, I knew later on I'd have a moment of pure anxiety, begin to overthink every possible thought that passed my mind.

But I had promised Nat, that Rayne and I would have this date night, and be as happy as we could.

That kid was too sweet.

She deserved the world.

Chapter Nineteen

JUNIPER

I rushed home, grumbling at my watch as I flung myself towards my front door. It was already getting dark in the sky, and the weather had become cold and breezy.

I shivered as I turned my key in the door, doing my best to ignore the lone car key that hung from my chain.

Oh just you wait Pebbles.

I was going to find you; you piece of–

'Juniper!' Rayne appeared just as I closed the front door behind me, and boy did she look handsome.

She stood with a silly smile, clad in black jeans, a grey shirt and a denim jacket, its collar faux fur.

'Wow, Red,' I giggled. 'You look handsome.'

Rayne stood still, shrugging her shoulders from the compliment. 'Well, not really, I just found this laying around,' she said.

I rubbed my shoes against the welcome mat, and listened to her babble on about how I looked much prettier, that I bothered to dress nicer, and so on.

'I mean, this jacket is my dad's again, I think I stole half of his clothes,' Rayne continued, examining the denim with a grouch.

I was at her front now, leaning up for a kiss, and she gasped gently. 'Oh! Sorry!'

I smiled when her lips touched mine, her hands on my waist.

I'd been craving this all day.

I let my lips fall open, and her tongue brushed mine. Through our kiss, I bent back as far as I could, humoured by the way she followed, it deepened the contact generously.

But hey, we couldn't stand in the middle of my hallway making out.

I broke off and patted her collar, fixing it for her. 'You're rambling...'

Rayne smiled sheepishly, itching her ear. 'Ah, sorry!'

I shushed her, and she cleared her throat.

'But you do look beautiful, really nice,' she said, examining my attire. 'Super cute.'

'You're awfully talkative,' I teased. 'Are you planning on proposing?'

Rayne's face flushed red, and she waved her hands a little, 'I forgot the ring!'

I liked hearing that, the fact she joked along with me, she was getting better at avoiding my flirtatious teasing.

It was a little upsetting, to be honest.

'Aw, no fun,' I sighed, grabbing her right hand. 'You're getting better.'

'I know, but hey,' Rayne pulled me along to Nat's room, and I leant against her arm. 'You'll still be the master.'

'Damn straight,' I chuckled.

Rayne paused before my sister's door and took a deep breath.

'I'm sorry, I'm a little nervous,' she admitted, facing me. 'I haven't been on a date in a while.'

I sympathetically smiled, holding around her waist. 'You and me both.'

'No way,' Rayne mumbled.

'Way,' I replied, kissing her chin gently.

She flicked my hat, and opened Nat's door with a laugh. 'I'll grab my things and we can go, alright?'

I nodded and followed her in, not surprised at all to find Nat and Arty together, playing video games.

Nat turned to face me, and smiled, 'Juniper!'

'Nat,' I rushed to her side, and filled her face with kisses. 'You little gremlin, how are you feeling?'

She eased her face from my lips, groaning in disgust. 'I was fine before you started doing this!'

'Shh, you love it,' I teased.

As Rayne packed her guitar away, Nat told me about her afternoon, and how Arty had been 'awesome'.

Arty was probably feeding my sister junk food, telling her stories of who she'd beaten up and what girls she'd kissed.

I grimaced at Arty, and she winked. 'I've been awesome, lovey.'

'You're technically living in my house,' I snapped.

'Yeah! Arty slept with me last night,' Nat interrupted, clinging to the redhead's arm.

Arty blushed furiously, and growled from her throat, 'Hey! I did not loser!'

She was embarrassed, she didn't want Rayne and I to know she was the world's biggest softie.

I saw Nat smirk, and turn to me again. 'She's secretly hoping Samantha comes around.'

I scoffed a laugh, and I could hear Rayne react the same way.

'What!?' Arty roared, she lifted herself and pointed to my sisters face. 'Hey, you little punk,'

'It's true!' Nat flinched playfully.

'No! I'm here because I'm undercover, from the bad guys, remember?' Arty had a serious look upon her face, that pretty much screamed 'Don't embarrass me, loser!'

Nat rolled her eyes, and I chuckled once more.

Arty was pretty open with my younger sister, and hey, knowing she was here? Was pretty reassuring.

'Well,' I mumbled. 'You stay as long as you want.'

Arty nodded once, 'I will.'

'But don't eat all my food.'

'No promises, lovey.'

'And don't drink too much.'

'Again, no promises.'

Nat giggled, and I felt my heart flutter from that sound.

Ah, I couldn't wait until she was running around again, going back to school and playing games with her friends instead of being alone here in this room of hers.

I looked at my sister, and savoured her company.

I was proud of her; she was stronger than I was.

Nat turned to face me once more, and grinned, 'You and Rayne are going on a date.'

I rolled my eyes at her teasing tone, more childlike than usual.

'Yes,' I replied. 'A date.'

'It'll be fine,' Rayne called, she was zipping her guitar up now, and turned to wink at Nat.

'I sang some of Nat's favourite songs,' she said proudly.

'It was awful,' Arty snapped back playfully. 'Like a cat.'

'Hah!' Rayne smirked, biting back a cuss.

'She was lovely,' Nat fought for my girlfriend, crossing her arms tightly. 'No wonder my sister is dating her.'

I shushed my sister nervously, 'Nat!'

But she only grinned and turned to Arty, who was giving both Rayne and me an unamused grouch. She was never a romantic type, but with this new formed crush on my sister's doctor, maybe she secretly was.

'It's okay, Arty,' I coaxed sympathetically. 'I'm sure Samantha thinks you're handsome too.'

Before she could fling herself from my sisters bed and tackle me to the floor, screaming about how she was the strongest female fighter in Boston, I rose quickly to dust myself off.

'I'll see you two soon!' I chuckled. 'I have to go back to college tonight, lodge a paper before tomorrow night.'

On the corner of my eye, Rayne looked at Arty with a sense of desperation.

And I saw the redhead roll her eyes.

'Yeah, fine,' she sighed. 'Drive her back, just make sure my car isn't towed.'

I was a little confused, wasn't that the plan anyway?

Before I could ask, Rayne swung her guitar over her shoulders, and stepped towards Nat.

'I'll see you soon kiddo,' she leant down to hug my sister, and surprisingly Nat held her first.

It wasn't something she normally did, even the tiniest bit of movement left her flinching in agony.

I could see her face ease, but she nestled into Rayne's left shoulder to hide her pain.

Rayne was taken aback, and I saw her glance at me.

Nat already loved her to pieces, she was in my sister's good books alright.

'See you soon, Rayne,' Nat mumbled as she let go, she looked upset.

Rayne rustled her hair in, and turned to grab my hand, 'I'll take Juniper on the best date, just for you.'

'Not just for me,' Nat corrected. 'For Juniper too.'

'O-Of course!' Rayne stammered. 'No problems there.'

Arty groaned to us, told us to leave and stop being sappy. And once we had left the room, I could hear Arty freak out at my sister, playfully of course.

'You blew my cover, lovey!' she whispered highly. 'I can't believe you!'

It was refreshing, to hear laughter from Nat Bridges' room, instead of agonising cries.

§

I offered to drive, but Rayne was headstrong and told me it was her job to pamper me tonight.

She sat in the driver's seat, smiled to me and then fumbled with the keys, mumbling how she hadn't driven a car in about a year.

She pouted when I laughed, I asked her if she should have even been driving in the first place. But she was stubborn about it, and gave me a satisfied wiggle of her eyebrows when the engine roared to life.

While we drove, Rayne and I spoke energetically. I spoke about other experiences at the restaurant we were going to, told her about the meals they had. She would add in her hungry groans, and a heavy sigh at the mention of salmon.

'I haven't eaten Japanese in years!' Rayne clenched the steering wheel. 'It's been so long.'

I smiled and glanced her way as we hit a red light, she focused on the road, but took a second to look my way.

I didn't know what it was, but Rayne and I instantly lost ourselves in our gaze.

Maybe it was because this felt, normal.

Going on dates, acting like there was nothing to worry about.

I had forgotten what it felt like, to relax and take a breather for once.

Rayne smiled gently when I took her right knee with my hand, rubbing softly.

And I kept my fingers there when she continued to drive, feeling that electricity run through me when she finally gained the courage to hold the steering wheel with one hand, just so she could hold mine.

I gave her directions, and she followed every detail correctly.

I told her about the time my dad got lost, ended up in the complete opposite direction, then gave up and bought us McDonalds.

Rayne could only chuckle and share her thoughts on a cheeseburger, that she wouldn't mind eating eighteen of them.

I agreed.

§

For a Monday night, the restaurant was surprisingly empty.

Usually they would be packed, full of people slamming down saké and sushi like it was the last pieces on earth.

Rayne parked rather safely, and finally exhaled when she shut the engine off.

I giggled and patted her knee. 'You did well, Red.'

'It was awful,' she replied. 'Let's just have a good night.'

I reached for my door, but Rayne shook her head and told me to wait. She unbuckled her seatbelt vastly, pushed her door open, slammed it shut then raced around the front of the car to my side.

She was being such a gentleman.

'There,' she smiled as she opened my door. 'How am I doing?'

I sat still for a moment, and laughed, 'You're giving me anxiety!'

'Really?!'

'Yes! Really!' I stepped from the car, and held her face in my hands. I saw her eyes dart to and from the public eye, to my own.

She was still a little nervous about being close around others, understandable.

'Doll,' I assured. 'Stop, stressing.'

She seemed to like that nickname, and pressed her cheek closer to my hand, like a cat.

'Alright...' she mumbled. 'I'll do my best.'

'You always do.'

Rayne grinned, and offered me her arm, which I took gently. 'Depends...'

'Oh?' I asked. 'Is that right?'

Rayne opened the restaurant door for me, and shrugged. 'Depends on the task.'

I found the perfect time to tease her, and waited until we were seated.

Rayne nearly hit her head on the low bamboo that hung in the doorway, and flinched angrily. I couldn't hide my giggle, and she playfully grouched.

Inside, the interior was exactly how I remembered it years ago, but a little more updated. Booths and tables reached the end of its small inside, lanterns hung from the ceiling, Japanese art covered the walls.

And oh look, there he was. Behind the counter slicing sushi like a swordsman, Takahashi.

He'd been here for ages, since I was a kid, before Nat was even born.

Behind that counter, at age seventeen he was slicing fish.

Now, to this day, at age forty, he was a pro.

Rayne was getting distracted by his skills, and gawked a little. So I took the reins, and smiled to the short Asian girl stepping our way.

I didn't know Japanese; I was awful at any other language apart from English.

So when she greeted us in Japanese, I mumbled nervously in reply.

'Two?' she asked sweetly, lifting her fingers.

'Y-yes!' I smiled back. 'Two.'

She guided me towards the nearest booth, but Rayne hadn't budged. I turned to tug at her, but she was literally stuck staring at Takahashi's skills.

'Red!' I whispered highly, tugging at her sleeve. 'Rayne!'

She responded to that, turning her head quickly. When she saw someone waiting for us, she widened her eyes gently.

'Oh!' she laughed nervously. 'My bad, sorry!'

She continued to apologise to our tiny waitress, but all she could do was giggle and comment on how tall Rayne was.

Finally, when we were alone, Rayne leant forward and held my hands with hers.

'Did you see that guy?' she asked. 'Mad skills.'

I couldn't even process the fact she was so excited; she was like a kid on Christmas.

'Yeah, he's pretty wild,' I replied, rubbing her fingers with mine. 'Doesn't say much, though.'

'With skills like that,' Rayne paused and chuckled. 'There's no need to speak, the skill itself does all the talking.'

We took a moment to sink in the environment.

I recognised every spot my family had sat at, I could picture Nat teasing me, and my dad scoffing down rice.

It left me smiling, those were great memories I had to definitely keep forever.

And here I was making another memory, with someone I loved.

Rayne squeezed my wrist gently, and I looked her way.

'I love it when you do that,' she said.

I blinked, waiting for her to continue, 'What?'

She brushed her hair from her face and leant back, letting my hands go slowly.

'That smile,' she pointed to my face. 'I love it.'

I blew her compliment off, and waved my hand a little. 'Stop that, Red.'

'What?' she teased. 'It's true.'

'Well...' I leaned forward, and so did she, over the table the distance between us was short.

'Hmm?'

'You said before, that you do your best, depending on the task.'

'Yeah?'

I licked my bottom lip and then smirked, 'So, what if I was the task?'

Rayne took a second to process my suggestive question, then choked on her own swallow.

I watched her cough quickly, tapping her chest with her hands.

'J-Juniper!' she laughed shortly, losing her breath again. 'You're awful!'

'Awfully good, Red,' I replied, grabbing the menu. 'Awfully good.'

She took a swig of tea, and swallowed loudly, shaking her head from the taste.

'Oh, if this is a challenge,' she pointed to me and smirked. 'You've got yourself a challenge.'

I hummed back, raising my eyebrows. 'A challenge, huh?'

'You're being so flirty!' she whispered highly, touching my foot with hers. 'I kinda like it.'

'Kinda?' I gave her puppy dog eyes, and she panicked again.

'No! I mean, I love it! Lots!' Rayne cried, lowering her voice when our waitress returned.

Rayne allowed me to do the ordering, it was easier, seeing as she'd probably forgotten what Japanese food looked like. I ordered everything I remembered I liked, and what my sister liked, this night was also for her.

Rayne agreed with everything I said, and gave the waitress a nervous shrug whenever she asked her anything.

We finished our order with a bottle of saké, and Rayne looked pretty excited about that. She turned to me and wiggled her eyebrows.

'Alcohol?' she smirked. 'Juniper...'

'Hey!' I laughed, raising my hands. 'I'll drink responsibly.'

'Mmhm,' she paused and leant forward. 'Is your side okay?'

'Oh, I'd completely forgotten to be honest. I cleaned it this morning before I went and saw Nick, and the pain had subsided quite nicely. It'd scar, most definitely,' I explained.

Rayne sighed relief, telling me how much she'd been worrying. She showed me her hand, and the tiny cuts upon her fists were clearing up as well.

I brought them to my lips, kissing them gingerly. I could feel her fingers lift and touch my chin, tickling.

'Stop being adorable,' Rayne mumbled. 'You're giving me heart palpitations.'

I let her hands go, and she winked.

'I like this, Red,' I said. 'This is really...'

'Great?' she interrupted. 'Because it feels amazing, sitting here with you.'

Rayne blushed and leant on her elbows. 'Sorry, that was super lame.'

'It wasn't,' I replied. 'At all.'

We paused, and it became hard to look at each other without laughing like little girls. I hadn't stopped smiling since I sat down with her, and I couldn't believe the energy emitting from her end. My heart had this constant pitter patter rhythm, and I asked Rayne if she felt the same.

She told me her heart hadn't stopped racing since she first saw me, and just her words made me emotional.

I pursed my lips and reached for her hand again, and this time, she lifted it to her lips and kissed.

'You're really something...' I croaked. 'Something truly amazing, Red.'

Rayne held me tight, and started to play with my fingers. She chewed at her words, and then smiled.

'Same goes for you, Juniper,' she answered. 'And everything's going to work out.'

I leant forward again. 'Yeah, I hope so...'

'They will,' Rayne sounded determined, just as determined as I usually got.

I scanned her face for any fault, but her expression hadn't changed at all.

And if there was anyone I trusted, it was Rayne Holmes.

We were getting awfully sappy, but I was fine with it. I glanced around the both of us, to make sure I wouldn't be seen, before I leant over and kissed her gently against the lips.

She deserved it.

Frozen against my touch, Rayne held me upwards. Her fingers touched my elbows, making sure I didn't fall.

She was always worrying, always.

I didn't like Rayne doing so, but I'd be lying if I said it wasn't a wonderful feeling.

Knowing someone was making sure I was safe and sound.

'So,' I said as I broke off. 'Tell me about this job.'

As I leant back, Rayne tensed up and avoided my eyes.

'Well, there's something I have to tell you,' she said.

Okay, that was scary, just a little.

I didn't know what was coming next, was she upset about something? Did I do anything wrong?

'Okay...' I eased.

Rayne noticed that my curiosity had instantly merged into fear, she panicked.

'Hey!' she laughed, patting my hands. 'Nothing to worry about, don't look at me like that!'

'Red, what's happening?' I mumbled back. 'Are you in trouble?'

She chuckled and waved the question off, shaking her head. 'Nah.'

Again, silence.

The restaurant continued to bustle around us, but we both sat rather still.

'I haven't been busking,' she paused and shrugged. 'Because of this new rule.'

'Rule?'

'Yeah, I need a licence to busk.'

'What!'

'Tell me about it,' Rayne groaned. 'And it's not cheap, like, at all.'

I nervously bit my bottom lip, playing with the webs of her hands. 'How much?'

'Six hundred,' she swigged some more tea. 'Six hundred bucks.'

Now, I knew that Rayne didn't have that money, even if she busked all day every day.

I saw her eyes flutter sadly, but she still smiled, like she was humoured by the whole situation.

'So, I've been looking around, for new jobs,' she sighed.

I turned as our waitress returned, handing us two plates of sushi, Rayne mumbled in awe at the display, they were big on that here.

As soon as the saké was handed over, Rayne took hold of it and gave me a sly smile. 'I'll take this.'

I grouched when she poured herself a small glass, thanking the waitress before she left. I was still curious of this so called 'job' she'd found.

'And so, what were you doing last night?' I asked. 'Not busking, clearly.'

'No.' Rayne answered, sniffing the sake. 'But, Christopher and MacCread y helped me out. At the mechanics, Christopher said he knew a few people, and Reedy was keen on my help.'

'Help for what...?' I lifted a pair of chopsticks, and couldn't hide my grimace.

I hated these utensils.

Rayne smiled to me, and lifted her own pair of chopsticks.

'So, I went over to the mechanics last night,' she explained, lifting a piece of salmon off her plate.

I watched her sniff it too, curious.

Before she shoved it in her mouth, and continued.

'And I sat with a bunch of big burly guys, real ugly,' she growled. 'But Christopher and Reedy were there too.'

That was interesting, I guess the work that Reedy was telling me about involved Rayne too, which meant he enjoyed teasing my girlfriend about being tall.

I watched Rayne savour the fish in her mouth, and she genuinely seemed impressed. She pointed to her plate with her chopsticks, nodding positively.

I could only smile and agree with her, chewing on my own piece. The fish was fresh, as per usual.

'Okay, so this job is pretty simple,' Rayne swallowed. 'Christopher and I are driving a shipment of, like.'

She paused and thought for a moment, chewing more before she proceeded.

'A shipment of electronics, or car parts, or something,' she said.

I could see she was shrugging the smaller details off, getting to the big picture instead. But something felt off about this job, something I couldn't figure out.

Maybe I was just worrying, overthinking. I knew Christopher, I knew Reedy.

They were two guys my age, working at a mechanic together, making the same pay.

I trusted them as well.

Rayne was chowing down on a piece of raw tuna, but she pulled a sour look.

'Ew,' she moaned. 'I don't like this one, what's this?'

'Tuna,' I told her, leaning against my right hand.

'It's gross,' she grumbled, picking the remaining pieces from her rice. 'It tastes like, paper.'

'Red,' I said sternly.

I watched her swallow, and sigh. 'So, we go to the drop off zone, hand over the stuff.'

She paused and leant a little closer, her elbows by each side of her rectangular plate.

'But,' Rayne hesitated, her brow furrowed. 'It's out of state, but only for a little while, I'll be back Saturday!'

I replied, with a croaky 'Oh...'

When she finished her words, I felt my heart shrivel up a little.

Okay, so the idea of Rayne leaving for a few days hurt like hell. I mean, it was natural to feel this way, she meant so much to me.

I looked at her, and she smiled weakly. I was trying hard to look tough, she was too.

'Where?' I asked. 'I mean, which State?'

'Philadelphia,' she answered. 'Passing through Connecticut.'

I couldn't hide my disappointment, my sadness.

I was going to miss her, and she'd only be gone a few days.

Upset, I said nothing, and only picked up another piece of sushi with my chopsticks.

I held uncomfortably, and my grip wobbled when I lifted them to my mouth.

Suddenly the fish tasted awful, my appetite was ruined.

Rayne ate slowly too, and her eyes glanced to and from her plate, to me.

'But, it's alright,' she mumbled, I felt her foot brush against mine. 'I'll be home before you know it.'

I shortly smiled, itching the back of my ear. 'Mm.'

'Juniper,' Rayne muttered. 'I'll be home, please don't worry.'

'How can I not, Red?'

'I know you're strong, everything's going to be fine, and I'll get back to busking before you know it.'

I felt guilty, knowing she may have had a chance to gain that money, if she weren't so preoccupied with my Fire Jackals issue.

'I'm sorry, Rayne,' I sighed, rubbing my temples. 'If I hadn't dragged you into this whole mess, you wouldn't have to do this.'

'Hey, hey,' her arms were across the table now, after she moved her plate from harm's way. The guilt was seeping through my veins, and I took a deep breath.

'Juniper, please,' she quietly said. 'There's nothing to worry about, I want to do this.'

'You want to?'

'Well, yeah,' she smiled. 'It's exciting, I mean, it's something new. Christopher is a great guy, and Reedy.'

'Don't know about Robert,' I joked, sniffling.

'Naw, he's alright,' she shrugged. 'He's going to Maine; kinda wish I could have gone there too.'

I agreed, Maine was gorgeous. And around this time of year would have been a great experience, even if all Rayne would be doing was shipping stock.

'It's weird though,' she mumbled. 'I'm a little nervous.'

'Of course,' I said. 'It's scary, and I'm worried already.'

'Don't be worried.'

'Already started, Red.'

She returned to her food, and playfully grouched my way. I felt a little relieved, knowing she was cautious. Just like I, Rayne rushed into things without thinking.

She told me about the money, how much she would making. And no wonder she said yes to this job so fast, it was a hefty sum.

Her rent would be paid off with no issues, the busking licence, and then she offered the rest to me.

'Red…' I warned. 'You're doing this for yourself, okay?'

'Juniper, if I have anything extra. It's yours, for Nat.'

'Red!'

'Juniper!'

'Rayne!'

'Emerald eyes!'

'Wait.' I stopped, confused. 'What?'

Rayne went red in the face, and her eyes fell to her plate. She shook her head and started scoffing down sushi, acting like she'd said nothing.

I could tell she was flustered, because she ate the tuna she had so cautiously plucked from her rolls.

The tension was lifting from our date, and I felt a little flirtatious. I mean of course I still had that pinching feeling at the back of my mind, but I did my best to ignore it.

'Emerald Eyes?' I asked again. 'Care to explain?'

'Explain what?' Rayne returned, grabbing the saké bottle.

She poured another glass for herself, and sculled it. I was curious to see how Rayne Holmes handled her alcohol, but she had to drive tonight.

I took the bottle from her, poured my own glass and raised an eyebrow towards her.

'Explain,' I ordered.

Rayne blushed again, and chewed slowly. She was savouring the last piece of her sushi, which was probably all mush now, she was stalling.

'Dollface,' I teased. 'Tell me.'

I could see Rayne's ears redden from here, and I smirked.

'Okay!' she whined. 'When I first saw you, I could only name you by...'

She paused and rubbed her neck awkwardly, 'By your eyes, they were green, so.'

Oh my god, how did I find this tall cute being?

'Aw!' I giggled. 'You already had a nickname for me, Red!'

'Stop!' she replied, her face buried in her hands. 'I'm sorry!'

'Sorry for what?' I coaxed sympathetically. 'It's romantic, super-duper romantic.'

'Romantic?'

'You bet, just the thought of it leaves my heart fluttering.'

Rayne looked proud, and her shyness vanished into thin air. 'Well, it's true, your eyes are gorgeous.'

I avoided her glare, and continued to eat, she had already finished her plate of food. 'Shh.'

'No, I get to spoil you!' Rayne fought back. 'Don't "shh" me.'

Even though it left me blushing like a total fool, Rayne and I discussed our first meeting. My coffee deliveries, her romantic choice of songs whenever I walked by.

I never knew, honestly. That someone could fall that deep for me.

When I first saw Rayne, I loved the way her voice sounded, and someone who had a voice like hers deserved a good tip.

But even I was surprised, to constantly have her on my mind after that.

When I told Rayne this, she beamed brightly, and excitedly held my hands.

'I was the same, it confused me.'

'In a bad way?'

'No, not in a bad way,' Rayne finished wiping her hands on a napkin. 'In a great way.'

I cocked my head, waiting for her to continue, and she crinkled her nose.

'I would always hope you'd come by, I had this silly wishful thinking. I would be looking around, always looking out for that red coat of yours.' She pointed to the clothing bundled next to me in the booth. I leant against my hand again and grinned, she shrugged gently. 'I dunno, Juniper,' she mumbled. 'You've made such a big impact on me, I wouldn't be the way I was today if it wasn't for you.'

I felt a wave of emotion roll over me, it stung me right in the heart.

I froze, the hairs on the back of my neck rose and I honestly felt like I'd lost my breath.

Rayne watched me crumble, my eyes had widened and my lips parted.

'Juniper?' she chuckled nervously.

Quickly, I avoided her eyes and grabbed my glass.

I sculled my drink next, hiding my ferocious blush. But it was too late, Rayne had seen my weakness.

'Oh!' she laughed loudly, slamming her hands against the table, that definitely gained attention from the public. 'Oh! I totally got you!'

I kept the saké in my mouth for a few seconds and downed it roughly. Shaking my head in denial, though Rayne was already pointing at me.

'I got you! For once!' she leant over to tickle me, I flinched and avoided her. 'For once, Rayne is victorious!'

'You are not!' I replied, pushing her hands from my face. 'You got lucky!'

Rayne halted, then flicked me across the forehead with two of her fingers.

'You got that right,' she sighed, leaning back against her booth. 'I totally did get lucky.'

She looked at me, with a genuine smile on her lips.

I was already giddy from the saké, I probably shouldn't have sculled it, it went right to my head.

'Stop that...' I returned. 'You're being handsome again, Red.'

'Like always,' Rayne winked, handing me some water. 'Always handsome.'

I took a moment to check my phone, see if Dad had messaged me, any emergencies.

But there was nothing, no warnings.

It was nice, not having to worry.

It didn't feel normal.

'It's weird,' I sighed, popping my phone back in my coat pocket.

'What's weird?' Rayne asked.

I set my plate aside, full from the meal. Rayne was leaning against her hands again, and I did the same. There was only a small distance between our faces, so I focused on her lips.

'You know, this,' I muttered. 'Sitting in a restaurant, eating and laughing.'

'It's a date, right?' Rayne asked, pouting. 'One of the best, I'm hoping.'

I lifted my right hand to brush her hair behind her ear, but she shook her head and let it fall back.

'It's normal,' I corrected. 'That's why I'm a little anxious.'

Rayne sniffled, then pursed her lips.

'Normal, in comparison to all the stuff that's been happening,' I explained. 'I thought I would never see the day, I'd be sitting here on a date with you, Red,'

Rayne huffed a laugh, and sipped a little water.

'I feel the same way,' she grinned. 'I was starting to believe sneaking into crazy clan meetings was a normal day to day task.'

I pouted, and she imitated the same look, eyes eased and playful.

'Well, I hope it doesn't come to that,' I replied. 'But really, Red. This is lovely, everything about this...'

'It's what Nat wanted.'

'But it's also what I wanted.'

Rayne nodded, and held my hands again. 'I wanted it too.'

I lost myself in her eyes again, and ripped myself back into reality as our waitress popped back up.

'Everything alright?' she beamed.

Rayne got nervous and let me go, shoving her hands to her sides.

'Uh!' she gawked. 'Yeah, really good!'

I loved it when she got flustered, it proved she wasn't as intimidating as she looked.

I thanked our waitress, and she questioned dessert.

We both couldn't say no to something sweet, especially me. I was obsessed with pastries and candy, heck, my workspace back at college was a mess of candy wrappers.

We ordered whatever looked the sweetest, cheesecake, for two.

After our table was clean, Rayne didn't hesitate to take my hands with hers again.

'So, you haven't told me about your day,' she said. 'Any luck with the car?'

I grimaced, because I realised that discussing the Fire Jackals situation was inevitable. It was always going to be a topic, no matter how much I wished it wasn't.

I inhaled and exhaled gently, playing with her thumbs. She had her eyes on me, but I could feel her fingers run along mine.

'I spoke to the police, actually,' I admitted.

I felt better telling the truth, such a weight of my chest. Though now Rayne looked confused, she twisted her lips, curious.

'You did?' she asked. 'Why?'

'Because,' I paused. 'Because I needed help, from people who know more than us.'

Rayne examined my face, eyes scanning to and from each aspect.

'At first I just needed answers on how to find a stolen car,' I could feel my lips hitch into an amused smile. 'But those cops are pretty good at their jobs, they could see I was hiding something.'

'And?' she mumbled.

'And now we have our most powerful ally, I was told not to continue searching, but...'

Rayne laughed a little, patting my hands with hers. 'That's not going to stop you, even if the police ordered you to. You're still going to look for the car?'

'Definitely,' I said. 'I need to find the truth, and I won't sit by and wait for someone else to.'

She seemed impressed by my determination, but I could see that look deteriorate into something else, fear.

''Juniper, you promise me something,' she started.

'Anything,' I replied.

Rayne's head leered closer, and her eyebrows furrowed. 'Be careful, don't get hurt, I won't be here...'

'I know that,' I replied, a little taken aback by her doubt. 'I'll be alright, Red.'

She breathed in quickly, and pursed her lips.

'I know,' she mumbled. 'I'm not saying you won't, I just... I won't be here, and I wouldn't know what to do if you got hurt.'

I hugged her hands close, lifting our bundle of fingers towards my face.

'Red,' I said sternly. 'I'll be alright.'

It took her a moment to be relieved of her worry, and even when she smiled, I knew that train of thought still lingered inside her mind.

When our dessert came, thankfully the topic changed.

The cake looked gorgeous, my mouth watered at the sight of its triangular shape; topped in glazed strawberries and cream.

Rayne's eyes sparkled, like she was seeing the galaxies and all the stars inside it. She leaned over the piece between us and gasped.

'Is it even edible?' she gawked. 'It looks fake; I don't trust it.'

I shushed her, pricking a strawberry with my fork, 'It's totally edible.'

Rayne went red when I pointed it her way, coaxing her into trying. I wondered how long it would take for her to ease up at the idea of acting this way in public.

She had a good reason, in every state there was at least one homophobic person in eye view. But I was the type of person who couldn't care less about what people thought of my current relationship, they stare at me? I look them right in the eye.

I smiled as Rayne opened her mouth and ate off my fork, she chewed nervously, but I could see her lighten up.

'Hey,' she chuckled, smacking her lips. 'Not bad, not bad.'

I grinned to her, and she gave me the thumbs up.

As we ate and spoke, Rayne's hand never let go of mine. We constantly made eye contact, even if it left us rather embarrassed.

I hoped every date we had from here on, had the same wavering happiness as this one.

Rayne squeezed my fingers, and I held tighter.

I didn't want to let go.

And in this tiny little Japanese restaurant, from my childhood.
I had created one of my most precious memories.
Here with Rayne Holmes.

§

As much as I denied it, Rayne paid for dinner.
I wanted to smack the money from her hand, whack it back in her back pocket and tell her to stop.
But she looked so content, on making me happy.
And that really hit home.
Plus, she told me not to worry, in her most sincere voice, she won.
We continued to joke around in the car, she spoke about Florida and her parents a little more, I opened up about my mother too.
Rayne said she wanted to meet her, and I shrugged, telling her that it may never happen.
It was true, I wasn't lying.
My mother was always on the move, she was in California one day, and Arizona the next.
Before the topic became too sour, Rayne clicked her finger and gasped.
'Hey! I have an idea,' she grinned, eyes on the road. 'I know this place, it's really great.'
I checked the time, it wasn't that late, nearly ten. When was the last time I'd been out with a super cute girl, joking and playing around like absolute teenagers?
I needed this, so did Rayne.
We were only ten minutes from my college, and I wasn't ready to check in for the night.
'You lead the way,' I chuckled.
'I will!' she replied.
With the radio on, my window partially open and my girlfriend in the driver's seat to my left, I felt relaxed.
I had to remind myself this was real, pinch my arm and touch Rayne's knee with my fingers, just to make sure.
Again, just like before, she took hold of my hand and brought it to the gearstick.
Did I feel guilty?
Yes of course, knowing that Nat was back home in bed, coughing and denying any meal my father gave her. She would probably be sitting there with Arty, playing video

games, telling my best friend she felt better and healthier.

Dad would be at his desk in the living room, scanning over hospital bills and financial documents. I could feel his anxiety from where I sat, it lingered on me.

And here I was, with the girl of my dreams, smiling as if nothing was wrong in the world.

I knew I'd feel this at some point in the night, just like discussing the Fire Jackals, that part of my anxiety was unavoidable.

If I took a deep breath, reminded myself that my happiness was also my sisters, my dad's, even my mother's; I relaxed enough to stay calm.

Things were going to get better, and that car was going to be found in the next few days.

Maybe this year would get back on track, move at a smoother pace instead of this rocky road of nightmare and fear.

'Okay,' Rayne muttered, knocking me from my thought. 'Here we go.'

To my discomfort, we turned left, into a dark alleyway.

'Wow, Red!' I teased, grimacing. 'You really know how to make a girl swoon...'

She sniggered from beside me as she drove, flashing the headlights.

I tried to peer through the darkness while we moved, passing grimy garages.

'I hope I took the right turn...' Rayne sounded concerned. 'I used to always come here when I was around the area.'

I held her knee tightly, smacking it once, 'You "hope?" Red!'

'Hang on!' she giggled. 'Just give me a second, Juniper!'

I crossed my arms and sighed, while she spoke to herself, lips twisting and twirling as she drove carefully.

'Hah!' she yelped and I jumped. 'See!'

'See what?' I asked, leaning forward. 'What?'

I saw it as soon as I asked, and my heart did a giddy leap.

There, hidden from the public view, was a perfect spot aside the river.

It was an old shipping dock, but no boats were vacant.

Just one long abandoned chunk of road.

Rayne turned the car to the right, parking against the wicket fence that held trespassers back, I guess it couldn't stop us.

'Neat huh?' Rayne turned and wiggled her eyebrows. 'Nobody will see us here.'

I watched her exit the car, and keep the door wide open. Just missing her head along the doorframe, she stood tall and inhaled the fresh river air.

I could feel the breeze, but the weather had really improved since last week. Usually around this time of the year in Massachusetts, it was constantly snowing, but it hadn't fallen in a few days.

I unbuckled my seatbelt and pushed my own door open, hanging onto it.

The river was absolutely beautiful, the layer of ice along its length was thin and sparkled under the moonlights feathered glow.

Rayne was right on the edge of the pier, holding onto the worn-out length of rope so she could get a better look.

We weren't too high up, but high enough to keep dry.

The streetlamp to our left was old, but flickered from bright to a mellow yellow glaze. I stepped around the car so I could join Rayne's side.

'Wow, Red,' I gasped, tightly holding the rope. 'This is awesome.'

'I know, I used to love coming here,' Rayne grinned, she took a deep breath and savoured the air again.

I focused on her face, she looked so relaxed.

'You haven't come here in a while?' I asked.

'Nah, I just stopped,' she admitted.

'Why?'

'Beats me.'

I hummed to myself, listening to the river as it gently flowed. I could hear the ice crackle to and from, the city of Boston on the other side bustling to life.

From the car, the radios volume was low, it was mumbling.

Cars wailed from afar, the wind rustled the trees and knocked loose driftwood against the cement wall.

And Rayne stood next to me, her warm left arm snaking around my waist. The setting was perfect, a little too perfect.

But it was real.

I leaned against her arm, holding tight to her shirt.

'Nice, huh?' Rayne asked. 'I don't think anyone knows its here.'

'More than nice,' I chuckled. 'It's beautiful.'

She rubbed my side, keeping me warm, 'I'm going to be majorly corny here, but you're beautiful too.'

I suppressed a laugh, tickling her stomach with my fingers. 'Stop...'

'No way,' she mumbled, bringing me to her front.

I nervously whimpered, just seeing the edge left me dizzy, but she held me tight around the stomach.

I wouldn't fall, if she was there.

'I got you,' she said. 'Don't worry.'

I felt her chin press down upon my head, and the rhythmic back and forth motion of her breathing against my back. Rayne made sure not to squeeze me too tight, she was obviously still worried about my wound.

I quickly glanced down, and noticed her bruised knuckles again, it pained me to see any splotch of damage.

I sighed and held tight to her arms, lifting them over my chest. She chuckled and watched the river with me, swaying me side by side.

It wasn't too quiet, nor too loud.

I could still hear her breathing, her tiny little sniffles, the clear of her throat.

Even when I closed my eyes, I felt safe.

Nothing else mattered.

Rayne kissed me quickly on the cheek, and pulled me back further from the edge of the river.

'Hey!' she called. 'Wait, wait I know this song!'

I was saddened when she let go and raced to Arty's car.

Rayne climbed into the driver's seat, and blasted the radio as high as it could go. The noise bounced off the alley walls and sounded crystal clear.

She turned to me and threw her hands out, a big silly grin on her face. It wasn't a song I knew, but it sounded like something I may like.

Something Rayne would love, definitely.

'You don't know them?!' she cried, eyes wide. 'Dr. Dog?, Keep a Friend?!'

I gave Rayne my fakest smile, hoping she could catch the signal that I had no idea what she was talking about. I felt silly standing in my spot.

She sighed loudly but raced back to my side.

'Dance with me!' she cheered over the loud music, excited. 'Please, please, please.'

'What!' I cried back, embarrassed. 'No way, Red!'

While she begged and grabbed me close to her, I laughed. It was so refreshing to know that Rayne was one hundred percent comfortable around me.

She was open, honest and told me about her feelings.

Well that last one might need some work.

This was so nerve wracking, I hated being startled, it happened at family events, school dances in the past, every party I went to.

Rayne held around my waist and lifted me, singing the lyrics loudly. I screamed in delight, clinging around her neck as she spun me around.

'Rayne!' I cried, I noticed my girly expression and quickly lowered my tone. 'Red! Put me down!'

I smacked her back gently, but she was way stronger than me, and held securely. She looked me in the eye, a humorous expression on her face.

'You can call me crazy ,' she sang alongside the vocalist, bringing me closer to her face. 'You can call me anything you like.'

'I'm calling you a nerd!' I laughed. 'Let me go!'

She wouldn't let go, and to be honest I was completely fine with it.

Until she began spinning me again, I yelped in fear, I was just waiting for her to fall.

I'd never seen this side of Rayne Holmes before, carefree and full of energy.

I felt special, that I could make her feel this way.

Hey, she made me feel the exact same.

While she sang at the top of her lungs, closing her eyes to roar the lyrics into the sky, I let my fingers race through her hair.

I couldn't look away from that cheerful face, that beautiful glow that surrounded her on this chilly night.

Nobody in Boston could ruin our fun.

Rayne had successfully reached the front of Arty's car. And as she set me upon the hood of it, I could feel the music booming below, rattling the car exterior.

Even when the song slowed its pace, the vibrations travelled through my body.

I kept my hands around Rayne's neck, touching behind her ears.

Her flirtatious side pushed through, when she finally stopped her singing and looked closely at me.

I smirked when she slipped between my legs, her hands at my waist.

I waited for a kiss, but instead she touched her forehead with mine, holding close.

When she closed her eyes, I followed.

Breathing in gently, I touched her nose with my own.

Ah, we lost ourselves again.

On cue, the emotions wavered over the two of us. I felt it my legs, my abdomen, finally in my chest. My pulse was fast, in rhythm with my heartbeat.

I opened my eyes, just as she did, so I could smile and press my lips to her nose.

'You make me happy,' I admitted, fingers trailing along the sides of her neck.

Rayne had become nervous, but she chuckled. 'You make me more than happy.'

'Hm?'

'I mean,' she kissed me quickly before she continued. 'You make me feel a lot more than just happiness, I feel alive around you. It's scary, and nice at the same time, I'm not used to it.'

I grinned when she did, and we embraced.

'Ah!' she groaned. 'I'm sorry, I'm being weird.'

'Not weird, honest.'

She pulled back, but kept the distance between us short. I focused on her eyes, dark orbs of brown; tinged with lighter shades of hazel. I was instantly lost in them.

Rayne leaned in close, and I was coaxed to do the same.

Our kiss was deep and secluded, private and full of emotion.

I felt my chest rise, a hitched breath longed to escape my lips.

Instead, I exhaled from my nose, hands gripping the sides of her face.

I beckoned for a deeper contact, so I brushed my tongue against her bottom lip. Rayne accepted my assertive gesture, the tip of her own tongue touched mine.

I croaked from the bottom of my throat, the sensation in my abdomen left my eyebrows furrowing pleasurably.

Behind us both, the speakers were blaring, loud and obnoxious.

The sirens wailed on, car horns echoed from the city, the wind was picking up pace.

But around the two of us, I could only hear her breaths, and my own, whenever we broke away.

I knew she was only leaving for a few days, and she would be back home in Boston before I knew it. But I kissed her as if she were leaving forever.

If this kiss continued to escalate at its current speed, the night was far from over.

And I was totally fine with that.

Chapter Twenty

JUNIPER

Rayne had me seated upon the hood of Arty's car, her lips locked on my own, arms around my waist.

I could still hear the music blasting from behind, and every breath between us. I think we kissed for a good three minutes, until the urgency of my desire grew unbearable .

I whispered into Rayne's ear, offering to let her stay over at my apartment. She was quick to accept, nodding her head with a blush.

She and I both knew, knew exactly what this was leading to.

My heartbeat was already so fast, but knowing she and I would be experiencing that again, left it aching.

I wasn't comfortable with anyone speeding while I was in their car, well in this case it was Arty's, but Rayne and I were heated, lust lingered between us.

So, I let her speed to school, and boy did she look attractive when she revved the engine.

We joked around while she drove, I teased her about the whole situation, flirtatiously of course.

And she groaned playfully, telling me to stop so she could concentrate on driving.

Rayne parked messily from across my housing complex, twisting the key from the ignition.

'Alright, c'mon,' I laughed. 'You're going to—'

Rayne kissed me deeply, silencing me.

Her hands clutched at my sides, fingers twisting around the buttons of my coat. I was taken aback by her action, but melted upon her lips.

Okay, she was really, really eager.

I muffled my chuckle, held her face, then broke off to breathe. Rayne's eyes were half lidded, she was breathless and rough.

I loved it.

'Inside,' I mumbled, tracing her bottom lip with my thumbs. 'Let's continue this, inside.'

Just twenty minutes ago, we were dancing on an abandoned pier.

Now, after unlocking it, I was kicking my dorm door open; my mouth wrapped around Rayne's. I was attempting too many things at once, and pulling my coat off while I longed to touch her was tough.

With a sly mumble, she held me around my waist, and followed me inside. I heard her bag drop, emitting a small thump. Her jacket was next on the list, I tore it from her torso, and threw it aside.

Piece by piece, we were becoming more and more heated.

The door slammed shut as I pushed my tall girlfriend against it, and she sniggered.

She was really enjoying this.

My coat fell to the floor, after I successfully shook my right arm free of its sleeve. I was still boiling hot, my skin was burning, but I wanted to be warmer, much warmer.

While I kissed her neck deeply; I felt around the door knob to lock it, didn't want anyone coming in at this point.

Rayne's skin tensed as I nibbled, and just as I was getting used to the idea of being dominant, she grabbed hold of my shirt.

I couldn't help but gasp when she tugged me forward. I smirked when she glared at me, her breath heavy, her lips inches from mine.

With one look, I knew.

When she clenched around my waist, then pushed me forward gently, I definitely knew that Rayne enjoyed being the dominant one.

I had no clue I was into rough foreplay, or enjoyed the idea of being submissive to my partner's touch. But when Rayne lifted me atop my desk, pushed aside my loose papers and books, then proceeded to tug my shirt free of its buttons, I had a pretty good idea that it was what turned me on the most.

While I gripped at her collar, she undid my shirt, quick fingers prying, longing for what was underneath.

A satisfied moan left both of us, when my chest was bared.

I glanced down to my bra, then into her eyes.

Rayne stopped, so she could glare towards them and smile seductively. I could feel her heart against my palm, it was going absolutely mental.

I thought that my own heart had reached its peak limit back at Arty's car, well I was obviously wrong.

Right now, it was stuttering, thumping in my ears, my blood was flowing.

Quickly, she dived into the crook of my neck, her tongue running along the length of it.

I think I swore, or said her name, or just groaned. But I lifted my head while she licked and held tight around her neck.

She pulled my pelvis close to hers, and I reached for her jeans, undoing her belt.

We were panting like we'd run a marathon, our faces inches from each other.

Rayne kissed me whenever she had the air for it, each peck was deep and heated, a little messy. But every touch left my body thriving, my head heavy and skin hot.

Her belt loosened, and I slipped my left hand below her waistband, squeezing the denim around her crotch.

I savoured the moment she lifted her head, emitting a tasteful sigh. So I continued to tease, stroking the material in one area I knew she desired.

Rayne's hands were already under the cups of my bra, her fingers twisting and turning, I could feel my eyes roll back, my breath hasten.

Okay, when we had sex back in Somerville, it didn't start off like this, but God, all I wanted to do was-

'...fuck you.' Rayne groaned, her forehead pushing against mine. 'I want to fuck you.'

Her breath heavy against my skin. I felt my head fumble at that suggestive tone.

I touched her bottom lip with mine, and her tongue raced along it.

'I'm fine with that.' I groaned, grinning lightly. 'T-totally fine with that.'

Rayne didn't hesitate, she went for my jeans, hitched the waistband between her fingers, then dragged roughly downwards.

I lifted my legs around her waist, undoing my bra as she continued pulling. I was absolutely throbbing once I was completely naked.

I clung around her neck, hoping she would begin.

'I-I've got something,' Rayne stammered, kissing me quickly. 'I mean if you don't want to—'

'Grab it,' I ordered, I think I got the hint. 'It's fine.'

'Juniper.'

'It's fine!' I moaned, tightening my legs around her waist. 'Red, don't be a jerk!'

Rayne laughed a little, she was teasing me and I was literally on the edge.

Before tonight had even started, I was hoping we would end our date with an intimate love making session. And I contemplated asking Rayne if she owned anything that could further our experience.

Glad we were on the same page.

Rayne kept close between my legs, while she lifted her shirt over her head, and her sports bra.

Once I was basking in the glory of her toned upper torso, I couldn't withhold one aroused mumble.

I heard her sigh pleasurably, before she closed the tiny gap between our bodies with a quick tug.

'Easy,' I whimpered as I leant back against the base of my desk, so I wouldn't slip,

I watched her tense, the tough boxes around her navel left my head swirling. I was a sucker for strong girls.

I bit my bottom lip, the temptation rising. Just the sight of Rayne's muscles had the butterflies duking it out in my stomach, sending vibrations down below.

She saw me hesitate, and quickly grabbed my hands towards her belly, allowing my nails to drag upwards, I felt each bump. As I examined her abdominal muscles, my eyebrows furrowed eagerly.

'B–Red,' I groaned, playful confusion in my tone. 'Are you real?'

My words weren't even full, but rather gasps of desperation, just seeing her like this was enthralling.

To answer my eager question, Rayne pulled me closer, picked me up, then dropped me against my bed.

I coiled my legs around one another, giving her my most seductive smile.

I knew what was coming next, and I was a little nervous to say the least. I hadn't experienced this with a girl before, ever.

Rayne grabbed my knees, and pulled them apart from one another. Afterwards, she positioned herself between my legs as they dangled over the side of my bed.

I breathed in quickly, my hands brushing through my hair.

Rayne was towering over me now, chuckling.

'Yeah,' she huffed, reaching for the waistband of her loose jeans. 'I'm real.'

I swallowed loudly as she dragged downwards, after her legs were bare, I was heaving from her display.

Rayne was absolutely stunning, her body was lean and toned, muscles evident in her arms. Her dark hair fell gracefully over her chest, and the look on her face was confident.

I absolutely ached for her touch between my legs. I was eager, too eager that I leaned up and reached for her crotch, but she pushed me back; roughly, so I hit the mattress with a thud.

I guess she had full power tonight, not that I was complaining.

I wasn't used to this side of Rayne, she was flirtatious, suggestive and most importantly, commanding.

'No,' Rayne smirked. 'Wait.'

I covered my face with my hands, but I peeked through the webs to watch her step around my bed to her bag.

I threw my glare aside, focusing on my pillows.

Oh okay, I was very nervous now, and I could feel the deep throbbing between my legs. I chewed the side of my mouth, trying to picture how this night was going to unfold.

I heard her shuffle around, and slide the straps upwards her legs. Then came a few clicks, then a small set of laughs.

She was being such a goddamn tease, and right now I was close to begging.

'Rayne,' I whimpered, lengthening her name eagerly. 'Come here!'

When I looked back up, she was between my legs again, her hands on both my knees. I glanced down and instantly turned red, and some sort of otherworldly whimper left the bottom of my throat.

'I'm glad you didn't pick the realistic one...' I snorted. 'Those are absolutely ridiculous.'

Before I could joke about how hilarious this was, wave my hand and snigger at how this was my first time using a strap on, Rayne smirked, and pulled my opened legs closer to her crotch. I wrapped my legs around her back, and she held me by the waist, tightly.

She smiled sheepishly to me, when she quickly ran her fingers along my sensitive flesh. I bit my bottom lip back, batting my eyes nervously.

Although it was slightly adorable knowing we were still a little immature, that we both saw the hilarity in our horny escapade. I think the seriousness of the situation hit me right after.

As the silicone length pressed into me, my smile faded from my lips. Instead I widened my eyes and gasped shortly, letting my mouth fall ajar.

Rayne kept her sights on me, even when I leaned my head back and released a satisfied groan.

Not only did it enter effortlessly, it left my legs trembling. Rayne's eyebrows furrowed, and she pushed inwards with one sway of her hips.

Unfortunately, in the past, I had been in the same position a few times. Before I accepted myself, accepted being a lesbian.

So Rayne's thrusts didn't hurt as much, but I wished she was my first.

I watched her move, she clenched her teeth whenever she thrusted, my breath hitched again.

She was my first woman though, and that meant a great deal to me.

Rayne had a sly smile on her lips whenever I whimpered and moaned. I tried so hard to look her in the eye when I did, and she would deliberately thrust slower, so my cry was croaky and short, stomach tensing from the pleasure.

When she picked up the pace of her movement, I found myself begging, loudly. Every time I felt the length slide in-between my legs, I cried in utmost pleasure, connecting my crotch to hers, hands clinging the bedsheets by my sides.

The walls weren't the thickest here in the student complex, but I couldn't find one reason to care.

Rayne's breath had become short too, as she tensed every time she pushed. Her hands clung at my sides, fingernails pressing into the skin of my thighs.

Her rapid breaths had become grunts, whenever she thrusted into me. Her jaw was locked and her collarbone was so defined from where I lay, I was lost in her rhythmic action.

I felt my eyebrows dip inwards, as I kept my eyes on hers, my moans vulnerable and high pitched.

'R–Red!' I tensed my neck as I whimpered.

Rayne pulled out quickly, leaving my whole body shaking, she could have warned me!

'Juniper,' she mumbled, breath short. 'Y–you alright?'

I watched her climb over me, her hands beside my head. I caught my breath, holding her arms.

'M–more than okay,' I shivered. 'Please, keep going.'

Rayne looked partially concerned, and pressed her lips to mine. She was being gentle, and right now I didn't want gentle.

I dragged her closer to me, so I could lean back in a more comfortable position, my head upon my pillows. Rayne held my side, especially where my wound lingered.

But just like the first time, I was focusing on another sort of pain, a pain that fuelled me to crave more.

Rayne positioned herself between my legs again, taking a deep breath before she continued. I bit my bottom lip once more, my left hand reaching out for hers.

Before she took it, she thrusted hardly into me, and I felt my back arch, my outstretched hand now clinging to my hair.

'Oh God!' I cried, my breath raspy.

She mumbled over my yelp, pushing deeper.

I was tempted to watch, so I lifted my head and glanced down, where Rayne's hands clung by my sides, her tattoo glistened with sweat.

She was unreal, and this probably wasn't her first time, no way.

I saw the black length insert, back and forth, and I gaped, sighing loudly. This was way better than the first time we made love.

I could feel it pressing against me, against the spot that left my body tightening, releasing, and repeat.

Rayne started slow, but the more I begged her to fasten her pace, the weaker she was becoming to my orders.

She lifted my lower body upwards, and dropped me against her kneeled legs. I saw her breathe in sharply, swallowing loudly before she positioned herself comfortably.

Not only was the feeling of Rayne penetrating me so satisfying, her hands lingering around my stomach added extra pleasure. They touched my exposed ribcages as I arched my back, nails digging into my sides.

'R–Red!' I groaned, my eyes glazing over. 'S-Shit!'

'S–say my name,' she huffed, breathless. 'Say my name, Juniper.'

Her words were mumbled, the tone in her voice high but absolutely desperate. My hands clung by my sides, but she leaned forward, reallocating herself closer against my naked body.

I held around her neck, my fingers through her hair. And I did what I was told, moaning her name with every pulsating thrust from her pelvis.

I noticed when I spoke, she would groan alongside me, every single time. I could feel her straining herself, but she wanted it just as much as I.

She was powerful, really powerful.

'Rayne!' I eased through a cry, my voice breaking.

The rest were wordless pleasure-stricken groans, I was close and I ached for a deeper touch. The faster Rayne moved, the more I realised how wet I really was.

'Juniper,' she gasped, pressing her lips to my jawline.

She sounded emotional, but my cries were overtaking her own, hands clawing into her back. I caught her open mouth with mine, whimpering in time with her thrusts.

God, she was so fucking amazing.

I was sure my heart would burst, my body melt from the heat she and I were sharing. I could feel my skin shiver under every touch, and I knew I was close.

I wanted to feel more, I craved it.

I broke off Rayne's lips, and grappled at her shoulders, pushing her further down. Thankfully, with one short glance, she picked up my command quickly, and pulled the silicone length out from inside me.

The movement left me groaning, and I tensed my neck as I strained my voice.

Rayne was between my legs now, and I desperately reached to touch her, any part of her.

She was the one to take my hand this time, hold it tight as she worked her tongue along my most sensitive spot.

My eyebrows furrowed, and I lost my voice for a moment, taken aback by the overwhelming feeling.

Rayne's breathless panting was sensational music to my ears, hearing her struggle to breathe and pleasure me at the same time.

She was as desperate as I was.

I bit my bottom lip tightly, lifting my crotch to her mouth, and she moaned back; enjoying the close contact.

I saw her eyes close, forehead crease as she strained, pulling and locking flesh between her lips. I was exceedingly loud now and held my mouth with my free hand.

From all the satisfied physical contact a few moments ago, to Rayne's trained movement against my hardened nerve, it was heaven.

Just when I thought it couldn't get any better, I started to climax. I felt the groan from the bottom of my throat travel upwards, I was feeling so sensitive that every stroke of Rayne's tongue was like a burst of electricity inside my body.

I panted, cried her name desperately, arched my back and begged her to keep going.

Rayne definitely delivered.

My eyes were forced shut, as the final pleasurable series of moans left my lips. My mouth was ajar, towards the ceiling, and everything in my body sprung to life, allowing the shivering sensation to take hold of me.

I could hear my ears ringing, my heart and pulse joining side by side to create a rhythmic wave. And finally, with an exhausted sigh, my back fell against the bedsheets. I was out of breath; my lungs were screeching for sweet salvation.

Rayne also exhaled tiredly, and shakily pressed her forehead to mine. I swallowed loudly, looking her in the eye, and she did the same. We panted simultaneously, lips close and ajar.

I realised in that moment, during an emotional display of undying devotion, that I had found someone absolutely irreplaceable.

Rayne then slumped lower, her head against my collarbone.

Our naked bodies were partially damp from our sweat, our movement, but my girlfriend had strained herself much more.

She swallowed loudly, her arms by my side, holding tight. I'd never felt so weak in my life, and I meant that in the best way possible.

Rayne slipped her head aside, pressing her nose up under my jaw. I smiled, breathing in gently as I wrapped my arms around her neck.

She was absolutely drained, and needed comfort more than her own release. I kissed her hair, feathered touches along her shoulder blades, coaxing her relaxation.

Rayne grunted from the touch, a relaxed croak of her voice. A moment ago I was aroused like no other, now I was full of undying emotion.

I wanted to cry, even if my eyes were already damp from my strain.

I felt my heart ache in the most compelling way, pouring out every speck of love and devotion in my very soul. This feeling was so addictive, I wish it were constantly lingering around me, around Rayne. It wasn't just perfect sex; it was so much more than that.

I saw the light in her eyes, every touch was caring and safe.

There was nothing to be afraid of.

Love was so frightening, but so riveting at the exact same time. I always pondered on the relationships I had before Rayne, even though they were short or either with men. I was never happy, never.

Love was always hard; I'd heard from multiple sources. The things I heard about it? I couldn't help but feel a little desperate.

I was told it was awful, made you weak and submissive to heartbreak.

I was told it was brilliant, left you on cloud nine, left you craving more.

I wanted to feel it, preferably the brilliant aspect of it all.

I was feeling it, right then and there.

And I was emotional about it, there was nothing frightening me, not here with Rayne.

'Oh, Red,' I sobbed, clinging close to her. 'I love you so much.'

Rayne could only respond with a short mumble; she was already drifting.

I drew a ragged breath, her hair between the webs of my fingers.

I couldn't understand why I was crying, or why I was pouring out heartfelt words through hicks and sobs.

Rayne was mumbling to me, her words muffled by the skin of my neck. They were sighed sentences, exhausted drabbles.

'I love you too...' she murmured. 'Lots and lots...'

I chuckled sympathetically, but laughing wouldn't get rid of the tears. I bit my bottom lip and positioned my head against hers, bringing it closer.

'I know,' I replied, whispered. 'I know you do.'

My eyes were set upon the ceiling, while Rayne's breathing calmed to a faint rise and fall of her chest. I sniffled and tried to collect myself as well, but I just couldn't.

Maybe Rayne held a lot more of me than I thought, one big important chunk that I couldn't bare losing.

I told myself, the idea of her going away for a few days was nothing to worry about. I thought I could sit back and be mature about it. But I felt myself slip, I was upset, disappointed and a little lost.

I clung to her tightly, and savoured the contact we shared. I felt my body relax, my bones ease.

Rayne's gentle breathing drove my own exhaustion to its extreme limits, I felt my eyes droop, once, twice.

I was instantly coaxed asleep, it felt like home.

It really did.

§

Rayne and I made love again in the early hours of the morning.

She'd woken up, kissed me against the cheek then proceeded to unbuckle herself from what left me absolutely shaking last night.

In the morning darkness, I could still see her stretch as she lay back, her head nestling in the crook of my neck.

I let my hands wander, touching her bare stomach once more, circling the muscles.

I was still exhausted, my head was heavy and my eyes were already drooping.

But when I lifted myself so I could grab hold of my mobile, I noticed the time and my heart dropped.

Seven in the morning.

Rayne was leaving in six hours, I had literal hours before I would be rolling into an awful anxiety filled state of mind. That sort of anxiety where the negative thoughts overruled the positive.

I swallowed, placed my phone back and cuddled closer to Rayne.

She noticed my warm embrace, tighter than usual I guess, I couldn't knock this awful feeling off myself at all.

Her hands took hold of me, fingers gently brushing to and from my elbow and shoulder.

'You alright?' she asked, voice hoarse and tired.

I inhaled quickly, shrugging my shoulders. 'Not really...'

Rayne leant up on her elbow, so she could examine my face. I blinked back, sighing.

'What's up? I didn't hurt you,' she paused, eyebrows furrowing. 'Did I?'

I shook my head in denial, last night was brilliant, and there was no unwanted pain at all.

'No...' I mumbled. 'Red, I just...'

My next breath was shaky, and my eyes were already watering.

God, why was I crying again?

She was literally leaving for a few days; she'd be back before I knew it. I couldn't understand the tinge of pain that lingered in my chest, or the way my heartbeat skipped to and from whenever the thought of her saying goodbye passed my mind.

Rayne was concerned, very concerned.

She fell beside me once more, head on my pillow instead.

'Baby,' she mumbled, eyes half lidded.

I blushed quickly, a shaky croak rumbling in my throat, pet names got to me too.

'It's because I'm leaving,' she murmured. 'Isn't it?'

I tried to hide my frown, but I just couldn't. I turned to face her once more, with big puppy dog eyes.

'What do you think?' I asked sadly.

Rayne breathed in and took hold of my face.

Oh no, don't do that. I'll burst into tears in one second.

I mumbled when she pressed her forehead to mine, then leaned up to kiss the tip of my nose. The contact was relaxing and left my cheeks warm, her hands were soft too. All I wanted, was to wrap her around my finger and keep her there forever.

'I'll be home, before you know it,' Rayne explained. 'I'll message you, call you...'

'I know you will, Red.'

'And I'm with Christopher, you know him.'

'I know.'

'And I won't ever stop thinking about you, every night I sleep there, I'll dream of you, and only you.'

She was being awfully romantic, and I giggled, my hands upon her shoulders.

'Red, you're such a hunk,' I whispered against her lips. 'You should be a poet...'

'I'm serious, Juniper,' Rayne whimpered. 'I know we've just gotten together, and you probably want space—'

'Are you kidding, Red?' I interrupted. 'Don't be ridiculous.'

She froze, and scanned my face for any signs of anger. But she wouldn't find any, I wasn't angry at all. Maybe I was a little offended, I always thought I was being the clingy one.

I smiled to her, and she grimaced in return.

'No, I don't want space,' I began. 'I've had enough space, and all I want to do is feel.'

Rayne was watching my lips move as I spoke, and her hands trembled just slightly against my face.

'Space frightens me,' I mumbled. 'I'm afraid to end up alone, and I'm scared that fear will push away everyone I meet, even you, Red.'

My fingers traced her jawline, up to her bottom lip.

'Don't be afraid,' she replied, eyes serious. 'I'm scared of being alone too.'

I could feel her sweet words against my lips, I ached to kiss her every time they left her mouth. She breathed in softly, shrugging her shoulders.

'I wouldn't know what to do, without you,' she chuckled weakly. 'I've been by myself for a while now.'

I listened, my eyes never left hers. Rayne chuckled anxiously, lifting her hand to tuck my hair behind my ear.

'I was afraid,' she admitted. 'Afraid the lack of human contact was my fault, that I was meant to be that way.'

She blinked quickly, a pained smirk upon her lips.

'Alone,' she muttered. 'Maybe I'm just used to it, and I don't deserve—'

'No,' I snapped, interrupting her. 'Don't you go doing that.'

'Doing what?'

'Doubting yourself.'

'Juniper...'

I sniffled and kissed her deeply, bringing our bodies closer. She was spiralling down again, convincing herself she was awful and unworthy.

Rayne thought she was some terrible being, that deserved nothing but pain and isolation. God, she deserved so much more, she needed me.

I broke from her lips, holding her head close to my chest.

'Don't, do that,' I scolded. 'Don't doubt yourself. You have nothing to be afraid of, nothing.'

'What do you mean?'

'\'I mean, you've got me now, Red.' I sniffled. 'You can lean on me, whenever you need to. Talk to me, scream and cry...'

She said nothing, so I continued.

'You don't have to be afraid anymore, or alone.'

'You shouldn't be afraid either.'

I swallowed harshly, remembering my mother for a moment. She left, she said she loved me but she still packed her bags and travelled.

Nat, even my sister could be leaving me, if I wasn't strong enough.

And Rayne? Losing Rayne would be the goddamn cherry on top of the cake of my misery.

I held her tightly, so tight she even chuckled gruffly.

'You're my girlfriend,' I said. 'And I'm going to protect you, no matter what.'

'Juniper, you don't have to.'

'I know!'I said. 'The great Rayne Holmes, made of pure muscle and badassery, doesn't need Juniper Bridges, a silly reporter protecting her!'

'Reporter in training,' Rayne chuckled. 'Still, I wouldn't mind it.'

'Wouldn't mind what?' I asked.

'You protecting me, I can't remember what that feels like,' she hummed. 'Being protected, I mean.'

I felt my heart drop, just the tone in her voice left tears welling up in my eyes.

She was tired, but not only from sleeping less hours than usual, I could hear the exhaustion in her lonesome words.

She'd been on a tough ride, maybe it hadn't stopped yet.

'Oh, Red,' I sighed, pressing my lips against her head. 'You have my full support, and my love.'

'That's all I want,' she croaked. 'I couldn't ask for anything better.'

'It's all I want too,' I replied. 'You'll protect me, Red?'

Rayne leant back, and I saw the stern look in her eyes. She was serious, very serious.

'If anyone touches you,' she grumbled. 'If anyone hurts you, in any way...'

She pursed her lips, eyebrows furrowing. 'I'll make sure they regret it.'

'Violence isn't the answer!'

'It doesn't have to be, but I want you to know if it comes down to it, I'll fight for you.'

I blushed, and got flustered real fast. She was so handsome; I couldn't deal with it.

'Stop that,' I laughed nervously. 'Red.'

Rayne treated me to something then, she not only kissed me roughly, but she straddled me.

I broke off and cleared my throat, this was very unlike her.

Usually I was the one hooking myself tightly around her crotch.

She tensed and I examined her biceps, then to her gorgeous face. She left my head swirling, I was still so tired, but something told me it was definitely her charming persona that left me swooning.

Rayne grabbed my shoulders, holding me down.

I prepared myself for a joke, something along the lines of bringing up 'round two.'

But she kissed me once more, silencing me.

I was taken aback, and my chest was already aching pleasurably.

Her kisses still left me breathless, every single one.

My tongue brushed against hers, and she mumbled through our heated connection. It could have been the early morning, but my arousal was returning, fast.

I broke off and held her close, she was having trouble keeping herself up.

Still sore from all that movement and strain.

'Hey...' I croaked.

'Yeah, I'm alright,' she denied my coaxing touches, maybe a little embarrassed.

'Red, lay back.'

'I-I got this Juniper.'

'Red.'

'...alright.'

She hissed as she fell, her head against my pillows. But she still flashed me a weak smile, shrugging.

'I guess I'm still a little sore,' she chuckled.

'You think?' I asked sarcastically, leaning up to trace my fingers along her arm. 'You blew my mind last night.'

Rayne got a little cocky, and proudly smirked. 'Yeah, well. I'm just too cool.'

I flirtatiously mumbled in response to her joke, kneeling close to her torso. I touched the sharp V-cut that dipped inwards, towards her crotch, with a smirk.

She breathed in sharply, a wicked smile on her lips.

'Hey, it's early.'

'And I still owe you.'

'You don't owe me anything.'

I brought myself between her legs, hands by her thighs. Rayne was denying the touch, saying I needed sleep, giving me those flustered excuses.

I decided to take it upon myself to quieten her.

'Look, Juniper,' Rayne muttered as I leant down to kiss her stomach, trailing pecks downwards. 'You honestly don't owe me anything, it's nearly seven in the morning...'

'Mmhm,' I purred back, licking towards the bottom of her navel. She clenched up, groaning a little.

I was at crotch level then, hands across her waist.

'Juni, you're going to be exhausted, and a reporter in training has to have all the energy—oh fuck.'

I was amused by her sudden halt, just as my mouth sat between her legs, I had to laugh a little.

Rayne lifted herself, just slightly, to breathe outwards.

I could hear her collecting herself, inhaling and exhaling, savouring my tongues motions.

'Okay...' she groaned. 'This is a good way to start the morning...'

I giggled again, lifting my head to scold her.

'Stop it!' I laughed. 'Let me concentrate.'

'Okay, okay,' she smirked, eyes still closed.

I focused on her face as I moved, so I could pick up exactly when she was in utmost pleasure.

I noticed when I just barely brushed the tip of my tongue against her sensitive nerve, she would clench her teeth and strain her neck.

I swallowed, a little nervous to step up my game, but I wanted her to relax, and my touches were affectively making her rather wet.

Rayne reacted as I slipped my index finger inwards, at first she jolted, and I thought she'd deny the touch.

But she did exactly what I hoped she would do.

She started to unwind.

I could feel it, oddly enough.

I could feel the tension lift, not only from where my fingers lay, but the energy around Rayne was also cool and content.

It was quiet between us, apart from the sighs that left Rayne's mouth and the distant hum of the heating system. I closed my eyes to savour the taste, she was sweet.

'S-shit,' I heard her cuss. 'Juniper...'

I broke away to shush her, pumping very gently. 'Just relax, Red.'

'Rather you call me,' she paused to whimper upwards, her left hand reaching for me. 'Rather you call me Rayne when you do...this.'

I laughed lowly, and accepted her wishes, positioning her against the headboard of my bed.

Rayne tried to return a grin, but it instantly left her face when I spread her legs apart, instead she looked at me with a lustful desire in her eyes.

'You look eager...' I chuckled. 'Rayne.'

Before I continued, I leaned forward to kiss her, positioning my arms above her head. She held my waist, but as I dropped between her legs once more, she combed her right hand through my hair, clutching.

I was a little envious, Rayne could last a lot longer. Stuck between that constant battle against moans and climaxing, she savoured each and every stroke.

I had a rhythm going, but she had taken a liking to manoeuvring my head in any direction she pleased.

I breathed when I could, exhaling against her skin, and she loved it.

'Juniper, faster,' she begged.

'Patience...' I teased.

'Don't be cruel,' she whimpered, high and vulnerable.

She spread her legs even further apart, holding my head tightly, roughly.

For another few minutes, I continued to run slow, steady, so I could enjoy her girlish begging. I'd gotten way better by the looks of it, Rayne was in a state of ecstasy, eyes shut and head arched against the headboard.

I loved teasing, but I knew what she wanted, what I wanted to hear as well.

I fastened my pace, my tongue curling forward and backwards, and she reacted with a low series of grunts.

There's the Rayne I know, trying to look and sound tough even when she was being dominated.

I chuckled as she came, she swore rather loudly, mixing it between a high pitched groan and thundering grumble from her throat.

She lifted herself against my mouth, and I held her up by her waist, eyebrows furrowing from the sounds that left her.

I smirked as I broke away, now I was getting pretty cocky. I must have been pretty good to get that response.

'C–Christ,' she coughed, her arm alongside her eyes. 'Juniper, my God, what even.'

I felt giddy now, and couldn't help laughing. She was chuckling too, breathing heavily.

'You're awful!' she cried playfully, swallowing. 'Stop teasing!'

'I'm sorry, Red!' I replied, standing to stretch. 'You're just adorable.'

It took Rayne a few moments before she lifted herself off the bed, legs still a little wobbly.

Even when I held her around the waist, she tried asserting her height, a big blush on her face.

I flexed my jaw, and she spluttered a laugh.

'I know, I'm a slow one to–'

'Come?' I interrupted, wiggling my eyebrows. 'For my second time, you seemed pretty impressed.'

'Oh?' she challenged me. 'Nah, I'm still the best.'

'Oh, yeah?'

'Yeah!'

We stood now, naked, with both our arms crossed. Rayne smirked, tall and proud. She could argue with me for hours, playfully of course. I could just imagine her silly comebacks, just to make me laugh.

I was the first to break, so I could hug her tightly around the neck.

'I win,' she mumbled softly.

'Mm,' I replied. 'Always...'

She held me softly and inhaled. 'Ah, I'm going to miss you.'

'Don't...' I whined. 'The morning isn't over yet.'

Rayne nodded, pulling back to examine my face. I sighed, shrugging my shoulders at her curious look.

'I love you,' she mumbled. 'A lot.'

'I love you more,' I replied, my heart aching. 'Way more.'

Rayne took me into her arms again, kissing the side of my neck. I held her close, breathing in her scent, the feel of her skin against mine, everything.

I wanted her around, I felt a little uneasy when she wasn't.

So I had to make this morning count, look her in the eyes whenever I could, kiss her and tell her how much she meant to me.

All because she was going away for a few days, it all sounded pretty childish.

Childish enough at least for Juniper Bridges to not understand why.

I couldn't put my finger on the emotion, happiness or sadness, want or lust.

Maybe it was all of those put together, maybe love was when it all balanced out.

Things weren't completely balanced though. Unfortunately, I could sense that.

Rayne, she sensed it too.

It was just something we had to work on, to create a solid tower, a tower of trust and respect.

Respect for ourselves, respect for our feelings.

Respect for each other.

But right now, in that moment, I just wanted to be with her, close to her.

I pulled Rayne back a bit, and smiled sheepishly.

'One shower?' I asked sweetly, hooking her fingers around my own. 'So you don't reek of day old sex.'

'Oh, what if I wanted to reek of day old sex...?' she whimpered playfully.

For a moment I thought she was serious, until she grinned and yawned loudly. I patted her cheek, winking at her grouch.

'C'mon, Red,' I muttered, pulling her back.

'Okay, a shower wouldn't hurt,' she responded, she sounded pretty excited.

Hey, I was too.

§

During our shower, Rayne completely relaxed.

We spent a good ten minutes embracing under the hot waters rush, allowing our bones and worries to ease. I was a little nervous about something this intimate, I'd never experienced it before.

But once I had stepped into the shower alongside her, her smile made all the anxiety drift away. It was almost addictive to see Rayne smile, and I wanted her to continue doing so. I never wanted to see her upset, hurt or worried.

But it was unavoidable, with how life was.

We couldn't control the future, or change the past, even if we prayed and prayed.

I spent a good five years of my teenage life, tossing and turning about what the future may have held for me.

That I completely forgot about living in the present.

But here? here with Rayne? I was definitely living in the now.

I was taking notice to every little detail, the way Rayne's wet skin felt against mine, the way my body reacted, the sounds and tastes.

Living in the present, was wonderful when I finally stopped to experience it.

I stepped back, leaning against the shower wall, as Rayne kissed my upper chest. The contact left a big smile on my lips, electricity through my body.

Rayne clung to me, tightly, hands by my sides. She told me she loved me, wanted to stay there right in my arms, and couldn't believe I existed.

Oh, Rayne, I wanted to say, you existing means so much more.

Was it too early to say I'd found my world?

I blushed deeply, clearing my throat. Rayne glanced to me, wet hair around her shoulders. If I thought she looked brilliant naked, naked and dripping wet was even better. She knew I was flustered, and thought maybe it would be hilarious to make me even more so.

Her arms were above my head now, crossed so she could lean down close to my face.

The stream was just above her head now, she breathed in gently, letting the water ease over parted lips.

Oh my God.

I groaned and hit her against the stomach, and she chuckled back.

'Hey! Watch it!'

'Stop looking so attractive, you dork!' I grumbled over the showers hum. 'Even when you're sopping wet, you look like some model for a grunge tattoo magazine.'

Rayne snorted and waved my comment off, glancing to her arm. I saw her eyes ease, like she was remembering something, that left a bittersweet taste in her mouth.

I brought her face to mine, so I could savour a deep kiss, hands against her chest.

Rayne closed her eyes, and pressed herself to me, fingers sliding to and from my waist. Not only was I savouring the kiss, this embrace was just as beautiful.

She was a little taken aback by my hold, and broke off to focus on my eyes.

'Juniper?'

It still left me shivering when she said my name, every time.

'Mm?' I replied, not ready to speak.

Rayne sniffled and brushed her fingers against my jawline, her eyes on my own.

'I'll say it again,' she began sweetly. 'I'll be fine, everything will be fine.'

'I know, I know,' I answered, a hot lump rising in my chest. 'I'm sorry I'm overreacting, it's as if you're leaving for three years, not days.'

'It's okay.'

'No, it's not,' I interrupted, feeling guilty. 'Here I am, acting as if you're about to up and leave for all eternity, making you feel like crap, ugh.'

'Stop it,' Rayne mumbled, her hands took my shoulders now.

I sighed and shrugged, looking to my feet.

I wanted to laugh it off, tell her I was only worrying because of how much I cared, which was true.

But I honestly couldn't shake another feeling off, like a deep rumbling anxiety that was sliding to and from my conscience.

I thought maybe it lingered because of all the past drama that took its toll recently, maybe it was normal for me to think this way.

Rayne brought my attention back, her eyes eased again.

'Juniper,' she started. 'I can reassure you, everything will be okay and I'll be home before you know it.'

I paused, held my left arm with my right, and finally exhaled my worrisome groan.

'Okay,' I replied. 'Okay, okay. Just, kiss me for a little bit more?'

Rayne chuckled, and grabbed me against her chest, roughly.

'Yes ma'am,' she grinned. 'Anything for the reporter.'

I felt the anxiety rush against me as soon as I had dismissed it, so I held her mouth with my hand when she sped in for a kiss, gently.

In her reflection, my face was stern, serious and distant.

'I mean it, Rayne,' I said, hearing her name left her swallowing. 'Please, be careful.'

I expected her to roll her eyes and repeat the same routine response, give me those intimidating and powerful Rayne Holmes eyes, eyes that proved she was strong and capable.

Instead, they calmed and her eyebrows furrowed. 'Yeah...'

Her words were muffled, so I let her mouth go, palming her left cheek instead. I wanted to keep her here, under the waters rush, for myself, for nobody else.

How selfish of me.

'I love you,' Rayne muttered. 'I'll come back.'

'I know; I'm not worried about that...' I paused, shrugging. 'I just...'

'What?' she asked, her look sincere.

I wanted to answer, I really did. But I wasn't so sure myself, so I decided to dismiss the whole topic.

'I'm just,' I mumbled. 'I'm going to miss you, that's all.'

Rayne smiled weakly, and leaned down to kiss me. 'Don't worry, please?'

I held the sides of her neck, pausing before her lips. 'That's a big ask, on your behalf, Red.'

She chuckled once more, and pulled me closer by the waist.

'Yeah, I know,' she pondered and winked. 'But at least try.'

'That I can do,' I mumbled, pecking her gently. 'I can try.'

Rayne paused before continuing, so she could press her lips to my nose. I flinched, giggling softly. At least when she kissed me, I was able to forget about my worries.

Even if it was just for a few moments.

It was bliss.

§

After our romantic and meaningful shower, Rayne got changed, dried her hair, and put one of my red hoodies on.

I watched her from the edge of my bed as she contemplated taking her things back home before she left to meet Christopher, but I insisted she let me take care of her guitar. She only took her duffel bag and flung it over her shoulder.

I knew I had only five minutes left with my girlfriend, so I wanted her to leave with something, other than an embrace and a kiss.

'Hold on,' I said, rushing to my desk.

The floor was still covered in my notes, from our previous night. Rayne realised this, and cleared her throat while picking piece by piece up.

I wanted to tease, gosh I really wanted to, but it wasn't the time.

I fumbled with my drawers, and scrounged through my loose jewellery, mixed with hair ties, bits and pieces. What I was looking for, had to be somewhere inside here.

'Hang on, let me just...' I paused and plunged deeper into the unknown abyss, feeling for the object's smooth, rounded edge.

Rayne sniffled and leant against the desk, watching me fumble. 'What are you looking for?'

I hummed to myself, and to her question. 'A ring.'

She gasped and jumped up, playfully grabbing at her mouth.

'You're proposing!' she gleefully teased. 'Oh, Juniper!'

'Can it, Red,' I chuckled. 'Or I'll propose to you with an onion ring, you big dork.'

She groaned loudly, and wrapped her arms around my stomach from behind, even as I stood searching.

I was about to lose hope, until I felt that familiar writing.

'Ah!' I grinned, pulling back. 'Here it is, little shit.'

Rayne snorted from my cuss, and turned me in her arms. 'Show, show.'

I brought the ring to my eyes, it was a little warn out, gold and scratched. It hung by a brown strap, my birthdate was engraved within the inside, the outside smooth.

'I got this, when I was four,' I chuckled, lifting it over Rayne's head. 'So, don't lose it.'

'Juniper,' she paused. 'Why are you–'

'Because,' I spoke over her. 'I want you to have something of mine.'

I was blushing, flustered and nervous.

'Y-you know, so when you're a little upset, I'll be there. I mean, not there, but you know what I mean.'

She listened to me ramble, but her eyes were set on the ring, twisting and turning its shape around her index finger and thumb.

I breathed in, rubbing the back of my neck. It was true, the ring was given to me by my father when I was younger, I was so excited when he handed it to me, I never wanted to lose it.

It held a big part of me, and now that Rayne was the one to hold an even greater chunk of my emotions, I wanted her to have it.

Rayne denied it at first, but I shushed her, kissing her across the lips.

'Wear it, and don't worry,' I said sternly, smiling. 'Look after it for me.'

'I will,' she said, determined. 'Don't you worry.'

I wanted to say that I wouldn't, but of course I would.

Rayne glanced to the time, and sighed softly. I felt the uneasy anxiety rise in my chest again, the thumping of my heart.

'Okay,' she muttered. 'Nearly one, I gotta get going.'

I walked her to the door, asked her if she had everything, wallet, keys.

She'd left Arty's car keys with me, told me to thank the redhead with a box of chocolates with the words 'fuck you' written on a piece of paper inside it.

I laughed at her idea, but told her; Arty would hunt her down in Philadelphia, and shove the paper in her face until she cried uncle.

We stopped at my door, and Rayne shot me a look full of sadness. I swallowed, and leaned against my doorframe, she was stepping on the spot, glancing to and from the hallway she stood in.

'Well, I'll be back before you know it,' she repeated, adjusting her bag around her shoulder.

I held her hands, and brought her close. 'You message me, call me.'

She nodded as I spoke. 'Yep, I won't forget.'

'And make sure you drive safe, tell Christopher to be careful too.'

'Christopher will be fine.'

'And you will too, yes?'

'Yeah, totally fine. I'll get you something from Philadelphia.'

I chuckled and fumbled with the ring around her neck, popping it under her shirt collar. Rayne examined me as I did, even when I kept my palm there, patting.

I felt her chest rise and fall, her heartbeat too. It was fast, she was either nervous or sad, probably both.

'See-ya, dollface,' I croaked, patting her once more against the chest. 'Don't get into any trouble.' Rayne's smile faded, and she leaned close to me, hugging my body tight.

'I won't,' she mumbled into my ear. 'I'll see you soon.'

Watching her leave was hard, harder than it should have been that's for sure.

Rayne walked rather slow towards the stairwell, but turned to give me one final wave. I did the same, raising my hand and wiggling my fingers her way.

'Love you,' she mouthed.

I winked and nodded once. 'I love you too.'

I kept my smile upon my face, until she turned. I could feel my anxiety successfully crash through the protective barriers of Rayne's assuring words. It kicked down doors and threw itself against my brain, and left an uneasy taste in my mouth.

I sighed and stepped back into my room, noticing how quiet it was without her.

I was already hoping for a text, and she hadn't even left the premises yet.

So it took me a few moments to process my past night, past morning and thoughts. All jumbled into one, was the biggest clusterfuck I had ever experienced, mixed with a tinge of every emotion a human could feel.

I drew my chair from my desk, and sat. I had to catch my breath, catch my train of thought before it hit Anxiety Station.

Besides, I had a lot of my own work to do. I had to get out of here and start searching, first would be the junkyard just outside of the City of Boston, then I would hit the smaller settlements that were known for scrapping old cars.

I was determined, but the pang of sadness that lingered, was overwhelming. I groaned and grabbed hold of my laptop, opening it so I could start searching.

I was going to find Pebbles, without a doubt.

Chapter Twenty-One

RAYNE

It was hard to leave Juniper, harder than I thought it would be.

After spending one hell of a night with her, of course it was difficult. I had become so comfortable with her, the idea of staying in one room for all eternity was bliss, knowing she'd be there with me.

But of course, with happiness comes second guessing, and with Rayne Holmes, there's always doubt.

I worried this was just our beginning, what if our end was closer than I'd thought?

No, think of the positive Rayne.

Remember how close you two got last night, think about those expressions she pulled, full of pleasure and satisfaction.

I caught myself blushing as I travelled downstairs, my face felt hot.

In the past, I'd shared a bed with other girls. I'd kissed their skin, touched them in places that left them squirming.

Last night felt different, there was lust in the air, a lot of it. But there was also another emotion, that engulfed the both of us.

When I was atop of Juniper, I made eye contact with her. Not to assert dominance, no, I wanted her to see that I was there, and I wanted her to know she was safe.

There was no feeling of pure trust with other women I slept with in the past, it was all pleasure.

We wanted to reach that climatic state and linger in it for as long as we could.

With Juniper, I longed for her release more than my own. I wanted to see her in that state of pleasure, that I had successfully left her feeling wanted and protected.

It was different, something never before experienced.

It left my heart racing and head wavering, mixing different emotions together into a swirling vortex of feelings.

But I was content with the bond between us, I couldn't have asked for anything better.

That's why I knew, Juniper Bridges was different.

Yeah she was a little nervous, awkward and flustered. As was I, but those traits slowly turned to confidence and eagerness.

We both wanted release, but we never tore our eyes away from one another.

That was love.

Pure, effective love.

And this job could very well destroy that pure love.

On the lower floor, I paused before the exit doors. I wanted to run back upstairs, stay in Juniper's room safely, without the worry taking hold of me.

I could back out, tell Christopher this was a mistake, and figure out another way.

But he could be there, that sick son of a bitch, Pebbles. And what if I missed that opportunity, to find the guy we've been scrounging around for?

The guy that Juniper had set her determination on, the one who made her sister's life a living hell?

I had to do this job, I wanted everything to be alright.

I had to, right then, there was no other way.

With the image of Juniper's smile plastered in my mind, I slowly walked towards the nearest bus stop. As my feet crunched into new snow, I realised I heard no storm at all last night. I was too preoccupied with my girlfriend to even process the weather.

Sure, I was living in the moment. Nothing else mattered last night, but her.

I think people lose themselves in pleasure, pleasure was an addictive emotion that I had missed. Alongside the feeling of being cared for, being told I was worth it.

But nothing was greater, than knowing Juniper was waiting for me when I returned. Nothing left my heart pumping more than her loving touch.

Whenever I was faced with something positive, the negative was absolutely ravishing, and took over almost instantly.

When you're used to it, you're simply used to it.

That's why the negative feeling that loomed over my chest, the feeling of upcoming sadness, was so strong.

I wasn't used to the positive, at all.

To shake this feeling from my bones, I had to get moving. To push through the negative, I had to waver in the positive, just until I could settle down, fix all that had come undone.

I glanced back towards Juniper's housing complex, imagining wishfully that she'd come running out to hug me and tell me she loved me one more time.

I think she knew; she knew that something was wrong. I was a terrible liar andI was surprised I could keep this fib intact for so long.

Last night, while Juniper and I made love, I could feel the guilt seethe through me. It was an awful feeling, whenever I looked at her, I saw flash images of her tear stricken and hurt, at my betrayal. I contemplated telling her, then and there. But I just couldn't, I was so content in her arms, she made me forget about the negative.

It was so selfish, relying on someone else to make my emotions stable.

Until I could do it on my own.

The hope that Juniper would see this act of selflessness as heroic, kept me going.

But who was I kidding? I wasn't doing this for myself, at all.

I wasn't even thinking about the money for the busking licence, all I could see was Nat and Juniper before anyone else.

I imagined beating the shit out of Pebbles, me photographed over his unconscious body and named the 'Hero of Boston.'

But the more I obsessed over that thought, the more it frightened me. It was me against a clan of murderous drug smugglers.

I shivered, pocketing my hands.

The weather was becoming clearer, and there were only a few inches of snow on the ground, which meant driving would be a little stressful.

It was almost like the snow was clearing, so my awful lies could be seen.

I clenched my teeth and examined the road beside me, icy roads meant possible accidents, and I'd already promised Juniper I would be safe.

The bus was just arriving as I turned the street corner, it was puffing in idle, almost coaxing me to my doom.

I sighed and rubbed my hands close together, it didn't often pass my mind these days, but a cigarette would warm me up. Juniper would probably scold me to all ends of the earth, but something told me she'd overlook it, if I came back and admitted to becoming a Fire Jackal.

I stepped onto the bus, the driver was chowing down on a bagel, its inside fresh cream cheese. I glanced to him once, before finding the nearest seat, a window seat.

I thought about Mrs Murphy, I hadn't seen her in weeks, maybe she was worried. Even Carla, she wouldn't admit it, but she was probably waiting for me to step in and drag snow all over her store.

I knew it sounds silly, but when the bus left its spot, and drove west, it felt like the last time I would see Boston.

I sniffled and pressed my left elbow against the window, its chilly touch sending shivers down my arm. I know I shouldn't have, but I watched Juniper's apartment vanish as the bus reeled off.

My heart dropped, alongside its heavy weight was a stinging guilt, that left me feeling quite sick.

Think of the positive, I reminded myself.

I closed my eyes, exhaustion rushing over.

I focused on a daydream that I hoped would become real.

Summertime, we would be on a great big oval field with green grass and huge oak trees. I thought of Nat running, laughing as I swung her around and around. She'd comment on how tall I was, she would sit on my shoulders and point at the sky, and I would hold her knees tightly. She'd bend her back as far as she could, and grab hold of her sister's hands, who would gently lay a kiss across her forehead.

Juniper would look beautiful; I couldn't wait to see her in summer. She already had such a radiance around her, but God, imagining her basking in the sun's glaze was a treat.

Juniper and Nat deserved the world, and although I couldn't click my fingers and fix everything, I wouldn't give up.

The bus jolted me out of my daydream, and the driver honked in response to another angry driver.

Seemed everyone was grumpy today.

I took a heavy breath, and rummaged through my duffel bag, which held a few shirts and sweaters here and there. I didn't bring too much but I knew I would be crashing at a few hotels here and there, I had to bring the necessities.

On the corner of my right eye sat a few elderly people, they glanced at me and whispered, commented on my masculine attire.

From the front, a few children laughed loudly, it gave me a splitting headache.

And finally, behind me a homeless person sat snoring.

Man, if I could just run back to Boston University and fall back asleep in Juniper's arms, that'd be great.

I grabbed my phone, and wondered if it was too soon to message her, tell her I was on my way. She was busy, she had that paper to file, she was probably tapping away on her laptop like a marathon runner.

I'd seen her do so before, she was unreal.

I thought about our date, before the brilliant end to it. Juniper mentioned she had gone to the police, and successfully acquired their support.

But hey, the police were a lot of talk, they promised a ton and sometimes never supplied.

I hoped Juniper would let the cops do the dirty work, but that was stupid of me to even consider, she was probably already searching for a missing car on her own.

This job was to make money, yes. But I secretly hoped I could find out who Pebbles was on my own, even find the location of the hit-and-runner's vehicle.

Juniper would be confused, really confused if I called and told her where to find him. Juniper also wasn't stupid, she'd figure out my lies sooner or later, I just needed to make the best out of it.

If you could even do that.

Make the best out of a lie.

I chewed my bottom lip, and remembered the meeting a few nights ago, though I tried my absolute best to shrug the memories off, they stuck to me like leeches.

This job started off as a simple meet and greet, on Sunday.

I'drocking up to Christopher' workplace, and he rushed to me instantly. I was a little frightened by his look, his eyes were wide, serious.

'Rayne, this isn't good,' he said, glancing around the dark shop. 'This isn't some simple job, this is,'

'Fire Jackals business,' I answered. 'I know.'

Christopher seemed to shudder at the name, and slowly crossed his arms. But I was curious, very curious.

'Uh,' I saw his eyes dart left to right, then he swallowed before he spoke. 'How did you know?'

'Why didn't you tell me?' I interrupted, breathing in the cold air. 'Why are you involved with them?'

Christopher was a good guy, I could tell by his sincere eyes, he couldn't easily lie without feeling guilty.

He shuffled on the spot, glanced behind him and then groaned a little.

'L-look, I didn't really expect you to come,' he stammered, leaning back a bit. 'I didn't want you involved.'

'Well,' I paused and shrugged. 'Now I am, so can you please explain?'

I was so goddamn curious to know why someone like Christopher was involved with a deadly gang. He was some sweet young guy who couldn't hurt a fly, at least, I thought so.

I glared at him for a moment, crossed my arms and waited for his response. He was nervous, he always was.

'I-I can't talk to you about it here. I lost my phone a few days ago, and I couldn't text you,' he muttered. 'I'll get into trouble...'

I felt a little disappointed, that meant Christopher' wasn't the anonymous person who warned me last night.

He paused and bit his bottom lip, rubbing his neck awkwardly. 'Reedy's done a job for these guys before, and he made it seem like something easy.'

'So, does that mean Reedy is involved with them too?' I asked.

Christopher shook his head, grimacing. 'No, he's not.'

'But you just said,'

'I know what I said!' he snapped.

I flinched, and saw a fiery burn in his eyes. Christopher sighed, rubbed his hair in and collected himself, waving his hands once.

'I'm sorry...' he whimpered. 'Reedy knows someone in the gang, someone pretty important...'

I instantly thought of Pebbles. I felt my breath hitch, my heart skip.

Christopher clenched his fists, and adjusted his varsity jacket, seemed he never took that thing off.

'So, he isn't technically in the group...' he laughed sarcastically. 'Lucky him, huh?'

I waited for more information, this all seemed a little fishy, and mixing it all together with a Fire Jackal on top made everything confusing. Christopher' brow creased, and he kicked a little snow with his sneaker.

'He was hesitant...'

'Why?'

'Because tonight is only a tiny portion of this job.'

I remember becoming even colder after Christopher spoke. I could still feel the goosebumps that rose on my skin that Sunday night, I think it was fear, or anger.

'What?' I asked, eyes leering.

Christopher nodded gently. 'There's more to it, this is why I hoped you wouldn't show.'

'I wish you guys warned me,' I chuckled weakly. 'Reedy in particular.'

Christopher smiled shortly, his bottom lip wobbling. 'No, don't blame him...'

I saw his eyes wander again, away from my own. 'Reedy likes earning big bucks, but he didn't expect the job to be this big.'

'How big are we talking?' I asked, rubbing my arms. I didn't want to show it, but I was nervous.

Christopher jumped when the garage doors behind him reeled upwards, I glanced towards two others, tall lanky males.

No females? I was the only one, great.

I knew I could protect myself against a couple of guys, thankfully Christopher wasn't an asshole.

Easing my eyes, I focused forward.

The guy on the right was twitchy, even more so than Christopher. He wore a grey sweater, black jeans and a dirty pair of tappers. His buzz cut blonde hair was absolutely filthy, like he'd swam in a pool of soot and oil.

He adjusted his goggles from his eyes, and grinned towards us.

Next to him, another male, a little older. He looked a little less intimidating to say the least, wearing a flannel shirt and red pants. His hair was brown, thinning and his facial hair made him look a little seedy.

I cleared my throat, and nudged Christopher.

'And these two are?' I asked, softly.

He turned to me, his face displayed the utmost guilt. 'These are our team members.'

I remember my first steps towards the garage, twelve uneasy footprints in the snow, twelve uneasy heartbeats.

Christopher was guilty that I'd shown up.

Maybe he expected Rayne Holmes to be a little smarter when offered uneasy jobs.

Maybe he thought I'd realise it was a little odd, with or without a text message warning.

Of course, when Reedy brought the job up, I saw Christopher curl up in his shell of anxiety, he seemed to be just as hesitant as I.

He was right, Christopher I mean.

Sunday night was only a portion of my Fire Jackal adventure, but it wasn't sugar coated at all.

I was introduced to Manny, the guy in the flannel shirt, and Crocker, the weird guy with the goggles.

They didn't attack me, or seem too uneasy, Crocker was too twitchy and it left me a little nervous.

I knew they were members of the Fire Jackals because they kept calling me a newbie, but not Christopher, that was odd.

We sat in the mechanic's garage, with cups of lukewarm coffee and stale biscuits to eat. It was cold, dark and a little spooky. I wouldn't mind it in the day, but it was just so desolate at night. Who knew there were Fire Jackals meetings happening in a local mechanic? Where would they be next? The local supermarket?

I didn't want to know.

Manny explained to Christopher and I, exactly what we were getting ourselves into.

But he never asked if we wanted to back out, he was serious when he glared at the both of us and said;

'No chickening out.'

My knees bobbed up and down in my seat, feet tapping the ground gently, a nervous act. Crocker made eye contact with me a few times, a sly smirk on his lips, he hardly spoke.

And I hardly looked his way.

Manny finished the smaller details, where we would be going, what we would be doing.

I wasn't too pleased with the goods being transferred across town.

Drugs, drugs and more drugs.

Shit.

I heard a croaky whine leave Christopher' lips when Manny showed us sealed tight packs of cocaine, ecstasy, syringes that were called 'Pyscho.'

I was curious, I'd never heard of that drug before. My facial expression must have shown obvious curiosity, because Crocker jumped in, grabbed one and shoved it towards me. I flinched, but he halted the sharp edge, right at the end of my nose, and giggled.

'You don't know what this is, huh?' he smirked, voice uneasy. 'This is my invention, actually.'

'R–really?' I muttered, trying to seem brave.

'Yes!' he laughed, turning to place it back down on its tray. 'It's got a powerful kick of adrenalin inside it, mixed with all the good stuff.'

He looked to me, eyebrows raised, and I cleared my throat.

'Good stuff?' I replied. 'Like?'

'Cocaine, liquefied stuff, the good junk.'

I didn't think there was such thing as 'good junk.' But I let the crazy dude go on to explain exactly what would happen if this syringe was injected, how easy it was to overdose and die.

Wonderful, I wouldn't be touching those at all.

I wasn't usually one to touch drugs, back in Florida I messed around a little with some of the bad kids. Smoked a little marijuana here and there.

I absolutely hated it, and chose tobacco over it.

But I was young, and stupid, so of course I'd tried stupid things.

But I was an adult now, at least, I thought I was.

'Why are you so shocked, Chris?' Manny laughed, leaning against the table behind him. 'You should be drooling.'

'H–hey,' Christopher warned, his eyes darkening. 'Don't.'

I saw Manny roll his own eyes, and chew on his stale gum. 'Yeah, yeah.'

I felt the tension around all four of us, I always had my hands by my side, in case one jumped me. I was always thinking of ways to fight, maybe I could grab the chair over in the corner of the room, grab a monkey wrench...

'So!' Manny smacked his hands down against his thighs, and I jumped. 'Tonight is easy, we're going towards the port, handing over to our buddies over there.'

I grouched to myself, the Fire Jackals really were everywhere.

'The cops are on our asses, twenty-four seven,' he paused and spat to the floor.

'They tend to flag us down in our most common meeting places, so here.'

I felt my heart sting when he rummaged through a bag beside his feet, pulling out two black handguns.

'They come near us? You aim right for the face,' he laughed.

I turned to Christopher, who was just as nervous as I. He looked at the weapons with the most terrified expression, like a child in a nightmare.

Manny was already fixing his own gun up, twisting and turning its exterior in his hands. He looked professional, and that left me queasy.

I'd only shot a gun back in Florida as well, with my dad at my grandfather's farm. And that was shooting tin cans with a goddamn BB gun.

'You ever used one of these, girly?' Crocker asked, handing me the weapon. 'You know? Guns?'

'I know what a gun is,' I snapped, watching my tone. 'But, no, not a real one.'

They both chuckled, but Crocker's laugh was way higher.

'Oh boy, Pebbles is setting us up with a novice?' Manny grinned. 'Great.'

I scanned each face for some sort of clue, to who Pebbles really was. I was expecting another joke, maybe his real name.

'Anyway, there shouldn't be any cops near port tonight,' Manny sighed. 'If there is, just duck, we'll take care of it, newbie.'

I nodded hesitantly, turning my head to Christopher. He was deep in thought, the gun in his hands. He stared at the barrel, his eyes quivering. I felt sympathetic for the poor guy, and I wanted answers to why he was even here.

Manny mentioned drugs, that would explain his nervous state.

When the other two blasted into conversation and began packing the drugs, I turned to Christopher.

'Christopher,' I whispered. 'Hey.'

He sniffled and glanced at me, waiting.

I sighed and kept my finger away from the trigger of my own gun, shivering at its cool touch. I had to constantly remain calm, I was close to breaking too.

If Christopher snapped, it could be messy.

'Hey,' I muttered, touching his shoulder gently. 'It's alright,

I wanted to tell him, that after all this we could run away from the Fire Jackals and never look back. take our well-earned cash and use it for good.

But Manny answered for me.

'So, Tuesday afternoon, we're leaving for Philadelphia.'

I froze, whipping back in his direction. 'We're what?'

Manny smirked, scoffed and patted Crocker on the shoulder. 'I think she expects the money right now...'

They both giggled like little boys, and I grumbled. Christopher was quiet, he was worrying already.

'Yeah, Philadelphia is where the big boys go,' Crocker grinned. 'We've got one important trade to do there, passing through Connecticut for another.'

I hadn't left Massachusetts once, I've only been to Florida and Boston. I wanted to be excited, but knowing we were shipping drugs through other states was bone chilling.

I wasn't a drug dealer, I was Rayne Holmes, a busker.

'Okay…' I swallowed. 'So when will we be back?'

Manny rubbed his chin, and chewed harshly on his gum. 'Give or take, a few days. Maybe get back in Boston by Saturday.'

I clenched my teeth, my attention on Christopher now. 'You knew?'

'No!' he answered. 'Honestly, I didn't. Tell her Manny.'

Manny groaned and rolled his eyes, like he was dealing with a bunch of children.

'No, this was something last minute,' he answered. 'But you won't get paid until the job is done.'

I breathed in, thinking about Juniper's reaction to me leaving, even Nat's.

God they were going to be furious with me, and I'd laid this secret on Nat already, maybe she'd break the news to her sister.

I kind of hoped not.

'Okay, Philadelphia,' I mumbled. 'Sounds easy enough.'

Crocker spluttered and pointed to me. I was instantly uncomfortable.

'Easy?' he laughed. 'Newbie you better be careful; this isn't "easy".'

I bit back my smartass reply that could easily get me killed. That wouldn't be the best way to go, talking smack to a Fire Jackal.

Think of the pay, I thought to myself.

Think of finding out more information on Pebbles, Juniper's smile when I gave her new information.

I watched Christopher rise and help Manny pack cocaine bundles, Crocker made jokes and examined each piece before shoving them into duffel bags.

I didn't move, I sat still and silent. My eyes were glazed, I was scared and vulnerable, but too cocky to admit it.

I was strong. I just didn't expect something this big to be put upon my chest, playing hero wasn't the best idea after all.

The night started smoothly, we drove half an hour out of Boston, Christopher and I in the backseat of a black van.

All I could think of as we drove, was the cops pulling us over, I would have to use the gun by my side, take someone else's life.

I was on edge, the worst type of it. Christopher too, he sat beside me and bit his nails nervously. But Crocker and Manny were fine, they blasted rock music, and wolf whistled to any girl walking along the way.

I hoped nobody noticed me, my cowardly self.

Every worry that lay dormant in my body, was appearing on the surface. I wanted to question Crocker and Manny about the meeting last night, if they knew anything we didn't.

But I had to remind myself not to, and not to worry either.

The two members Juniper and I bumped into, were nothing to second guess about.

One was piss drunk, the other couldn't even see me clearly, his punches missed.

I thought to mention Arty, know a little more about her story, but that would just put her in more trouble.

I knew she loved Nat, but living in Juniper's house forever probably wasn't on her to do list.

Plus, she was already going to kick my ass, once she figured out I joined the Fire Jackals.

I was definitely putting myself in danger, the exact same danger I told Juniper off about.

How hypocritical.

We reached the port safely, and I glared outside. It was cold, damp and rickety. But I could see a familiar mark upon the big shed against the shoreline.

That dammed mark that I was going to learn to have to love.

Crocker hummed to himself as he exited the car, smacking on the window to frighten me. I cussed under my breath, this guy was a total jerk.

'Alright, let's go,' Manny said, his tone relaxed. 'Before we're late.'

I didn't exactly know what he meant, but I rushed out just as Christopher did. Outside was awful, windy and icy due to the shore being so close. It was a bittersweet moment for me, as I saw how the ice glistened over the water's surface.

Crocker shoved me out of my moment, by handing me three bags, all filled with drugs. I cleared my throat and nodded once, and he smirked, teeth black and rotten.

I was starting to notice there were no good-looking Fire Jackals, except Arty, she was charming as much as I hated to admit it.

Christopher held a few bags as well, and nervously looked around. He was getting closer and closer to that edge of mentality.

I gave him a soft glance, a calm and collected look.

A totally fake collected look, but he seemed to gain some sort of confidence from it. Manny led with Crocker behind him, followed by Christopher and myself.

I kept on my toes, and listened out for any odd noises, but there was nothing, at all.

That scared me even more.

Manny paused before the metal door, rimmed with grime and sea snails. I grimaced nauseously, there was nothing I hated more than the smell of rotting fish and metal. Crocker yawned and knocked upon the door, smacking heavily in a rhythm.

After he halted, I waited for a response, listening to the wind around the four of us. It took a total of two minutes before another knock was returned, and Manny grinned.

'Easy,' he chuckled, lifting his chin to peek through the small window. 'Ey, its Spark.'

I heard a muffled laugh, then the clicking of keys. I thought the door was rusted shut, but with one tug it opened with a screech.

I eased my eyes, shutting them for a moment, and when I opened them, I was looking into the barrel of a gun.

My heart froze instantly, the blood in my body had turned cold.

The man who held the weapon to my face was a blur, I was already about to cry.

'Relax, man!' Manny laughed, to my relief. 'She's with us.'

I took a deep breath, holding the ends of the bags with such force I thought they might burst. The gun stood still, before it wavered and fell by its owner's side. I shakily exhaled, locking eyes with the elder member. He was tall, not as tall as me, but he looked absolutely terrifying.

I thought Nick Rodgers' scars were odd, this guy had a whole goddamn party of cuts on his face. Above his cheeks, on his nose, through his lips.

He was grimy and smelled like liquor and weed, the worst kind of mixture.

He smelled like he couldn't be trusted, just as much as he looked it.

I was starting to really believe that all members were butt ugly.

'Sorry,' he said gruffly, running the gun through his short hair—odd choice of a comb. 'I haven't seen this one around.'

His eyes were wandering my body now, and I absolutely hated it. He was glaring at me with that disgusting lust, the one people feared.

'Yeah, well. She's one of us now,' Crocker answered, stepping inside.

Oh god, I didn't expect that to sound so gross, but it left my head swirling.

I was one of them now.

Christopher looked me in the eye once, and I swallowed deeply, relieved I wasn't dead.

I passed the grimy guy with a scowl, and he chuckled roughly. The thought of his manhood being blown off by my newly acquired gun wasn't too bad.

'So you got the goods?' another voice asked, female this time.

Thank God! I was waiting to see my second female Fire Jackal, well, third if I counted myself and I wasn't ready to do that yet.

I turned my body right, expecting a woman my age, but she was just as grimy as the others. She was in her late forties and looked like some sort of drug overdose warning picture.

I shouldn't have been thinking humorously, but I smirked a bit, they were all fucking awful looking.

Maybe I was just keeping myself sane, so I wouldn't end up like Christopher, who looked like he was about to spontaneously combust.

'Yeah, here we go. A lot of good shit,' Crocker grinned, grabbing a bag from me.

I made quick eye contact with the female, she was blonde and might have actually been quite pretty before turning into a murderous crack addict.

I wasn't going to end up like that at all, I was out of this whole goddamn group as soon as I found out Pebbles identity and gained a few bucks.

I was ready to be on the run, just like Arty.

Hey maybe we could bond over it, become even closer friends.

'Hey, missy,' the female snatched the other bags from me, and I flinched. 'Pull your head out of your ass.'

I contained my feelings and ignored her cuss. She scoffed my way, threw the bags against a decaying couch along the back wall, and sighed happily at the contents.

'Wow, this stuff is good,' she grinned, reaching to take hold of it.

'Hey!' the other growled. 'It's for our group, don't fucking touch it.'

I was expecting guns to start blazing, from the verbal abuse being thrown around the room now. Crocker and Manny joined in, argued with the other two, pushed and shoved. Christopher and I stood still, poker faced, we didn't want to get involved, as much as we already were.

I breathed in gently, collecting myself. I thought to run, but a bullet in my back would be pretty awful.

I watched the commotion die down, just as the female injected herself with some psycho, and grinned. Crocker chuckled and pointed to her, nodding once. 'Good huh?'

'You fuckin' bet,' she replied, jumping on the spot. 'You make some good shit, Crocker.'

Her male partner looked pretty angry, but held back his furious cuss. He crossed his arms and pulled Manny aside, they spoke vastly.

I wanted to leave, man I just wanted to bail.

This wasn't where I wanted to be on a Sunday night, I wanted to be back in Boston with my new girlfriend, maybe watching a few crappy flicks on TV.

Christopher sniffled and held his gun lazily, pocketing it behind. 'Sorry, Rayne.'

I shrugged my shoulders, it wasn't his fault. I was supposed to be strong right now, use cunning skills to find out answers, but I was a mess.

'It's not your fault,' I replied.

'The job I was offering wasn't this, it's just Reedy had to open his mouth...'

'Don't worry about that,' I answered, quietly. 'Let's just get this over and done with.'

I wanted to tell him of my progress, the truth about Pebbles and Nat, everything. But if I opened my mouth, I'd be a dead girl walking.

I'd been a Fire Jackal for approximately two hours, and I'd already had a syringe at my face, a gun too, and watched a middle aged woman shoot up right in front of me.

I didn't want to know what was next.

Christopher shivered from beside me, his bottom lip trembled again, so I took his arm and squeezed gently, coaxing him.

He seemed to calm under my touch, he needed a friend, and I was going to be there for him, through this shit storm we'd gotten ourselves into.

That was two days ago.

Two long miserable days of constant lies and guilt rushing through me.

Sunday night I couldn't sleep at all, I tossed and turned in my crappy apartment bed, worrying.

When I'd taken Juniper out on a date the day after—the date that Nat wanted, what I wanted too—I'd told her I was going away, with Christopher, to ship electronics.

I was surprised I could even hold a straight face when I said it, without blabbering and falling to her knees.

Juniper wasn't dumb, she was one of the smartest individuals I had ever met. But she trusted me, she trusted me so much that she couldn't see a lie, and that left me hurting even more.

I was going to break her apart, I could feel it rumbling in the earth, the lies coming through and smacking me in the face, the harsh reality of being a fool.

I tried hard to change the subject Monday night, I was lost in her eyes, yes. But that harsh bite at the back of my head, constantly reminding me of my awfulness was strong, irritating and pressured.

I lost myself in her touch, her kiss and the sounds that left her mouth when we made love. I felt the anxiety and tenseness of my bones ease, only for a moment.

I was angry at myself, I didn't deserve someone like Juniper, I was a lying piece of garbage.

I did my best to live in the moment last night, there with her. With her arms around me, the feel of her skin and heat.

I lingered in that plane of existence, and nowhere else.

I was in love with this girl, so in love that I was ready to take a bullet for her.

Juniper told me the harsh reality of not loving myself.

She explained how loving yourself was important, that putting yourself aside for those who wouldn't was a mistake.

Of course, I would put myself aside for her any day, but she thought I was smart enough to know when and where, smart enough to be responsible about it.

She trusted me, and joining the Fire Jackals definitely betrayed that trust .

I'd be miserable, and I told her I would listen.

But here I was, on a bus west, to meet up with two crazy Fire Jackal members and my nervous friend Christopher.

I swallowed and leaned my head back, touching the necklace around my neck.

It felt heavy.

As if it held all my responsibilities, my maturity and guilt.

It burned.

The bus jolted along the freeway concrete road, making my elbow bump to and from the window lining. I swallowed, glancing towards my destination.

For now, in the spot that I sat in, I relaxed.

I closed my eyes, and thought of Juniper. I thought of her smile, and her hands around me. I had to think of the positive, I needed to escape the negative.

I had to, before I lost myself.

§

The town of Newton was glowing in sunshine by the time I arrived. I wasn't happy with this weather, all the crappy snow days just had to be before I became a member of the Fire Jackals.

I stepped off the bus and inhaled that fresh air, it pinched my nostrils.

Manny set our meeting place up just a few blocks away, and the city was already bustling. I saw elderly shopping with their grandchildren, couples holding hands at cafes. It seemed like a completely normal day, for them at least.

I sniffled and held my bag close, listening to the sounds surrounding me.

I heard dogs barking, chatter and birds, almost like a dream.

I was used to honking and yelling, thick Boston accents around my apartment, the smell of weed and alcohol.

Newton was stylish.

I wrapped the strap of my bag around my shoulder, walking forwards.

Even as I made my way towards our meeting place, I felt uneasy. This was so weird, stepping through a pretty town with the weight of the world upon my shoulders.

I wondered for a moment if Juniper would like it here. Would she hold my hand and sway it around? Hold my arm tight and examine the shop windows when we passed them?

I sighed, everything sounded wonderful when Juniper was involved.

I turned the street corner and continued up north. I made no eye contact with salesmen as I passed, not into the eyes of women who smiled my way, or children who giggled.

I kept to myself.

For the past hour on the bus, I continuously thought about last night, tried to enjoy the thought of Juniper's touch.

But God, the guilt was so strong, it was overwhelming.

With one more turn, I saw a familiar black van, it stood out.

Jeeze, they could have borrowed a nicer car, something that didn't have 'we're shipping drugs' written all over it.

If I thought Christopher was nervous on Sunday night, he looked like a complete mess today. He was leaning against the boot of the van, biting his nails harshly, and when he saw me, he grimaced. Manny cheered and raised his fist towards me, he was wearing the same clothes I'd met him in, maybe it's all he owned.

Crocker reacted to Manny's knock on the car window, and pulled himself from the driver's seat, grinning towards me.

'Hey guys,' I eased. 'Ready to hit the road?'

I wanted to sound somewhat positive, even though I felt like bolting.

This afternoon I was tempted to make a no show, but they knew my face.

I'd be dead by nightfall.

Christopher cleared his throat loudly, made no eye contact with me, and turned to step into the van. I glanced to Manny, and he smiled sheepishly, shrugging his shoulders.

'What's with him?' I questioned. 'Seems a little more on edge than usual.'

'He's a nutcase,' Crocker laughed. 'He's lost it.'

I waved Crocker's comment off, if anyone was a nutcase here, it was him. Manny examined me for a moment, and nodded once.

'Pack the necessities?' he grinned. 'As in, the necessity.'

I nervously glanced around, only a few people here and there, laughing at cafes and restaurants. We were parked on the side of a church, probably Crocker's idea of a bad joke.

Manny was talking about my gun; a new weapon I'd acquired the night before my date with Juniper. Which meant that last night I was lugging around a pistol and a strap on before arriving at Boston University.

I cleared my throat and nodded slowly, patting my duffel bag.

'Yep,' I muttered. 'She's here.'

'Great!' Manny smirked, teeth yellow. 'You might need it.'

I hoped not.

Before I entered the van, I took one more refreshing breath of air. Letting the relaxing sounds around me sink in, the church bells, wind in the trees.

When I sat down next to Christopher, the sounds vanished, all that lingered was awful silence.

Crocker yawned loudly and started the engine, burping loudly before he grappled at his beer. Drinking and driving? I'd be dead before we reached Hartford.

'Dude are you seriously–'

'It's diet, beer,' Crocker growled over me. 'Leave me alone, shithead.'

I gritted my teeth and buckled up, tightly.

'First stop is...' Manny grabbed at his phone, and snickered. 'Framingham, gotta hand some stuff over there first.'

I was confused, just slightly.

'So we're not going straight to Hartford?' I asked. 'Won't we be short for time?'

Crocker spat outside his window, and I nauseously watched it splatter against the outside of my window.

'Nah, new plans,' he chewed loudly. 'Got a few lil pit stops.'

I wasn't happy to hear that, at all. I wanted this whole plan to be over and done with, I was so close to opening the door and rolling against the road.

It would probably be less pain then the look of Juniper's distraught face, when I arrived home at a later date.

Christopher had his headphones in, and I tried to catch his attention, but his eyes were wide, on the road ahead of him.

I had to get through to him somehow, maybe he was just trying to stay awake, he was third in line to drive.

I was fourth, thankfully.

The meeting in Framingham was annoyingly long, and we had to sneak around a huge abandoned plaza, because police were patrolling the whole place.

When I stepped foot into the wobbling old hotel, I could see the asbestos in the roof, and the rotting wood left my stomach queasy.

But we found the right place, right down in the basement.

Christopher was the one to hand over three bags of cocaine and psycho, and the money returned looked brilliant.

There had to be at least five thousand dollars in that bundle, I wished I could take it and speed out, kick Crocker in the balls too.

But I kept my mouth shut, just as Christopher did.

By late afternoon, Manny parked the van outside Shrewsbury mall and I was thankful to find that I could wait this one out.

But I had a job as well, I had to watch the van.

Crocker told me that if anyone came up to me, and questioned my business? I'd have to knock them out, so we could deal with them later.

I was shocked to hear his words, but he pinned my collar with two pointy fingers, and told me he'd lay a bullet into its very spot if I got caught.

I hadn't felt that fear in a long time, but his eyes were serious, dark and murderous.

This was no game, not at all.

I wasn't used to being a scaredy cat, but when the other three left, I felt like crouching on the concrete gravel and sobbing.

I'd only texted Juniper twice in five hours; I'd told her I was safe and sound and she'd replied with a short thanks. I'd panicked, afraid she was mad at me.

I sat there, by the front wheel of the van and typed away slowly, keeping my eyes peeled ahead and on each sides.

It was a quiet day at the mall, which made it even freakier.

I was always awaiting a bullet to lodge into my leg, or a cop to catch me off guard. It was a life or death situation, every fucking second, now that I was a Fire Jackal.

We hit the nearest hotel in Worcester at around eleven at night. I was a little relieved to know there was no drug dealing business for the rest of the night.

Christopher parked, took a deep breath and glanced to Crocker, who smiled.

'Well, we rest for the night,' he sniffled. 'And then off to business tomorrow morning, as per usual.'

'Morning?' Manny bit back from the passenger seat. 'You? Getting your ass out of bed before ten in the morning?'

Crocker leaned forward to grab the other by the neck, and they blasted into laughter. I couldn't perk a smile at all, not with these guys. Instead, I followed Christopher out.

I grabbed my bag quickly, but Crocker took it and grinned again. 'I got it, newbie.'

I eased my eyes, and pocketed my hands. 'Okay, thanks.'

Crocker threw the bag to Manny, who caught it and shoved it in the boot, aside the rest of the drugs.

'We should move the car somewhere else,' he mumbled. 'I'll drive it around back, Crocker come on.'

Crocker groaned and raced into the front seat, pushing Christopher aside as he did so. I caught the guy before he stumbled, but he flinched by my touch, instantly.

While the other two drove off, I turned to my friend, I was alright with calling him that.

He wasn't looking my way, instead he chewed his gum roughly and kicked his sneakers against the grit below him.

I sniffled gently, the hotel looked warm enough, big windowed apartments with neon lights. It was probably way better than my home back in Boston.

'You're awfully quiet,' I muttered, patting Christopher against the back. 'Kinda freaking me out.'

'I–I'm fine.' Christopher replied. 'I'm just tired.'

I saw his eyes, dark heavy bags held along the bottom of each. I could feel the exhaustion linger on his body, his whole persona was fidgety.

I glanced towards the vending machines against the outside shed, and had an idea.

'Hey, hang on,' I mumbled, grabbing for my wallet in my back pocket. 'Don't go anywhere.'

He didn't respond, so I took that as an okay, and made my way towards the Zoom Cola machines. They were red and awfully bright tonight, I couldn't even focus on the pricing, so I just shoved my last ten-dollar note in the money receiver.

I felt pretty generous, so I pressed in two Zoom Cola Quantum's, the pricy stuff. Four dollars a pop, I was loaded.

I chuckled to my awful mind joke, grabbing hold of the ice-cold red bottles as they fell. I hadn't tasted a fresh Quantum in ages, I was a little excited to say the least.

Christopher looked as if he was about to bolt, I felt like I was approaching a scared cat. He was hunched, his eyes set on the ground still.

Something was bothering him.

I cleared my throat when I reached his side, glancing around for anyone else.

Oddly enough, nobody was out this late, not even on the freeway alongside, it was empty.

I handed him a drink, and it took him a few seconds to take it.

'It's fine dude,' I coaxed. 'Just take it.'

He shook his head, but I pushed the bottle into his grotty brown t-shirt. 'Take it, Christopher.'

Christopher looked into my eyes, and I nodded again. 'Don't worry, dude.'

I found a spare picnic table, and sat alongside the seat. Christopher sat opposite me, and clicked the pop open.

We didn't speak, not just yet. I was interested in the stars above, the faint sirens in the distance. I actually felt a little relaxed.

The heavy guilt was still hazy in my chest, like a sharp point. So, I breathed steadily, inhaling and exhaling loudly.

'Christopher?' I asked.

He didn't respond, so I continued.

'I never saw myself doing this, Juniper's going to kill me.'

I smiled weakly, easing my eyebrows his way. He was sliding his fingers to and from the wet bottles edge.

'I'm sure Reedy is having a better time in Maine, hey?' I asked.

No response.

I shrugged my shoulders, took a sip and bit back the awkwardness. The taste wasn't as good as I hoped, it was flat and fell down my throat like knives.

The guilt was lingering there too.

'I didn't want to do this,' I admitted, the words fell from my lips. 'I just...'

Christopher was looking at me now, his eyes weak.

I gritted my teeth, and played with the strings of Juniper's hoodie. It still smelled like her, and I found myself lifting the collar to my nose, to feel her presence throughout the day.

'I'm not here for me,' I said. 'I'm here for someone else.'

I let my eyes trail off into the distance, I was doubting as well as giving myself a lecture.

'I fucked up,' I groaned. 'I shouldn't be here; I shouldn't have joined this group. I wasn't thinking straight, and now look what we're doing.'

I glanced to Christopher, and he nodded weakly. 'Yeah.'

'Why are you here?' I asked sternly. 'Tell me what's going on.'

I leaned forward, the bottle of pop between my hands. Christopher was shivering, and he seemed hesitant. But I edged closer, patting his nervous hand.

'Christopher, you're bothered by something,' I said calmly. 'I know you're a good guy, so just talk to me.'

I saw his eyes change then, a faint realisation rushing into his senses. I think I was the only one who had said that to him in a while, because he looked a scared little boy, about to cry.

'R–Rayne,' he grimaced, shaking his head. 'I–I can't.'

'Yes,' I answered. 'You can, tell me why you're here, then after we can bail, get away from it all!'

I made sure Crocker and Manny weren't around, and continued.

'If we just finish this job, we'll be free right?'

'Maybe you, but not me.'

I paused, and leaned back, my head eased.

Christopher grimaced and took a deep sip, his fingers shivered.

I wanted to know more, I needed to open his brain and pick at it, it didn't make any sense to me.

'Christopher,' I started. 'There's a lot I have to tell you.'

I was opening up too easily, I couldn't look at Christopher and think he was a Fire Jackal, the guy was too sincere.

If a boy who'd rushed to my girlfriend's side, and asked for self-confidence tips was an eager Fire Jackal? Then the kids at the preschool down my street were murderers.

I breathed in deeply before I spoke, and kept a clear eye out for the other two. I asked Christopher to keep it a secret, and he nodded to that.

I could trust him; I knew that much. Christopher wasn't happy being a Fire Jackal, he wanted out.

So I told him, about Juniper and Nat, Arty too. About our adventures, if you'd call them that.

He reacted only to a few things I said, but he looked as if he was about to pop, and I watched him swallow deeply.

'I...' Christopher croaked. 'I got involved with them before all that.'

'What do you mean?'

'I mean, I needed something to numb the pain.'

I froze, and itched the bridge of my nose. 'Pain?'

Christopher grabbed at his head and sniffled, I saw his eyes flutter, really fast.

'I'm pretty messed up, if you can't tell.'

'Well I wouldn't say messed up....'

'I'm messed up Rayne, I've got anxiety, depression, OCD the whole fucking bunch.'

His voice was a soft hum, he was disappointed in himself and it hurt to hear. I'd doubted myself as a human being for a long time, I never thought I was good enough.

Christopher and I were alike.

Not so much in the OCD area, nor the harsh amount of crippling anxiety he described to me. But he and I shared a mutual problem, we both doubted ourselves.

It'd only been twenty minutes, but Manny and Crocker hadn't returned, they were probably drinking.

'I needed something to ease it...' Christopher sniffled, he sounded ashamed. 'I needed drugs, and these guys had them.'

'Crocker and Manny?' I asked.

He nodded, then smiled weakly, a pained grin. 'Now I'm stuck with them.'

I felt bad for him, really bad.

'So I stopped doing drugs, I couldn't deal with them anymore,' he explained, squeezing his fingers to the rough table edge.

The wind picked up around us both, and I shivered under its breeze.

'I thought I could get away, but I was stuck… I'm still stuck.'

Christopher held his head between his hands, elbows locked. 'I fucked up, too.'

I wanted to reach for his arm, pat it and tell him everything would be okay, but this had clearly been going on for a long time.

Longer than our new unpolished friendship.

He breathed in harshly, and glanced up to me, eyes wide. 'I have a little brother; I love him a lot.'

I nodded, listened to him, I didn't speak.

'He was upset, that I was—he would always make sure I was okay…' Christopher was on the verge of tears. 'And I told him I'd stop coming home late, told him I'd get better.'

He paused, his eyebrows furrowing. 'But I just, fell deeper into his clutches…'

'His?' I asked, sternly.

I was awaiting his response, and he seemed to bite back his words. I felt my heart thump in my chest, and I couldn't stand being on the edge now.

'Christopher!' I muttered, smacking my hand against his. 'You mean Pebbles?'

He bit his bottom lip and shook his head, constantly now, like a mad man. I shook mine too, and watched his every move.

'No…no.' he started to mumble. 'No, no.'

'W-What?' I asked, shaking his arm. 'Tell me, Christopher!'

I saw his eyes water, his face pulled in distraught. I began to rise, as his eyes focused behind me.

'I think he's said too much, to be completely honest.'

Manny's voice was cold; he was closer then I'd expected. I felt a gasp leave my parted lips as I was hitched around the neck and thrown back, against the rough pavement.

Everything was a blur then, but the pain was unreal.

I felt legs pin me down, fists against my face. I tried my absolute hardest to fight back, but his knuckles were cold, harsh, made of brass.

I growled and pushed upwards, and he leered over me, eyes wide and manic. I coughed when his fist interlocked with my jaw, the metal splitting my lip.

Oh fuck, what the hell was happening?

I couldn't process any of it, all I could see was the rage of another human being, upon me.

After seconds of constant beating, I swallowed loudly when he lifted me. I gritted my teeth to him, but he only sneered at my face and threw me back down.

The force left me groaning, he was heavy against my body now.

I was panicking, I tried to think of something positive, something, anything.

I felt the knock of a boot against my head from behind me, and I glanced up towards Crocker. He was blurry and splotchy due to my consciousness fading, but he held a white syringe in his hands.

'Don't worry,' he coaxed, leaning close to my face. 'This'll only pinch...'

I tried to muffle my scream as the needle was injected, I couldn't pinpoint exactly where, but I could definitely feel it throughout my whole body.

My yell turned to an awful wail, and my eyesight instantly turned foggy. My heartbeat was slow, and my pulse followed its every move.

I saw only Christopher now, as he leant over and sadly grimaced. I couldn't understand, but I maintained eye contact.

Crocker sighed deeply, and huffed once. 'Well, better get her out of here.'

I watched the world around me wobble to and from, the three of them had become jelly in my peripheral.

Manny grinned and leant over my face, giving me a sympathetic grin.

'Once a Fire Jackal?' he mumbled, tapping me across the nose. 'Always a Fire Jackal.'

I finally closed my eyes, Manny and Crocker's voices becoming soft hums, rumbling in my ears.

Juniper, please be the one to wake me up.

Chapter Twenty-Two

RAYNE

Today was wonderful.

There wasn't a cloud in the sky, and that was something absolutely crazy for Boston. Boston was always muggy and wet with a cold thatbit at your skin with sharpness. I was so used to walking to South Station with a cold shiver down my spine. I was terrified of what would attack me in the night, but even terrified of what I could experience in daytime.

It'd only been two months, I met Juniper in January, and here I was in February, in her home.

Surrounded by the people I cared about, with not a care in the world.

I was sitting on Juniper's father's recliner, with a big smile on my lips. Arty was playing video games with Nat on the couch beside me. Though Nat stood proudly, she was standing and she looked so goddamn happy about it, she could bend her back as far as she could with no strain at all.

She stood in jeans and a loose T-shirt, she wore my red jacket, and flashed me the biggest grin she could. I winked back; Nat was ever so grateful to be able to wear my almighty jacket, Juniper even admitted to being a little jealous.

I glanced towards Christopher and Reedy, who were currently in a heated discussion with Juniper's father. Mr Bridges was tall, taller than his daughters. He had this calm look about him, being a man in his forties, he'd aged pretty well.

He was covered in freckles, brown hair tough and rough. He was big, and muscled, but he was a huge teddy bear.

He grabbed Christopher with a laugh, showing him his baseball card collection against the wall, which was framed and dusted.

Juniper told me he was awfully careful with his memorabilia, a little too careful.

I saw Christopher smile, and that was pretty important. The boy was hardly talkative, and was always shaking. But here he was, grinning like a complete dork, with Reedy by his side. I noticed he and Reedy were inseparable friends, just as Juniper and I were.

I tore my eyes away and brought my glass of Zoom Quantum to my lips. The taste was savoured, as it dribbled down my sore throat, I wondered why my skin was heated and felt irritated. I sniffed and continued to sit comfortably, my head pressed into the leather backing behind me, I felt my eyes flutter.

I was happy here, in this little Somerville home with the people I cared about, surrounded by good food and drinks.

Arty even gave me the thumbs up, which meant a great deal. She and I weren't as close as I hoped, but she was a powerful friend, and having her around was a little reassuring in awful moments. Awful moments that Juniper and I had caught ourselves in, filled with guns and ugly Fire Jackal members. I took a deep breath, glancing towards my girlfriend. She was perky today, and passed her father with a smirk, he tried pulling her into conversation, but she slipped from his grasp and held her drink tight. I chuckled when she pouted and told her father he had to pull his head out of the sport, jokingly of course. But he responded with a laugh, a big hearty laugh that shook the house walls. It was brilliant, and everyone reacted to it, chuckling to themselves.

Juniper was embarrassed to say the least, she groaned and stepped towards me. I popped my drink down and welcomed her with open arms.

I was in awe of her beauty again, it was awfully sappy of me, but I focused on the smaller things. Apart from her gorgeous legs and slim waist, I focused on the way her shirt hugged her body comfortably, or the way her hair draped over her collar. I wished to touch her, hold her tight and close my eyes, let the worry and angst drift from my body.

I loved that moment, oh, how addictive it was. To feel all that anxiety, escape my aching bones, slither down my veins and slip from my fingertips.

Juniper smiled, stepped between my legs and finally sat upon my knee. I held her waist and glanced up, I think she enjoyed knowing she was just a tad taller than me.

I let her coaxing touch wander, her left hand took my shoulder, as the fingers of her right brushed my hair from my face.

I was aware of the others, but they kept to themselves, so Juniper and I could lose ourselves in our own movements.

I sniffled and locked eyes with her, calmly. She was absolutely beautiful, I'd begun to doubt myself, wonder if I was good enough for her.

I froze up to that nagging anxiety, and leaned forward, pressing my forehead to her collar. Juniper kept her hands around my neck, fingers running down my back.

Ugh, it felt unbelievable. How could the touch of another leave me so breathless, so calm and content?

'You should wake up, Red,' Juniper muttered. 'Okay?'

I paused, what was she on about?

I leaned up, and caught her eyes again, giving her one confused smile. 'What?'

Juniper sighed gently, and pressed her index finger underneath my chin, I swallowed.

'You asked me to wake you up, right?' she asked. 'So, wake up.'

Her words were gentle, coaxing and calm, but the more she repeated her words, the more I panicked.

I froze, even when Juniper leaned forward, close to my lips.

'Wake up, Rayne,' she whispered.

§

I did wake up, but I wished I hadn't.

The first thing I felt, was my neck. It was painful, ached and creaked with every tiny movement I made. My head was lowered, low to my lap, it was the first thing I saw. I eased my eyes to bloody and ripped jeans, the seams at the knees open and cut. I'd been dragged.

I swallowed loudly, my lips were cracked and dehydrated. There was a throbbing in every nerve, the chattering of my teeth had begun. I struggled, but I couldn't move, no, not one part of my body except for my upper torso and a portion of my legs.

The feeling was odd, a lucid wavering of my head and motion, I was still foggy. I tried to recap when my head twitched upwards, very slowly because the blood was still rushing.

I focused on the sounds around me, before I examined my surroundings. It was quiet, but I heard dripping, tinkering of metal against metal. The sounds echoed, all around me, empty.

I blinked tiredly, every flutter was sore and singed.

I furrowed my brow, flexing my pained jaw.

The images faded to and from, like the flickering of television channels. I remember seeing Christopher, he was smiling at first, but then he was crying.

Why was he crying?

He was telling me about his brother, his drug addiction, he was opening up. It's all I wanted, I wanted people to open up to me, see that I was worth trusting. But then what happened next?

Oh, Crocker, and Manny.

I groaned from the bottom of my throat, remembering the way they grinned, the pain and struggle they inflicted on me.

The smaller details were spared, but I couldn't forget the rage in Manny's eyes. They were blinded, and I was his target.

I eased my own eyes from the light, it was so bright where I sat, and every time I tried to move, my legs wouldn't cooperate.

After I had successfully lifted my torso, I glanced downwards. My legs were tied, bandaged with old computer cords and rope, wrapped around the feet of the wooden chair I sat on.

I swallowed, my heart had begun its frightful dance, stuttering and reaching for my throat. I struggled with my hands, but they were tied too, behind the chair head. The more I woke to my senses, the more I panicked.

I gritted my teeth, glancing to and from my elbows. Any movement hurt like an absolute bitch, I don't think I'd ever been in such pain in my whole entire life.

'Fuck...' I whispered lowly. 'Fuck, fuck...'

My voice was hoarse, I hardly recognised it for a moment. It was shrill and high, and echoed along the metal walls surrounding me.

I breathed shakily, and finally examined where I sat. It was dark, even when the lights above me flickered and jolted with every blow of the wind. I eased my eyes from the painful scorch, dust fluttered to my feet, the smell was awful.

I swallowed again, trying to savour any slither of saliva in my mouth, but nothing was helping my aching throat. Nothing would sooth it when my spit was mixed with blood.

I paced myself and glanced to my right. In the corners of this warehouse stood old machinery. On the floor, dust and broken rubble. The walls were rotting; I was waiting for this whole entire building to come crashing down.

It was dark, looming and frightening.

Oh god.

I struggled again, the wooden chair scuffing against the concrete below me.

Where the fuck was I? what the hell was going on? And what the fuck was that awful pain in my arm?

I tried to glance behind, try to pinpoint the exact location of its stinging. But my neck, it hurt so much.

I groaned gently, leaning forward to breathe shakily.

I was scared.

I felt my whole face, it was convulsing and throbbing. Manny did a number on me, I didn't need to see my reflection to know that.

The pain was enough.

Manny, Crocker and even Christopher.

Where did they go? And why was I tied up in some abandoned warehouse?

I tried to figure it out, in my already thumping head. I couldn't understand, why would Christopher turn on me like that? I thought he was a friend.

I wouldn't let my own anger consume me, for I knew the truth.

He was a friend.

I knew, the moment I was ripped from my seat and beaten, it wasn't something Christopher wanted.

I could see the pain in his eyes, he didn't want any of this, and I didn't either.

There was more human in that boy then Manny and Crocker, he was being used.

I furrowed my brow again, sniffing deeply. The mucus was rising now, and I had to spit forward. My breath was shaky, there was way too much blood in that hunk against the dirty floor.

I wouldn't cry, not yet.

I felt all my emotions crash into each other, fear, sadness, anger. A bad mix, a really bad mix.

I inhaled again, hissing from the stinging sensation above my eye. I tried focusing on what was around me again, even if it left a deeper hole in my gut.

To my right stood a surgical tray stand, a grotty, dirty and wobbled metal object. My breath was fastening when I saw the objects sprawled along it, tweezers, scissors and plyers, the whole fucking set up had tools of destruction written all over it. I swallowed, eyes adjusting when I saw something completely different. Next to one dirty canister was a wad of bloody tissues, a tattoo pen lay beside it.

Fresh ink poured from its tip, I knew I'd been the canvas to its disgusting touch.

I groaned and eased my eyes, leaning my head back against the wooden chair backing. I felt my teeth chatter, the fear was taking over fast.

I wasn't used to this feeling.

The last time I felt unimaginable fear, was back with Juniper, when we nearly lost ourselves to one dumb Fire Jackals member.

But this was different, I was vulnerable, tied up and beaten. I closed my eyes tightly, and tried to not jump at every sound I heard.

Oh god, Rayne what are you doing?

What the fuck are you doing?

You're sitting here, you're stuck and feeling sorry for yourself.

You've left the loving arms of a girl who would tear the sky down for you, and yet you're here, doing this.

I swallowed loudly again, heaving a sob.

I'd made a fool of myself, trying to play hero. And I was stuck in a big pile of gunk.

Now the realisation was hitting me hard, taking me by the throat and shaking.

I furiously struggled now, yelling as if to gain more power in my tugs. Juniper's necklace jingled when I pulled, it was still heavy, it bared all my regrets.

'Fuck!' I cried, tensing my wrists in their bounds. 'Fucking, fuck!'

'Now, now!'

I flinched from that response, and whipped my head aside.

Walking forwards, with a big old grin on his face, was Manny.

I focused on the crowbar in his right hand, he spun it and clenched it tight. If I thought the fear was rising before? Now it was all that drove me.

'You're making a mess,' he chuckled, pointing towards my bloody surroundings. I eased my eyes to him, I had to seem somewhat tough.

'What the fuck is going on?' I asked, my voice low. 'Where the fuck is Christopher?'

He sighed as he passed me, tinkering with the objects along the tray. I breathed shallowly, and listened to him scoff at the name I spoke. The wind was picking up outside, shaking the walls and windows.

'Christopher...' he grumbled, eyebrows sarcastic. 'Christopher, Christopher...'

He turned to me, and stood close.

'Christopher!'

I didn't expect the blunt end of the crowbar, as Manny corked me right in the gut with it. It sunk deep into my flesh, and I widened my eyes in response. The yell that left my mouth was a mixture of things, a groan and cough, I could feel the blood rise in my temples.

He pulled a face as he leaned back and watched me splutter to my feet.

Aside the stinging pain, I felt my anger rise now, alongside with my fear.

'It's always about Christopher...' Manny grumbled. 'Little fucker.'

I glanced up, breathing hollowly.

He stood still for a moment, looking me deep in the eyes. I couldn't lift myself properly, without the aching, so I sat hunched.

But I didn't dare speak.

Not after that.

Manny sniffled once more, and shrugged his shoulders.

'He's around, but he's a lost cause that one,' he rambled. 'He doesn't know when to stop, saying too much...'

I listened to him continue, even though I ignored most of it, to focus on my own pain. But Manny seemed so cool and collected, like he'd done this plenty of times before.

I watched him pick the wrench up, examine it for a moment and then chuckle.

'Hm,' he mumbled. 'Yeah, Christopher is a mess.'

I gritted my teeth, struggling once more. 'Why the fuck are you doing this?'

My words were muttered, quiet, I was afraid to speak too loud.

'Because!' he yelled, throwing his hands up. 'You know too much now.'

I wanted to deny that, say I knew nothing.

But what did he mean exactly? With whom?

'You've seen what we do, you've been sneaking around us for weeks now.' Manny scoffed, sticking a finger my way.

I tensed up, he knew?

How?

'I–I don't know what you're talking about,' I muttered.

Manny pulled a face, and waved my words off, scoffing once again.

'I know what I'm talking about,' he replied, fiddling with the wrench again. 'And Pebbles needs you gone, as soon as possible.'

I shivered to that name, remembering just how close I was to finding out his identity. Christopher seemed to know, he was biting back the truth.

I was right about this job; I would find out who Pebbles was.

Before I was brutally murdered.

I felt my stomach reel, so I tensed and shakily huffed. Manny laughed and stepped closer, grabbing at my chin. I flinched from his touch, shaking my away.

'Don't fucking touch me,' I spat.

'Oh, fierce,' he replied, patting my jaw. 'But you're still just a woman.'

Oh man, if I wasn't tied up, I'd beat the absolute shit out of this guy. There was nothing worse, then being looked down upon by a man.

Especially one like Manny.

Hey, I was a fool.

I believed him and Crocker too to be somewhat, bearable.

But I was ridiculous to think that the Fire Jackals were a clan to be trusted.

But did I trust them? Or was I fool to think I was able to swindle my way into their private archives?

'You see,' Manny began. 'Us Fire Jackals aren't stupid.'

'Really?' I replied, snarky.

I was still frightened, but boy was the anger rising.

Manny paused and chuckled to himself, clicking his neck to both shoulders. He sighed and stepped forward, swinging the wrench around his index finger.

I watched it, I focused on every motion.

'You really think Pebbles, is that stupid?' he asked me. 'He's one hell of a guy, close to the big boss, all that.'

'He seems like a pussy.'

'Nope, just a smart, loyal, guy.'

'Aw,' I sympathetically said, giving Manny my biggest smoulder. 'You're in love.'

He laughed, his eyes sweet for a moment. But they quickly turned fierce, and he threw the wrench down, smacking me right in the shoulder.

The heat was unbearable, and I yelled loudly. I could feel myself fail, numbness wavering over the punching stinging.

I flinched, struggled in my seat and glanced to my bleeding right shoulder.

I could hear Manny's heavy breaths, mixed with chuckles and cusses. He was enjoying this, inflicting pain on another human being gave him pleasure.

What a sick bastard.

'You should watch your mouth,' he snapped. 'I won't hold back, no matter how much Christopher tells me to.'

I focused on his words, as they echoed off each wall and rusty metal slither. I was in so much pain, so close to closing my eyes, blacking out.

That dream world didn't sound so bad, Juniper was there, Arty and Nat.

I felt my eyes moisten, but I had to be tough, I needed to get out of this alive.

That, or have some sort of reasoning to die, so Juniper could pick up from where I left off.

'You and that Bridges girl, have been nothing but a fucking issue,' Manny gritted. 'At first we let you twerps sneak around; Pebbles knew you were after the truth.'

You're damn right we were, I felt like yelling.

Juniper wasn't going to give up on Nat, and someone was willing to give us information, that would aid the search, we had to find out who and why.

I was starting to really understand why Juniper fought me so hard, fought against my worries, she was always on the edge.

Of course she wanted the truth, and I was so stubborn to do the same.

But now, where I sat, tied and bleeding.

I felt so much more.

The truth was just a few words away, I could find out, I had to.

'Who the fuck is he?' I ordered. 'Who the fuck is Pebbles?'

'You really think I'll tell you?' Manny laughed, pulling a cigarette from his back pocket. 'Kids.'

I watched him light it, roughly with a match. Under his white T-shirt was his gun, tightly in in the back of his pants.

I hoped to God he wouldn't take that out next.

I controlled my breathing, flexing my wrists around tight bounds. I'd already tried lifting my whole entire body weight, like they did in the movies.

But I was as stiff as ever, the pain was too furious.

Manny whistled to himself and touched the tattoo pen.

'I'm not telling you shit,' he started. 'Pebbles fucked up, yeah.'

He paused and took a suck from his cigarette, blowing. 'Moron hit the Bridges kid, got too cocky, ended up messing up big plans.'

I wanted to know what these plans were, but it was hard to speak. The wrench knocked a lot from me. I realised Manny was being cocky himself, he was sharing a bit too much.

Not that I was complaining.

'The head honcho was pissed off, and Pebbles looked like an absolute moron, I say he deserved it, just this once.'

'He hit a girl.'

'Eh, shit happens,' Manny turned to me, and smiled. 'But, he got careless, and look where we are.'

I eased my eyes to him, and he grinned.

'Bridges' girlfriend, tied up and vulnerable...' he sighed and leant forward, pointing the wrench at me. 'What a shame.'

'Bite me, asshole,' I grimaced. 'We're close, we'll find out who he is.'

'You sure about that?' he asked, eyebrows raised. 'You've got guts; I'll tell you that.'

I bit the inside of my cheek, tensing forward. I was afraid to talk, but also petrified to not talk at all. All he had to do, was reach into his pants and grab his gun, lodge a bullet in my brain, and I'd never see the light of day again.

I needed to bluff.

'And the drama with the car, and all that mishap,' Manny rolled his eyes, and offered me a cigarette. But I pulled away from his fingers, pursing my lips.

It was like the devil, beating the shit out of someone then offering them a piece of candy. I wouldn't have it.

'Did you think we were that dumb?' he asked.

'A little,' I growled under my breath. 'You're not the brightest bunch...'

'Hah.' Manny sniggered, taking another puff from his cigarette. 'Honestly? Pebbles thought you and Bridges were just bluffing...'

I raised an eyebrow, though it hurt to do so, I was curious. Manny leant against the metal table, the clutter below him shifted.

'I mean, two puny girls against a big ol' gang?' he chuckled and flicked the ash from the stick between his fingers. 'It was a joke.

'Not so much now, huh?' I grinned, my teeth were bloody, I could feel it. 'You got careless too.'

He stood tall now, and grinned my way.

'Yeah, you two were sneaky for a little while,' he sniffled. 'But rats usually get caught.'

I smirked back, biting down on my cuss. This meant Pebbles was fooled, successfully fooled by a reporter in training and her busking girlfriend.

'Took him a while huh?' I asked. 'Pebbles doesn't seem that smart,'

My words were cut short, as Manny threw a punch across my face, once, twice.

I counted seven smacks, before he leaned back and caught his breath. I was groaning, loudly. I let my shoulders drop, my head fumble.

'He's a smart guy, trust me!' Manny yelled, pointing back at me. 'He just didn't expect you two to be so fucking dumb, walking into trap after trap.'

I let my mouth part, my bottom lip was split open once more, and blood dribbled down my chin. I'd bitten my tongue after his third punch, and it was aching.

I didn't like showing weakness, but I couldn't muffle my whine.

'And yet here you are,' Manny gasped, hands stretched wide. 'Falling right into Pebbles' trap.'

I sniffled and shook my head, a lot of thoughts were going through my mind, but I found myself concerned about others again.

Juniper, did that mean she was a target? She was looking for the car, that fucking car. The car that held the exact answers we needed.

I wondered if Pebbles knew, if Manny and Crocker knew.

Knew that we held the key, that we were one step ahead of them.

Manny rubbed his hand through his grotty hair, then wiped them across his pants. I saw slithers of my own blood upon his palms, I was worried, how many more scars would I have now?

'It didn't take us long to realise it was you and Bridges who snuck into our meeting a few days ago,' he paused and threw a finger my way again. 'Sneaky little fuckers.'

I got my answer.

'You thought you'd find him, didn't you?' he chuckled, his grin widening. 'You're the stupid one.'

'You sure about that?' I spat aside again, smiling back weakly. 'She's stronger than you think.'

He looked confused but waited for me to continue.

'Juniper, she'll find out who did it,' I croaked, swallowing back. 'Were close, and she'll find him. No matter what you do to me, she'll be the one victorious.'

'Well, listen to you!' Manny laughed, crouching to glare up at me. 'You're playing the hero, all for some girl.'

'No,' I answered back, leaning forward to scowl. 'For the truth. You assholes can't do this and walk away from it.'

Manny smiled, nodded once and hummed to himself. After he rose, he turned to grab another tool, the tattoo gun. I grimaced and leant back, my breath hitching.

'Oh don't worry,' he mumbled, nodding his head towards me. 'We already branded you, so.'

I felt my gut drop, my heart falter.

'What do you...' I paused and felt the sting in my arm again, in my wrist.

'So, now you're always reminded...' he popped the gun down, and wiped its dirty end with the same bundle of tissues beside it. 'You're always reminded, of being one of us.'

He paused and sniggered, crinkling his nose. 'If you make it out alive, that is.'

I swallowed and ¬controlled my breathing, I hoped Christopher would come soon, talk some sense into this maniac.

But he and Crocker were nowhere to be seen.

A big part of me worried, for Christopher.

Of course, I worried that maybe he wasn't the sweet guy I faintly knew. Maybe I was putting all my eggs in a basket, trusting someone who seemed like an innocent puppy dog.

Manny sighed and checked the time, his watch was the only expensive thing on his body. 'Hm.'

I leaned forward, and tried to shake the blood from my chin, it was irritating. But not as irritating as Manny's smug ass smile.

So my questions were answered, they knew it was Juniper and I who snuck into their meeting, they knew we had the key and they also knew I joined solely for one reason;

Not for money, not for myself, but to find Pebbles.

I breathed hollowly, and focused on Juniper's face in my mind, her smile.

But it quickly fell to a frown, disappointment.

If I was to get out of this alive, I'd have their mark, I was branded. This wasn't a tattoo I wanted.

I felt my tears well up, my bottom lip wobble. And as Manny began loading his gun, I felt my chest heave.

'Juniper,' I mumbled quietly. 'Juniper, I'm sorry...'

I was repeating my words, to myself, faint whispers that he couldn't hear over his humming. I wonder why he'd kept me alive, why they didn't just lodge a bullet right into my head. I'd thought that ever since I woke up in this goddamn place.

I wonder what death felt like, when the time came.

Would he torture me for a little while longer, drain me of all my strength, then finish the job with Crocker by his side?

Whatever was going to happen, I would think of Juniper, it'd numb the pain right?

'Hey, you've obviously had all the fun,' Crocker's voice came, so did the rustling of his footsteps.

I swallowed and glanced towards him, he was striding forward, as confident as ever.

Behind him, was Christopher.

'I leave you alone for ten minutes, and you've bruised that perfect face,' Crocker sighed, he shoved another bag beside the tray, sniffling roughly.

I didn't enjoy that compliment, at all. I cussed his way, and he chuckled, wiggling a finger my way.

'Oh, yeah she seems fierce,' he giggled.

'That's what I said.' Manny smirked.

They spoke among themselves, but my eyes were only set on Christopher. He stood, meters away from the other two, and stared right at me.

His eyes were eased, saddened and weak. Eyebrows dipped inwards, concerned and frightened. I looked at him, with utmost disappointment, and I could almost feel his heart break.

I was right about him, if he wasn't different from the others, what was stopping him from killing me?

Christopher was frozen, but he quickly breathed in.

'You guys didn't have to...' he lost his voice. 'You didn't have to mess her up that bad...'

Crocker paused, Manny did too. And they both turned to face his stuttering self. I saw the scene unfold in front of me, Manny was the first to groan and step forward.

'Do not chicken out!' he yelled, pushing into Christopher's frail chest with the end of his crowbar. 'Pebbles asked you personally to do this...'

The name drained all blood from Christopher's face. He swallowed, glanced to me and then back towards Manny.

'You wouldn't want to disappoint him, even further right?' he asked, smacking him once.

'N–no...' Christopher mumbled, stumbling on the spot.

'What?' Manny growled, pushing closer.

'No!' Christopher repeated, louder now.

'Then don't be a fuck up!' Manny snapped. 'You've already disappointed him once, being a little snitch.'

Crocker was chuckling, but Manny looked very serious, so serious that Christopher seemed to flinch under his touch. I watched him lay a hand upon Christopher' shoulder, clutching tightly with a smirk.

'You owe us, right?' he asked. 'From all those times, the good stuff.'

I breathed hollowly, coughing towards my lap. Crocker was easing forward, another syringe in his hands.

Oh, God.

'No,' I mumbled weakly, 'Don't.'

Crocker smiled, a small crinkle of a grin that sent shivers down my spine. I wanted to focus on Christopher' mumbled words, but this mad scientist was getting closer and closer.

'Don't fucking touch me!' I spat, pushing myself back. The chair made an awful screech, and my growl was heavy as he leant over me, the syringe pointed at my neck.

'C'mon, you must be tired, being so agitated,' he sighed, his breath smelt awful. 'This'll calm you down, then we can talk.'

'I don't want to talk, you lunatic.' I tried freeing a leg, to smack him in the crotch, but I was honestly stuck.

Crocker leant back, greased me off, then motioned to Manny. 'Permission?'

'Granted,' the other grumbled.

I wasn't sure what he meant, until Crocker's fist hit me fast in the face.

Over my cry, I heard Christopher whimper. The smack echoed, off the metal walls. Christ, I didn't think I could hurt one more bit, but one more smack proved otherwise.

I gritted my teeth again, my neck sore from leaning forward. My left eye hurt to open, so my right was my only source.

I watched Crocker's syringe, closely.

'Jesus, she's rough!' he laughed. 'Pebbles told us to keep her alive?'

'No,' Manny mumbled, he gave Christopher a close look. 'No, he wants her gone.'

I felt my breath hitch, my panic rise. I tried scurrying back from Crocker's smile, but he was so close, too close.

'Christopher!' I cried. 'You're better than this!'

He was still standing in my peripheral, like a lone wolf.

But I was about to die, they were finishing me off. 'Please!'

'Begging, like a dog,' Manny sighed, he took the wrench in his hands again, flipping it. 'What a surprise.'

I kept my glance on Christopher, his chest was rising and falling, body stone cold from the looks of it.

'Christopher isn't going to save you, love,' Crocker whimpered, touching my chin with his grubby hands. 'He's as fucked up as we are, drugs, booze the whole bunch.'

I escaped his grip once more, and saw Manny scoff.

'Yeah, he's just as much as a mess. Christopher used to ask for drugs, we used to give him drugs,' he continued, shrugging his shoulders. 'Simple as that.'

Crocker nodded along, leaning back to pull the sleeves of his shirt up. I saw the large tattoo on his wrist, and could only hope that mine wasn't plastered with the same mark.

'Christopher, Christopher, Christopher,' Crocker groaned. 'One of Pebbles many pets.'

'I'm not like that,' Christopher muttered. 'Don't...'

'Yeah, you are!' Manny continued, a groan escaped his lips. 'You're weak, and a traitor. Now come here, finish the job so we can go home.'

I swallowed when Crocker turned my way once more, his hand was awfully close to my face now.

'Now, just like before...' he mumbled, concentrating on the needles tip. 'This'll only pinch.'

My eyes were wide, I had to do something, fast.

With a yell, I lodged my teeth into the side of his right hand, biting roughly. I was nauseated to feel his skin break, wound open and splatter my cheek with dirty blood.

He threw his hand back, and the needle sliced my jaw, more scars.

Crocker wailed loudly, his tone high pitched. I watched him step back, hold his wounded right hand with his other.

Manny's eyes were widened, as he took his friend by the shoulders.

'Crock!' he cried, examining the gory mess.

I swallowed and loudly huffed, my chin was practically drenched in my own and Crocker's blood.

I must have looked like some sort of war child, brutally bruised and beaten. I spat whatever lingered in my mouth, and ignored Crocker's cries of despair, it only took me a few moments to realise his pinkie finger was on the floor.

I didn't even feel the bone.

I knew I was about to die, why not end my life with a mark. Manny reached for his gun, and I saw his wild eyes, just like before.

'You're fucked! You're absolutely fucked!' he yelled, teeth yellow and stained. 'Christopher was meant to do the deed, but I'm going to fucking ruin you!'

My heart was loud, even over Crocker's screams of despair. They echoed all around me, into both ears, my head was ringing.

There was a familiar sound, a clicking of a trigger. I swallowed and examined Christopher, he had his gun pointed, right at Manny's torso.

Crocker's screams had become wails, he also turned his head and focused on the sight. Christopher was still shaking, his gun wobbling to and from each side.

Manny smirked, lifted his hands and chuckled. 'Now, Now. Christopher...'

The emotion in the room had changed, and I sensed a sort of panic in Manny's voice. It wasn't completely shrill, but his gun lay in his pants, he didn't grab hold.

But I knew Christopher hadn't held a gun on anyone before, he was practically sweating from head to toe. His bottom lip wobbling.

'Christopher,' Crocker swallowed loudly, his wounded hand by his side. 'Don't be a fucking moron...'

'No more!' Christopher cried, the gun was aimed at the both of them now. 'No more.'

Manny stepped forward, laughing loudly. 'So, you're turning on your own men?'

Christopher looked guilty, but his face turned stern.

'You would turn on us, for this?' Manny pointed at me, and I swallowed in return, the awful metal taste of blood in my throat. 'You were supposed to prove your worth tonight! You were meant to change!'

'I have changed!' Christopher cried, his voice nervous. 'I'm not like you!'

'Yes, you are!' Manny patted Crocker against the shoulder, his tone was calm. 'You're exactly like us.'

I saw Christopher falter, his gun fell, but he lifted it once more.

'You were stuck, in that awful place, up here...' Manny pointed to his head, tapping once. 'You were stuck, and we got you out.'

'With drugs!' Christopher cried. 'That wasn't escaping! It made me worse! I got stuck with you guys!'

'You were achieving so much Christopher!' Crocker groaned, his eyes were lidded, sore. 'You were such good friends with Pebbles...'

Christopher flinched, and stepped forward. 'Stop it!'

'You let him down, Christopher!' Manny yelled, his voice was high, it left me jumping. 'You're going against your own!'

'I'm not!' Christopher finally snapped. 'I'm not!'

I felt bad for him, even when I was so close to death, the guy was practically having a meltdown. But Manny still couldn't reach for his gun, I wondered why.

Even if it was such a bad moment to do so, I was pondering about the smaller details of this sudden situation.

They were both holding back.

Manny growled then, and threw his hand out. 'Pebbles saw this coming, I just hoped you would change!'

'What do you mean?' Christopher sobbed, the gun wobbled once more. 'What do you fucking mean!?'

Crocker grinned softly, pointing his bloody hand at me. 'You were too soft, you feel guilty.'

'Pebbles is smarter than you think, he knew you'd back out.' Manny paused and stepped closer, I was expecting him to take the gun from Christopher' hands.

'You're fucked either way, kid,' he mumbled. 'Pebbles had this all planned out.'

Christopher' eyes were wide now, and he glanced to me, then back at the other two. There was a sudden silence, until I heard it.

Sirens.

I swallowed and felt relief, but even that disappeared. I was screwed either way too.

'Oh fuck!' Christopher cried, his hand shaking. 'No!'

'What are you going to do Christopher?' Manny asked, taking his gun out with one swift move. My breath was high now, when he pointed it my way, right in my direction.

'Are you going to end this? So, we can get out of here?' he asked, nodding his head my way. 'Or are you going to make a bigger mess?'

Christopher eased his eyes, then sobbed my way. His body was stiff, but he pulled his way towards me. I felt the room shift, when he lifted his gun towards my head.

I wasn't focusing on it, I was focusing on him.

I pleased with him, my eyes did all the talking, I couldn't move my mouth. I just expected it, I expected the black veil to cover my existence, and I'd wake up somewhere warm and comfortable. I awaited death with baited breath. I wondered about Mom and Dad for a moment, Cole and all the people I knew.

I was going to vanish.

There were two gunshots, but I didn't see the end of the tunnel.

I only saw Christopher turn, aim his gun towards both Manny and Crocker, and yell when he pulled the trigger.

Manny was down first, I watched him fall limp against the cold floor, and Crocker went pale. He glared at Christopher, his bottom lip wobbling.

But he then smirked, pointed at Christopher and laughed.

'The car is outside! You know!' he huffed, crouching to his knees. I tried my hardest not to focus on Manny's dead body, his eyes limp.

'The car's outside!' Crocker repeated, singing. 'The car's outside, and Pebbles wins!'

Christopher wasn't facing me, but I saw his shoulders drop. The car? Did he mean the car?

'Both of you weren't going to make it out of this!' Crocker yelled. 'You're both royally—'

He couldn't finish his words, because Christopher shot him too.

I cried from the sound and leaned my head back. I didn't want to see this, I couldn't process murder. I waited for my turn, but Christopher only sobbed and threw his hands out.

'Fuck!' he screamed, loud and exaggerated. 'Fuck! No!'

I opened my eyes to see him pace forward and backwards. He whimpered and touched both dead bodies with a shaky foot. He then leaned up, held his face in his hands and sobbed in desperation.

'Oh god, I shot them,' he whimpered. 'R–Rayne, I didn't mean to... I didn't want to.'

I swallowed again, catching my breath. I couldn't speak, not over the amount of noise. There were sirens, and Christopher's cries.

'C–Christopher,' I said, coughing. 'You have to tell me!'

He turned, eyes wide. The gun was by his side now, and he gripped at his hair with his left hand.

'You have to tell me who he is!' I huffed, struggling in my chair. 'You tell me who Pebbles is, and this is all over!'

He shook his head now, sobbing loudly. 'No, you're wrong!'

Christopher stepped closer, and I flinched from his cry. 'The car! The car is out there!'

I focused on his face, and asked the question. 'Did you hit Juniper's sister?'

He paused, and contemplated saying something, but he still whimpered.

'He's going to kill my family, he said if I didn't get rid of you, he'd kill my family, he'd make their lives a living hell...'

He stepped back, repeating the same lines over and over. He was completely lost, with sweat rushing from his pours, blood against his shirt and jeans, face and hands.

'He's going to kill my little brother, Rayne!' he yelled at me, his shoulders slumping. 'I tried to warn you!'

I felt my heart stop, my blood run cold. 'W–what?'

'I tried to fucking warn you two! I tried to warn you two!' he jumped up, crouched to the floor and let out another cry. 'I wanted to help! I told Juniper where to go, I told her where she could find answers! Because I wasn't allowed to tell!'

I heard pairs of footsteps echo from the hall on the left, but I was too focused on Christopher' words. He glanced towards the same direction the sound emitted from, and whimpered.

'He was too smart! He found out, he found me out,' Christopher wailed. 'I warned you! You didn't listen, why didn't you listen to me!'

I shook under his words, he was the one that texted me, that night back at Juniper's.

'He's got me, he's got me under his strings...' Christopher laughed, manic. 'He's had me this whole time...the car...'

'The car!' I yelled over his sobs. 'Did you hit her!?'

'No!' his answer was lengthened, his eyes wide towards me. 'I didn't want to leave her there! I didn't want to!'

I swallowed back my tears, the pain was excruciating and all these noises were driving me insane. I heard the voices closer, until they stopped right in the room.

There stood two cops, guns out and thrown our way. Between them, stood Detective Rodgers. He had a sore look on his face, more or so shocked to see me.

He held his own gun, and cleared his throat.

'Now, son,' he started. 'Put the gun down.'

Christopher sobbed again, and glanced to me. 'Rayne, I didn't want to leave her there. He hit her, he hit her and left her there and I wanted to go out and help, but he was angry! He was so angry!'

I widened my eyes, even if it hurt like hell, his honesty was appalling.

He was practically shaking, the gun swinging back and forth.

'Put the gun down!' the cop on the left yelled, stepping forward.

I couldn't even hear the other three, I was too focused on Christopher, as he shook and trembled.

'I was guilty! So guilty!' he stepped closer, and I heard the three react. 'I didn't want anything to do with it! He said he'd make my life a living hell if I didn't get rid of you! He knew you and Juniper were close to finding him, he knew!'

I shivered, my jaw tensed. Christopher smiled softly, and raised the gun to his temple. I felt my own sob fall from my lips.

'Christopher!' I yelled. 'Don't!'

'I'm screwed Rayne!' he laughed. 'I'm so screwed, there's no way I'm getting out of this. Even if I live, he'll rip my family to shreds...he'll hurt Simon.'

I watched his eyes well up with even more tears, even though they were already sprawling down his dirty grubby cheeks.

Christopher wasn't Pebbles, but he was right, Pebbles had him under his strings.

Christopher was just a puppet, and now here he was, guilty for a crime he didn't commit.

Framed.

Christopher turned to the cops, and looked Detective Rodgers in the eye.

The older cop looked concerned, but he was listening too.

'I didn't do it!' Christopher cried. 'I'm not Pebbles!'

'Gun down! Now!' the cop on the right called. 'You don't want to do this!'

I swallowed when Christopher looked at me once more, he grinned, a pained smile.

'I can't tell you...' he mumbled, his chest rising and falling. 'You have to understand, I can't. He'll hurt them all.'

I felt my own tears, as they welled. He stood there, a gun to his temple, with a sincere face.

'Tell Juniper, I'm so sorry.' He said, pushing the gun closer. 'Tell her I'm so sorry.'

He nodded once, and kept his smile there, before I saw his index finger twitch.

I remember hearing a gunshot, a splattering sound that left my ears shaking.

I remember hearing an awful scream, a wail of desperation and fright.

It took me just seconds, to realise it was my own cry of anguish.

Chapter Twenty-Three

JUNIPER

Tuesday was red skies and sunshine, something Boston hadn't seen in a while. I could smell the fresh air from my open window, the sound of the public as they walked along footpaths that were covered in thin layers of snow, and the blissful tune of birds as they sang at the top of their birdy little lungs.

It all sounded so swell.

But I wasn't really feeling the whole 'rejoice and wave your hands in the air'. No, I was a little upset, okay little was pushing it, I was really upset.

Rayne had left, on her job adventure, which, mind you, seemed a little suspicious.

But I trusted her, and whenever I found myself stressing I reminded myself that Rayne was an adult, and she knew that as well, she'd be careful.

Besides, I had my own job to do, even if it was super mischievous and dangerous. And as I sat in my room, lodging my nearly overdue paper, all that wandered on my mind was Rayne's handsome face. Hey, it was only natural for me to worry, right?

My girlfriend was six feett of pure power, strong and willed, with one hell of a voice. But I knew Rayne, she was a puppy dog, someone who crumbled under pressure just as much as anyone else. She was hardened, but only in certain areas, she was still working on the confidence aspect of it all.

I was fine with speaking publicly and getting along with new people—unless it's a handsome busker in South Station.

But that was a while ago; now we shared something absolutely amazing and I couldn't stand the idea of losing her.

I leaned back in my chair and sighed, my fingers slipping from the keyboard. Somewhere, surrounded by other journalism documents, was one file. A file that I'd taken a liking to, it served as a sort of diary, of my own life.

With eighteen pages, a vast majority of them consisted of my adventures with Rayne and Arty, finding the truth about my sister's attacker.

I wasn't confident with publishing it, no, not until I found that car and Pebbles.

I lost myself in my writing, made things a little too personal, but in the end it was still a story. But stories were important, they consisted of memories and feelings, something everyone cherished. I envy other journalists; they have no fears and publish the truth easily. I, on the other hand toss and turn at night at the thought of my first article even making it into the paper.

People read the news, and they wanted the truth. But some didn't, some wished to keep the veil of ignorance over their eyes.

The truth scared people, fuelled anger and a bunch of other emotions.

Was I even ready for that?

I watched the ceiling, nibbling my bottom lip gently.

I was close, so close to finding out where and who Pebbles was. But I questioned my strength, finding the truth on my own. I was a little cowardly to say the least.

I came across as a confident girl, who would kick down doors to expose those who defied the law, but God, I was just as scared.

What fuelled me, was Nat.

I couldn't wait to see her standing again, and every moment I stood tall was a moment where I wished she were instead.

It's funny how a human being can drive motivation through another, like a sharp iron stick. Whenever I found myself faltering, the thought of Nat smiling, was enough to kick me onto my feet.

I sniffled, rubbed my hands together, and leaned up. I had to find my first location, take Arty's car back to my house, then continue searching till the moon rose.

I'd already found a few car dumps here and there, but whether they had Pebbles' car was another story all together. I could be walking in and out of these dumps with nothing at all, but I had to try right?

I'd printed a few maps, circled where to start, I just had to get going.

When I stood from my desk, I turned to my empty bed. I could still feel Rayne's arms around me, her intimate glare, the lust.

Whenever I found myself thinking of last night, the biggest blush took hold of my face, burning the tips of my ears. Ugh, how did that girl do so much to me.

But there was a sense of loneliness, the type of loneliness that I felt silly about. Rayne wasn't far, just a few states away. That was nothing.

There were people, struggling with relationships in different countries, what right did I have to whinge about her vanishing for just a few days?

I sighed and stretched, quickly giving my desk a clean-up, Rayne had already picked up most of the mess she'd made earlier.

After that, my bed needed to be fixed, and boy were the images just hitting me one after the other. I felt giddy, sad and bashful at the same time.

I'd never really experienced sex like that before, it was honestly so comfortable, there was no issues.

It could definitely be because it was with Rayne, someone I trusted and felt safe around, but all my other experiences were absolute garbage.

I had to quickly avert my thoughts when I started remembering the past. There was no good in remembering what made me uncomfortable, the past was the past.

I dwelled in that motion for a while, remembering all that left me feeling worthless.

I still pined over my mother leaving, still thought about the mistakes I made years ago. And again, I'd find myself wasting precious time, on things that had already happened.

It was so important, to live in the moment. Heck, I could worry about the past, but only if I knew it had happened, and there was no way back.

Rayne's guitar stood still, leaning against my cupboard doors. It was lonely too, but it reminded me of her gorgeous voice and face, so, I didn't mind it there.

Rayne was lost without her guitar, it looked pretty damn expensive too. It may have been her most expensive item to date.

After I'd had my late breakfast, packed my bag full of notes and directions, I grabbed Arty's keys and vaulted for the door.

Before I turned the knob, I checked my back pocket, and sighed relief. It was still there, Pebbles' key, safe and sound.

It was my only lead, if I lost it? What would I even do?

I'd be lost without it, I'd have to go sneaking into more Fire Jackals meetings, maybe even get shot again.

Oh, there I go again, worrying about the future as well. It was tiring pining for the future, being stuck in the middle between what is and what could be. After I was positive that I had everything I needed, I ventured out into my dorm hallway and locked my door quickly.

As I walked down towards the parking lot, I jingled Arty's car keys in my hand. I wasnot really keen on driving the bomb, but as much as Arty loved Nat and my dad, she needed to drive her own car and do her own things.

Come to think of it, I didn't even think she had anywhere to live right now. She was always on the move, and it was understandable, seeing as she was an ex-member of the Fire Jackals.

I had to constantly remind myself that telling the judge about Arty would be a big mistake, if I ever made it to court that is.

But, if I found Pebbles, then I would see myself in that building. Not that I was excited about it.

I shivered when I hit the outside of my school building, and instantly caught sight of Arty's car, parked in the same messy place Rayne positioned it.

Of course I smiled, remembering her eagerness for me. It was rather flattering, she was lost in my eyes, and that made me feel, well, worth it.

It was an addictive feeling, something that left my heart stuttering and swirling. Rayne loved me, not only when we made love, even when she glanced over at me, I felt that overwhelming feeling of mutual want.

What a funny story, to tell those around us. When all this Pebbles-Fire Jackals mess was over. I'd start to see my friends more, hang out and have coffee.

Whenever I dragged Rayne around, I would be expecting the old; 'Oh how did you two meet?'

And just describing our ridiculous adventures, would be humorous to say the least.

Ah, I couldn't wait for moments like that. Having more time to spend with Rayne, I'd bring Nat with me too.

I had to focus on those thoughts, that was the future to look forward to, I was allowed to pine after that part of life.

Even if it wasn't real, yet.

After I was seated in Arty's car, I breathed in gently. It still smelled like cigarettes, that awful musky smell. I crinkled my nose and shoved the key in the exhaust, twisting and focusing on the engines roar. I didn't drive much, only here and there. When I was on break, I'd live with dad and Nat back home, and drive her to school and such.

I enjoyed our little drives, she'd be so grumpy about going to school, that she'd sit there pouting. I remember one summer day, she was so stressed about an upcoming test, that she burst into tears before leaving the car. Even though it was common anxiety, I couldn't stand watching my sister cry. She was a good student, she tried her absolute best and didn't take shit from the boys on the playground, or even some of the girls.

Nat said she wanted to be like me when she grew up, and although that was super adorable, I wasn't ready to watch my sister fall into the life of journalism and exposing the truth. I remember telling her she'd do great on the test, and she cried and sobbed about how she wasn't ready. So, I simply took her to the mall that day.

Dad still doesn't know, but Nat was so happy and relieved. She took the test the next day and passed it with flying colours.

I smiled as I drove towards my first circled location. It was a dump just east from South Station, it was worth a look.

I decided that focusing on Nat's happiness was the be the best, so I wouldn't falter and fall back into depths of no motivation.

With Pebbles key in my back pocket, I drove carefully and quietly. I usually loved blasting music, but right now I was too stern, too tense.

This was the first time I was exploring on my own, and I was a little frightened. The first worry was the car I was in, Fire Jackal members were everywhere on that dark Saturday night and maybe one caught a glimpse of Arty's car, in that case I was a sitting duck.

As I stopped at a red light, I kept glancing to and from my right and left, I was half expecting some movie villain with a gun pointed at me.

But an elderly woman sat on my right, and a teenage boy on my left, he wiggled his eyebrows at me, and I nervously glanced away.

Gross.

I passed the police department, and shuffled in my seat. Nick was a good helper, and he seemed to definitely care.

But I was prone to trusting everyone I met. When you do the right thing, you half expect others to do the same, right?

But that wasn't how people worked, I'd met my fair share of assholes too.

Nick was a cop, and yeah, most cops were assholes. But he was so sweet and confident about helping me, my story moved him.

I grumbled and reached for the radio, turning it on with a click. What I expected was the popular radio tunes of this month, what I received was the most awful CD music I had ever heard.

I yelped at the loud blast, of heavy metal. The light was still red, so I smacked the radio, hoping to stop its yelling.

How could Arty even like this music?

'Jesus!' I cried, hitting the off button. 'Fuck!'

The guy in the car beside me was watching, I could see him chuckling on the corner of my eye. *Yeah? Laugh it up buddy, I'll fling this CD into your engine!*

After another few smacks, I successfully turned the awful sound off, and sat in silence. I sniffled to myself, turned my head and made eye contact with my friend, who sniggered and gave me the thumbs up.

Before I mustered up the strength to give him the bird, the traffic began to move. Instead, I gave him a smug smile and drove forward, regretting my decision to be a mature human being.

I visited three junkyards and tow depots, and not one had any Fords. They were full of old dump trucks, cars with their seats all ripped up and pulled to pieces.

Most of the junk in each yard was old appliances and ping pong tables.

And the people who worked there, had no interest.

The more I drove, the more I felt useless and hopeless. The more I drove, the more I expected disappointment.

I travelled till the mid-afternoon, until I stopped at my final destination before Somerville.

When I pulled up aside Molecular Junkyard, I groaned. I could smell the awful burning rubbish already.

The junkyard was ginormous, not only that, but it smelled like burning rubber and garbage. I groaned as I walked towards the entrance, it was fenced off. I sighed and held my backpack around my right shoulder, glancing in through the gates small opening. Around piles of scrapped metal and wheels, were a few intact cars. I tried focusing on each, trying to pinpoint if any would match up to a Ford.

The more I looked, the more I expected to find the right one, but from standing all the way over here, I was literally achieving nothing.

I pursed my lips and turned to the information kiosk, I couldn't see anyone around, but I could see the no trespassing signs. I grimaced and stepped towards the desk, and quickly knocked on the window. It was grubby, dirty and slicked with oil, and I shivered.

Nothing was worse than one big smelly junkyard, with wet sloshy mud and snow.

I waited, first I was patient, but after three minutes of nothing, I groaned loudly.

'Hello?' I called through the little plastic gap. 'I need to uh, look for a...car?'

I didn't think that was the right thing to say, but it was all that left my mouth. I sniffled and lifted my fingers again, tapping once more.

Nothing, nothing, and nothing.

I sighed and shrugged my shoulders, glaring at the fence again.

Hey, I'd snuck into an abandoned building before, this would be no different, right?

Quietly and carefully, I roamed around the front once more. The gate was flimsy, as was the lock keeping me back behind it. I tinkered with it slightly, okay, I had to remember Rayne's pick locking technique.

So I fumbled with the lock once, twice, then groaned loudly. I was not a lockpick at all. I had no idea how to sneak into abandoned places, this was why I was better with a partner.

I crouched, with a big old pout on my face, before something caught my eye. It wouldn't be the safest way, but thankfully I could spot another way in.

It did require a few climbs, a few broken boxes to hold myself up. But once my feet touched the ground, I was facing each massive pile of junk. The length and size of this place was huge, but mostly full of scrap metal. It wouldn't hurt to look around, but my sights were set on the cars a few feet away.

As I walked, I kept an ear out, and an eye, in case the patrol would find a girl roaming around a junkyard. I wouldn't know what to say, and Nick would definitely scold me for breaking the rules.

But at this point, I honestly didn't care.

I was dead set on finding the truth.

It was my only excuse.

I rushed towards the cars, parked rather messily next to each other. A few trucks lay lopsided, even a neat old convertible.

Man, I missed driving, even sitting in Arty's car was nice.

I felt and heard the slish slosh of puddles below me, and nearly lost my balance a few times. I had to hold my hat to my head before it fell into a puddle the size of a kiddy pool.

The weather was no help; I was going to smell for weeks.

After I finally reached the cars, I examined their fronts and backs for any indication of them being the one I was after.

I checked hoods, wheels, and finally every front to see if it matched the key in my back pock et. I could feel my frown strengthen, my shoulders slump with every upsetting realisation that none of these machines affiliated at all.

I was disappointed.

The wind kicked up, blowing that awful smell of oil and dirt my way, and I held my hat once more. Ever since I was young, if nothing really went my way, or I didn't find the answers immediately, I was a pouting ball of anger.

I knew it wasn't easy, to find a lone car over all of Boston. I knew that my questions weren't going to be answered with a click of my fingers.

'But it would be nice if one of you assholes,' I paused my verbal thinking, then lifted my foot. 'Was the car I was looking for!'

I kicked the hood of an old broken down sedan with a huff, and it clanged in response. I listened to the dull echo around me and widened my eyes as the bumper bar wobbled and creaked.

'No, no,' I whispered highly, coaxing the old thing to stay put. 'Don't, don't, don't.'

I stepped back, then forward, should I grab it? Leave it? Ugh!

It creaked and whimpered, and finally fell into the pile of muck and dirt below it. I stood still, and watched it sink lower, the dirt and grime seething through open parts.

'Oh man,' I mumbled, touching the piece with my foot. 'Sorry old fella.'

I felt guilty, until I realised that the goddamn car was in a junkyard. It was obviously here to be scrapped, and it didn't have feelings!

The wind made this awful howling, whispering hiss into my ears. It travelled through hollow pipes and rusted metal holes, against leaking shack walls and thin plywood.

It was actually rather spooky, and I wouldn't have found myself here any other day. Slowly, I grimaced, huffed again, stepped back, and turned on my heels, right into the face of another. I couldn't really catch a good glimpse of him, but he glared.

'Hello, missy,' he mumbled, face tired and grumpy.

I yelped, stepped back and lost my footing, but he threw his hand out and caught me by the left arm. Quickly, I examined his attire and facial features. He was middle-aged, with mutton chops for sideburns, his hair was swept back like some awful Danny from Grease impersonator, and he wore blue overalls over a grubby brown shirt.

And he looked pretty pissed off, with a piece of tobacco rolling around his mouth.

'Uh, hi!' I stammered, pushing myself off from his grip. 'I uh.'

He crossed his arms, gave me a limp eyebrow and waited. I was stuck, not only was my right foot buried deep in mud, but I was lost for words.

I was in trouble now.

'You what?' he mumbled. 'Sneak into junkyards for fun?'

He had a gruff voice, and it sounded agitated. Slowly, he raised his arm and pointed towards the gate, at the giant no trespassing signs.

'You must have just, missed those huh?' he asked.

When he turned to me once more, I had the guiltiest smile on my face, but I had to get out of this somehow.

I was okay at bluffing.

'Y–yeah! I just,' I paused, collected myself and smiled. 'I thought one of these, uh...'

I presented the cars surrounding the two of us with jazz hands. 'Was one of my friends', um, missing cars!'

I smiled, widely and watched him glance behind me, nodding his head towards the sedan I stood by.

'And you thought kicking them, would benefit...how?' he asked, eyes peering.

'Oh!' I glanced to the bumper, and laughed weakly. 'Well, I just, my foot you see...'

'Cut the crap, kid.' he sighed, 'You're awful at bluffing.'

I felt my face flush, but I was not in the mood to be told off, nor arrested. Yes, I knew I was trespassing, and yes it was for a good cause. But I had no time, to stand here and explain it to some grumpy stranger why.

It fell silent between the two of us, and I kept processing how I missed him, I honestly thought there was nobody here, mid-afternoon.

'Okay,' I paused, raised my hands and sighed. 'Honestly though, I'm looking for a car.'

He quirked his eyebrow again, and chewed silently. I pursed my lips, and wiggled my foot free from the grub.

'I'm looking for a car, and I thought maybe, it'd be here.'

'Here in the junkyard.' he paused. 'Where every car, is in pieces.'

I grimaced and waved my hands again, pointing at every full car. 'Clearly not.'

He laughed shortly, sarcastically and rubbed the bridge of his nose with his thumb.

'So tell me why, I shouldn't call the cops right now and get you arrested?' he asked.

I felt my heart drop, my anxiety levels rise. I had to think of something fast, even if I couldn't make eye contact with this guy at all.

I couldn't have this, no way.

'Look, I'm sorry alright?' I eased. 'here look.'

I grabbed at my back pocket, and wiggled the Ford car key in his direction. 'The car to this key, is missing.'

He listened, his eyes following the gentle sway of the key.

Again, I was giving too much information to someone I literally didn't know. But I noticed his eyebrows quiver, surprisingly at the sight of it.

'And, a friend of mine told me, that junkyards might be the best place to look.'

'Why is this car so important?' he asked. 'Not every day someone trespasses into a junkyard to find a car,'

He stepped forward and reached to grab the fallen bumper. He held it in his grubby hands, then threw it into the nearest pile of scrap metal, wiping his palms of any dirt.

'That could easily be a bunch of metal, scrapped and salvaged.'

He was right, so right. I don't know why I kept thinking that this missing Ford was intact somewhere along the lines, but I had to somehow believe it, it was all I had left in this case.

'Yeah, well,' I paused and cleared my throat, wiggling my foot again. 'I need to find it, ASAP.'

'And again,' he turned to me, raised his finger and grumbled. 'I ask, why is this so important?'

My breath wavered, not only from the cold weather, but I was super nervous.

'It's important...' I gritted my teeth. 'Because, this car has something in it...'

Good one, Juniper.

He patted the sedan on the hood, and chuckled. 'Right.'

I panicked when he reached for his back pocket, grabbing his phone. I jumped his way, holding his arm tight.

'Whoa wait!' I cried. 'Look! This car has something really important in it, and I've been searching everywhere for it.'

I felt how grotty his arm was, and slid my hand from him, I wasn't a fan of touching strangers. But I also wasn't a fan of panicking.

'Look, just understand,' I sighed. 'I'll leave; it wasn't here anyway.'

He watched my eyebrows furrow, because I was honestly upset that Pebbles' car was missing. The tone in my voice wasn't as quirky as usual, it faltered and sounded disappointed.

Who was I kidding, I shouldn't put all my eggs into one basket and expect the car to fly down by my side.

'I'm sorry, Mr,'

'Sturges, just call me Sturges,' he said gruffly. 'But this doesn't stop me from calling the cops on your ass.'

I felt like kicking this guy in the balls, and rushing out of this junkyard. But I was stuck, like I said. I grimaced and shrugged.

'Please?' I asked. 'Just understand this car is super important to me, and I wasn't trying to steal anything.'

'I know that, nobody wants this junk,' Sturges snickered. 'It's just dangerous, and a girl like you shouldn't be prancing around places like this.'

I nodded, but couldn't help but smile. This guy wasn't as hard as I thought he was, he was either worried about the wellbeing of others who snuck into his yard, or he was making further fun of me. I played along, and nodded again.

'Yeah, I know that,' I muttered. 'I'll leave you be, sorry again, Sturges.'

His name was definitely not 'Sturges' there was no way someone would call their kid that. I slowly backed off, and he watched me. But he seemed to be fighting the urge to say something, a grit of his teeth made that quite evident.

'Wait, kid,' he grumbled. 'Look, maybe I can help you.'

First of all, why would someone who, a second ago wanted to arrest me, want to help?

I didn't question him, no, I thought to myself and stood still, clearing my throat.

'I don't think anyone else can do much,' I answered, clearing my throat. 'It's a tough search.'

Sturges spat aside, his chewing tobacco becoming smaller and smaller in between his teeth. He seemed taken aback by my words, distraught.

'I've been ripping apart cars all my life, if it's a certain car you're looking for, I would have been the one to smash it to pieces around here.'

I nodded to his words, but honestly couldn't get my hopes up again.

'It could be anywhere, not just around here,' I answered, pocketing the key once more. 'I'm worried it's in another state.'

'Hah!' Sturges laughed. 'Trust me, I know my locations, I know my people.'

He ranted on, about how he knew the top junkyards around Massachusetts, that he was well known in the junk industry.

I acted like I cared, but his words went from one ear to the other. He was babbling, but he seemed proud.

I didn't have the time though, to sit around and listen to him, as mean as it sounded in my head. 'Heck, I've even done work for the Fire Jackals, those fuckin' lunatics.'

'Wait,' I snapped. 'Wait, what?'

He froze, mid words.

'What, you don't know them?' he asked, puffing. 'They're always coming around for scrap metal, and I know I shouldn't sell it to them, but hey, I run a business here.'

I glanced around, towards the giant piles of rubbish. I think a few were teetering over each other, and there were always seagulls laying upon tires.

But he honestly lost me at Fire Jackals, now I was curious.

'I know them,' I answered. 'You bet your ass I know them.'

Surges roamed towards the kiosk, and threw his tool belt over the counter, sniffing loudly.

'Oh yeah?' he asked, 'They're a bunch of morons, always sneaking in here too.'

I followed him, my arms crossed.

'But sometimes, they're civil, believe it or not,' he spoke as he popped tools upon the rack in his little office. I stood by and listened to his words.

'Wait a second,' he turned, and raised his finger again. 'You're not a part of the group are you?'

I was honestly shocked to hear those words, and the anger was rising fast.

'Like hell I am!' I raised my voice. 'You have to be kidding, there is no way in hell I'd join them, or be associated with them.'

'Okay, my bad, relax,' he raised his eyebrows, hands up. 'Jeeze, you must really hate their guts.'

'You have no idea...' I whispered to myself.

I fumbled on the spot and cleared my throat when the awkwardness hit. Sturges was doing his own thing now, and although his words were promising, about knowing people and what not,

I couldn't trust every stranger I met.

If my mother and father taught me anything, trusting strangers was a big no-no.

'Seems like the Fire Jackals are a sensitive spot,' he said. 'This missing car wouldn't have anything to do with them, would it?'

Busted.

I tensed my neck, rubbing my hands together.

Said too much, Juniper! So stupid!

'N–no.' I answered. 'Why would you think that…'

Sturges chuckled and swung a monkey wrench around his index finger, then gave me a smirk.

'A girl comes sneaking into a junkyard,' he sniggered. 'Looking for a car, then reacts like that? To the mention of the Fire Jackals?'

I smiled awkwardly in return, and he shook his head.

'Yeah?' I eased, my head cocking. 'What a coincidence!'

'Cut the crap,' he said again. 'just say yes.'

I sighed, and shrugged my shoulders. 'Maybe, okay?'

What was I doing? I should have just turned, ran and ignored his question. Why was it that I was so bad under pressure? I was supposed to be a tough cookie, but man, this whole Fire Jackals situation had burned me to the bone.

I was getting weaker, the closer I got to finding answers.

'The car has something to do with them, yeah,' I truthfully answered. 'And its super important that I find it, because my family is in trouble, and I'm desperate to find answers.'

'Well okay!' Sturges laughed, slamming his hands down on the bench near his tools. 'Why didn't you just say that in the first place?'

I sarcastically glanced around and shook my head. 'Uh, because I don't know you?'

'True! I don't even know your name,' he smiled, he seemed too kind now.

I bit my tongue, and grouched. 'It's Juniper.'

'Juniper, well,' Sturges pulled his hand out. 'Lemme see the key.'

I was hesitant, the key? My only source? Hand it over?

'Uh…' I stepped back as I spoke. 'Why?'

Sturges looked annoyed, he frowned. 'So I can have a look at it?'

I touched my back pocket, swallowing deeply. 'Look at it? Why?'

'So I can match it with any car I've scrapped in the last month? Or however long you've been searching?'

'Why do you want to help, just a moment ago you wanted to arrest me.'

'Can't a human being help?'

'Yeah, they can, but not after threatening.'

'Kid, just let me see the key,' Sturges leant forward, and smiled crookedly. 'I can probably give you a hand.'

I grimaced, pursed my lips and mumbled to myself. Oh man, what now, hand over the key and watch a full-grown man run away clicking his heals?

I held the key tight, and glanced over his shoulder, trying to find any signs of a computer. Sturges followed my look and blinked.

'No computer? How are you going to search?' I asked, curious.

He rolled his eyes and handed his palm my way again. 'I don't need a computer...'

Sturges reached underneath him, and my first response was to flinch, I'd seen too many guns in the last week. Instead, thankfully, he pulled a bunch of clipboards out instead, and slammed them against the grotty tabletop.

'I use old stuff, paper, you know what it is?' he smirked.

I felt like snapping back, that I was a journalist, paper was my best friend you egg head!

But, instead I stayed still and held the key tightly.

'I write down every car that we get here, every name of the deadbeat that wants a few bucks for scrapping stolen cars, or old ones.' Sturges dragged his finger along the spine of paper, tapping the board behind it. 'So, if you show me the key, maybe I can link it up to something, I'm guessing the real owner had two sets of keys.'

'I'm not too sure, honestly,' I replied.

'Could have been towed,' Sturges thought.

I rolled my tongue, and shrugged again. 'Yeah.'

I shivered from the weather change, the clouds had become dark, and the sun hid behind them like a coward.

Boston was so temperamental, it never suited one weather choice.

Sturges stood silently, his hand out.

And I stood nervously, my hands by my side.

I wasn't sure about him, call it a hunch of some sorts, but not only was he a stranger, but he was a stranger that worked in a junkyard.

I'd met a bunch of odd people, through this adventure with the Fire Jackals, I could only trust a few, a handful.

I sighed and pulled the key free from my jeans, and handed it over.

I guess Sturges would have to be trusted, for now.

He smiled and reached forward, took the key and then brought it to his eyes.

'Hm.'

'Yep, not much to see... so...' I cleared my throat and reached for it once more, but he whipped it further away.

Sturges took his time, he stopped to ponder, then looked again, pondered, then looked. I was getting a little frustrated, I just couldn't stand here and wait.

'Well, it's a Ford...'

'Yeah, I established that...' I grumbled.

'Looks like a Ford Fusion series...' he mumbled back. 'By the way the key bends in, and out here...'

He was mumbling to himself, but he seemed to recognise everything. His eyebrows dipped inwards, and outwards with every rotation, until he huffed to himself and sighed.

'Honestly kid?' he finally said, stretching slightly.

Here it comes, bad news.

'I haven't scrapped a Fusion in years.' He handed me the key as he spoke. 'Sorry, bud.'

I grabbed it back, rather quickly, and shoved it in my back pocket. Man, just when I thought the day couldn't get any worse.

I smiled shortly, shrugged my shoulders and sniffed.

'It's alright,' I said. 'I wasn't expecting you to know, I mean, not that you don't know your stuff or...'

I paused, and Sturges crossed his arms. He could probably see my disappointment, and his eyebrows seemed to relax.

Truth was, I was close to giving up. But not on Nat, no.

I was close to going back to college, signing some forms, and dropping out of school.

Nat was my first priority, and she needed to be okay.

School, well... school could wait.

'Anyway,' I muttered, waving my hand once. 'Thanks for the help, Sturges.'

'Sorry to disappoint.' He replied, clearing his throat. 'Not a cheap model.'

I nodded again, and patted my thighs.

'Well,' I eased. 'Thanks for not, y'know, busting me.'

Sturges smirked, and waved his hands a little. 'Well, hold on there now.'

'Oh, no,' I whimpered. 'Don't tell me you're still headset on arresting me?'

Sturges laughed again, and stepped forward, his arms tight against his chest.

'Well, no,' he grumbled. 'You milked your way out of that.'

I waited for the rest of his words, and shivered from the afternoon cold. We were expecting a storm tonight, it wasn't the worst, but I'd hate to be caught in it.

Sturges reached for his phone again and handed it to me.

'But look, I can ask around for you,' he paused and rubbed his neck. 'I mean, it's not something I do normally, but you seem pretty troubled, and I hate it when people are troubled.'

I was hesitant, and slowly eased my head. 'What's the hitch?'

'Nothing!' he replied, grouching. 'I just don't like that crowd, and if they've hurt someone, I'd like to help bust their asses.'

He started to grumble again, whinging about how members would sneak in and steal his stuff. I wasn't too fond of giving my phone number out, but he knew a lot more than me, probably a lot more than Nick too.

'Okay,' I replied, grabbing his old phone from his hands. 'So, you'll look for me? really?'

I tapped my number in fast, and he nodded. 'Yeah sure, I'll call a few of the boys, see if they've dealt with any Ford Fusions here and there.'

'Thankyou!' I grinned, he pocketed his phone after I returned it. 'That would honestly be a great help, I don't have much time left.'

Those words hurt to leave my lips, because I hadn't processed just how hurtful they were. I swallowed when he took his phone, and I kept my tears back.

Of course it brought an awkward silence, but it was getting harder and harder to hide my sadness.

Sturges cleared his throat, and then clapped his hands a bit.

'Well, off you go then,' he ordered. 'And don't sneak in here anymore, just wait for someone to come around before you go jumping fences.'

I laughed weakly, and nervously rubbed my neck. 'Yep.'

As I walked away from Sturges, every step was rough and heavy. I'd come here, expecting to find a missing car.

I left with another ally, at least I thought so.

It wasn't any good for me, giving my number out and hoping for the best, that's why I took it upon myself to find the real truth.

When I reached Arty's car, sat in the driver's seat and closed the door after myself.

I sighed.

Maybe I wasn't cut out for this, maybe the answer this whole time was to give school up and do everything I realistically could for Nat.

Feeling sorry for myself, I backed out of the junkyard. As I moved slowly, I spotted another car parked a few feet away, a dark black SUV.

But I couldn't pinpoint who sat in it, and honestly?

I couldn't have cared less.

§

The drive back to Somerville was quiet.

I wasn't one to pop music on as I drove, especially after Arty's rock music fiasco a few hours ago. The freeway was empty, so I sped up a little.

I really wanted to see how my little sister was holding up, and Arty was probably eagerly awaiting her car.

Although I kept my eye on the road, my mind wandered. I thought about one thousand things at once, Rayne, Nat, Arty my dad and the past few weeks.

Even my Slavic boss made it on the train of thought, I felt pretty bad that I wasn't doing my all at work.

How could I? I was constantly teetering on the brink of sanity. This whole situation I had gotten myself and others into was enough to cause traumatic anxiety.

I nibbled my bottom lip, and sighed gently.

Things didn't always work out, I understood that.

I saw it with my father and mother, they didn't work out, but Dad still did all he could. Nat was bloody bedridden, and even she smiled.

Maybe I was being selfish, to the extreme limits.

This day wasn't going as planned, at all.

Once I reached home, it was dark out. It was only five in the afternoon, but it felt like midnight. I was tired, sore and dirty from the day. I could use a bath, a few drinks and a nice nap.

But there was no time for relaxing! No way.

I had work to do! Google searching and college business. I had to check up on Dad, and make sure Nat was eating properly.

I parked Arty's car, and finally let out my exhausted yawn. I was tired, and I hoped that whatever the day had to throw at me next was put on hold.

Dad's car was gone, which meant he was working again, a late shift nonetheless. He was always pushing himself, but for all the good causes.

When I unlocked my home door and stepped in, Arty was already waiting for me in the hall. She smiled, her hair was messy, which meant she just woke up.

'Hey, love,' she muttered. 'How are you?'

I shrugged and closed the door behind me, the wind was already picking up. 'Could be better.'

She hummed when I stepped forward, shoving my keys along the coat rack. We didn't use it for clothes in this house; it was full of random things, hats, and mobile phone cords.

Arty was ready to leave, she had black jeans on, a white shirt and her leather jacket. She looked pretty darn cool, but also fierce, she'd smack anyone that got in her way.

'I looked for the car today, but, no luck,' I mumbled, stepping to her side. 'I think it's time I...'

Arty saw me falter, and I did, awfully.

It was like all the emotions from today were hitting me tight in the chest, and I honestly wanted to sit down and cry.

I wanted everything to be alright, finish and clean itself up. Not only that, but I missed Rayne, a lot.

Arty touched my arm, and I smiled shortly. 'It's alright, I'll stay with Nat tonight, but thank you for the car, Arty,' I rubbed her hand, and patted it once. 'Rayne owes you too.'

'Oh I bet she does,' Arty sniggered, wiggling her eyebrows. 'You both do.'

I rolled my eyes and blushed, 'Stop that.'

'So you're not going to tell me all about your wonderful, romantic...' Arty paused and sighed sarcastically. 'Date?'

I paused and turned to her, throwing her car keys her way. 'Absolutely not!'

She grouched and winked, then lifted her hand. 'Oh!'

'Mm?'

'Nat's um...' Arty pursed her lips, lowered her voice. 'She's not feeling too good.'

I felt my heart drop, the panic rise. 'Oh, okay...'

It was all that left my mouth, but I had to stay strong, just until Arty left. 'Flu? Sore?'

Arty twisted her lip, and nervously shuffled on the spot. 'I dunno, lovey. She just seems, tired.'

It was rare to see Arty fumble and fall, for real emotion to take her by the shoulders and shake her. But she wasn't one hundred percent strong every day, she was soft too.

'Okay, I'll look after her,' I said. 'Tomorrow I'm going back to school; I'll talk to the headmaster...put in my leave.'

'Oh, Juniper,' she mumbled sadly.

'It's fine,' I replied, a smile on my lips. 'It has to be done, I can't have Nat get y'know, sicker.'

Arty gritted her teeth, and nodded sadly. 'If it's what needs to be done, we all want that gremlin better.'

I chuckled weakly, and waved her off. 'I'll text you, get going!'

She nodded once more, and paused at the door, her expression was saddened.

'Just, message me if you need me, alright?' her voice was sweet, calm, but still lingered deeply with her accent. 'I worry about you, Juniper.'

My heart was punching itself, eating its strings. 'I know.'

Arty waved again, and left, leaving me in the hallway with a lump in my throat.

Arty rarely said things like that, I knew she cared, she didn't have to remind me.

But this meant business, she could see things clearly too.

That Nat was getting worse, just as Samantha said.

§

When I stepped into Nat's room, she lay still and silent, her chest rising and falling sharply and hesitantly.

'Hey honey,' I coaxed. 'How you holding up?'

She glanced to me, eyes tired and bloodshot, but she still smiled. 'Juniper...'

I nodded, glanced around her room and checked her vitals. 'The one and only...'

It was very silent in the room, usually she had her TV and game on, but she lay quiet. I breathed in sharply, sat by her bed and held her weak little hand.

Nat cocked her head, tiredly blinked and rubbed my fingers with hers. 'I'm okay...'

I scoffed playfully, and leant closer. 'You going to tell me the truth?'

Nat was one to hide her pain, but it was pretty easy to see, especially in her state. She was gaunt in the face, her skin pale and cold. On other nights, I found myself sleeping in this seat, to check her pulse every few minutes.

I knew tonight, I would be doing the same.

'I'm sore...' she answered truthfully. 'But I'm going to be okay.'

I wanted to cry, her voice was hoarse and tired. Here I was whinging about my problems, finding some car, while she sat in bed, in horrible pain.

I held her hand tight, lifted her knuckles to my lips, and left butterfly kisses upon her skin. She was coaxed by the touch, and slowly chuckled. 'Gross.'

I grinned back, and asked her about her day, how Arty was while I was gone and what she was excited about. Nat told me about the recent level in her game, how she blew some guys brains from his skull, then felt bad about it.

She told me she accidently kicked a cat in the game too, and had to restart just so she could apologise.

Arty had made a few trips to the store down the road to buy snacks for Nat throughout the day. She was apparently confident about showing her face, I couldn't blame her, she was strong, she could beat up any Fire Jackal punk.

'Where's Rayne?' she asked, voice low.

My chest tightened from her words, but I smiled. 'She's working; she'll be back soon don't worry.'

'Did you have fun on your date?'

'The best fun, Japanese was great,' I answered. 'We ordered everything you liked, and Rayne was so excited, the big baby.'

Nat seemed thrilled to hear it, and she poked me for more questions. I answered every single one, thankfully she wasn't like Arty, who asked the riskier questions.

Hey, she was twelve, Arty was twenty-four.

'I'm glad you had,' Nat couldn't finish, she coughed loudly, held her chest and hobbled over. I rose from my seat, and held her back, shushing her sore cries.

She had these moments, when the pain was so unbearable that she burst into tears almost spontaneously.

I coaxed her, told her everything would be okay, and she clung to me. The more she did so, the harder it was to hide back my tears.

This wasn't fair! I hated the world for her pain, her agony.

Nat swallowed loudly, and leaned back, but I held her, as close as ever.

'Oh, Natalie...' I cried gently. 'Everything is going to be okay, I promise.'

She could only heave back, her little fingers tight around my wrists. She was so thin in my grip; I was afraid to break her.

The positive vibes that she had a chance to get better in the long run, were in the trash.

She was worse, progressively leaving this world.

I couldn't have that, and that's why tomorrow I'd quit college, and hand my scholarship over for her wellbeing.

The Fire Jackals plan was over, fuck Pebbles, he'd won this time.

But he wouldn't take my sister, no way.

Nat was exhausted after her moment, but she still mumbled words my way. I sat back, and sniffled.

'Nat, I'm going to book your surgery tomorrow,' I mumbled. 'Okay?'

She glanced to me, confused, but eager. 'R–really?'

'Yep,' I answered slowly. 'And I'll be right by your side, throughout the whole thing.'

When Nat was hit, the first thing we did was go to the police. Dad and I were positive that they'd find out who did it, and we spoke to lawyers too.

But we were sick of waiting, sick of seeing our Natalie suffer. I couldn't care less about my degree, it'd been nearly a month now, and I couldn't stand one more day of seeing her in pain.

She deserved a painless life, and she'd get it.

'Nat...' I muttered. 'I love you, alright?'

Nat would usually blow her tongue my way and push my face. But she was already welling up with tears, her body shaky and tired. She was scared, as was I.

'I love you too. You know...' she started.

'Mm?'

'When I woke up in the hospital... I thought I was dead.'

I swallowed tightly, my throat rough and dry. I couldn't deal with her talking about the afterlife, she was so young.

But I listened, it hurt, but she wanted to speak.

'I saw you and dad, and I couldn't feel the pain for a while...' Nat croaked. 'But then it hit me, you remember right?'

I weakly grimaced, and shrugged. 'Yeah, I remember...'

I did, it was awful. She woke up, glanced to us and then started sobbing, wailing and crying about the pain. Dad had to shush her and keep her close, he had the most hurt look in his eyes, and I was numb to the bone.

Nat smiled gently, touched her chin and prodded. 'Y'know, I couldn't remember much.'

I cocked my head a little, and rubbed her fingers with my own.

She was quiet before she breathed in to speak, I could hear the distant hum of the heater, the beeping of her IV drip.

'But I remember walking home, I remember hearing the car make that awful noise...'

I'd heard her say this before, when the police questioned her as she lay in this exact spot. She didn't have much to say, but it seemed right now her eyebrows furrowed in realisation. Like she'd thought long and hard about that awful moment she was hit by a car.

'I remember seeing the front of the car... I think it was black...' she paused and coughed softly.

I soothed her arm, and waited to hear her continue. A part of me was eager, maybe if she told me more information I could go out and try finding the car again.

Oh, wait. I already realised that was a done deal, a no breaker.

'I remember the front of it, all scratched and rusty, and the tire on the right was red...' Nat tiredly blinked. 'I think I saw a fluffy bunny hanging from the mirror.'

I giggled when she did, she still found something to smile about. She poked her tongue my way, even that part of her was sore and dry.

I reached for her water, and handed it to her, but she denied the offer. 'It was scary, but I'm here.'

It was wonderful to hear those words, the last part of course. After I popped her drink down, I sighed and leaned over her, to give her the biggest kiss on the forehead.

Nat held my hand, tightly, though she still shivered.

'I'll be here,' I whispered, pressing my forehead to hers. 'I will always, be here.'

'I know,' she replied, looking deep into my eyes, hers were watering just as much as mine. 'I'll be okay.'

'You will,' I said sternly, not knowing the answer entirely. 'I'll make sure of it.'

It was false hope, but she couldn't deal with any more breaking news, she had to stay positive. But I was frightened, so frightened that she would vanish.

'When I can walk again, can you take me to the zoo?' she asked, a cheeky smile on her lips. ‘So, I can see the monkeys.’

I tickled her gently, placing my hat by her head. ‘You’re monkey enough.’

I still loved the sound of her laugh, though it was weak and sore, she was happy.

It’s all I wanted.

§

I didn’t remember falling asleep, but my phone reminded me of my spontaneous slumber.

It vibrated loudly, alongside my head and woke me with a startle.

The room was dark, but Nat’s bedside light was on. I sniffled to myself, lifted my head from my crossed arms and flinched.

Nat was fast asleep, the vibration didn’t wake her at all, but it was awfully loud. I groaned and grabbed it to my ear, not even checking the time once.

‘H-hello?’ I croaked, clearing my throat. ‘Hello?’

‘Juniper,’ a voice came, but it seemed out of breath. ‘This is Juniper, right?’

I rubbed my head, blinked tightly and glanced at the window. It wasn’t storming yet, but the wind was awful.

‘Y-yeah,’ I mumbled. ‘This is Juniper...’

I yawned deeply, and the voice on the other side mumbled.

‘It’s uh, it’s me Sturges,’ he muttered.

I paused, blinked and finally realised. But I was absolutely exhausted, his words were muffled.

‘Sturges?’ I asked, confused. ‘W-what’s up?’

I pulled my phone from my ear quickly, and noticed the time. My eyebrows furrowed, it was four in the morning? I didn’t even remember falling asleep, the last thing I remember was Nat and I playing a game of cards.

‘Um,’ Sturges cleared his throat again, he seemed pretty troubled. ‘Darlin□ I found your car.’

I widened my eyes, his words echoed in my mind.

‘What,’ I stammered. ‘Wait, what?’

He huffed from the other side, I could hear faint rustling too. ‘I, uh, I found your car. The Fusion.’

I swallowed and rose from my seat, holding the phone close to my ear. I had to pinch my arm a little, worried that I was dreaming.

It wasn’t the first time, that’s for sure.

‘Sturges, are you serious?’ I asked, I was awake now. ‘You’re kidding?’

'N–no, well,' he paused, swallowed loudly and grunted. 'I called a few people up, and they spotted it...'

'And?!' I asked loudly, I swallowed when Nat shuffled in her bed. 'Where? Where is it?'

Sturges paused, before he made this awful whimpering sound.

I was confused, he called me at four in the morning sounding as if he was stuck on the toilet.

'It's in Marlborough,' he answered. 'Near the old lead building, you know the one?'

'No,' I replied, honestly. 'But I'll find it!'

I was already rushing for the door, but I could hear him calling to me. I sniffled as I shoved my boots on, but I paused at the key rack.

Fuck! Arty was gone with the car.

'Shit!' I whispered highly. 'Shit! Shit!'

'You can't go alone!' Sturges called, he rushed his words. 'They might be there.'

'They?' I asked, turning to check the time once more. 'Who is them?'

I waited for his reply, but all I heard was the dialling out of our call. He hung up.

I swallowed deeply, stood still and clenched my phone tightly.

This was a lot of information in five minutes, a lot of dire information. I groaned to myself, thought quickly and clicked my finger.

'Nick, Nick,' I repeated, rushed. 'Nick will help.'

I wasn't sure if Sturges was being honest, he was a shady guy.

I was desperate.

I dialled Nick's number, was he even awake at this time? I hoped, I really hoped as I stood still and tapped my foot against the floor.

Two rings, three, four.

Finally, that brilliant sound, of a phone being answered.

'Nick!' I cried. 'Nick, I'm sorry for calling! I really am!'

'Juniper, you caught me just as I was leaving the office,' He grumbled to me. 'What's going on? It's four in the morning,'

'Someone found the car,' I snapped, interrupting his words. 'Nick, they found the car.'

'Who found the car?' he asked. 'Who found the–'

'Some guy!' I rubbed my head, pulling my hair behind my ear. 'S–Sturges, a guy I met today at the junkyard out east, it doesn't matter! He knows where it is.'

'How are you so sure?' he asked back. 'You can't go believing strangers!'

'Nick, please!' I cried, he was right, but I was desperate. 'Please, the car is in Marlborough.'

My breath was fast, hastened and panicked. I couldn't take no for an answer, but I needed at least one answer.

'I don't usually do this for people,' Nick grumbled. 'Give me your address, I'll be there soon.'

I swallowed and nodded quickly, rushing my address out. He could sense the urgency in my tone, and I could too.

I thought the day was over, my rushed scare-filled day of disappointment.

But here I was, waiting for a cop to rush over to Somerville and pick me up.

I swallowed and held the key tight in my hands, checked on Nat once and twice.

She was sleeping soundly, and I think she'd be alright for a few hours. But I left her a note, told her I was out doing an errand, and I'd be home as soon as possible.

I was a little excited, to know the car may turn up.

But there was a lot of anxiety, especially with the distance, and Sturges panicked tone.

But I had a cop on my side, with a loaded gun, hopefully.

It took a few minutes for Nick to pull up, he'd obviously sped here, because the lights were flashing above his car.

I bet the neighbours thought I was being arrested, but I couldn't give a shit.

I rushed towards Nick's car, just as he was leaving it.

'No!' I called. 'Go, go, the old lead factory! That's what he said!'

'The one that's always having issues? In Marlborough?' he replied. 'What?'

He had his arms wide, confusion written all over his old face. 'What are you,'

'Nick!' I groaned, rushing into the passenger seat. 'Please! We have to go check, at least check!'

He sighed and pulled back into the driver's seat, raised his finger my way then grimaced.

'You scared me,' he grouched. 'But you're lucky I was around.'

I nodded, swallowed and eased my head from the loud wind. 'I'll explain it in the car, c'mon.'

He cleared his throat, throwing his cigarette out into the street as he backed out of my driveway.

'You owe me some coffees...' he mumbled. 'Maybe a breakfast burrito...'

I laughed weakly, and nodded once. 'Deal! Let's go.'

§

The drive was short, shorter than my map app told me. it was usually a forty-minute drive, but with Nick's sirens blasting, we were nearly there in fifteen, max.

I explained my day to him, every small detail a cop needed to know. He listened, to every word, but hung onto the ones I was nervous about too.

Like, Sturges sudden change of heart, and his offer to help.

Nick brought up that he may be working for the Jackals and as he spoke, he realised what he said. I saw him blink, focus on the road and then grab for his radio.

'What are you doing?' I asked, grabbing his arm. 'We have to suss it out first!'

'Miss Bridges,' he replied. 'If we are driving into a trap? We are in big trouble. I need to call some back up, some of the guys in Marlborough.'

'You can do that?' I asked, glancing his way.

'Yes, I'm technically above them.' He answered. 'They follow orders; I give them... not that I enjoy ordering people around.'

I raised my eyebrows, pretty impressed by my strongest ally. The head honcho cop was actually a sweet man who drove around at four A.M.? I'd struck gold.

I went to make a joke, but his radio screamed at the both of us. A panicked yet monotone voice called our way, a group message but important none the less.

'We have a, uh, situation at the old lead factory, in Marlborough North,' the voice mumbled.

Nick glanced to me, and I stared back, eyes wide. 'We have a car patrolling the area, said they heard gunshots, requesting back up in case of assault...'

I yelped when Nick kicked the pedal, speeding forward, sirens blasting. If I wasn't so scared already, I would have opened my window and cheered like a teenage girl.

It's not every day you drive in the car with a cop.

'Your friend Sturges....' Nick called over the engines roar. 'Might just be right.'

I was already sure of Sturges being correct about the car's location, but this popped the cherry on top.

Something was definitely going on at the old factory, it was too coincidental.

I just wasn't sure I was ready to find out.

§

Nick parked the car hastily outside the huge building, opened his door and paused. I tried to get a good look at the area, but it was dark and murky out, especially here in Marlborough.

I saw a few cop cars; two officers were already rushing towards us. I heard yelling, faint muffled cries from the building.

'Holy crap,' I whimpered. 'This is serious.'

I seemed to realise it myself, that there really was Fire Jackal business going on, or some thugs shooting up inside.

Nick turned to me, raised his finger and sternly glared my way.

'You stay right here, in the car,' he ordered. 'Do not, leave the car.'

I nodded quickly, swallowing in my seat. 'Y–yep! I'm staying right here.'

He grabbed his gun, nodded and rushed outside. I felt my heartbeat, thumping like a drum. I wasn't awake for this at all.

Nick messily left the door ajar, so I could hear exactly what was being said.

'Fire Jackals, sir,' The taller blonde cop muttered, he looked my way once and sniffled. 'We've had a few men scout the area earlier tonight, four members are inside.'

'And are we positive they are members?' Nick asked.

'Yes, sir,' The other cop sounded out of breath, that, or he was nervous. 'It's positive.'

I heard another gunshot and yelped gently. It wasn't every day you heard that, especially when it echoed.

I couldn't stand the sound, I'd heard a shotgun once, I thought it was my limit.

Nick turned to me, his eyes widened.

'Alright, let's go in boys,' he called, holding his handgun close. 'Keep your head up, more forces will be here soon.'

They continued to talk to each other as they raced to the decrepit entrance. I watched them become smaller and smaller, my eyes widened.

I was worried, Nick was rushing into a disaster, alongside two other police officers. And I sat here, in my seat, slumped down.

I would have sat still, but with the echo of yelling, and clang of metal, it was awfully hard to do so. I swallowed loudly, glanced around the car, and lost my breath instantly.

There, deep in the grotty parking lot, parked absolutely atrociously. Was a black vehicle.

On cue, I felt my breath hasten. More or so then before, it was pumping in my chest. I'd forgotten, just for a moment, what I had originally come here for.

Lost in the moment, of criminal activity and worry, I almost missed that godforsaken car.

I stepped out, shakily, knowing very well that I shouldn't have.

My legs were wobbling, my hands trembled and reached for my back pocket.

As I walked, I could still hear the yelling, the commotion from just inside the building. But my eyes, they were widened and set on one thing only.

As I walked, the wind picked up, the rain started. It was soft, against my cheeks and ice cold. My adrenalin was rushing, but my blood was chilled.

I remembered my sister's words, as I reached the hood of the car.

I remember seeing the front of the car... I think it was black...

I swallowed and circled around the front, easing through the small gaps. It'd been used recently; the engine was still hot when I touched the hood of the car.

My head was fumbling, especially when I saw the dent. It was a huge mess, the whole right of the bumper was destroyed, covered in, oh god.

Scratches.

I remember the front of it, all scratched and rusty, and the tire on the right was red...

Nat's voice was the only thing I heard, in my mind. Her voice was just as hoarse as before, quiet and sad. I held the key tight in my hand examining the tires, and my heart dropped when I saw it

A red wheel.

I was shaking now, my breath was loud, the rain responded to my feelings and poured down a little heavier. I didn't want to look; I knew a few hours ago I would have jumped for joy at the sight of the car, but right now all I wanted to do was run and hide forever.

I raised my head, groaning to myself. I had to look, c'mon, this is all I wanted, to find the truth.

I raised my head fast and spotted the keychain hanging from the rear-view mirror. Even in the dark, that fluffy pink bunny mocked me.

I felt my bottom lip wobble, my fingers tremble and waver. I was scared, so scared and I couldn't understand why.

I'd lost myself in this whole situation, and now here I was, in front of the car I'd been searching everywhere for.

I wasn't used to this, the positive winning over the negative.

Not in a situation like this.

I popped the key in the driver's door, and flinched when it unlocked. Sturges was right, about all of this.

Now I'd find out who Pebbles was, get Nat's surgery, expose the truth. I pulled the door open and flinched from the muggy smell. I saw a few items, pieces of clothing, papers scattered here and there.

Precious DNA that could find our man.

But again, something else caught my eye, and I reached almost spontaneously for the driver sun visor. When I opened it, my heart dropped.

There was a photo, two actually. And a familiar face was plastered on each, with a younger boy.

'No,' I mumbled, but it was more of a moan of agony. 'No, no.'

I focused on Christopher' face, and his smiling brother.

When I stepped away from the car, in sheer shock and surprise, another gunshot echoed. With all this newfound news rushing through my brain, I reacted to it, and stumbled to the concrete floor. A scream rang in my ears, and it frightened me.

Instead of fleeing, I was up on my feet, I ran towards the sound.

Everything was a blur, as I sprinted I could hear my heartbeat, the thunder roared from above me. My breath was short with every pump of my legs, every sway of my hands.

I roamed through rotten rooms, until I spotted Nick's back. He was standing, still, with both cops beside him. And I wasn't thinking, not one bit.

I rushed between two of them and brought the scene to my attention.

I wished I hadn't.

Rayne sat, shackled and tied, beaten and bruised. She wept over the dead body of Christopher, his head blown to pieces.

I couldn't hear anything, I only saw her and three bodies lying absolutely still. I swallowed deeply, held myself up and glared towards Rayne, my chest pumping.

All four of us stood still.

Rayne was weeping, she hadn't noticed me yet, she was lost and torn in her own misery. She threw herself around in her seat, calling out to Christopher' body, begging him to come back.

I was numb, I couldn't speak, I couldn't scream.

I just, stared.

All my questions had been answered, every single detail was coming together.

I wasn't ready for the truth.

No, not at all.

Chapter Twenty-Four

RAYNE

Death was bittersweet.

Many feared it, saw it as the end of the line for us humans.

Who could blame them? You live a life full of emotions, love, happiness, sadness and anger. Then watch it crumble to pieces when you reach a certain age. It could be eighty, thirty, even four years old.

Some laugh in the face of death, talk about it as if it's some great moment of life. That without death we wouldn't really be living our lives to the fullest.

To some, death was seen as an escape. An escape from the hurt, the heartbreak and trauma. Some feared death, some craved it.

To me, death was game over. All those memories, happy and sad, they meant nothing once the grim reaper extended his finger and touched your shoulder with a frosty tap. I was never one to listen to those who called out into the streets that time was running out, that we had to live every moment of our lives like the last.

Some days I wanted to sleep and do nothing else, some days I wanted to run across town and experience something different.

To me, life was a clock slowly ticking, we had no idea when that clock would stop, when the hands would shatter and break.

I didn't enjoy talking about it, nor did I like the idea of a clock above everyone's head, ticking away their lives.

I wondered, if we had that.

If we really did hold a clock that told us when we would die, would people change their minds about the activities they indulged in during their days?

Or would people turn into fear driven humans, slowly driven to madness with every slow tick?

I didn't like to think about it, death.

I found no enjoyment in the idea of vanishing from the earth, nor did I enjoy seeing those I knew slowly drift from the conscience that was life.

When my grandfather died, I was numb. He and I were close, he was the only man I looked up to as my own father, when my drunken real father stood on the sidelines. We did everything together, listened to his old records, cleaned the horses stables on his farm and drove around every paddock together.

He was my escape at the time, from a life of misery. The guitar I inherited was his own, every lesson I learned about playing was from him.

He was a saint, a man of his word.

That's why I never expected death to take him, he was too pure and he didn't deserve it.

I remember hearing the awful news through a small crack in my door. Dad and Mom stood in their own doorway just across the hall from my own, and discussed his cancer, the way he went.

I was only fourteen at the time, but I remember the words echo through my ears, jump off the walls and pierce me right in the gut.

But what surprised me, is that I didn't cry.

I felt like bawling, felt like punching the walls, felt like kicking and screaming. But I never did, I just sat in my room in the dark for hours, until morning.

I held his guitar close, watched the trees dance outside my window in the awful Florida wind. When my father entered my room that morning, I didn't even listen to his words, I knew already, why would I want to hear that fatal news again?

My father was a cruel man, though he spoke to me with sincere sadness. He stood in front of me and told me he could hear me that night.

Hear me? I thought, confused.

That's when he told me I was sobbing all night, that he could hear every rack and hick from my body.

When he left my room, I was brought aback by his words.

I wasn't aware of my own emotions, my numbness was stronger than my feelings, to the extent that I couldn't even remember crying.

When my grandfather passed away, a part of myself did too. I think his death sparked my emotions to run wild, sparked my depression to hit home.

I ran away from Florida when I was old enough, there was too many memories I wished to let go of.

They hurt too much.

That's why I hated death, I never enjoyed thinking about it, I wanted to forget it existed. Why would I want to think of something that destroyed lives, and those around them?

I never wanted to experience it, but I guess life had different plans for me.

Around me, was nothing but silence. I could feel my chest vibrate, my lungs pull and stretch. My eyes were wide, my head spinning.

The gunshot was the only thing that echoed in my mind, the only sound I could really concentrate on, as Christopher fell sideways very slowly.

When he pulled the trigger, life made me suffer and stopped time itself. I watched him stumble and melt, the hairs on the top of his head flutter from the force of his shot. His eyes were closed, but mine were peering into them, waiting for them to open.

When he hit the floor, his gun clattered to my feet. I felt the tip of it hit my toe, but it scattered forward when I strained, pulled and strained in this chair.

I could hear my breath, whatever I had left of it. It was high and raspy, pained and rough. He lay there, covered in his own blood and misery. I didn't want to believe it was real, so I shook my head, over and over.

Maybe if I shook enough, I'd open my eyes and be back home in bed next to Juniper. Maybe if I blinked over and over again, I'd open my eyes and see Christopher sitting at that picnic bench again, with his Zoom Quantum and shaky personality.

Maybe I could go back in time and fix everything, if I believed hard enough.

I'd experienced death again, and it was painful, the numbness was back.

I was aware of my struggle, of my hatred towards the whole concept, but I couldn't stop my reaction.

I felt my gut pull when I looked again, Christopher still lay there, his blood was gradually rushing faster, and mine was gradually dropping.

I knew I was screaming, I was not only sad but I was angry, at so many things. I was furious at Pebbles, whoever he may be. Another human being was the madman behind one's death. Christopher lay dead on the floor, while Pebbles lay calm on his bed.

I was certain I would find the true identity of that man, I knew without a doubt that Christopher was not the crazed asshole we were looking for. Nobody stood there denying, in tears and a manic realisation that they were screwed either way, and then end their life.

Christopher had been framed.

Before he ended it all, I had trouble believing it. But there were too many holes in this string of deadly situations.

They knew I was after Pebbles, but Crocker and Manny made it pretty clear that Christopher wasn't him. They spoke about Pebbles like he was some god, a crazed mastermind.

And although I wouldn't believe it at the time, I finally understood when Christopher broke apart. He was a kind soul, a guy who'd gotten himself in a shitty situation, much like myself. If he were Pebbles, why would he try and warn me, text me and message Juniper clues in order to find the truth?

He admitted to being in the car that hit Nat, he was honest before he left this world. But who was he with? He wouldn't tell me, even with Detective Rodgers in the room with us, he was still hesitant on telling us Pebble's true identity.

He was worried, about his brother and his family. Worried that they would suffer the consequences of his mistakes even after death.

That's why I knew Christopher wasn't Pebbles, I just hoped Juniper and the police agreed.

Something told me that they wouldn't, not with all the fake evidence that Pebbles planned together.

With my mind running at one hundred miles per hour, I only started to calm down when two hands touched my cheeks and held tight.

I hadn't blinked in a long time, and I was a little annoyed to see Christopher' body blocked by another. But when I snapped my eyes from his limp state, and locked them with a pair of green orbs, I instantly started to cry again.

Juniper held my face closely, and I froze. She was talking to me, but I couldn't hear her, I couldn't hear anything but my heartbeat and my sobs.

She was shocked, I could sense it and see it.

Her eyebrows were creased, her face pulled in utmost fear. She shook me a few times, but I couldn't make out her words. My head still ran with all the information I'd consumed in the past two hours, a headache full of pain and whispered truth.

I swallowed and tried to focus on Juniper's shaky hands, the feeling of each digit pressed into my jaw, but I was too numb.

Instead, I gave my ears the sweet satisfaction of the sound of environment.

I still couldn't understand Juniper, because I finally heard myself. I was a mess, a sobbing mess. I was mumbling the same thing over and over again to Juniper, to anyone who surrounded me, maybe even myself.

'It wasn't him!' I cried. 'It wasn't him!'

Juniper was coaxing me, telling me everything was alright. When I focused on her eyes, I could see tears welling up around her bottom eyelids, but I could also sense the disappointment. Boy, was I in trouble, not only with the police, but with Juniper too.

Just as I started to feel the satisfying touch of her fingers on my face, Juniper was pulled back by Detective Rodgers. She didn't force herself forward, she didn't fight to grab me back, she just stood on the sidelines and looked away from the three dead bodies surrounding us.

I watched Christopher again, and mumbled the words once more, it was all I could say.

Realising that only those words left my mouth was frightening, and I was sure this trance I'd found myself in would last days.

A flurry of black began untying my feet, and I could feel another pair of hands behind my chair fumble with my strains.

I was forced to my feet, no matter how much it hurt, and thrown to my knees. I struggled from the grip, and reached to touch Christopher' face, I wanted to feel his skin and make sure it was warm and alive. No matter how much it pained me, I wanted him to be okay.

It was silly to think he'd wake up, but I still tried.

'You have the right to remain silent and refuse to answer questions.'

The Miranda warning was a mumble of words to me, though one cop spoke loudly, I didn't care. I heard the click of handcuffs and quickly threw my head back. I felt the satisfying contact with another, and it left my vision blurry.

He groaned from the smack behind me, and I rushed forward to Christopher, even if it pained me to do so. My body was aching, and now that the adrenalin was slowly drifting, God I could feel the awful pinching throughout every bone. I fell by his body and sobbed loudly, but before I could even touch him, I was thrown down again, one pair of hands held my arms behind, and another swiped a familiar object around my wrist.

I only recognised the handcuffs because I'd been in them once before, after I stole that stupid gum packet.

'Anything you say may be used against you in a court of law. You have the right to consult an attorney before speaking to the police and to have an attorney present during questioning now or in the future...'

I swallowed and lowered my head, it was starting to hurt the more I lifted it. The sharp coldness of the metal around my wrist stung, especially in one area. I hadn't seen my new tattoo, but I hoped it would vanish before I saw it.

I watched Christopher slowly melt from my vision, as I was pulled up and turned. I denied the touch and pleaded with those around me, to let me stay and wait for Christopher to wake up. I was manic, just as Christopher was a few moments ago. Moments to me, could have easily been hours, the concept of time right now was messy and fumbled.

I was pushed a little forward, and I stumbled. I wished to hit the floor, though I was kept up by another pair of tight hands. My sense of smell had returned, the aroma of my own blood was strong, and it left me awfully queasy. I felt my eyes droop and my head waver, I couldn't walk properly.

'Sir?' the cop behind me asked. 'The media is probably outside, word spreads fast here, and we've created a commotion.'

I breathed heavily as he spoke and turned to spot Juniper. She stood beside Detective Rodgers, the man I once sung for in South Station, the man who I lied to and saidthat I wasn't one to mess with the wrong crowd.

How embarrassing.

Juniper was close to him, and he pulled a face my way, an angered yet concerned face. I watched the scars dancing along his face follow every pull. He popped his gun back, and started commanding his two men, that tightly held onto me.

But I couldn't bother listening, I was only set on one thing, and that was Juniper. I knew she was letting all of this settle, inside that bustling mind of hers, she was realising.

That her girlfriend had lied, told her she was going to be okay, did exactly what she warned me not to do.

Put another before myself, in such a deadly situation.

I wanted to get on my knees and plead to her, as pathetic as that sounded, I needed her to know that I too didn't expect this to turn out the way it had.

I had no idea Pebbles knew about my sole reasoning behind joining the Fire Jackals, I wasn't aware the guy was so smart.

He had this all planned, and Christopher was doing his absolute best to warn me, I just wasn't listening.

Now look at this mess.

I was pushed forward again, even as I turned my head to focus on Christopher, as he slowly vanished from my sight.

We walked slowly, my breath was still short, my body ached. I only focused forward, not at the rotting corridors was pulled through, the rusty doors and dirty ground.

Just forward.

I heard more commotion outside, and I knew as I was shown outside that I was going to be the main attraction.

I flinched from the cold air, the sharp touch of fresh rain, it stung my wounds. Not only did the icy rain leave me in pain, so did the flashing of cameras.

I eased myself away from the crowd of raincoats, held myself back from their nagging photographs.

There was such a commotion of voices, blasting questions, pointing, pushing and shoving. I couldn't stand it.

'Alright! Alright!' Detective Rodgers stood in front of me, his trench coat was drenched from the rain, but he didn't seem to care one bit. 'Nothing to see, go back to your cars, it's dangerous here.'

He turned to me, then motioned a spare set of cops inside, mumbling a few words to them. They nodded, both big burly men, then stood beside the door.

They were locking the premises down, before photos of Christopher, Manny and Crocker could be taken, the awful scene where I once sat.

I flinched from another photo, I could only see white for another three seconds afterwards. I felt the anger rise in me, but I had to remain calm.

I was already in a messy situation, with a lot of people, an angry mob of photographers and journalists wouldn't help.

I saw Juniper being questioned, but she was ignoring every word, she only stood by, she wasn't looking my way.

When I was pushed forward again, I spotted another set of photographers, they were shooting at a car, a lone car parked terribly in the carpark just outside this joint.

It didn't take me long to realise that it was the doomed car Nat was hit by, the doomed car Pebbles had set Christopher up with.

I knew there was two people involved, the hit and run couldn't have been Christopher' fault entirely.

Not with all the evidence that he was innocent. Christopher was no way near capable.

Again, I was only thinking to myself, I was ignoring all that went on around me, I had a lot of thinking to do.

I was forced into a police car, photographers followed and snapped shots, and all I could hear was a flurry of cops telling them all to back off, go home.

It was a surreal feeling, something I only saw on television, in the movies.

I was a bit naïve, I never expected it to be real, nor did I expect myself to be a part of it.

When the door shut, I was basked in an eerie silence. I could still hear the voices outside, as well as see the camera flashes. But I didn't care at all for any of it, I just stared at my feet, and mumbled to myself. I had to think of a plan, something to get myself out of this, something to convince them that Pebbles was still out there.

The driver's door opened, and Detective Rodgers slipped in, halfway through a conversation with a journalist.

'This is none of your concern, we will take our suspects into custody and question them,' he closed his door, wound the window down and shot the camera a view. 'Now if you'll excuse me.'

The passenger door opened as he spoke, and Juniper was next to sit down.

I felt my heart ache, she was here too. I didn't really expect her to find herself in this situation too, but that also added to the mystery, it left my mind boggled.

How did she find herself here? How did the cops find us at all?

They would be called the heroes on television and in the papers, when in reality Christopher was. He was the one to step up and push Manny and Crocker down, he was the one to save me.

But he couldn't save himself, I couldn't help him either.

I leant back, my hands still behind my back, the guilt rushing over me. If I hadn't joined the group, come along with him, I could have saved his life.

I could have fixed this, even if I did an awful job at fixing my previous plan.

If I thought I was screwed before, now I was definitely in trouble.

We drove out rather fast, it was dark in the car, so I couldn't make out Juniper's face, nor Detective Rodgers's.

As he drove, he spoke on his mobile, spoke through his radio and kept shoving me glances from the rear view mirror.

I could sense it, but I never had the heart to look back, he'd be disappointed too.

Outside, the rain was pouring, shoving itself against the windscreen, the wipers made a rhythmic squeak every sway.

Detective Rodgers kept moving his head, sideways to glance at Juniper, who hadn't moved one inch. I could only make out her silhouette, slumped and shaking. She didn't speak, nor did he—and I wouldn't, not yet.

The sirens were blasting above me, and we were speeding, even on this awful road. I sat rather still, the ride was so smooth, a seatbelt would have been nice, but I couldn't flex my fingers at all.

The silence was horrible, there was anxiety in the air, sadness and building tension. I was the reason for it all, I knew I was.

Outside, on the corner of my eye, the sun began to rise. Over the horizon of cornfields and dirty terrain, its beauty only left me guiltier.

I was watching the sun rise, though it hurt to peer through my left eye, I could still feel the warmth from the star.

The clouds surrounding the glowing orb were painted red, orange, yellow.

I didn't deserve its beautiful sight.

I glanced to Juniper, and watched as the red reflected upon her eyes, she too stared, her face pulled in thought.

I could see the tears; it shook me to the bone. She didn't make a sound, her lip didn't even quiver, the tears just fell. Even in this time of misery, I still wished to focus on the beauty, every teardrop that slithered down her face glistened, gorgeous warm colours upon her face.

Another sight of beauty, I didn't deserve.

Juniper Bridges was broken, and I had done all the breaking.

The rest of the morning was a blur, especially when I was guided into Boston Police Station. Detective Rodgers held me by the right arm, not as tightly his colleagues. A part of me wanted to run, but I knew it wouldn't do any justice to my situation.

I had no strength to run anyway, none at all.

Every pair of eyes were on me, not so much Juniper who trailed behind the two of us. I still didn't have the strength to look at her, the same went for Detective Rodgers. I just stared forward, flinched with every step.

My body was weak and cold, I shivered, my throat was dry and rough. But nothing hurt as much as my heart did, the awful anxious feeling of knowing everything was falling apart.

Not only that, but the only image that flashed to and from my mind's eye, was Christopher as he lay lifeless.

Every time I saw it, I felt my eyes well up.

I was brought to a room in the far back, behind a locked door. When I finally turned, Juniper was nowhere to be seen, and I felt like panicking.

I swallowed and glanced to Detective Rodgers, who hadn't spoken one word to me, even if he had, I probably wouldn't have heard.

Not over the screaming headache I had going on.

I was lead into a bright room, one that made me close my eyes and cuss. It smelt of disinfectant and hospital, I hated it already.

A blonde woman sat at her desk and eased her eyes when she saw me and the man beside me. around her stood a few medical devices, a sick bay with beds.

Thankfully I was seated, though I couldn't shake the other seat I previously sat in out of my mind. Detective Rodgers brought his hands behind my back, I could hear and feel the metal weight fall from my wrists.

'Don't move., he grumbled, paused and realised how angry he sounded. 'Please.'

I swallowed and brought my wrists to my thighs, then slowly lifted them to my sights. I focused on my left wrist first, and saw nothing but a few cuts and bruises. Crocker and Manny must have tied me up really tight because the marks were still evident.

With a shaky breath and a thump of my heart, I brought my right wrist up. I felt a groan escape my lips, hollow from the bottom of my throat.

The tattoo work was messy, and tiny bits of tissue surrounded it. It was a blank staring Jackal, the size of three dimes, trailing alongside the veins. It was decorated with dark lines, triangular shapes pointing down beside its slick face.

I lowered my head, clutched the mark with my other hand and heaved my shoulders.

It hurt, but it pained me more to know I'd have a constant reminder of this mistake I had made. I kept glancing down at it, hoping it was a temporary tattoo, that it would vanish if I itched it enough. But it wasn't going anywhere, at all.

I could overhear Detective Rodgers speaking with a female cop, he told her to check me for any signs of a concussion. But as soon as he left, and as soon as she stepped my way, I panicked.

'Hello, Rayne. I'm Officer Ellen,' she said, pulling gloves over her hands. 'Hang on now, I have to do a few checks,' she mumbled. She stood clad in uniform, but her face was sweet.

I pushed myself from her touch, shaking my head. 'Don't.'

Officer Ellen paused, blinked and stared up at me, I was a whole two feet taller than her tiny state. She raised her eyebrows to my face, and I could tell she was uncomfortable.

I heard my breath again, and flinched when I stepped towards the mirror plastered above a faucet. When I saw my reflection, my legs wobbled.

I'd never seen myself so beat up before, not even after a hard training session back in Florida. I swallowed and touched the bruises upon my eyes, my forehead and my jawline. Trailed the needle-sharp cut that slithered up my left cheek. Crocker's needle had done a number on me, and Manny's punches had left me with one big black left eye. there was cuts everywhere, still red and bloody. My chin was drenched in dry blood, bottom lip split and grubby.

I shakily took a breath, and stepped back, turning to hold my head with my hands.

'Not a nice sight, hey kiddo?' she asked, pulling a few things from drawers. 'So, you better let me clean you up.'

I wasn't comfortable with anybody touching me right now, but I let her examine me for any concession signs. I was knocked out once, but I could still feel its aftermath.

She sat me down, and waved a flashlight into my eyes, asked me basic questions, what was my name, when was I born.

I answered them all truthfully.

I told her I was knocked out via syringe, that I only remembered a few things before I woke up. She wrote these down, but I never made eye contact with her, I only stared forward. I remembered every small detail, surprisingly.

As another ten minutes passed, of questioning. She reached to touch my face, and that's when I reacted and pushed back once more.

'Don't touch me!' I sobbed, shaking my head quickly. 'Don't.'

She stared at me, her blue eyes full of concern, but there was a slight annoyance in them. Especially when she had to follow my nervous state around the room, I didn't want her anywhere near me.

'We have to get you cleaned up, Rayne,' she explained, holding the gauze in her hand. 'So please, let me.'

'No,' I barked back, lifting my shaky hands. 'Don't come near me, okay?'

I didn't understand my current state, why I didn't want anything to do with her. I was really quite dizzy, and every step ached.

She tried to coax me, but I wouldn't have it, I just needed to be alone, I didn't need her hands on me. I glanced to her waist, she had her belt on, and I could see the gun plastered into it. I shivered at the thought of its fire, the sound.

I was crumbling again.

Officer Ellen didn't invade my space, but she pulled her walkie out from her pocket and started mumbling into it.

I breathed steadily again, and touched the cut above my eyebrow, right next to the one scar I already had.

I worried about the way I looked, but I didn't have the guts to look in the mirror once more. I leaned against the counter at the far left of the room, my hands trembled on the cold porcelain. I watched Officer Ellen press her hand to her hip, and listen to the response, which was static mess to me.

She glanced my way, nodded once and twisted her lip between her teeth.

'Alright, bring her in,' she mumbled. 'This isn't something we'd normally do, how come this kid gets special treatment, sir?'

I didn't understand what she meant, but Detective Rodgers was the other person mumbling over the system, after a stern wording, Officer Ellen sighed and nodded.

She gave me once small look, and raised a finger.

'Hang on tight,' she said. 'Someone will be in soon.'

I didn't respond to her, I looked to my feet instead.

When I was alone, I held my arms and clenched tight. Oh God, I was in a heap of trouble, they were just cleaning me up before they locked those cuffs on me again and threw me into a cell.

Maybe there was still time to run, maybe I could sneak out the window.

I glanced around for any sign of one, but the only opening was fenced off, barred.

Go figure.

I jumped from the door, as it creaked open slowly.

'Just take it easy in there,' came Officer Ellen's voice. 'She's shaken up, very reactive.'

I didn't look, I didn't want to know who or what was coming through that door, a big nasty syringe? To put me to sleep, like the one Crocker had?

I swallowed and shivered, my back was pressing into the countertop, and I felt like sitting again. Getting up fast wasn't the best thing to do right now.

'Rayne.'

The guilt that had previously settled, exploded once again.

I sniffled and glanced to Juniper, as she stood affront of the door. I breathed heavily and lifted my head higher, so I could examine her.

Our roles had turned, she was the one avoiding my eyes, but all I wanted was the contact. I opened my mouth to talk, but nothing was leaving my voice box.

'I have to clean you up,' she said sternly, her voice crackled more than usual. I knew why, she'd been crying too.

I waited for more, but that's all she said. I watched her walk my way, grab at the medical supplies on the other bench. When she turned, I expected her to scream at me, throw a fit and tell me I was the worst person on the earth.

Juniper pointed at my chest, and flicked upwards. 'Take that off, you've got blood all over it.'

I bit my lip, and nodded to her orders.

I slipped out of her hoodie, and it fell to my feet. I saw her look once, but bring her attention to her hands, as she examined the disinfectant she held.

As I grappled the end of my shirt, I could feel my stomach turn and twist, any sort of movement hurt, and I couldn't lift the shirt entirely without the need to throw up.

I did my best to hide my struggle, but I hissed and dropped my arms.

Juniper stepped my way, grabbed the bottom of my shirt, and lifted gently. I half expected her to rip it off me, but she was being soft. She was careful lifting it over my head, I finally saw how much red had covered up the white.

I shivered, it was freezing in here. I examined my shoulders, especially my right. The blade was bruised, cut and infected. I groaned and went to touch it, but Juniper smacked my fingers down.

I focused on her eyes, but she avoided, grabbed at my chin and began wiping it. I trembled, not only from the numbness, but from her touch.

I examined her face closely, every line under her eye, the crease between the bridge of her eyebrows. Her hair was messy, and I longed to touch it.

'Juniper,' I mumbled.

'Don't.' she replied, wiping the dry blood harsher. 'I'm not ready to talk to you.'

It hurt to hear, but I shut up entirely.

I could only imagine the things going through her mind right now, the trust we'd formed was breaking apart, and it was entirely my fault.

Juniper always told the truth, even if it hurt her to do so.

It was the right thing to do, not telling the truth ended in situations like this, a big mess.

She kept her hands to herself, and cleaned only what she had to. The disinfectant stung, especially on the cut across my cheek. It twisted downwards and rolled over a little of my jaw.

I still couldn't think straight, and when I tried focusing on how I had ended up with that cut, I remembered my teeth crunching down on someone's bone, pulling the socket.

With a mumble, I held my mouth and leaned forward, my chin against Juniper's head. My eyes had widened again, but she only flinched and stood still.

I was breathing heavily, my chest heaving. Had I really done all that? Had I really been punched and bruised to all ends, beaten and spat at like I was some sort of terrorist?

I was heaving heavily now, my arms by my side. I waited for Juniper's embrace, but she wouldn't touch me affectionately.

And I didn't blame her.

She wiped down my shoulder, as I sobbed above her. My cries were quiet, but evident, even to myself now.

The numbness of feelings had subsided, I brought in every single emotion I thought I had lost. But I knew this was because of Juniper's presence, if this were Officer Ellen, I would have been as numb as a doorknob.

My shoulder fell under her wiping, but though I could feel the tension surrounding her, her touch was feathered and sweet.

Juniper couldn't be an asshole even if she tried.

'Juniper...' I croaked. 'I...'

'Stop.' She spoke over me. 'Just...'

I swallowed and listened to her voice, she pulled me back, and patted down my face once again. I could see the blood on every wipe, there was so much.

Juniper's bottom lip twisted, and she eased her eyes. 'You've made a mess of yourself.'

I nodded with another sob, and she shushed me sternly. 'Stop crying.'

'I'm sorry,' I replied. 'I'm sorry!'

'Stop it,' she grumbled.

I wanted to fall into her arms and sob for hours, tell her how sorry I was for being an absolute moron, for joining the clan that left her sister bedridden. But how was I meant to tell her? She seemed to hate my guts, I'd ruined any sort of chance now.

'I just wanted to...'

'Rayne!' she raised her voice then, and I jumped.

I could hear her breaths now, they were high and hurt, it made me crumble.

'I'm doing this because they told me to.' she cried. 'Just stop talking, this isn't easy for me either!'

I tried to grab at her face, but she pushed my hands away, sniffled and left me to grab more supplies. I decided it was best to stay quiet now, try to hold back my tears and shut up. I had no right to talk, especially not to Juniper.

She'd reached the other side of the room, pressed her hands to the counter and hunched her shoulders. The room was shrouded in light, but I'd never felt this much darkness in my life.

This whole situation frightened me even more.

I could lose my light, the girl that stood only feet away from me.

The clock on the wall above Officer Ellen's desk was loud, and although I was heavily focused on Juniper's back, I noticed the ticking.

It could have been an awful reminder that I had only moments before we'd split up, before I was in jail or put away for good.

How was I meant to go along with this?

She turned, sniffled, collected herself and rubbed her hands together. I was on the edge, waiting for her words to come, but she'd said enough.

But I'd never wanted to hear her voice as much as right then.

Juniper finished cleaning my face, it took quite a while but I wouldn't lie, I enjoyed the close contact, no matter the situation.

I did my best to look away, to not focus on her smouldering saddened eyes. I couldn't bear the thought of her crying over me, crying over the mistake someone else had made.

For all I knew, I'd broken her heart.

They'd brought Juniper in because she was the only one I'd allow the touch from. I must have been in pretty bad condition, if I needed to be cleaned this badly.

She brushed the blood from my hair, cleaned my bloody lip and bandaged the soreness over my nose. In just moments, my face was stinging from every bandage that covered my wounds. I counted almost six, the longest being the one along my new scar.

I couldn't help but yelp when she wrapped a gauze around my shoulder, and then my wrist.

When she saw the tattoo, I watched her eyes close sadly, her eyebrows dip inwards. It was another emotion, something I'd never seen between us.

Disappointment.

I'd be seeing a lot of it now.

Juniper didn't linger, she turned to the other bench, grabbed at a new shirt and then placed it beside me.

I'd begun to panic when she turned to leave, so I reached out and took her hand with both of mine. She struggled in my grip for a moment, before her shoulder dropped again. I wanted to embrace her, beg for her forgiveness.

I wasn't respecting her space; I was being selfish.

'Juniper, please,' I said. 'Please, look at me.'

'Why?' she asked. 'Why, Rayne?'

I missed the pet name 'Red' more than ever, my name was like poison right now.

I paused and held my breath, especially when she turned. I saw her eyes, lock onto mine. But she only shook her head and scoffed.

'Look at you,' she said, with one shake of her head. 'You've made a fool of yourself, gotten yourself into trouble? And for what?'

I didn't know how to respond, but I squeezed her wrist. She pulled it back to her side, then held back her tears. Not only was she annoyed, but she was tired.

'I did it...' I swallowed and held back a cry. 'For you,'

'Don't!' she cried back. 'Don't say it was for me!'

I froze under her yell, shook under her saddened eyes.

'You're an idiot!' Juniper sobbed, I could tell it pained her to say. 'You're an absolute idiot, and I was an idiot for trusting you!'

Before I could grab her, tell her I was sorry, she turned and left.

Instantly, the light in my eyes vanished. I was weak, weaker than I thought, I couldn't even rush after her and tell her why I was so sorry.

I was guilty, guilty of breaking someone's heart, guilty of causing more pain.

I was an idiot.

Alone in this room, I considered breaking everything I could get my hands on. I needed to take my frustration, my stupid choices out on anything I could touch.

But I knew, if I was to act upon that idea, I'd just add one bad choice to my list.

I'd lied.

Broken down one big ol' tower of trust, all because I tried to play hero.

Just how was I meant to explain that?

'So...'

I sat still, silent.

Opposite me sat Detective Rodgers, a cigar in his lips, a coffee and a bunch of files by his right hand. I'd been cleaned and changed into a new shirt, but I still hobbled over myself like a child. I kept thinking of Juniper, I knew she was watching me from outside this interrogation room. If I knew one thing, one of these mirrored walls wasn't a mirror on the other side .

I glanced around a few times and tried pinpointing just which side it was. I could feel Detective Rodgers's eyes on me, but I had no need to look his way.

'Full name is Rayne Claire Holmes?' he spoke softly, calmly. 'Am I correct?'

I paused before I spoke, parting my dry lips. 'Yes.'

'Now, Rayne...' he started. 'Firstly, tell me where you live?'

I swallowed and pressed my fingers together, shrugged my shoulders then sighed. There was no use lying here, he was a cop, this wouldn't be the last time I was explaining my life story.

'I live here...' I mumbled. 'In Boston.'

Rodgers touched his files, lifted one to his scarred face and blinked quickly. He'd taken his hat off and his coat, so he sat with a loosened tie, his cigar in his parted lips. The room was bright, but a dull sort of lightness, that was good to my headache.

'Says here, you're originally from Florida yes?' he asked.

I paused, he knew this already. Did he not recognize me from the station that day? He kept his eyes on mine, and I felt uncomfortable.

'Yes, I'm from Tampa.' I answered. 'My parents... live there.'

I hadn't even thought about my parents at all, it was quite mind boggling. Would they need to be notified about this whole situation? Would they help me pay bail of some sort?

I could just imagine my father right now, he'd be scolding me, so would my mother. The whole Holmes family would be disappointed in me, which I didn't really care much for.

But I didn't need them to know about this, no way.

'Now, we don't have your families contact numbers...' Rodgers mumbled. 'Did you need us to,'

'No,' I answered plainly. 'No need.'

He examined my eyes, and scribbled a few notes down, which I didn't bother reading.

'Rayne, I'll just ask you simply...' Rodgers slapped the notes down and leaned forward. 'Why were you involved with the Fire Jackals?'

I pondered for a long moment, which he noticed and told me to take my time. I was glad he wasn't going along with the whole good cop bad cop situation.

I don't think I could handle that at all.

I lowered my head and sniffled, taking in a deep breath. 'I thought,' I froze and swallowed. 'I thought I'd find him.'

'Find who?' Rodgers asked.

'Pebbles.'

'But you did,' he answered. 'You were working with him, are you telling me your intentions were not to work with the Jackals, you and the members were seen a day before, dealing close by."

I shook my head almost instantly.

'Christopher wasn't Pebbles,' I answered. 'he said so himself.'

Rodgers eased his eyes, and leaned back against his comfortable chair.

'You do know who you were involved with, yes?'

'Yes,' I replied. 'I know.'

'So, again I ask,' Rodgers took a suck from his cigar, and sniffled. 'Why were you involved with the Fire Jackals?'

He was confusing me, but I knew he was waiting for a more detailed explanation. I examined the room again, and focused on each camera, positioned in the corners of each wall. I wouldn't admit it, but I was frightened.

This was something I only saw on television, read in books and the newspaper.

'I…' I froze and pressed my hands to the table. 'It was only a week ago…'

I'd lost all concept of time before I was able to see the date plastered on the walls of the police station. It hadn't been days, just one.

I was a fool to think the Fire Jackals would trust me, there was no way they were going to allow a spy in their clan.

'I busk… as you know,' I glanced up at him, and he made no face, nothing to tell me he'd caught on. I sniffled and lowered my head again, remembering my conversation with Carla.

'I found out about the busking licence, and I had no money at all,' I answered truthfully, a little afraid Juniper could hear. 'Juniper and I had already begun searching…'

I paused and bit my tongue, would speaking about Juniper get her into trouble? We had trespassed after all.

'Go on, Rayne,' Rodgers pushed. 'Continue.'

I breathed in, every breath racked in my chest.

'C-Christopher,' I swallowed back my tears, ignored the image of his dead body, and pressed on. 'Christopher and his friend Reedy told me about a job, a job that paid good money. I'd only met the two of them a few weeks prior, and they seemed like nice guys.'

Rodgers was writing, very vastly.

'I had no idea it was Fire Jackal business…' I held my breath before I spoke. 'But on that same day, that night I was given a warning.'

'A warning?' Rodgers asked. 'What kind of warning?'

I raised my head and pursed my lips, wondering for a moment where my phone was. It was a silly thing to think about, but I honestly couldn't remember.

'A text message, from an anonymous sender…' I said. 'But now I know who warned me.'

There was a small pause, before Rodgers cleared his throat. 'And who was that?'

'Christopher,' I answered sternly. 'Christopher was the one who warned me, and helped Juniper.'

I could hear the defence in my voice, I was aware of Rodgers's suspicion, that Christopher really was Pebbles.

That thought scared me, and I fumbled a little.

I too, had been framed.

Pebbles really had thought it all through, of course!

Get Rayne Holmes involved, the right hand woman of the girl sneaking around and finding the truth, brand her with the Fire Jackal tattoo, and allow her to join the group.

I was really screwed, Rodgers had every right to think I was a liar.

But what about Juniper?

She knew the truth; she knew I wouldn't have joined for any other reason but to find Pebbles myself. She could be hanging onto the suspicion that I was doing it all for the money, but even Juniper wasn't that stupid.

Juniper knew me, she knew Rayne Holmes.

And she trusted me, well, did.

Rodgers wrote down another few lines, then he nodded his head. I breathed in before I continued, and flexed my sore shoulder.

'I thought…' I halted, and sighed. 'I thought joining them would help… help me find Pebbles. Help find the guy who put Juniper's sister down…'

When I told the truth, the guiltier I felt.

'But I was wrong,' I said simply. 'I was wrong, and I got myself in a mess.'

'That you did,' Rodgers answered back. 'So, you joined under the idea that you'd find out who Pebbles really was?'

I nodded.

'And yet you do not believe Christopher was the one who hit Natalie Bridges?' Rodgers asked. 'Even though we have a handful of evidence that he did?'

I slammed my hands down against the table, it shook everything, his coffee, his papers.

'No!' I yelled, anger taking hold of me. 'It wasn't him, I knew Christopher!'

'After just a few days?' he asked back, calmly. 'That's a lot of trust for someone you hardly knew.'

'Christopher didn't do it, he said so himself, and it makes no fucking sense!' I'd sworn in front of many people before, but a cop was a new one

I sat back down, and before Rodgers could tell me off.

So I described every single detail before I was knocked out cold. I told him about our journey out of Boston, and every pit stop we made. My vast words had surprised even myself, I was rushing everything out, getting defensive.

I finally reached my conclusion, and told Rodgers about Christopher' connection with the Jackals, how he described Pebbles as someone he feared, and that Manny and Crocker spoke about the leader as another person as well.

I did everything to back Christopher up, tell Rodgers that there was no way he could have been the almighty Pebbles.

When I reached his personal life, I paused and leaned back in my chair. My shoulder dropped, ached and left me shivering.

Did I have the right to talk about Christopher's personal life? Was it my job to tell the world of his drug addiction and depression?

I swallowed loudly, wiped my face of fresh tears and fisted my hands. I had to muster up a lot of strength to bring up Christopher' past, but when I opened up about the drugs and his story, Rodgers's concern was high, his curiosity evident.

I mentioned Christopher' family, his brother, that he was stuck once he stepped foot into the group.

'And what about this, Reedy figure?' Rodgers asked. 'Where does he stand in all of this?'

I shrugged my shoulders, I hadn't really thought about it. But I wondered how he'd react, knowing his best friend had shot himself.

Would he blame me? for Christopher' death?

Would Christopher' parents, his brother, also blame me?

I breathed in shakily, and tried my hardest to not think of that awful job, of telling a mother their son had died.

I collected myself, brought my hands to my thighs and mumbled.

'Christopher told me that Reedy knew someone important…I instantly thought of Pebbles,' I explained. 'Christopher also said that even Reedy didn't expect the job to be so dangerous, he should be in Maine right now.'

I was telling Rodgers about Sunday night now, the drugs and the plan Manny and Crocker were explaining.

I described everything I could remember, even if I wished I didn't have to. I finally reached my awful moment back at the old factory.

Waking up in a cold abandoned area and being brutally beaten. I told Rodgers everything Manny explained, the little add ins that Crocker spoke about too.

I was very clear when my story hit peak point, when Christopher turned on Manny and Crocker and told them he wasn't like the clan hoped he would be.

I described Christopher's deeds as heroic, something a so called 'mastermind genius' wouldn't do. I hoped Rodgers was beginning to believe me, because all that left my lips was the truth.

Finally, I told Rodgers about the setup, that Christopher killed himself because he knew Pebbles would make his family's life a living hell.

Rodgers was there for half of Christopher's confession, so I didn't need to relive that awful moment when I lost a friend.

I felt my bottom lip wobble, especially when I remembered the sounds, the smells and energy around Christopher's death.

I sat in silence, and shook my head slowly.

'Please…' I begged now, not something I was used to doing. 'Please, Sir. Christopher is innocent, he's been framed, I couldn't help him.'

'It wasn't your job to help him, Rayne,' Rodgers's voice was soothing, soft. 'None of this was your business, yet you still wished to get involved.'

I looked up to his calm eyes, but his eyebrows were crooked, inwards.

'I understand you did all of this to help, to help Miss Bridges,' he said. 'I know you and her share a close relationship, you have met her sister, indulged in the heroic act of finding out the truth.'

I could feel my bottom lip wobble; his words left nothing but a pang in my heart. Rodgers took another suck from his cigar, and let it fall into his ashtray.

'But you've made a mistake, many, many mistakes,' he told me. 'You're now involved with one of the biggest criminal groups of the state.'

I held my breath.

'You're a good kid, and I understand your intentions were not to hurt those around you,' Rodgers sighed. 'But you've broken the law, and consequences are to follow…'

I was scared now, my heart was thumping and I wanted to run. I was trying to hold a strong face, but I was falling apart again.

I glanced up to Rodgers, and he blinked sadly. 'I understand, some of us wish to find the truth ourselves,' he paused and stood up.

My eyes were eased, saddened to say the least. I sat still, watched him pace the back of the room then slip his hands into his pants pockets.

'But you've chased the truth, found it, and now you're in a lot of trouble,' he pointed to me, and grimaced. 'This won't be easy to get out of, Miss Holmes.'

I let my head fall, my hopes of leaving this station and sleeping in a warm bed with Juniper Bridges, crushed.

I'd royally screwed myself.

Rodgers pushed his chair in, glanced at his watch, then sighed.

'I will be back in just a moment, there are still many questions I need to ask,' he mumbled. 'Sit tight.'

When he shut the door, I let my shoulders finally fall the way they wanted to.

I could show my weakness, let the emotions take over.

I wasn't one hundred percent sure, who was watching me through the cameras, or through the one-way mirror.

But I hoped it was Juniper.

'Juniper,' I called. 'I only wanted to help, I didn't expect this to happen.'

I could have easily been talking to myself, but I needed to release. I lifted myself from my chair, and stepped towards the nearest wall.

'I didn't want anyone dying!' I sobbed. 'I didn't want anyone getting hurt, I just wanted to find the fucker who put Nat down!'

I felt the anger rise now, that uncomfortable feeling. I was a sitting duck; I couldn't believe one act of heroism had put me in this place.

I raised my finger to the camera and prodded the air.

'You can be angry at me!' I yelled. 'You can hate me, never trust me again!'

It pained me to say these words, so I turned and grabbed hold of my chair backing.

'But I did all this for you!' I cried. I didn't even feel the weight of the chair as I lifted it angrily. 'I did all this for you, for Nat!'

I threw the chair down, and watched the wood splinter, the plastic backing fly into the wall beside it. I'd pulled my shoulder again, I could feel the blood rush down the gauzes. But I was so upset, angry, that I couldn't even care.

I threw the table next and watched Rodgers' coffee and cigar sizzle into each other.

'I wanted to catch that motherfucker for you!' I roared, kicking the table forward. 'I wanted him dead! Not Christopher!'

I was making such a mess, but I was the biggest mess of them all. In this small interrogation room, surrounded by piles of paper, photos of Christopher' dead body, photos of the old factory, locations and faces, I stood and heaved.

I was losing myself, more and more. I breathed in, slumped to my knees and scrunched a few pieces of paper by my sides.

'I'm so sorry.' I cried. 'Juniper, Nat... Christopher.'

As I lay back, I watched the light above me fade, I was so tired, that I couldn't be bothered fighting the exhaustion.

Maybe if I fell asleep, I'd wake up from this bad dream.

Chapter Twenty-Five

JUNIPER

What would I call this feeling?

Numbness? Anger? Disappointment? Sadness?

I'd call it a mess.

A goddamn mess.

It was hard to process, anything to be exact. I'd caught myself trying several times throughout the morning, but nothing settled.

From the moment I received Sturges' call, I was constantly teetering on the edge. I was stuck in this sickening feeling, a constant wavering between emotions.

Whatever it was, I wished it would vanish. But the more I wished, the worse felt.

It was early, eight in the morning to be exact.

A lot had happened in the past two hours. I was questioned by Nick, again. In a cold room surrounded by white walls and a one-way mirror. He asked me to explain again, just what happened before I called him that night.

So I did, I told him; Sturges called me, out of breath and revealed the location of a missing car I'd been stressing over for weeks. I described the urgency in his tone, how it frightened me; but the adrenalin was rushing so hard that I only noticed later on.

Nick had given me a concerned look, he had noticed my dazed voice, my lonesome eyes. He asked me another question, tapping his pen against his clipboard. He asked about my day before the call, and I described Sturges change in personality, his eagerness to help.

The more I described it, the more I wondered if Sturges was trapping me, maybe if I had left a few minutes later, he could've bludgeoned me with something from his scrapyard of doom.

Nick was silent for a moment, he sat opposite me, a cigarette in his lips. He was a kind man, no other cop would have driven all the way to Somerville to pick someone up, to drive willingly into what could have easily been a dud.

But, it wasn't.

It wasn't a dud, and I was really experiencing all of this. First the interrogation room, where Nick Rodgers gave me worried glances, asked if I was comfortable. Now the waiting room, surrounded by Boston police officers, giving me the same glances.

I sat still, my hands on my lap, head angled downwards. I was out of it, lost in the thoughts that trailed my mind. Where did I even start?

Sturges had given me the correct information, I'd found the car. A part of me wished I hadn't, due to the offender being Christopher.

Christopher, the boy with speech issues, the boy who told me I was one of his friends. He was a bumbling mess, an anxious wreck, but he was still a kind soul.

At least I thought so.

I couldn't wrap my head around the conclusion that he was the one who hit Nat. That he was even a member of the Fire Jackals. I'd thought he was a mechanic working for his father at the mechanic shop down west. Not some bloodthirsty group member who drove around hitting little sisters for fun.

It didn't add up at first, but the more I obsessed over the thought, it made a little more sense. His anxiety was guilt, his trembling persona around me, was because of his crime.

How could I have been so stupid?

That was definitely him in those photos, plastered inside his car. That was definitely him, laying still upon the floor, a bullet hole lodged into his head, at the feet of my screaming girlfriend.

No, that was definitely Christopher.

I thought that image would fade, maybe not straight away, but slowly. I knew, as I sat there silent and still in a warm police waiting room, that image would never fade.

I'd never seen a dead body, not so close up. Of course, as I ran to Rayne's side, I did my best to ignore Christopher, but just knowing a dead body, three to be exact, lay around my feet was traumatising.

It was a gory scene, something nightmares were made of, something my night terrors would take advantage of.

It was going to be a long healing process.

Christopher was Pebbles.

Of course, I would have never expected it, and that was easily part of his crazy plan. He was so close to me, always coming into the shop and asking for a hot chocolate, asking for confidence. It made me feel pretty ill, to know he had secretly done something so awful.

Nat, she'd be shocked too. To know one of my friends was the asshole behind her pain, put her in that bed of hers.

But maybe she would rejoice, knowing very well that we'd found him, found Pebbles.

Should I rejoice? I didn't really feel like doing so. If this were a week ago, and I'd found Pebbles to be some chubby gang member's son, I would have raised my hands in the air and cheered.

Finding Pebbles, suing him, getting that money for Nat's surgery? It was a dream come true.

But this was different, Pebbles was Christopher. Rob's friend, my friend, even Rayne's friend.

Oh, here comes that flurry of emotions again, mostly disappointment.

Rayne had done the unimaginable. Joined up with the Fire Jackals, gotten herself into danger, putting herself aside for others.

Typical of her and I was a moron to trust her.

When I found her tied up, crying, screaming. I didn't know what to think. What was I supposed to think?

When I first found the car, saw Christopher and his brother smiling happily in those photographs, it all started piecing together. Like a muddled puzzle, as I ran into that decrepit building, my heart pumping back and forth, every piece was coming together.

It was forming a picture I feared, a picture of betrayal and disappointment.

I knew Rayne was involved once I'd figured out that Christopher was the owner of the Ford. I ran towards the gunshots, when I should have headed the other way.

I ran with fear pumping in my veins, but I needed to see, see the truth unfold.

God, I wish I hadn't.

I tried to tell myself otherwise, when I found her sitting there, struggling to catch her breath and cry at the same time. In that moment, I rushed to her side and held her face between my hands, she was panicked and scared.

In some situations, in moments of pure fear and vulnerability, sometimes putting your own fears aside for others was the right thing to do.

I brushed aside my anger and disappointment at the time, left one emotion, concern, lingering through me. Rayne was struggling, but when she took one look at me, she realised, I know she had.

She realised the mistake, the many mistakes she had made.

Lying, sneaking around, putting herself aside for another.

I didn't like thinking about it, I didn't like thinking about the girl I loved joining a team of mass murderers for whatever reason.

Was it money? She'd joined the Fire Jackals to make amends? I understood she needed that busking licence, but surely she could have picked a few shifts up somewhere else, why the goddamn Fire Jackals?

I felt the fire burn deep inside me, the tenseness of my bones. What about that trust? All that trust we'd built, only for her to throw it on the floor and rub it into the dirt.

I was pissed, beyond angry, ready to snap any time.

And I had snapped, just a few hours earlier. When Nick held me by the shoulders and told me that Rayne needed cleaning up; that she was lost and panicked even though she was surrounded by what we as society called the safest people on the planet.

Cops.

I was angry at her, yes. So goddamn angry that I could stamp my foot and call her an idiot over and over again, but I was worried.

Even though she did the wrong thing, I was so worried about her.

It wasn't every day you found your girlfriend tied up, bleeding like a fountain.

I was being stubborn, but I had to remain calm and content. I couldn't lose myself, not just yet.

Rayne had other ideas. She had snapped.

I watched her throw herself around that interrogation room, flip a table off the floor. She knew I was watching her, knew I could hear everything she said to Nick. Seeing her broken state in that seat, staring at her cuffed hands with a distant look upon her face, I didn't know how to feel.

I didn't know.

A part of me wanted to stride in there, slam my hands down on the table, before she threw it, and give her a stern talking.

I could yell at her for hours, tell her she was a complete fool, that she played dirty with our trust. But when she began to throw her emotions around, point at the one-sided mirror, almost exactly towards my location near the back door, and yell at me?

I froze, I had no desire to fight back, I was too fragile.

All I could remember, was watching her break down, sob and slam her hands against the wall. And the last thing I saw was Nick's scarred and barren face, as he took hold of my shoulders and told me to leave, sit in the waiting room and wait for my father.

I think he knew I was about to break; I think Nick had dealt with this before.

Maybe.

'Juniper.'

I ignored my name at first, continued to think about how I'd been betrayed by my other half, someone I thought about nonstop, wished to be close to.

How could she be so stupid? She was under arrest, involved with Boston's biggest crime lords. Now she was branded, most likely going to jail.

Rayne Holmes, you're such a—

'Juniper, honey.'

I snapped back to reality, to look upon the eyes of my tired father. He'd crouched to knee level, his right hand touching mine. I swallowed and blinked, examining his concerned face. I saw every line under his eyes, every weary worry that he held upon his shoulders.

He was scruffy and tired, brunette hair a mess, facial hair unshaven. He rushed here, that's for sure.

'Are you alright...?' he asked. 'I got here as fast as I could.'

I blinked again, every time I closed them, I wished to fall asleep there and then. Around me, cops bustled and spoke, cleared their throats and typed away at their computers. It ran in my ears, every single small noise, I was hyper aware, I didn't like it.

'Is Nat alright?' I asked, voice croaky. 'Where's Nat?'

Dad had this concerned look upon his face, something I knew I'd be used to now. I'd seen it from Nick, the cops around me, even Rayne.

Ugh, just thinking about her left me wanting to cry.

'She's at home, sweetie,' he answered. 'Arty's there.'

Oh, Arty. I'd completely forgotten all about her. I wondered what she was thinking right now, she must have seen the news. Oh, I hadn't even thought about that too, the news must have my face plastered all over it.

'She wanted to come, but Nat was still fast asleep...' Dad answered, gently whisking the hair from my face. 'She came rushing over as soon as she saw the news, just this morning...'

I shivered from his touch and sniffled quickly. The news? Ever since I was a little girl, I wished to be the one shoving my recorder into some news, into the face of some corrupted leader of Boston, and then throwing a tantrum when security pulled me away.

But I was the one who had microphones in my face, flash photography everywhere.

This was a big story, three bodies found in some abandoned factory? One survivor and a gruesome discovery?

It was all unfolding pretty quickly, I had so much catching up to do.

'Juniper, honey. You need to tell me what happened,' Dad's voice echoed, to and from both ears, ringing. 'What is going on?'

He was doing the right thing, comforting me in a time of absolute chaos. I needed someone there, and I never stopped to think my father could have been the one to go to in the first place.

If I were to go to him about this whole situation, trying to find Pebbles, sneaking into buildings, he'd tell me I was silly.

And I was, I was silly.

All I needed to do, was jump out of college for a while, pay off Nat's surgery. Yeah sure, we'd be in debt for a little while, okay maybe a few decades. But we'd live, we had aunts, uncles. There is no way they'd put us on the streets.

I was feeling more and more like an idiot as I thought of all the possible turns this could have taken, instead I was stuck with the awful ending.

He shook me again, gently so I'd respond to him. I swallowed again, looked into his warm eyes and shrugged my shoulders.

'Christopher shot himself,' I answered, blatantly. 'He's dead.'

'I–I know that,' he replied, sounding a little shaken. 'I heard that news already. But why are you involved?'

I held my hands together, and he laid one warm palm over them. Any human contact right now left me biting back tears, but I had to be honest.

I was all for the truth, but here I was keeping my father from all that I'd done. It was hard to talk, but I did my best.

'I…' I paused and bit my tongue. 'I haven't been honest with you.'

He was taken aback, just slightly. His eyebrows curled inwards, freckles above following their every move.

Dad and I never lied to each other, of course our private lives were strictly confidential, I didn't snoop into his property, he respected the same.

But we told each other everything. But these past few weeks had been absolute terror, we were never in the same house anymore.

I sighed and opened my mouth to speak, but I found my bottom lip wobbling.

'I wanted to find the guy who hit Nat,' I began, my voice was low, croaky. 'I wanted to find him and put him in jail, sue him and fix Nat up.'

I realised my tone was higher, my voice was quivering, weakening. I looked into my father's eyes, and he glared back, worried.

'I… I thought I could do it, with Arty's help, Rayne's help…' I paused, smiled painfully and chuckled. 'I found clues, snooped around, snuck into abandoned buildings, just to find out more.'

'Juniper…'

'I know!' I cried, heaving forward. 'I wanted to help Nat, I couldn't bear watching you lose your job, lose the house, I know how much that house means to you.'

Though I sobbed now, I knew the cops around us continued their work. I could feel some eyes on me, but that may have been the concern for my shaky body, my breaking state. I swallowed loudly, leant back and breathed in gently.

'I couldn't bear seeing Nat die...' I croaked, glaring at the ceiling. 'I just couldn't bear it...'

I listened to the heaters growl, the soft chatter around us, but my dad said nothing. I knew it was a lot to process, especially now that I was sitting in a police station waiting room. I felt his fingers twitch, his nerves tense and loosen.

'I'm sorry Dad,' I whimpered. 'I just needed to do this.'

'It's alright,' he muttered back. 'I'm surprised, but I'm glad you're alright.'

I was brought into his embrace, after I thought he'd surely tell me off. Tell me I was an irresponsible adult who could have gotten killed. He pulled me into his big strong burly arms, the scent of home lingered all over him.

It left my tears welling up, my heart aching. Right now, there was nothing else I could have needed, then a hug from my father.

He shushed me when I sobbed again, muffled in his strong shoulder.

'I know, everything is okay,' he whispered back. 'It's all over now.'

It was typical words after an awful event, but God they were brilliant to hear. But I knew, I knew deep down that it wasn't over at all.

There was so many unanswered questions, the ones that I originally needed answering, were unfolding into more.

'You did all you could, Juniper,' Dad sighed, he kissed me against the temple, shushing me once more. 'No more crying now, alright?'

I couldn't reply to him in words, so I mumbled, and held tight around his neck. A part of me wished he would lift me over his shoulder like he did when I was younger, take me into my room back home and tuck me into bed.

I was a wreck, and I needed a good sleep.

But this didn't stop the swirling, the mass of information in my brain. The event was over, yes, but the aftermath was only beginning.

A large thud of the doors prompted Dad and I to break apart. He lifted himself first, held me down in my seat and watched another awful scene unfold.

Two adults were being ushered in by a few cops, a female and a male. The male was tall, lanky and wore glasses. He'd just gotten out of bed, because his black shirt wasn't tucked into his blue jeans, and his shoes weren't on properly. His hair was a mess, and his eyes were red and puffy. I noticed him straight away, I'd seen him at the mechanics here and then, Christopher' father.

Next to him, was a snivelling woman. Her long brown hair was tied up in a messy bun, her coat covering her satin pyjamas. She was whimpering loudly, and sadly.

I stepped beside dad, watched them walk in, watched the woman fiddle with a tissue, back and forth between her fingers.

It was a neurotic thing to do, of course, who could blame her? Her son had died.

Not only had he taken his own life, he had joined a murderous team of grade a asshats.

But I couldn't help feel for her, she was a total wreck, even more so then Rayne. I lost myself in my thoughts, as she slowly walked by, but when she caught my sights, she widened her eyes and sobbed loudly.

I'd never met Christopher's mother before, but she seemed to know exactly who I was.

'Oh, honey!' she sobbed, rushing forward.

The cops beside her tried holding her back, but I was already in her grip, after three steps. I swallowed and focused on her eyes, her grip was shaky and so was she.

'Oh, honey, Christopher didn't mean it!' she cried, shaking me. 'He's such a good boy, he would never do something so awful!'

I was stuck in her grip, even my father tried to hold her back but she continued to moan. My eyes were widened, as hers were too. They were red, bloodshot and she smiled like a complete lunatic. 'Christopher is a lovely boy, you know!' she chuckled, heaving her sobs. 'A lovely boy!'

She was practically dragging me down to the floor, her body arched and angled. I focused on her, the way her hair whisked around her teary eyes, left me swallowing back my own sobs.

'He did so well in school, grades were perfect! There is no way he could have done this!' Christopher's mother was lost, and I was frozen in her grasp.

I'd never seen a human being act this way, I'd never experienced the loss of a family member. I wondered for a fast moment, just exactly what could have been going through her head. Would I act the same way if Nat passed away?

I swallowed when the cops pulled her back, well attempted to. Even her husband looked me in the eyes, his were mellowed, tired and lost.

He focused on pulling his wife from my grip, and dad focused on ripping me back too. She was fighting the hands, telling them to back off, telling them she wanted to stay with me and describe how 'wonderful' Christopher was.

A part of me felt angry, I wanted to tell her off, tell her that her son had put my sister through hell.

But I just, couldn't.

Not when someone was like that.

Dad and I watched a broken woman being pulled into the main office, she still cried to me, her hands waved, and she had this smile upon her face like everything would be alright.

Were humans really that delusional when the world broke apart around them?

I couldn't fathom the idea of losing Nat, and seeing that left my knees shaking. I was being held up by dad, his hands tight around my shoulders.

I huffed, swallowed and blinked quickly. That was too much in a few seconds, way too much.

'C'mon, honey,' Dad mumbled. 'Let's get you home.'

I turned to follow his lead, follow him through the stalls of confused cops. But yet another sound left me turning, one familiar voice.

Nick was escorting a messy Rayne out of the interrogation room just a few doors away, he held her not forcefully, but rather gently. She was shaky, her legs wobbled and she kept pulling at the cuffs around her wrist.

Even from here, I could see the Fire Jackals emblem, red and purple on her right wrist. It left my stomach whirling, made me shiver.

What was she thinking?

Nick was smoking yet another cigarette, eyebrows concerned and rustled. He mumbled something to Rayne, then to another cop who stood by. He turned his attention my way, lifted his hand to halt me, and quickly dismissed himself.

Rayne glanced up too, saw me and grimaced sadly. I was doing my best to forget our little tumble in sick bay. Oh, I wanted to yell and cry at her then, but my job was to simply clean her up, and leave. That wasn't the right place to have an argument, not one bit.

But, it was hard to not hold her face and scold her, tell her how much I was worrying. Seeing the pain and strain in her eyes, was heartbreaking.

Dad stepped to my side again once Nick reached the both of us. He shook Nick's hand tightly, and shared that mutual worry.

'Detective Nick Rodgers,' Nick mumbled, the cigarette hopping with his lips movement. 'You must be Juniper's father.'

'Yes,' Dad replied, shaking Nick's hand as he spoke. 'I'm her father yes.'

'Your daughter needs some rest; she's been on her feet for quite a while now,' Nick cleared his throat, he wanted my attention.

But I couldn't look at him, not when Rayne stood only feet away. She had those smouldering eyes, a sorry look upon her face.

She knew exactly where she had gone wrong.

'A–about that, Detective.'

'Call me Nick.'

'Nick.'

I sniffled and watched Rayne shuffle on the spot, the cop who held her arm glanced our way too.

'What happens now? With, the parents of the deceased,' Dad mumbled. 'Their son was the boy who hit my daughter, is that correct?'

I shivered and glanced to Nick, his eyes had softened, cigar sizzling. 'It appears so, I was there when the boy confessed, as did two of my colleagues.'

I must have missed that part of the morning, but that just made me believe there was no way Christopher wasn't Pebbles.

He even admitted it to Nick.

'So...' Dad replied. 'What should we do now?'

'You do nothing, Miss Bridges, that goes for you too,' Nick pointed my way, and I tore my eyes from Rayne again, just to look at him.

Nick and I shared that mutual understanding, he knew exactly where I was glaring, and tried to sidestep in my direction.

'We'll take it from here,' he said. 'We need to talk to the deceased's parents, get some information from them before anything legal occurs.'

'My youngest daughter is not well, Nick.'

'I am aware, and so I ask you to transfer her to the nearest hospital, all bills leading up to the surgery will be covered.'

Dad blinked, cleared his throat and lowered his hand a little.

'Oh, Okay,' he mumbled. 'Is there anything we have to sign, any...'

'No,' Nick answered sternly, the scar under his right eye twitched. 'We've got everything under control, I understand the funeral for the deceased will be held as early as possible. Given the situation, I understand if you would rather stay clear.'

I listened to Dad and Nick converse, speak about the upcoming issues they may or may not face. But I drained all that out, Rayne and I had made eye contact again. Even when bustling cops rushed back and forward, blocking our view, we never took our eyes off each other.

She watched me, looking more and more eager to throw herself out of the clutches of the big burly cop beside her, and rush to my side.

I pictured that happening, and wondered what exactly I would do.

Would I push her away, tell her to back off and turn from her?

Or would I hug her tight and tell her I was scared, needed her comfort.

Ugh, both of them would end badly.

Rayne's eyes flinched, her chest rose and fell, she swallowed more than usual.

'Alright, I will contact you when we have more information,' Nick said, voice husky.

His voice knocked me into reality once again, and I was whipped from Rayne's eyes.

'For now, go home, get some rest,' Nick softly said, touching my shoulder. 'I'll speak to you soon.'

The urgency in his tone left me panicking, he was ushering Dad and I out now, and I couldn't have that.

'And Bl–' I paused, swallowed, and caught myself. 'And Rayne?'

Nick froze, his lips pursing around his cigarette.

I was confused, where did that even come from? Dad stopped beside me, he too looked Rayne's way. They hadn't officially met, but he was aware of who she was, especially if the news was repeating over and over.

Nick turned his head, focused on Rayne, who was aware of our looks, then grimaced shortly.

'Oh, Miss Holmes?' he asked. 'Don't you worry, we'll be keeping a watchful eye on her, for the majority of the day. There is still much more to cover before she goes anywhere.'

That scared me. Although I was furious at her, I still feared for what happened next.

Jail? Court?

I set my eyes on her again, and she was on the verge of panic, seeing me leave. When Dad patted my back, I continued to walk. I was tired, sloppy and I needed rest.

I wasn't sure there was going to be much sleeping, but I needed out of this place.

Before we walked through those glass doors, the ones that swung back and forth, I turned my head to glance at Rayne Holmes once more.

Her bruised and battered face was pulled in utmost pain, I half expected her to run after me, but she was under the watchful eye of twenty cops.

She wasn't going anywhere.

It was hard to turn away, harder than I expected.

There were many things in this life that I hadn't experienced before. I hadn't hiked the mountains of Maine, or seen the Grand Canyon. I'd never eaten a whole jar of Nutella on my own, or skydived. Life was something to rejoice about.

To live was something extraordinary, and we as humans always forget that. I wasn't one to wake up and think of all the positives about living. Sometimes I wished to stay in bed all day and waste away twenty-four hours of life. Sometimes I wanted to sit in my dorm room and research old articles from the forties and fifties, see how they wrote in those times.

I've been surrounded by people who told me to live every day like it was my last. But honestly, who thought about that day?

Thinking about the moment of death frightened me, like it frightened many others. I didn't like thinking about death, or talking about death. Nobody in my family had died, thank God. So I was spared of that awful gather of family, mourning over the death of blood.

So why was I here? Why was I standing beside a shaky boy with his eyes closed, head down? Why was I next to a random family member of Christopher's, who glared upon a coffin with bittersweet sadness?

Why was I here?

When I came home yesterday, I kissed Nat upon the head, told her she was getting her surgery, and fell right asleep next to her.

I remember her asking Dad and I one hundred questions, she saw the news, cried about Rayne. But I was so exhausted, I couldn't respond to her. Arty left as soon as I had arrived, I tried to stop her, but she looked absolutely furious. She threw herself from my grip, and rushed to her car.

I hoped she wasn't going to the police station; Rayne would be in much more danger now.

When I fell asleep, I told myself there was no way I would attend Christopher' funeral. There was no way I would sit and mourn over a guy who did such an awful thing.

So then why was I here?

It was cold that morning; the rain was drizzling absolutely everywhere. The mud wobbled at my feet, the scent of wet dirt drifted. The priest mumbled, even over the light thunder in the distance. Boston was weeping today, as was Christopher's mother, who stood close to her sons casket, her tears evident even through the rain.

Next to her, was Christopher's brother, the same boy as in those photos. He was small, maybe Nat's age, but he looked absolutely broken, his eyes wide, mouth ajar. He had one day to process that his brother had passed away, I could only imagine how hard it was.

I was close to Christopher' coffin, a brown closed casket, slim and slick with water.

I couldn't look at it, it only left me shivering. Knowing there was a dead body in that wooden box? Only made me think of how it could have easily been Nat.

Nick had gotten back to Dad and I before nightfall, told us the great news. That Christopher' parents would pay for Nat's surgery, get her fixed up in no time.

I would have rejoiced any other day, if it were any other person.

There was something awful about celebrating the death of Christopher, but I would be lying if I didn't say I was so happy Nat would get her surgery.

I wouldn't have to drop out of college, Dad wouldn't have to do a bunch of double shifts.

Nat would be running in no time, going back to school, being herself.

The priest began blessing Christopher' casket, flicking an essence over it. I focused on each drip, flinching every time he whipped the plant back and forth.

Reedy was beside me, he'd come home from Maine. I had my suspicious about him as well, especially knowing he was along with the whole job. As soon as he was home, he was taken into custody for questioning. I wondered what he was asked, what he was doing in the woodsy part of town.

But it wasn't my right to pry, he too had become a bumbling mess. He greeted me with tears as soon as I stepped foot in the cemetery, a lot of eyes were on me actually.

I didn't blame them, the victim's sister appearing at the offender's funeral? They must have thought I was mad. Or awfully rude.

But I was here to give my condolences to Christopher, enemy or not.

He was still someone I knew.

Reedy flinched when the priest passed him, his bottom lip was trembling, his hands shook. I didn't know how to react, but I held his hand tightly, it wasn't every day your best friend passed away. He squeezed back, the sign of comfort left him sighing and swallowing.

I glanced up, looking forward past Christopher' coffin. While the words of the Holy Bible continued to be read, I focused past the group of black and grey suits. Another small group stood feet away from the main, at a distance that was respected.

At first, I wondered how Christopher' parents and family would react, but then I realised this event was closed, personal. They would have had to be invited to be here. I expected Christopher's mother to be the one who invited her; she was already manic and lost, I'm sure she didn't think it through at the time. She would invite anyone who was 'Christopher's friend.'

And Christopher was her friend, after all.

I blinked, my face dry thanks to the man beside me, who held an umbrella over my head. Another pair of eyes did the same, blinked sadly and tiredly. Nick Rodgers held his own black umbrella over her tall state.

There she stood, only feet away, battered and bruised in a slim black suit, surrounded by three cops. Yet even from here, in the dreary rain where I stood mourning over the death of a man I called my friend, a tiny portion of myself wished to be holding onto her hand. Allowing comfort, touch, anything to pull us through this misery.

Rayne was mourning, I could see it in her face, even from so far away. She was clean, her hair and her face wiped of any blood. I tried to look away, especially when Christopher's casket was being lowered, the cries and sobs around me continued, but I needed to focus on something else. Flashing images, of Nat vanishing, her funeral, and the pain she was enduring were leaving my head spinning. All this emotion was too much to handle, why did I come here?

I heard Reedy break beside me, he covered his face with his free hand, and I held his arm now, comforting him, pressing my forehead against it.

Christopher's mother sobbed loudly, tried to throw herself forward, but many family members held her, even her younger son.

It was something I never wanted to experience, a funeral.

I knew in life's many miseries; I'd experience it someday or another.

But I didn't think it would be this hard.

Minutes of agony continued, many tears were shed, even I held back my sobs. Christopher had always come across to me as sweet, caring.

It was hard to believe, as much as I wanted to deny my own conflicting thoughts, something told me he wasn't the one who should have been in that casket.

I closed my eyes, listened to the sounds around me, but they had become too loud, too extreme.

The cries of many, the wavered emotions of people I hadn't even met, it was all too much.

When the ceremony ended, we were all handed a lone rose, something to leave Christopher as he ventured somewhere else.

When I was handed one of its thorny stems, I swallowed and held it close. The edges pricked at my finger, but I was numb at this point.

I watched family member after family member throw their rose into the deepened hole. Some kissed them, some whispered prayers. It was surreal, too surreal.

MacCready turned to me, brushed his hand against my cheek and wiped something away, he looked saddened to know a tear lingered there.

I was just confused.

He stepped forth, mumbled something to his rose, and threw it inwards. I think he stood there, watching it flutter below, before he turned and nodded once my way. I saw his face contort, tense and falter as he walked.

Many who passed Christopher's coffin looked my way, whispered, but I blocked all that out.

All I focused on, was another who strode forward. Her presence left me a little uneasy, not in an awful way, more like a 'confused bundle of emotions' kind of way.

Suddenly the stem thorn broke skin, it hurt.

Rayne had no handcuffs on, so she held her rose tight. I could see every new scar on her face, every pain ridden scuff.

Her left eye was bruised, black and purple. Her upper lip cut, her left eyebrow split open once more, and the biggest cut of all, lingered from the left side of her face, up her left cheek. It was thin, but I could still see it, I wanted to comfort her in that time, drag my fingers alongside the length and tell her she was still beautiful.

She caught my eyes staring, and I glanced to my feet. I wasn't ready to give her the satisfaction of eye to eye contact, not this close.

Nick nodded to me, tipping his hat, it was drenched in rain. I returned the same, a simple nod and a purse of my lips.

Nick and his officers let their roses go, I watched them fall, heavily over the rain. The thunder was picking up now, and I could still hear Christopher's mother cry, tell her husband he would come back, she that she could make him pancakes and freshly squeezed orange juice. I needed to get out of here, especially now that Rayne looked my way, from the opposite end of this pit of misery.

I gave her a sideways glance, dropped my rose and turned to trudge off. I was completely drenched in the rain as I did so, but I couldn't look back at all.

I knew she was staring at my back, with lonely eyes, hurt.

Well I was hurt too, and I couldn't stand being there.

I had experienced death that day, seen the emotions surrounding it.

I never wished to experience it again.

By the mid-afternoon, I was showered dressed and clean. I packed up Nat's bags and prepared her for hospital,, my chest still lingered with that awful feeling, bittersweet agony.

Outside the thunder continued, grumbled and groaned. The house shook under its mighty boom, the wind chimes mom left up outside rang eerily.

This day was just miserable.

But the positive was here, she was sitting in bed, watching me pace and pack. Nat was thrilled about the news, that she'd be getting her surgery and she'd heal over time. Of course, she was a little scared that the whole thing could backfire and she'd be crippled for eternity. But Samantha had already spoken to Dad and I, and told us that things would be alright.

And this time, I knew she was right.

'Are you coming with me?' Nat asked. 'To the hospital?'

I turned to her, rubbed my hands upon my jeans and nodded. 'Of course, why?'

She breathed in tiredly, the machines were the only thing I had to pack up, but that was the ambulances job, not mine.

'You don't have to go to the police station?' Nat asked another question.

I paused, rubbed the bridge of my nose and stepped her way.

When she found out, about everything, she feared I was going to jail. She was worried I'd stuffed up, and I'd never come home.

It was a little amusing to me, she was so worried about me, when I worried nonstop about her.

I sat beside her, and examined her face.

Nat had cleared up, knowing she was going to be alright. She was still gaunt, wispy hair around her eyes and ears. But she had a certain glow upon her face, happiness.

I smiled, tucked the hair behind her ears and nodded.

'You know everything is going to be alright.' I told her. 'I'm not going anywhere.'

'You promise?'

'I promise, you ninny.'

She giggled when I pulled her ear, but that smile quickly faded. I blinked, and waited for her to continue. But she froze, kept her tired eyes on mine, I pushed my question.

'What?' I asked. 'What's the matter?'

Nat shrugged her shoulders. At first I thought she was frightened about the surgery, so I held her hand and grinned.

'Hey, you're a trooper!' I cheered, voice crackling along the tone. 'You'll be running around annoying me in no time—'

'It's not that,' Nat interrupted.

I paused and swallowed the rest of my words, I wasn't used to Nat overbearing me. She sniffled, glanced to her TV and then chewed her bottom lip.

I followed her eyes, wanted to see what she was seeing. The room was warm, but there was a certain coldness lingering.

'Arty was really mad,' Nat said. 'She said she hated Rayne.'

I shivered at that name, I thought I'd avoided that conversation with my sister. Honestly, I wasn't exactly sure how to explain what happened, or what we were doing messing with the Fire Jackals.

Nat loved Rayne, she was over the moon when she heard about our date, how brilliant it went.

Remembering that night, left my heart aching. All that love and contact, only for Rayne to go and do something stupid.

'Do you hate Rayne?' Nat asked.

I leaned back a little, my breath was kicked from my chest. Did I hate her? Did I really despise the girl?

Of course, right now I couldn't stand the idea of her around me, but could I ever hate Rayne Holmes?

No, never.

'No,' I answered, I told myself too. 'No, I don't hate her.'

Nat blinked, eyelashes fluttering once and twice. She opened her mouth to speak, but lost her words when the doorbell rang.

I sighed, patted my hands to my lap and tried pinpointing who it was. Was Dad home early? Maybe Arty was coming by to say goodbye to Nat.

I jumped up from her bed, with a sour taste in my mouth.

'I'll be one minute,' I muttered.

As I left her room, I gained speed, even though I wished to dawdle, someone was waiting for me on the other side of that door.

They didn't ring again, thank God, be a little patient.

I sniffled as I opened it quickly, but boy did I feel like slamming it shut.

Rayne stood before me, still in her suit, hands pocketed. She wasn't drenched in rain, but she was still a little wet. I held the side of my front door, and froze under her glare.

'Juniper,' she mumbled.

'Rayne, now is honestly not the time,' I started.

She fumbled, rubbing the back of her neck. I saw Nick parked in my driveway, he was smoking again, keeping that watchful eye on Rayne's back. She couldn't go anywhere without an escort, that was understandable.

I would have expected a cop to be beside Rayne at all times.

Why not now?

'I wanted to see Nat,' Rayne said. 'If that's okay.'

I paused, eased my eyes at hers and clenched my teeth. 'Not really.'

Rayne flinched, then swallowed awkwardly. The rain was becoming heavier, whisking leaves towards the doorframe. I shivered under the winds frozen touch, the hairs on the back of my neck rising.

'Juniper, please,' Rayne's voice was stern. 'Look, I don't have much time. Nick gave me ten minutes.'

'Then we'll stand out here for ten minutes!' I sarcastically bit back. 'I'm not letting you in my house.'

'Could you please, let me see Nat.'

'No.'

'Juniper!'

'Nope!'

Rayne was getting frustrated, if she weren't under the watchful eye of Nick Rodgers, she'd probably push past me. I saw her hesitate, ease her eyes and groan lightly. I finally had a closer look at her scars, and they left my heart pulsating. I couldn't imagine the pain she endured, what did they do to her?

'Juniper, please,' she repeated. 'You need to let me see her, I have to see her. Just give me five minutes, and I'll be out of your hair.'

I listened to her, crossed my arms and chewed my bottom lip.

'I get it, I'm not wanted,' Rayne snapped. 'So just let me see her, and I'm gone.'

I wanted to reply, but the energy was lost. She wasn't wanted, at this time, but I didn't have the heart to tell her myself.

I grimaced, stepped by and let her in.

'Thank you,' Rayne grunted as she walked forward.

I glanced to Nick before I closed the front door, he was still glaring this way, was I even allowed to close it?

Rayne stood still and waited for me to pass first. I did, rather sternly. I was furious to know she was here, and furious with myself.

I wasn't strong enough to kick her out and tell her to back off, but I knew Nat would be excited to see her.

I was right.

'Rayne!' Nat gasped, she tried to lift herself from her bed, but fell back gently. 'You're here.'

Rayne grinned and stepped forward, I should have drawn a line between her and my sister, a certain spot where she could reach. But Rayne took my sister into her arms, hugged her tight.

'Hey, kiddo,' she replied. 'I'm here.'

Nat pulled back to smile, but it vanished at the sight of Rayne's face. I couldn't blame her; Rayne was beaten up beyond recognition.

'Rayne, your face,' Nat quivered. 'What happened to your–'

'Aw this?' Rayne grinned, she touched her black eye, the scars, the cuts. 'This is nothing! Don't stress, how are you feeling?'

'Rayne, but.'

'No buts, tell me, what's new?' Rayne chuckled. 'Excited to finally get that surgery, yeah?'

I grimaced, rolled my eyes from her happy persona. She wasn't fooling anyone, she was a mess, through and through.

Nat glanced to me, and I swallowed back.

'You did all this?' Nat asked, she blinked. 'You said you'd save me, and you did.'

I raised my eyebrows, confusingly glanced to my sister. What was she on about? Rayne? Saved her?

Rayne listened to her talk, but she shot me a nervous look.

'You really did do something stupid,' Nat sighed. 'You got into trouble didn't you? You said you would.'

'I'm sorry,' I paused, lifted my hand and blinked. 'What's going on here?' I stepped forward, flipping my finger between the two of them.

Rayne cleared her throat, but Nat weakly smiled.

I wasn't smiling, not at all.

'Natalie?' I asked, sternly.

'Sorry, Rayne...' Nat eased, her face a little childish.

'Look,' Rayne interrupted, she lifted herself from the bed. 'I told Nat I'd do something stupid, and I did.'

'She told me not to tell you, Juniper!' Nat was frightened. 'But she wasn't doing anything wrong, she just wanted to save me!'

I gaped, and shook my head. I was smiling, not a happy grin, no, I was astounded by her pure stupidity.

'You asked my sister to lie for you?' I asked.

'Juniper...' Rayne started.

She stepped forward, her hands reached for me, but I veered back, no way was she touching me now.

'You,' I said again, eyes wide. 'You asked, my sister,'

I pointed at Nat, who was nervously looking at the both of us.

'To lie, for you?'

My heart was racing, as was my anger. There was no way this was happening, just when I thought this day couldn't get any worse.

I looked at the both of them, I wasn't as upset at Nat, then I was Rayne. She'd asked my twelve-year-old sister to keep something from me, she knew all about Rayne's stupid idea.

And she couldn't speak a word of it.

I swallowed, contained my anger for a moment, and pointed at Rayne.

'We need to talk,' I said, my tone lower than usual. 'Now.'

'B–but Juniper!'

'Natalie,' I barked back, my hands raised. 'Please, not now.'

I turned, and started my walk, my mouth was still gaped, I was still letting that fire ignite inside me. Rayne wasn't ready for this rage, not at all.

She followed me, and I listened to her footsteps, all I could honestly hear was my own heartbeat.

When my kitchen door was closed behind Rayne, I didn't hesitate to turn and push her roughly. She stumbled back a bit, her shoulders recoiling.

'Are you fucking kidding me?!' I screamed, shoving her again. 'What is your issue, Rayne Holmes!?'

Rayne's eyes were wide, she looked taken aback standing there.

'Why would you be so stupid?' I yelled. 'How dare you make my own sister lie to me!'

'I–I just.' Rayne was trying to speak, but I wasn't going to let her, not yet.

I turned on my heels, touched the sides of my head and turned to flip them towards her.

'To protect you?' I scoffed. 'You asked Nat to lie, to protect your dumb ass!?'

I was being rough, even my words surprised me, but I was done with this, done with all this lying.

Rayne was struck for words, even when I prowled my kitchen and threw my hands with every word.

'Give me one good reason, why I shouldn't kick you out of my life, right now!' I yelled, pointing my index finger at her chest.

She still hadn't moved from the last place I pushed, she was glaring at me, eyes wide, hurt. I wanted to tell her off for that, but she began stuttering, struggling to push the words out. I was already out of breath, close to crying, close to screaming my lungs out.

'T–this wasn't the reaction I was expecting,' Rayne stammered.

'Oh?!' I laughed sarcastically. 'What were you expecting then? For me to jump for joy?'

She stepped closer, and I pushed her back again, she didn't move much, but she still wobbled on the spot.

I didn't want to hurt her, but I just had to push some sense into her.

'Were you expecting me to thank you?' I cried, dabbing my finger sharply into her collarbone. 'Wow! Okay!'

I stepped to my kitchen bench, leant over it, breathed in and turned with a smile.

'Wow, thanks Rayne!' I sneered. 'For joining a murderous team to be a hero!'

'I don't think you're being fair!' she answered back.

'Oh, I'm not being fair?' I cried back. 'Me?'

She swallowed when I stalked closer, expecting another push.

'You say I'm not being fair?' I asked, my tone low. 'You lied to me! We built all this trust, and you threw it all over the floor!'

I felt my chest tighten, my lungs pull and pull.

'I didn't want to lie!' Rayne said. 'This wasn't what I wanted! I didn't want to lie! I just wanted to help!'

'When did you know the job was with the Fire Jackals!?' I asked over her babbling apologies. 'Tell me!'

Rayne swallowed again, her eyes darting to and from the floor and my eyes. She had more bad news for me, just great.

'Tell me!' I yelled, pushing her again.

She held my wrists, and I flinched from her touch. I was frustrated, and I continued to arch forward.

'Saturday,' she answered sternly. 'I got an anonymous message, Saturday.'

I gasped, let my struggle fall, and shook my head.

'Before we?' I croaked. 'B–before we...'

Rayne nodded weakly, and she didn't hold herself up when I pushed again. She stumbled to the floor, and I cried loudly in even further frustration.

'Why didn't you just tell me!?' I yelled. 'Why didn't you just tell me when you first got the message?!'

Rayne tried stumbling to her feet, but I powered over to her, leaned over and kept her down.

'Because!' she cried back. 'I didn't want to see you go through that!'

'Through what?!'

'The pain!'

'Oh for God's sake!' I groaned and leaned back.

I was out of breath, and I had started crying. I didn't even notice it, but they were rushing down my face like waterfalls.

I was so hurt, so betrayed and pushed to the edge.

I didn't expect more pain, so how come more and more was piling up?

'Juniper...' Rayne croaked. 'I'm sorry I lied, I didn't want you involved.'

I stood by the kitchen counter, shaken and weak. I tried to keep a stern face, but my emotions betrayed me. I was sobbing now, covering my mouth with wobbly hands.

'Juniper, please,' she spoke from the floor. 'I thought I could find him, and fix all of this. I thought they wouldn't see me coming, and I could find him...'

I breathed in and held myself up weakly, I hoped she wouldn't touch me, or I'd lash out again.

The kitchen was usually a bustling place full of food, my father's awesome cooking, and my sister's silly jokes.

But right now, it was a cesspool of disappointment and dread.

'I saw Nat...and I.'

'Don't bring her into this!' I sobbed. 'Don't you dare!'

She was brought back by my tears, my shaky breath. She was on her feet again, but didn't dare step towards me.

'I couldn't bare seeing the pain she was going through, all those machines. You saw how I was after that,' Rayne paused. 'At the time I thought I could pull it off... you were already in so much pain as well, why would I want to add this to the list?'

'Because Rayne!' I snapped back. 'You completely ignored what I told you to do!'

Rayne froze, but maintained eye contact.

I was lost, my anger had turned to sadness now.

'I told you to think! Think before you do this.'

'Do what...'

'Put others before yourself! You always forget about you!' I cried back. I had to inhale before I spoke, the croakiness of my voice shook my chest. 'You didn't care one bit about the busking licence didn't you?'

She lost her words, and her eyes fell to the floor.

That was a good enough answer.

'You took this whole situation upon yourself!' I sobbed. 'You grabbed an awful opportunity, and thought you could save the day!'

She watched me raise my hands and laugh again, a breath of defeated air.

'And you came out looking like completely stupid and reckless!'

'Why are you being like this!' Rayne yelled.

It was I who was shocked now, to see her retaliate so loudly. I hadn't heard Rayne yell like this, not for a long time.

But even now, it was serious, a little too serious.

'You're being ungrateful!' she cried, pointing her finger to the floor. 'I did this for you! For you and Nat! For your whole fucking family!'

'And you expected me to be happy about it!?'

'I expected you to thank me!'

'Thank you?' I cried loudly. 'Thank you for getting yourself in danger? Getting beaten up? Arrested?'

I paused and took a breath, Rayne was firing up.

'Nearly dying?' I growled. 'Thank you?'

Rayne lost her words once again and brushed a shaky hand through her hair. I watched it fall through the webs of her fingertips, but I had to focus on her face again, I was watching her crumble.

'News flash, Rayne!' I started. 'I don't need a hero; I need a girlfriend!'

I swallowed and turned again, wiping the tears from my face, there was just too much tension between us right now.

'I trusted you…' I croaked. 'I trusted you, Red…'

I was baffled, I couldn't understand how she'd do such a stupid thing. Why wouldn't she tell me? Did she think I wasn't strong enough? Was she trying to play hero and expect things to just work out?

I jolted when her hands wrapped around my waist, tight around my stomach.

If this were three minutes ago, I would have pulled myself away, told her to go forth and multiply.

But I was tired, exhausted from all the anger and sadness.

Rayne held me tight, her breath was shaky, she was crying again. I couldn't stand it when Rayne Holmes cried, it was so unlike her.

'I'm sorry…' she sobbed. 'I would never lie to you on any other occasion.'

'But you did, Rayne.'

'I know... But I just wanted to fix everything, I wanted you to be happy.'

'Now you're in so much trouble...' I paused and wiped my face again, her forehead was against my head. 'You'll go to court, maybe even jail.'

When I said that, my voice fell into a sore whimper. I'd been so blinded by my rage, my sadness, that I'd completely forgotten about her consequences.

Yes, I was so sore at her for lying.

I knew she was only trying to protect me, protect Nat.

But she lied, and I couldn't handle liars.

I sniffed, turned and held her face quickly. She seemed to tense up from my touch, maybe she expected me to slap her.

No, I would never, I already felt awful for pushing her.

But I knew I had the right to be mad, I had the right to be upset. Rayne knew that too.

I lost myself then, in the contact we shared. Rayne Holmes wasn't a monster; she wasn't someone who lied on any occasion.

I knew she wanted to do right, I knew she only wanted to help.

I sniffled and watched her eyes, she was practically shivering.

'Look at you...' I stammered, brushing my thumbs along her scars. 'I could have lost you.'

Rayne's bottom lip trembled, and she was coaxed by my touch. I saw her eyebrows crease, she craved this.

When I mentioned the word 'lost' I knew she was thinking of Christopher. She really must have liked him, to be as shaken up as she was.

'I could have lost you, on Saturday...' she countered, voice vulnerable. 'I just wanted you to be happy...'

I let her kiss my forehead, she reached for my lips but I wouldn't let her touch them with her own. She didn't try again, but I felt her swallow, when she hugged me tightly.

'Juniper, I'm so sorry,' Rayne mumbled. 'I'm so, goddamn sorry.'

'I...' I paused, eased my eyes and breathed in her scent. 'I know...'

She released, just so she could look into my eyes, see the sincereness that dwelled inside them. But I was still hurt, this didn't change anything.

'But it's going to take more than this, to gain my trust again,' I said.

She let me go, and I was torn between hugging her tighter, and letting her walk away. She sighed, rubbed her face and nodded once.

'I'll leave you be,' she mumbled. 'I don't know what happens next.'

I agreed, opening my mouth to continue. But a flurry of red caught my eye, standing in the doorway of my kitchen.

I widened my eyes, as Arty stood tall and furious. She'd paused once she set her glare upon Rayne.

They both made eye contact, Arty like a lion, Rayne like a gazelle.

'Oh, I think I know what happens next, lovey,' she cussed, her neck cracking.

Rayne had begun to step back, but she was no match for Arty's pounce.

Chapter Twenty-Six

RAYNE

You know, after hours of emotional loss, mental trauma and a whole bunch of stomach aches. You'd think being numb to everything afterwards was expected. When someone sits in a rotten chair, watching the knuckles of a junkie fly towards their face, the bone crunching feeling of breaking skin upon them, they would never let anything afterwards hurt them. I watched a friend die, I watched him declare his innocence before ending his life in the most brutal way possible. I'd never seen death so close up, I'd never wanted to taste the warm blood of another in my mouth, I'd never, ever wanted it.

But I'd experienced it, death.

Not once, not twice, but three times.

I knew that the pain of my wounds would be mediocre compared to the image of dead bodies, the smell and wavering emotion in the air.

When you're exposed to so much pain, it was only natural to become numb to it.

It meant I hit rock bottom.

That I'd hurt Juniper, Christopher and most importantly, myself.

I only realised I was crying when I felt the tears, only realised I was angry when I saw the mess I made in the interrogation room. Only realised how lonely I was when I slept in a jail cell, with the constant battle of happy and traumatic memories fighting against each other in my already muddled mind.

I couldn't spare one emotion; my poker face was tougher than ever before.

It scared me.

Was I ever going to feel happiness again? Was I ever going to find myself smiling without realising it?

I'd seen my loved one cry; those emerald eyes had never looked so distraught.

The truth had unfolded, messily.

Juniper knew about my lies, biting back the truth from her was my biggest mistake.

I knew the consequences when I accepted that godforsaken job, even after the text message that warned me not to do so, the text message I now know Christopher sent.

Yet, I walked right into a trap.

I took Juniper out on a date, with the acid of guilt settling in my mind. By the time I took her to the pier, the guilt had hit my stomach. By the time I kissed her upon her desk, the guilt had pushed its way to my throat, it was hard to breathe.

I ignored it, held my girlfriend close and tried my absolute best to indulge in the massive amount of love that lingered between us.

How could she ever trust me after that?

I'd betrayed her, in the worst ways. And the only positive thought that lingered in my mind as we acted, was the silly idea that I was being a hero. The silly conclusion that I was saving the day, that Rayne would make everything better.

I'd made everything worse.

I thought I'd lost the ability to feel physical pain after Crocker and Manny's actions. I thought there was no way anyone's touch would leave me bleeding the way they did. If they tried, I wouldn't feel it.

I'd had my share of pain, hit maximum level, no way would anything hurt me now.

Boy, was I wrong.

I saw her eyes, crazed and furious as she lunged at me. Unlike Manny's motions, I was seeing Arty in slow motion. My pulse was racing, but I forgot to react in time.

I felt the sharp pain of elbows in my stomach, my already bruised belly. Arty's eyes peered into my own, as her forehead hit impact on mine. I couldn't speak, couldn't object, she was faster than usual.

'Fuck!' I groaned as she shoved me back, the rest of my words were disembodied gurgles of pain.

I fell, heavily against the kitchen cabinets behind me. The wood hit the bottom of my back, leaving me lurching forward. Which just aided Arty in her fury.

'You!' she yelled, throwing her fists into my chest, her voice was shriller than usual, thick and accented. 'You piss ant!'

In such a blind fury, I could only see wisps of her, colour, black and red, the occasional freckle along the bridge of her snarled nose.

I was against the wall now, thrown into a messy position before she took me by the legs and pulled my tall body underneath her.

'You fucking little prick,' she cussed, I felt the spit upon my face as she leant over me. 'You lying, asshole!'

I caught one glimpse of her face, eyebrows furious and hair wet from the rain, before another fist skyrocketed into my nose.

I felt it break.

I felt everything, actually.

Surprisingly enough, my body wasn't as numb as I thought.

The guilt was also adding to my pain, it was on Arty's side, I couldn't blame it. But like every normal human being, I wanted out, I wanted the aches to stop.

I pushed her back, hands grappling her shoulders. But she was tough, tougher than usual.

Arty was in full power mode, she was a ton of bricks against my weary hands.

I breathed in sharply as she hit me again, I could feel my lip split again, my blood rush free.

I'd forgotten that just moments before, Juniper had me in her grip, my face in her hands. There was some sort of progress between us, something I craved.

For her to see that I wasn't a nuisance, that my lying intentions were not to hurt her, that I was aware of my mistakes.

I was in enough trouble as it was, I couldn't add anything else to my list.

'You. Lying. Sack. Of. Horse. Shit!' Arty yelled, a punch following with every word.

I coughed whenever I could, breathed in at every pause between hits. But there was something constantly crying out to me, in my mind, it told me I deserved it.

Arty lifted me, threw me against the wall again and lifted my right wrist above my head. We were close, close enough to feel our furious breath against one another. She grinned furiously, pushed my arm back tougher and laughed.

'Oh, lovey,' she chuckled, grabbing my chin with her free hand. 'I had to see it to believe it!'

She nodded her head to my new tattoo, scabbed and sore. I swallowed loudly, looking past her eyes. I couldn't move, I wouldn't throw a punch, Arty didn't do anything to me, why should I hurt her?

I mean, I could feel the fury rise in my chest at every kick, every shove. But I just, had no reason to hurt her.

'Arty!' Juniper had been calling, following our brawl around the kitchen hastily. 'Arty! Let her go! Enough!'

They'd been arguing as she threw me like a ragdoll. I heard Arty attack Juniper, tell her I deserved this and I was a lying sack of shit.

Fair enough. I felt like saying.

Arty had me on the floor again, she spat once, twice. I only glared back, unable to stand, unable to snap back.

'Oh they have you on watch do they?' she asked, out of breath, kicking my left ankle.

I flinched, feeling the plastic object wrapped around it. I wasn't so fond of an ankle bracelet; Nick could see that as he wrapped it around me before the funeral earlier today.

House arrest scared me. That being said, any sort of criminal-based objects did.

I wasn't a dog, but it seemed like Arty thought otherwise.

'That's fine!' she laughed, leering at me. 'Traitorous dogs need to be on leads.'

Quickly, she lifted me by the collar with her bloody fists, and brought my face close to hers to cuss more thick accented profanities my way.

It was until Juniper grabbed around the redhead's shoulders, tried pulling and telling her off, and then shoved back by Arty's pure anger, when I finally flickered back to life and threw myself over the redhead.

She was brought back by my hands, coiled around her tense neck, hers the same around mine. I couldn't bear any pain brought Juniper's way, especially Arty's, someone who was tougher than me. I could feel my nose dribble, my lips purse and my growl rumble in my chest. Arty looked at me with widened furious eyes, her eyebrows dipped inwards, her teeth clenched.

I could see the betrayal in those murky green orbs of hers, pent up anger that had seethed through, every ring of darkness surrounding her iris was peering into my own.

She hated me.

'That's enough!' Rodgers yelled, pulling me back with two strong arms. 'Goddammit!'

I wouldn't budge, I could feel my fingernails dig further into the flesh of Arty's neck, she looked partially concerned, but her lips slowly curled into a smug smile.

I couldn't stand being made fun of, not in this case. I smacked her in the face once, twice, and she reddened up quite fast.

I watched her nose bleed, her bottom lip wobble as she grit her teeth my way.

'J-just...' she gasped through tight lips, I felt her legs kick. 'Just like a F-Fire Jackal.'

Her words skyrocketed through me, and I let go almost instantly, allowing myself to be ripped from Arty's grasp and into Rodgers'.

I watched the redhead rise, pulling herself forward for more with the same fury in her raging eyes. If it weren't for a pair of gentle hands that took her by the shoulders and pushed back, I'm sure Arty would have continued.

'Are you two finished?' Samantha asked loudly, 'You're both acting like animals!'

I swallowed to myself, loudly and out of breath. Rodgers held my arm tightly, he was watching Samantha scold Arty, glancing to the both of us constantly.

'She's a fucking idiot!' Arty cried, her hands wide. 'Don't tell me that moron didn't deserve it! She has no right to be here!'

I was still catching my breath, but I could see Arty turn at Juniper, her hands still raised. Juniper herself was frozen, she'd been leaning against the fridge, her eyes almost astray.

I couldn't blame her, that push was rather rough, and her best friend didn't even realise.

Nick patted my back harshly, grabbed my attention as Arty argued with Samantha and Juniper, her words were being shut down by the doctor, it would have been amusing in any other situation, if I wasn't the core of it all.

'What the hell do you think you're doing, kid?' Nick cussed, his old fingers tensing into my shoulder. 'You want more trouble?'

I looked him in the eye, my head a complete mess of unwanted memories. Every punch and every smack reminded me of that night, and it only took me a moment to realise.

My nose was broken, and the adrenalin had passed, so the blood kept coming. The floor was starting to look like a crime scene.

My fury was over Juniper's pain, Arty pushing her just threw me into overdrive, I couldn't stand the sight of her in any sort of agony, whether it be weak or strong.

Arty pointed at me again, wiping her nose and forehead of sweat. 'You better stay the hell away from Juniper,' she threatened, out of breath.

Samantha had one hand above her strong chest, keeping her back from pouncing.

'You go anywhere near her, and I'll kill you myself,' Arty sneered.

'Nobody will be killing anyone!' Nick yelled, lowering his hands mid torso. 'You shut it, or I'll arrest you.'

Arty greased the cop off, but kept her eyes on me, her chest heaving back and forth from our spar.

'This is utter childish behaviour!' Nick continued to scold the both of us, like we'd been caught stealing a cookie from the cookie jar, instead of brawling in the Bridges home kitchen.

'Absolutely!' Samantha agreed, her nose crinkled in annoyance before she pointed at me. 'You need to leave, now.'

I glanced towards Juniper, who had her eyes set on me. Just like before, back at the Station, the words left us anxious.

We both knew we needed space, Juniper needed it especially. And I had a lot on my plate, financial issues, court dates, police officers on my every trail.

But the thought of being apart, left us ripping at the seams.

All four of us stood silently, before Nick cleared his throat and bent down to grab his fallen hat. I tore my eyes from Juniper for a moment, as he took hold of my shoulder and steered me forward, tipping his hat towards the doctor.

'Ma'am,' he muttered to Samantha, who was still standing upright, trying to look tough in front of Arty who looked quite nervous under her glare.

'Go to the North West Clinic up the road,' she muttered, shooting a glance Nick's way. 'Tell them I sent you, get that nose fixed up.'

I swallowed the excess saliva dripping down my throat, and sniffled, even if it hurt to do so. Nick thanked her again, and took a handkerchief from his front pocket, handing it to me quickly. I took it hesitantly, but it stopped the dripping when I pressed it to my nose.

'Thanks,' I grumbled.

Under Arty's glare, Nick looked Juniper's way, who was following the both of us with her weakened eyes. I couldn't stand it when she looked like that, I just wanted to hold her in my arms and tell her I was sorry, for the hundredth time.

I touched her ring around my neck, lingering in the relief that it was still safe and sound.

'I hope Natalie's surgery goes well,' he smiled shortly. 'Apologies for the mess.'

'I'm not sorry,' Arty snapped.

I grimaced her way, and she pumped her chest forward proudly. I could distinctly see Samantha's fingers fumble from her collarbone, lowering it to her side again.

'Rayne,' Rodgers muttered. 'Let's go.'

I wanted to scream in denial and stay, try and talk out everything with the three of them. Samantha was probably aware of my mistakes; she would have seen the news. She would have seen Juniper and I leaving the warehouse together, photos of me, blurred out photos of the dead bodies.

I glanced to my girlfriend for the last time, if I could even call her that anymore. I hoped we would still be together, the thought left me shivering.

She pursed her lips, looked to her feet and rubbed her neck gently.

Damn, our only chance of talking like civil human beings, and Arty the almighty had to come crashing through.

Samantha had begun examining Arty's face, pulling her chin back and forth, Arty looked annoyed and kept growling in response.

'Stop that,' Samantha scolded. 'You're a mess.'

When I turned, I followed Rodgers' every step.

I closed my eyes as I walked, holding the fabric to my nose.

Christopher. You'll always be on my mind now; won't you buddy?

I didn't mind it, I know we just met and all, but I'd try and remember clearer times, times that I felt positive we would be better friends.

As I passed Nat's door, she was sitting up, awake, looking my way. I couldn't bear the look in her eyes, she'd been crying, sobbing more likely.

I swallowed and raised my hand to her, and watched her do the same. As much as I'd love to run in there, hug her gently and tell her everything was alright.

I wasn't welcome here.

I knew that now.

Rodgers cleared his throat, and I tore my eyes from Nat's. He raised his eyebrows, pointed his head to the left. I couldn't deal with this mad rush anymore, I needed to stay in one place.

I was finding myself lost, time moved so fast and I couldn't catch up with it.

I nodded once to Rodgers, glanced back at Nat's sore eyes, and did the same. If I could show her any sort of support, through a doorway, I would.

Just like leaving Juniper, it was hard to leave Nat.

I followed Rodgers down the hall and memorized every paint chip in the old family walls. Every photo that hung on the walls, just in case I would never see it again.

It felt like that.

As soon as he opened the front door, we were both hit with the chilling rain. It had worsened since I last stood outside, the clouds were almost black.

I pursed my lips and stepped forward, letting Rodgers shut the door behind me. It was an awful feeling, and I had to catch myself from sobbing.

What made me so weak?

Wasn't I meant to be a hardened person now? After all that?

Maybe it just made me weaker.

I spent forty minutes in the ER.

It was rather embarrassing, Samantha was trying to make a point, that's for sure.

Because the medical clinic she had Rodgers bring me to, was for children.

So I sat, surrounded by kids with broken bones and bloody noses just like my own, in a colourful waiting room with crayon drawings almost everywhere.

I wondered if Arty would be taken to the same hospital, it seemed the doc was rather annoyed with her too.

I sat in silence, until the young boy next to me, with a missing tooth and bloody gums smiled. I awkwardly grinned back, and he pointed to my face.

'You okay?' he asked, voice high. 'You look sad.'

I wanted to turn to this kid and tell him to shut it, but I wasn't that mean, especially to a six-year-old. I glanced to Rodgers, who was sorting out papers with the nurse, who wore a colourful smock instead of the normal white one I usually saw. He made a few glances to me, she did too, and I felt even more awkward.

With a clunky sniff, I looked back to the boy beside me, his hair a rugged blonde. I nodded once.

'I'm okay,' I lied. 'Thanks.'

The kid instantly shut up once his mother told him off, talking to strangers was a no-no, rule number one.

When I was called up, I hoped the procedure would be speedy. I couldn't stand sitting in that chair getting my nose fixed up in a children's goddamn clinic.

If Samantha and I ever spoke, I'd definitely never let this die down. But I got her point, she wanted me to know I acted rashly, like a child.

I couldn't help it, Juniper was in trouble and Arty was being a total madwoman. I wondered if anything else would go wrong on this second day of my house arrest.

Knowing my recent luck, shit would definitely hit the fan.

Rodgers didn't say a word to me in the car ride back to my apartment. I sat in the back seat of his black cop car, looking guilty to any person we stopped next to at a red light.

I felt what they thought I was, that's for sure.

It was really quite scary how much this car ride reminded me of Florida. Every trip was in utter silence, I wasn't allowed to speak, I wasn't needed.

I felt like that right now, not needed.

After trying to talk it out with Juniper, being smacked around by her ex-Fire Jackal best friend, and then scolded by a gorgeous doctor, it was one hell of a mess.

At least it diverted my mind from Christopher, and his family at the funeral.

I caught myself before I fell into a depressed state, if I could even dig the hole of sadness deeper. I had his dead body painted in my mind, his casket, his mother's tears, even his poor little brother.

I bit my bottom lip and leant against the right side window, glancing towards the sky.

I knew that Christopher wasn't Pebbles. It wasn't that hard to see.

I hoped that Rodgers saw that, and his other two members. They watched Christopher sob, outcry his innocence and tell the four of us that he was doomed either way.

It was frightening to know that Pebbles was capable of so much, so much disaster. Christopher was in trouble either way, he could have told me who Pebbles was, but then find no peace in the afterlife; knowing quite well that this mysterious individual would be making his family's life a living hell. Of course, I pleaded with him to tell me, put the gun down.

Surely if Pebbles was just a man, he was no stronger than the rest of us.

But he had an army, a strong army of drug addicted morons, who could obviously do his bidding. God, I wanted to wring that guys neck, whoever he was.

Rodgers wasn't open about the whole case. Last night, as I sat in his office and played with my thumbs, I could distinctly hear his members talk about it. I only heard small things, things I already knew.

That his parents were a mess, that the Fire Jackals were involved, etc.

But it still hurt hearing his name.

I wasn't able to save him.

I was so ready to join the group and sniff out Pebbles, kick him in the head, get him arrested and walk out free.

That was a stupid thought, of course it wasn't going to be as easy that.

I just didn't realise until now.

Silly me, huh?

The tattoo on my right wrist was irritating, and I was getting frustrated as I itched and itched every second. A part of me hoped that if I itched it hard enough, it would disappear. It was a constant reminder of my mistakes, I wanted it gone.

I couldn't even look at it, without the rush of guilt wavering over my stomach. It twisted and turned and left the positive walking out the door.

The negative had bared arms.

I was tired, so tired that I could fall asleep right there and then. Yet every time I found my eyes closing, the images of death and decay flashed before my eyes, Manny and Crocker too. I knew sleeping would be an issue now, for however long.

I touched the bandage over my nose, flinching at it. There was two there now, locking my nose into place, the canvas that was my face was absolutely trashed.

It was hard to look at myself.

Yet when Juniper held me in her grasp, she looked at me, like nothing had changed at all. It was hard to not kiss her.

One look and she left me feeling worth it.

I needed that more than ever.

'Rayne,' Rodgers muttered, ripping me from my trance.

I sniffled and glanced towards him, he kept his eyes on the road but made little eye contact with me. his monotone voice rumbled through my already weakened chest, I couldn't handle another lecture, not now.

'Are you alright?' he asked.

I swallowed and nodded once, looking to my shoes.

I was glad Detective Rodgers was the cop in charge of me. from the first day I ever met him, he seemed very welcoming, like he cared.

You didn't come across that here in Boston, most of the cops couldn't care less and only did what was necessary.

Yet here I was, in the car with a scarred man, who chain smoked like crazy. He'd arrested me, been disappointed in me and told me I'd made a huge mistake joining the Fire Jackals, and he was asking me if I was alright.

I didn't deserve this either.

'I apologiseapologise,' he said. 'I should have come in with you. I wasn't aware that Juniper's friend would be that way.'

I huffed to myself, Arty? Of course she would.

But Rodgers had no idea who she was. I was careful talking about the progress Juniper and I made in our quest, I knew that Arty was guilty of more crimes then I.

I protected her, knowing very well she'd be at the same level of anger when she saw me.

Even then I was thinking of others, and not myself.

'It's fine,' I murmured. 'I was expecting it sooner or later.'

My voice was wobbly, croaky.

'Well,' Rodgers returned, a little concerned by my response. 'She did a number on you, and for that I apologise, you are my responsibility and–'

'I'm no one's responsibility,' I snapped back.

There was that awful silence.

I shouldn't have attacked him about this, but I couldn't stand hearing that.

I made this bad choice, I did all the wrong, I was nobody's goddamn responsibility.

Rodgers pulled a cigarette from his front pocket, his coat was folded on the seat beside him. He clicked the lighter over the tip of it and watched the road carefully.

It was funny how cops broke the rules too.

I could have used a cigarette right about now, it would help me mellow out, and the smell of burning tobacco was leaving me heavy headed.

'You are my responsibility, because you have committed crimesh' He told me off. 'You're under house arrest, you can only go so far without us knowing.'

I swallowed and rubbed my neck, itching the back of my head. I hated hearing all this stuff, it made me feel like I'd murdered someone, stolen candy from a baby.

'So, until the court of law decides your outcome, will you continue to be my responsibility,' Rodgers cleared his throat, turning the car into a main street. 'Do you understand?'

'Yes,' I mumbled back. 'Yes, sir.'

'Call me Nick, Rayne.'

'Nick.'

It still felt odd, calling a cop by his first name. We weren't friends, but he was doing his best to make me see that we could be.

Shouldn't he be upset with me twenty-four seven? Shouldn't he think I'm some guilty crime lord that deserves nothing?

He was being careful, yes. But he had shown compassion, and I wasn't used to it.

First it was handing me a fresh pillow and blanket to have a nap in last night.

Second was making sure I ate at the station, handing me a double cheeseburger meal in a brown paper bag, even with a Zoom Cola.

Next was being kind about me signing police statements and whatnot, making sure I did everything correctly.

I knew about the whole 'good cop, bad cop' scenario, but boy he hadn't shown one bad side since I was arrested. Only little scolds here and there, but nothing violent, nothing over the top.

Maybe he believed me, believed I was only in this situation because I tried playing hero.

The whole case was messy, so messy that he looked stressed about it.

I'd hate to be a cop.

'Now, let me lay down the basics about house arrest...' Nick mumbled.

I held my breath as he explained, every small detail, every problem it could cause if I were to run away, or step foot on off-limit turf.

I nodded, I never spoke back, I never added in that it hurt me to hear all of this.

It also hurt me knowing Juniper's dorm and her home in Somerville was off limits without police escort. I was stuck in my part of town, the furthest I could go was South Station.

I was also not allowed to busk, without the licence and all.

So I was stuck, to stay at home and loathe and writhe in my own misery. I hated it, I didn't find strength in being upset, I had to move on, be strong.

But my ladders of strength had been kicked down, they clambered all over the floor like piles of junk. I was scrambled.

'So,' Nick hummed, turning into my apartment street. 'The court date is set for Monday, but that's just the first...'

I swallowed again, the first of many? Or the first and final?

'I'll pick you up, at eight on the dot,' he said, parking the car next to my neighbours Vespa. 'Wear that suit...'

He turned in his seat after the breaks were set, then examined my bloody white shirt. I glanced down too, and grimaced.

'Maybe, you ought to take that off and give it to me,' he mumbled, itching his nose. 'I'll take it to the drycleaners, before Monday.'

I nodded once, touching patches of dry blood, Arty really did a number on my nose and lip that's for sure.

'Alright, let me walk you in...' Nick mumbled as he opened his door. 'I need to have a word with your landlord.'

'Oh, have fun with that,' I huffed, undoing my belt. 'She's a real keeper.'

Nick shot me a concerned look, then smiled shortly. I returned the same look, my eyebrows dipped inwards.

Nick grabbed my duffel bag from the boot before we moved, seeing it left me a little anxious. My phone, clothes and wallet were somewhere in there.

They'd rummaged through Manny and Crocker's car before taking it into custody, I guess the two crazies were polite enough to bring my bag along with them.

The tiny amount of cash in my wallet was probably gone, as well as my credit card.

Not much they could do with it now.

The rain didn't bother me as I walked side by side with Nick. He held his hat as he half jogged and commented on how awful Boston's weather had gotten. When I first met him at South Station, I never expected him to be the man in charge. He seemed welcoming, a little too nice for a big head honcho of a police department.

I second guessed a few times, thought that maybe he was secretly the biggest asshole on the planet, but he never broke character.

Either I was anxious and overthinking, or he was a great actor.

The stairs were slippery as we walked, Nick was humming a tune, but glanced my way quickly. I was keeping to myself, lingering behind him.

The rain was deafening on top of my apartment complex. The timber roof made awful sounds, I'm pretty sure my bathroom would be flooded.

As we passed my landlords door, she opened it rather fast and pointed at me. she was wearing a grotty white shirt, and ripped jeans, she arched her nose to me and huffed loudly.

'Ah! Trying to sneak by me!' she sneered. 'You owe rent, asap!'

I opened my mouth to talk, but Nick stepped in, a smile on his face.

'Evening ma'am,' He nodded once. 'Detective Rodgers, Boston Police.'

I watched her beady eyes widen.

'What?!' she cried. 'What do you want, I told your boys I had nothing to do with what happened!'

I watched her ramble on, and Nick stood perfectly still, his hands by his side, his attention sharp. She was going off at him, telling him she was innocent of a crime that I couldn't even understand.

'Ma'am,' Nick mumbled.

'And another thing!'

'Ma'am.'

'I told him, I don't want that stuff in my apartment! And he didn't listen!'

'Ma'am!'

Nick raised his voice, making the both of us jump. She eased her eyes towards him, and waited for his continued words.

I saw him smile, then tip his wet hat her way.

'I am not here for any of that,' he chuckled, collecting himself. 'I'm here to talk about Rayne Holmes.'

I shuffled uncomfortably behind him, like a child in trouble.

I just wanted to run into my apartment and sleep, well, try to.

My landlord glared at me, held her doorframe and arched her nose my way. 'What about her?'

Nick turned to me, smiled and then cleared his throat. 'I would like to organise her rent for the next couple of weeks.'

'Why?' she sneered. 'She can't pay it? She needs to leave.'

I felt the anger fuel inside me, I never liked my landlord, she was such a tool. Ever since I moved to Boston, she made it her job to piss me off, had some odd grudge against me.

Could have been the guitar playing, my apartment was right next to hers after all. And there were multiple times where she smacked her fist against the wall between us, telling me to shut up.

I continued playing, of course.

'Rest assured, her rent will be paid,' Nick said. 'She needs to stay in your complex for a few more weeks.'

'Why?' she snapped. 'Is she in trouble?'

'That's classified.'

'Hah! She is!'

'Ma'am, please,' Nick interrupted. 'Please leave your bank details with me, so I can forward you the correct amount.'

'But'

'Please.'

I saw the two of them make eye contact, hers was nervous, Nick's was calm.

I knew she wanted to say more, snap at me and tell me I was awful, but she grumbled and turned into her apartment.

'Hang on,' she mumbled. 'I'll go get it now.'

I felt relief wash over me, my rent was just another worry on my plate, and now that was cleaned up. But hey, I'd have to owe the money back sooner or later, that is, if I wasn't going to jail.

I swallowed, my anxiety was at peak point again, I almost felt like throwing up.

Nick spoke with my landowner for a while, before he nodded his head once and turned to walk my way. I was lingering around my door, waiting for Nick to hand me my bag so I could find my keys. I goddamn hoped they were in there.

Or we'd be annoying my already annoyed landowner further.

'Well,' Nick chuckled as he stepped by my side, handing me my bag. 'She's quite something.'

I felt like smiling, but it was hard to do so.

On the corner of my eye, Nick watched me rummage through my bag. I couldn't look as my hand dipped in, it reminded me of my mistakes.

Everything did.

I sniffled when I felt the familiar feeling of keys, and pulled them out to unlock my door. I hoped that Nick would just come in, take my suit and leave, but I had a strong feeling that he'd stick around, talk to me more.

A part of me wanted it, the comfort of a strong person, someone to tell me that they were going to help.

But another part of me wanted to be alone.

I was hit with the familiar smell of my temporary home as the door creaked open, it was just the way I left it, messy and unprepared for any guests. I threw my duffel bag to my couch, Nick lingered behind me, closed the door and hummed to himself.

'It's...'

'Awful, I know,' I answered quietly. 'I'll go get changed, hang on.'

'Rayne,' he interrupted.

I paused in my steps, listened to the heaters buzz, focusing on anything but the awkwardness between the head detective of Boston city and a mess of a twenty-two-year-old.

'I understand you're an independent young woman,' Nick started. 'But you need to know, I'm here to help you.'

I grimaced, shrugged my shoulders and weakly smiled.

'You need to talk to me, I need to understand you,' he continued.

'You don't need to,' I said, turning to grouch. 'I made a mistake, now I'm in trouble.'

He stood still, examined me speak.

I averted my eyes, raised my hands and dropped them.

'What do you expect me to tell you?' I asked, scoffing. 'I joined them to find the truth, and I never found it!'

'but the court won't believe that.'

'You think I don't know that?' I snapped again. 'I know I'm screwed, either way.'

I paused and swallowed, forgot who I was talking to, then sighed.

'I just...' I bit my cheek. 'I messed up, okay?'

Nick's face fell, as mine did. I felt the tone in my voice, it was crumbling.

'I just, felt like I could do this,' I explained. 'I felt like I was doing the right thing, finding out the truth, helping Juniper find the guy who did what he did to her sister.'

I felt as if I'd explained this many times, but I needed it to be set in stone. Nick had heard this all before, but he seemed to be fine with hearing it all over it again.

I stepped towards my kitchenette, kicked my shoes off and touched the countertop softly. I wasn't one to enjoy feeling sorry for myself, but I was so tired.

'The drugs? The violence?' I eased. 'I did my best to stay clear from it, I couldn't hurt anybody.'

'From what we've gathered, you did most of the bystanding.'

'No,' I replied. 'I hurt people...'

Nick's eyebrows furrowed, he was curious now, and I should have finished explaining.

'I hurt Juniper,' I grimaced. 'I hurt her, her sister, her dad.'

My voice wavered, I was so close to breaking down again. I couldn't have that, not in front of Nick, not again.

'I made a stupid choice, to get involved with awful people,' I tensed up, gritting my teeth. 'And now look at me!'

I raised my voice, pointed to my face and breathed in sharply. 'I fucked up, Nick.'

'You're still young,' he countered. 'A lot of kids get involved with the Jackals...'

'Yeah but, who would be dumb enough to walk into a trap, like me?'

'You were not aware.'

'I should have been.'

I watched Nick fix his tie, loosen it more so he could comfortably sit on my couch armrest. He sighed, took his wallet from his front pocket then popped my landlord's details into an empty slot.

'Rayne,' he started again. 'We all make mistakes, and were all not aware until the circumstances.'

I rolled my eyes, turned and rubbed the back of my neck.

God, lectures were the goddamn worst.

'You acted rashly, jumped to conclusions,' he explained. 'Just like most of the kids who join.'

'But I'm not a kid!' I snapped, turning to point at him. 'I'm an adult, a really dumb adult.'

Nick gave me a look, one stern look that pretty much told me to shut up and listen, as much as I didn't want to.

'Rayne, sometimes when we're desperate...' Nick paused, collected himself and rose from the couch. 'We do stupid things, sometimes we get caught, sometimes we don't.'

'What would you know, you're a cop.'

'Yes, a cop that used to be young once.'

I twisted my lip, rummaged through my fridge and tried finding some sort of alcoholic beverage. I could feel Nick's eyes on my back.

'Believe me when I say, that I understand you did what you did for the right reasons,' he said softly.

I turned, my chest felt tight.

Did he really just say that? The head of the police station believed me?

Nick nodded once, smiled and wiped down his hat.

'You've come to, you've understood your problems, your mistakes,' he pocketed his hands. 'Most of those who join, do.'

He paused, lowered his head and gave me a stern look.

'Some, don't.'

'Well, I surely have,' I added, grimacing. 'I've realised my mistakes, realised I was an idiot...'

I pocketed my own hands, and flinched from my shoulder. 'But now I gotta pick up the pieces.'

'With help, you will.' Nick added. 'I will do my best, but I cannot promise anything. You have still broken many laws, drug dealing, illegal transport.

'Why are you doing this?' I interrupted.

Nick froze, his scarred face tense. I could only imagine what was going through his mind right then, what he was thinking of me, I'd interrupted him many times now.

But I was curious, I needed to know why he was willing to help me, why he didn't just throw me in a cell and swallow the key.

Why was he being so compassionate? Did he really see me as innocent?

'Why are you helping me?' I asked. 'You're the head honcho, big name.'

I lost my words, grumbled and lifted my right hand. 'You're the boss.'

'I'm just a man,' he replied. 'And I like helping people.'

'I'm a criminal.'

'You are far from a criminal,' Nick chuckled. 'More like, a silly young adult who got herself in a bad crowd, which I warned you about a few weeks ago, did I not?'

I felt my cheeks flush, a little embarrassed.

So he did remember our first meeting.

'From the day I met you, I knew you were a good person,' he chuckled. 'I mean, I hoped you were.'

'I am.'

'And I trust you.'

'Do you?' I muttered. 'Do you really trust me?'

Nick seemed taken aback. He pursed his lips, smiled to the floor and shrugged his shoulders.

'That's for you to prove,' he answered. 'If everything you have told me, is the truth.'

'It is,' I replied. 'I wanted to find out the truth, and I got into trouble.'

'Rayne, you don't need to justify yourself anymore,' he spoke over me. 'You've done all you can, now you have to let the people in charge do all the work.'

I nodded, sighed and pointed to my room.

'I'll get the suit for you, let me get changed,' I muttered. 'One second.'

'Take your time,' he replied, sitting back against my couch. 'No rush, the weather is awful anyway.'

I swallowed and cleared my throat, rushing to my room so I could get out of the wet suit Nick had lent me.

Just another nice gesture from his end.

I closed my door quietly, pushed my back against it, and exhaled. I couldn't do it from my nose very well, it hurt like a bitch whenever I inhaled too.

I didn't move for a moment, my room felt too drafty and empty. The more I looked around its interior, the more I realised how dreary it really was.

It was only my bed, bedside table and bathroom on the right, my cupboards with whatever clothes I managed to shove in a travel bag before I left Florida, and my busking gear. I missed my guitar, Juniper was still looking after it, that or she'd broken it to pieces.

Highly unlikely.

Undressing was rather tough, especially on my shoulder.

Arty's actions left my stomach swirling, my nose aching. She only added to my messy body, decorated in bruises and scars.

Seeing my reflection only made me upset, even when I caught a short glimpse of myself. When I did, the guilt seethed through me like venom.

I hoped the guilt would vanish, over time, however long it would take.

But my positivity was running short, especially now that I was going to court, my fate would be decided by some random person, with more power than me.

At least Nick trusted me, but I knew he was thinking otherwise when I fought for Christopher's innocence. A lot of people would be thinking the same, especially Juniper.

I wondered if she would ever believe me when I told her he wasn't Pebbles, she got what she was after, after all.

Nat would be getting her surgery, what else was there to do? Find the real Pebbles? I think Juniper's snooping was over.

But not for me.

No, I wanted to find out the truth, even if it hurt me.

But this time, I would tell her, tell everyone around me that I wasn't finished. I wasn't going to be, until I found the original Pebbles, who framed my friend and got me beaten up.

I pulled my coat off first, unbuttoning my shirt. I wished Juniper was here to help me.

I hissed in pain as the shirt slipped from my shoulders, I took one glance at the bruises upon my bare body, and sharply inhaled.

God, I was a mess.

Bruises on my stomach, my arms, my chest. Some black, some red, some green and red.

I was a fucking walking painting.

I changed into whatever I had laying around, plain black shirt, grey tracksuit pants. It was comfortable, and man I needed that right now.

The uncomfortable feeling of my ankle bracelet was another reminder of my guilt, I wished I could rip it off.

As I walked out of my room, Nick was busy checking out the antiques that came with this apartment. He tinkered with a model boat of the Titanic, and hummed to himself, a tune I could tell was Cole Porters 'Anything Goes.'

I smiled shortly, clearing my throat. He turned, smiled nervously and chuckled.

'Titanic,' he mumbled. 'This yours?'

'Nope,' I answered, handing him my folded suit. 'Came with the mansion.'

He huffed humorously to my joke, grabbing the clothes from me.

I stepped back, crossing my arms. Nick tucked the bundle under his shoulder, checked the time and blinked.

'Well, I'll be off,' he grinned, his dimples evident. 'I will keep in contact with you, mobile phone is still active, but it's being tracked.'

'Nice to know.' I grumbled.

'I understand that's a bit, unnerving,' Nick explained as he walked towards my door, I followed. 'But it's necessary.'

'I get it,' I replied.

Nick paused at my door, turned and patted my unwounded left shoulder. I smiled weakly, and waited for him to speak. The silence between us wasn't as awkward now, but I still felt shallow.

'I will pick you up Monday, take this time to, relax...' he sighed. 'Remember the rules, you cannot go far, especially with that around your ankle.'

'I know, as far as South Station.' I muttered. 'Or I'll be arrested, yeah.'

Nick crinkled his face, chuckled weakly and opened the door. I shivered from the cold, and he groaned loudly.

'Boy, this is awful,' he sighed. 'Well, I will see you then.'

'Yeah.'

'Rayne, remember what I said,' he spoke as he stepped forward. I held the doorframe and watched him rug up, turn to me and nod.

'You are far from a criminal,' he spoke softly, popping his hat back on. 'Remember that.'

His words left a bittersweet feeling lingering around me. I watched him walk carefully down my apartment complex stairwell, humming the same tune.

I wasn't sure how I should have reacted, knowing I had this compassionate person on my end. It seemed to me that everything was falling to pieces, but Nick Rodgers was there, he was doing all he could.

I wasn't used to it.

Especially from a male his age.

My father was around the same age as Nick, and I absolutely hated his guts. And here was a man with more heart than the whole Holmes family.

I respected him.

I closed my door gently, and instantly felt the warmth in my apartment. It was quieter than usual, calmer too. With a grimace, I stepped towards my room, my bare feet digging into the awful carpet. I was exhausted, my eyes were drooping, my head becoming a fumbling mess.

What I used to think was an annoyance, like the bathroom sink dripping, was lulling me to sleep. I fell upon my sheets and didn't even feel the pain as I did so.

I would in the morning, or whatever time I slept till.

I didn't care right now.

Maybe if I slept enough, time would race fast, and things would fix themselves.

Yeah, keep dreaming Rayne.

Chapter Twenty-Seven

RAYNE

I had mixed feelings about it.

We've all been there, when an annoying fly zooms around your bedroom, its bellowing hum driving you absolutely crazy. Or when the next door neighbour cuts his lawn at eight in the morning, even when you can hear the church bells from up the road ring louder then Notre Dame.

You wish for nothing, but silence.

Silence is peaceful, but your thoughts are often louder.

To be able to completely shut off your thoughts could be a gift to many.

But thoughts are important, they drive your actions, keep you sane, keep you focused. But when your mind is shaken, full of multiple hit and miss emotions, anger, depression, anxiety.

You make poor choices.

I should know, I made the worst choice of them all.

Silence was also frightening.

I had trouble sleeping last night, could you blame me? I was tossing and turning, drinking until I passed out.

I found myself on the living room floor, smacking my lips and clearing my dry throat.

The dust in this apartment was otherworldly.

I couldn't remember what time I actually zonked out last night, or maybe this morning? All I knew, was getting up right now would be a mistake for my poor old head.

Usually, the cars outside would be honking angrily, the woman next door screeching at her husband, or ex.

The city of Boston would echo, and I would hear it, always.

I learned to ignore it, but sometimes it was so overbearing it was hard to shut it out.

Today was eerily silent, no voices outside, no profanities being thrown around, no thumping from the guy who lived above me.

Just me, myself, and I.

I hated it.

Never before have I wished to wake up to the sound of my parents fighting, or the construction workers fixing the road down the road from my house.

Never before have I wished that sort of negativity.

But here I was, laying on the carpet of my dingy apartment, wishing for the loudest sounds to drown out my bustling thoughts.

I swallowed, watched the stains dance on the ceiling, the shapes they made. The only sound I could hear was the tap as it dripped. Focusing on it was all I could do, before my own heartbeat was driving me mad.

As well as my face, my eyes were sore and itchy. I sniffled, and that hurt too, some crazy Irish woman had her time with it.

Gently, I reached over and touched the bandage over my nose, rubbing the bridge. They patched it up pretty-well at the children's hospital but boy,thinking about that was embarrassing.

I touched the fresh wounds on my face, some still stung as I dabbed my fingertips along the length of them. I would be reminded of Manny and Crocker for a long time, knowing how prominent these scars were going to be.

I wondered if I would learn to love them, or always hate them.

Ached and sore, I rose from the carpet, clutching a big chunk of its dirty texture to keep myself from falling back against its roughness.

My head was dizzy, eyesight blurry, and I smelled awfully like old whisky. I think I finished off the bottle I had stowed away, but the morning aftertaste was atrocious.

Okay, the loudness of my thoughts was becoming too much, I had to get up and do something.

The roughness in my throat was awful by the time I reached the kitchen, so I grabbed whatever glass I had close and shoved it under the tap. As I watched the water fill it, I thought about the past day, Arty's wrath and Nick's kind words.

I lost myself in the thoughts again, how conflicted I was, confused and muddled. Nick was willing to help me, and I really didn't know how to react to that.

Maybe he just didn't want to see a girl my age go to jail, or court.

Maybe he wanted me off the hook because he truly knows that I meant no harm whatsoever.

Maybe he felt sorry for me, felt sorry for the whole goddam world. Christopher wasn't around anymore, it was scary to think about, really frightening.

I struggled to sleep because of his dead eyes, the bittersweet conversation we had over Zoom Quantum.

I never made friends with people like Christopher so fast, but I genuinely wanted to help the guy. He needed someone there, and I wasn't so sure how Reedy was doing with the whole anxiety thing his friend had going on.

I knew what anxiety was like, maybe not to the extent that Christopher had, but somewhat the same level.

It left you feeling lonely, hopeless and selfish.

At least that's how it left me feeling.

I cussed as the water overflowed, dripping over my right hand. It flowed over the side of the sink, all over my bare feet.

I quickly twisted the faucet, placed the glass down and examined my wet hands. I could see every cut and bruise now, and every memory alongside them.

C'mon, pull yourself together Rayne.

I slipped my hands to my sides, rubbing them on my black jeans. I should probably shower, but I was afraid of how my cuts and bruises would react.

They would either soothe under the water's rush, or burn relentlessly under its scorching touch.

I glanced towards my microwave, shoved on top of the fridge. The time was harsh red on my tired eyes, I had to squint, which left my black bruise twitch. It was mid-afternoon, but an awful day outside. From my window, I could see the grey sky, the trees waver under the harsh wind.

It'd been days and days of depressing weather.

It fit the situation.

I touched my shoulder and growled from its pain. The necklace around my neck dangled as I leaned over the kitchen counter, it was still very heavy from the guilt I bared. But before I could even feel sorry for myself, another girl came to mind.

Whenever I felt pain, or agony, I instantly thought of Nat. I wondered how she was, how she was reacting to the surgery, if it was finished.

I overheard Nick speaking with some of the other cops before we hit the funeral yesterday morning. Nat was scheduled for this morning, really early, five am.

I guessed the surgery was really lengthy, took a lot of skill.

Took a lot of money.

I wish it were the real Pebbles they had caught, and not Christopher, a poor framed man. His parents were more than willing to pay for Nat's surgery, they felt nothing but sympathy for the Bridges family.

But they shouldn't have been the ones to fork out all that cash. I hoped when the real asshole behind all this drama was caught, they would get that big sum of cash back. Juniper was starting to believe, at least I thought she was.

I could see a part of her didn't believe that Christopher was the one who hit Nat, they were a little close too after all.

I'd seen Christopher around Juniper a few times, and he never seemed to be a possible offender. It just didn't add up.

But boy, Pebbles sure did a good job at making it seem like he did the bad deed. And got me involved in the long run.

Man, the thought of whatever that idiot looked like boiled my goddamn blood.

I tensed, but instantly regretted it, as the sting of my bandages hit home.

I was angry, fed up and felt like kicking the ankle tag off. I thought I was supposed to get this after the trail.

Maybe they didn't trust me as much as I thought? Maybe they thought I'd bail.

But hey, it did cross my mind.

Except I wanted to stay, Juniper was here, after all.

I missed her, but I was in her bad books, as well as Samantha's and Arty's.

Arty I didn't really care about, she and I never got along, but I could potentially see a friend in her, she jumped to conclusions too much.

Samantha, she seemed like a calm soul, I think she was more determined to get Nat's surgery, then the man who put her in the state she was in.

I wanted everything to blow over, be okay, for Pebbles to fall down the stairs and break his neck.

I wanted Nat running and jumping, I wanted Samantha and Arty to finally converse together, I wanted Nick to come to my door and say I was innocent; clear of all charges.

And finally, I wanted Juniper here, with me.

I paused before I lifted the glass to my lips, savouring any beautiful thought of Juniper's persona in my mind.

I sculled my water quickly, it was lukewarm, typical.

But it soothed my throat, and even though my voice was still hollow and croaky, I was pleased.

I wasn't too keen on sitting back and thinking, pondering on what would happen on Monday, if I was going to end up in jail or with a big fat fine that I wouldn't ever be able to pay off.

I hated the thought of being in jail, and the panic would often rise in my chest awfully fast. How was I meant to respond to that? Knowing very well that the city of Boston would throw me in a cell for getting involved with a shitty group.

I was numb to it.

I had to keep occupied, before I ripped my eyes out at the thoughts.

So I rummaged through my duffel bag to find a fresh set of clothes.

I swallowed as my fingers touched a familiar object, flat and cold. I sighed, took out my mobile and tinkered with it, seeing the old messages from Juniper.

Asking if I was okay, wanting to know where I was, and that she loved me.

More guilt to add to my bucket.

I shoved the phone back in my bag, zipped it up and threw it across the room, I couldn't stand it, not right now.

The shower wasn't sounding that scary after that, I almost felt like I deserved the scorching pain.

Whenever I felt strength, good vibes and positive emotions wave over me, they were quickly filled with negative tar and gunk.

I was trying to warm myself up after my shower, convince myself that things would be alright and I'd make it out of this mess fine and dandy.

I just didn't understand why it was so hard to keep thinking that way, why did my brain have to jump to the worst conclusion?

I was dressed in another pair of jeans, dark blue this time, with my old black hoodie. I sat upon my bed, tried to picture what court would be like in three days' time. But honestly, all I could think of was Nat and Juniper.

The fight with Arty was replaying over and over again, what she called me, how she pushed her friend aside to hurt me.

It was all so muddled.

I had to stop feeling sorry for myself, but honestly, it was hard when it was just myself and my mind, alone.

At two on the dot, I jumped from a knock at the door.

At first I thought it was Juniper, so I rushed to the living room, but I quickly paused. It wouldn't be her; the only person I could think of was Nick.

I cleared my throat and collected myself, before I unlocked the door and opened it. I was right, Detective Nick Rodgers stood with a tired face, a cigarette in his lips and a freshly washed suit folded in his hands.

I still wasn't used to his appearance, or how someone so kind could have such terrible facial scars.

But he wasn't here to tell me I was innocent, nope.

'Hello, Rayne!' he smiled. 'Sorry to come around uninvited, but they finished with this early and I thought I'd drop it off.'

'Hey, thanks,' I replied slowly, reaching out to grab the suit from his hands.

After putting out his cigarette, Nick handed the bundle of clothes to me, but I noticed how tired his eyes were, even more so than usual.

'Uh, come in,' I muttered, stepping back to open my door wider.

'Oh, are you sure?' he asked, blinking slowly. 'A quick glass of water would be swell.'

'Well, all you're getting is a lukewarm glass of Boston's best,' I sarcastically joked.

Nick closed the door behind me, and chuckled gently.

It was still odd, having the head of department in my home. It was even odder to know that he was paying so I wasn't kicked out of it.

'I was going to ask you,' I paused, contemplated continuing, and sighed.

Nick waited for my words, his eyebrows raised in anticipation. He stood in my doorway, his coat shoulders wet with rain, his hat also damp.

I pocketed my hands, shrugged my shoulders and grimaced.

'I know I can't go there alone,' I mumbled. 'But I was wondering if you'd take me to see Nat.'

Nick opened his mouth to speak, but I turned quickly to grab a glass, I wasn't ready for the denial.

Of course he wouldn't take me, that was asking for too much. And after my fight with Arty yesterday? I was lucky to even hear the Bridges' family name.

'Alright,' Nick replied.

I was halfway through filling his glass, when I abandoned ship and turned quickly. He smiled again, tired eyes crinkled on the sides.

'Why so surprised?' he asked. 'I would be supervising you, after all.'

'I know that, I just thought you'd say no, after yesterday and all.'

'You are curious about Nat's surgery; you would like to visit a little girl in hospital.'

'Yeah...'

'So, I will take you.'

I was this close to pointing my finger at him, telling him I didn't trust his friendliness and will to help me. I was close to telling him to back off and leave me alone, that he was a cop doing his job.

But I just couldn't, I couldn't do something like that.

I turned to grab Nick's overflowing glass of water, and poured a little back down the sink. I was muddled, thoughts running wild, but at least I'd be able to see how Nat was doing, if she was alright.

Maybe this time, without Arty rushing me and beating my face to a pulp.

'Here,' I mumbled, handing Nick the glass. 'I'll go get my shoes on.'

I left him, alone in the living room again, with the small scale model of the Titanic, and a dusty couch to sit on.

I had lots of questions on my mind as Nick drove me towards Somerville Hospital.

Most of them were for my own wellbeing, how court would play out, if I was innocent of the charges. But there was no motivation for asking, I just sat in silence, watching the city of Boston get smaller and smaller.

Nick was checking his cell as we drove, he constantly checked, his anticipation was high and his tiredness was leaving him crazily aware of his surroundings.

I wondered if all cops were like that.

Finally, I popped a question, but it had nothing to do with me.

'Why are you so tired?' I asked.

Nick chuckled and itched the back of his neck. 'Been waiting for an important call, was up all night contacting them via email.'

'An important call?' I asked, wondering if it had anything to do with me. 'Who from?'

'That's confidential, Rayne,' he replied. 'Sorry.'

I grimaced and shrugged, it didn't bother me. I was just curious, but I should probably learn to tone my curiosity down a notch, after the backlash I had received just lately.

'Sorry,' I mumbled, rubbing my knee.

'There's no need to apologise,' Nick muttered, clearing his throat quickly. 'I just have some important work on the go, as you say.'

'Right,' I replied, touching the scar along my cheek, I was noticing it too much, almost always rubbed my index finger on it.

On the corner of my eye, Nick gave me a few sideways glances, before he smiled and huffed. 'If it's any consolation, Rayne,' he said. 'The scars suit you.'

I chuckled and hummed sarcastically.

'Sure.'

'I mean it! They give you character and they're not as bad as you think,' he paused, grabbed my attention with a click of his fingers, and pointed to his own scarred face. 'These are the ones you have to avoid gaining.' I took a closer look, at how each spiral scar rolled over his withered skin, the way his cheek was indented and tough.

I felt pretty bad for the guy, who knew how he received that damage, and I wasn't ready to ask him, it wasn't my business after all.

Cops were usually the people who got involved with other people's business, but I never stopped and thought that maybe the police themselves had issues too.

I was under the impression that when you're an officer, someone of the law, you're impervious to that sense of distress.

I was pretty clueless.

I saw Nick purse his lips, making the scar above his upper crinkle and fold. He was patting his fingers to the radio, but his radio receiver was propped up and close to view, guess he was supposed to be working today.

'Sorry,' I said. 'For making you drive me.'

'Oh, no!' he replied. 'Not an issue at all, I was curious to see how Natalie's surgery had gone too.'

'You were?'

'Of course. Juniper was very positive that her sister would be alright, and I promised I would check up when she had finished.'

I flinched to Juniper's name, clearing my throat to hide my vulnerability. Her name left me shaky, I kept wondering if I would bump into her again, be able to hold her and apologise for the hundredth time.

I watched the road ahead, pulling my sweater sleeve over my bandaged tattoo, I was waiting for the day I'd take it off and the Jackal tattoo would have vanished.

I hadn't even thought about how I was going to cover it, maybe get some art done to merge over it, if I had the chance to anyway.

Who knows where I'd be in three days' time.

I held back my questions about Nick Rodgers's scars, any sort of conversation that may bother him. I found the awkwardness in the car more amusing than concerning. Nick was old fashioned, the CD he played was Ella Fitzgerald, the scented tree hanging from his rear-view mirror looked old and dusty.

He himself seemed dusty and old, but he was only in his fifties, or even forties, no doubt. What mattered here was that I was opening up to him, that nothing scared me knowing he was there.

I usually relied on myself, and good God that was stressful.

I mean, it was expected. I was raised to be independent, I was told to never trust strangers, even the law. But that was my crazy parents speaking, the parents I should have contacted about this whole situation. I wondered how they would react, it was always on my mind, and I never liked thinking about it for more than three seconds before it drove me absolutely crazy.

I took a deep breath and glanced back at Nick. He was focused on the road ahead, but stopped to look my way and smile, a reassuring grin that left me conflicted.

Was I meant to feel comfort in his smile? Forget that he was most definitely just a man doing his job, a cop? He was doing his absolute best to keep me comfortable, keep me occupied, sending positive vibes.

I smiled back, a short grimace that he acknowledged and looked appreciative of.

It was the least I could give him, for all his effort, at least for now that's all I could do. I had nothing to give, no money, no gifts.

I hope my word was enough.

The first time I went to hospital was back in Tampa.

I was eight years old, just got my first bike from my grandfather, and took it for a ride down a dirt road. I broke my leg.

I remember the smell of antiseptic, the uneasy feeling it gave my already warped stomach-ache. I remember the sounds pretty clearly, the mechanical echo throughout cluttered hallways, the dial of a phone, the ring. There was a sense of uneasiness, a sense of dread and worry.

People died in these places, human beings, things that existed. We're born, we live life, and we rot away, and that terrified me.

Hospitals reminded me of one thing, sickness.

Cancer, poisoning, old age, coughs and the flu.

It was all awful.

I walked in silently with Nick, who pocketed his hands and nodded to the nurses as he passed. The halls were decked in white, the pure colour.

That pale colour was easily stained with red, I'm sure it was an occurring thing here.

I kept my head lowered; a lot of the nurses were glancing to my freshly bandaged wounds, raising their eyebrows at the state of me.

They probably thought I was some loose patient.

I wanted to turn around and wave my hands about, make it even more obvious, but to make a scene in a Hospital wasn't on my to do list either.

We stopped at the children's ward, and Nick cleared his throat to the woman at the front desk. She was small, petit blonde and her nurse smock was decked out in childish attire. I noticed her name, Kelly.

I stood nervously beside Nick, my own hands pocketed and still. They spoke for a moment, he told her who he was, what he was doing and who he wanted to see. She gave me a few sideways glances with her beady blue eyes, but I made no contact.

I was worried she'd say no, I mean, I was involved with the gang, even for just a moment. But it was enough time to make me feel guilty, feel as if I deserved nothing.

'She's in the last door to your left, room forty-five,' Kelly smiled, handing Nick a slip of red paper. 'But she's still asleep, the surgery was—'

'Did it go okay?' I blurted, stepping forward to catch her attention.

That movement wasn't needed, because she was already glancing at me. I swallowed and kept my hands by my sides, I didn't even notice the words spring from my mouth.

Nick chuckled weakly, but the nurse only returned a nod.

'Yes, she did very well!' Kelly said gently. 'I'm proud of her, her big sister left a few hours ago, slept over. What a wonderful girl.'

'Y-yeah,' I returned.

It was music to my ears, not only hearing about Nat's successful surgery, but the fact Juniper had been around as well.

Hearing her name, thinking of her, anything remotely to do with her?

Left me a little lightheaded.

Nick and I walked along the children's ward, I tried my best to not peek at the sick kids as we passed, but I couldn't help it.

Some glared at me, some smiled and pointed, I felt absolutely awful seeing them here.

They deserved to be outside, at school, doing what they loved.

Life was cruel.

But life was going to get better for one particular girl.

Nick stopped at the right door, pointed to it and nodded his head.

'I will watch you from out here,' he mumbled. 'Take as long as you need.'

I swallowed and glanced at him, nodding once.

'Okay.'

He was concerned by my awkward standing, not being able to move at all. I was nervous, not used to confronting sick people.

I was anxious the first time I saw Nat, and now I was even more.

It could have been because she'd just come out of surgery, who knew what she looked like, who knew how she was feeling.

I didn't want to add any stress, I'm sure she was upset over my absence the other day, the fight that broke out in her own house.

My stupid choices.

I turned into her room quickly, kept my head down and only lifted it when I reached the chair by her bedside. There were those familiar sounds, the monotone clinkering, the drip.

I mustered up the strength to look at her, and was instantly brought to tears.

Nat's face was still a little gaunt, but she seemed to be comfortable. She was still bedridden, but she slept without creased eyebrows, she looked relaxed.

God knew she deserved it, we all knew she deserved the relaxation a young girl like herself should have. I finally exhaled that big breath of air I had trapped, the anticipation of how she'd look, or react.

She was sound asleep, hands curled up by her sides, the right hand open a little, like someone had been holding it.

I swallowed and turned to Nick, who was occupied on his phone from the hallway, he took a seat and glanced at me, smiling gently.

The hospital ambience was uneasy, but I felt safer here with Nat.

With a clear of my throat, I took my place on the seat next to her bed, second guessing before I took her hand in mine.

It was warm, comforting me already. I was worried she'd wake up from the horrible chill on my fingertips, but she only flinched and continued to sleep.

I examined every aspect of her face, every device that surrounded her, before I brought her hand to my lips and kissed the back of her palm.

'I'm sorry,' I mumbled, creasing my eyebrows. 'I'm so sorry, I made a big mistake.'

My words were small, not at all loud. I was talking to Nat, to Juniper, to my parents and to Nick, to everyone I had hurt.

To Christopher.

I squeezed her hand again, bringing it to my forehead as I held it.

I lost my words, took the time to breathe, collect myself and continue. A few seconds, became a minute, a minute became ten.

Ten minutes of silence and uncomfortable tension, all emitting from my body.

I glanced to Nat again, watched her parted lips, as she breathed gently. I had to speak. I had to tell her everything, she wouldn't say anything back, but all I needed was to vent.

'I was scared; I'll tell you that,' I chuckled weakly. 'I jumped in headfirst, had no idea that this would happen, honestly.'

I sighed, watched my legs bop up and down nervously, my boots were unlaced. I cleared my throat again, confused by the moistness around my eyes.

'Y'know,' I started. 'I thought that I'd find the guy who did this to you and get him.'

I smiled at Nat, half expecting her to be listening to me.

'I thought it was the best plan, but I was so scared to scare your sister,' I grimaced, lowering my head against her hand again. 'That's why I asked so much, I asked you to lie and that was awful, I don't know what was going through my head. I thought maybe, just maybe; things would work out.'

I paused and shrugged my shoulders softly, breathing in to sigh.

'Obviously not,' I finished.

Nat breathed in, and out. I watched her chest rise and fall, her eyelashes flicker. I held her hand close, with both of mine. I hoped she would feel my touch, maybe she'd see me in her dream, if it was a happy one, or even a sad one.

As long as I existed in her world, that's all that mattered to me.

'I was really scared,' I chuckled. 'So scared, thought I was going to die.'

I was laughing to myself, but that quickly turned to realisation.

I could have died.

'Oh man,' I gritted my teeth, bringing her fingers to my forehead again. 'I remember sitting there, realising that I'd screwed up.'

I was choking up, shaking my head to forget every painful aspect of my past few days. Manny and Crocker's face was flashing, to and from my perspective, my mind's eye.

I couldn't stand it.

'I wasn't thinking; I was being really stupid,' I admitted, feeling even more ashamed of myself. 'I just wanted to help, find out who was doing all this, and in the end I got someone killed.'

A part of me knew that wasn't my fault, I didn't ask Christopher to join the Jackals, but obviously the real Pebbles knew I was making a guest appearance that night.

I felt like I was the blame, of all of this.

'I'm sorry I hurt you, and Juniper,' I kissed Nat's hand again, chewing my bottom lip. 'I'm sorry I made a mistake, I played with Juniper's feelings, your feelings...'

I finished my words, opening up was tougher than I thought, it hurt a goddamn lot. I was being honest; honesty was what mattered.

If there was one thing my parents taught me, one good thing, was that honesty was so important.

I think that was the only positive aspect of life they told me about.

Being honest was important and lying had backlash.

'I lied to Juniper,' I swallowed, shaking my head at my own stupid self. 'I flat out lied to her, told her nothing was wrong. I wanted her to have peace of mind, you were already in so much pain, I didn't want to add to any of that.'

I was getting annoyed, heated with myself, so irritated.

'I'm an idiot, Juniper was right,' I muttered. 'I should have told someone.'

I squeezed her hands, tight but gently, I wanted her to know I was honestly so sorry for the trouble I caused. Knowing this could very well be the last time I would see her, was burning my brain. I sniffled, kissing her hand once more;

'I'm so glad you're okay, Nat,' I said, smiling shortly. 'I wanted to help you, but I never lied because of you, that was my own choice, and I made a mistake.'

I gritted my teeth, swallowed that leering lump in my throat. 'I made a mistake...'

The room felt smaller when I lowered my head, hoping when I leaned back up, Nat would be awake, smiling at me, telling me everything was alright.

I let the silence overcome me, allowing the tension to become heavy and unwanted, I needed to feel these emotions.

It was the first step of forgiving myself.

It was hard, but I felt as though in the end? I would have myself and that was it.

At least I was taught to think that.

So I sat in silence, loathing myself, thinking the worst.

Until two hands took my shoulders.

At first I thought it was Nick giving me a sturdy pat, of reassurance, that everything would be okay.

But these hands were soft, gentle and smooth.

I swallowed and glanced back, and instantly froze, it was Juniper.

She had her eyes on me now, hands still on my shoulders. I couldn't speak, I couldn't really react.

Juniper's face was exhausted, the bags under her eyes were prominent, she hadn't slept well, that's for sure.

'H-how much of that did you hear, huh?' I joked weakly.

'Enough,' she answered.

I paused, watched her mouth move and struggled out of her grasp. She was confused by my movement, but I honestly felt like I didn't belong here.

I glanced towards Nick, who was still nose deep in a newspaper, he must have known Juniper was here though.

He wasn't that clueless.

'I'll go,' I muttered. 'Sorry.'

I cleared my throat, nodded to her and sidestepped, but Juniper took hold of my hands, and that was enough to leave me swallowing back tears.

'Rayne...' she said. 'Stop...'

I did what I was told.

Juniper was close, one step and we'd practically be pressed against one another. I looked aside, anywhere but her eyes.

'Are you going to look at me?' she asked.

'I didn't think I deserved to.'

'Don't be ridiculous.'

'I'm not.'

We both paused, Juniper kept my hands in hers.

I wasn't really sure what I was supposed to do, or what she was supposed to do. The contact was full of tension, but untouched tension.

There was no Arty rushing in, no Samantha and Nick.

Just Juniper and I.

'Juniper, I'm sorry,'

'Enough,' she interrupted. 'I know you are.'

Those words definitely tugged at my heartstrings, she knew I was sorry? She knew I'd loathed myself since the day I accepted that stupid job?

I glanced back at her, those green eyes of hers had never looked so tired. I couldn't help but feel a little guilty, maybe I was also the reason she was losing sleep. Juniper pursed her lips, looked to our hands and then sighed.

'You were really scared,' she said, rubbing her neck quickly. 'Weren't you?'

I felt my bottom lip wobble, especially when she turned her attention to Nat and I could see the tears welling in her eyes.

I lowered my head, pressing my forehead to hers. 'Petrified.'

This had been the closest we'd been in a while, but she stood still. I felt my chest heave, but I had to contain my feelings. I had to.

'I've been tossing and turning over you,' Juniper admitted, nodding a little. 'You've driven me crazy.'

I opened my mouth to reply, but she touched my lips with two of her fingers. The contact left me shivering.

'I've been mad, upset, betrayed,' Juniper's voice hitched. 'But God, I can't stay mad at you.'

I finally looked into her eyes and saw the same sadness. She pushed my chest a little, and touched my shoulders again.

'You lied,' she muttered. 'Snuck around, joined the group that put my sister in this position...'

Every word shot me down, but I continued to listen.

'And you put others before yourself, because you wanted to fix everything on your own,' her hands were massaging, touching both sides of my neck. 'You made a big mistake, and you got yourself hurt...'

I felt ashamed, hearing the words from her mouth especially.

We stood together, in Nat's hospital room, with the monotone drone of her appliances surrounding us. The tension was high, but it faltered from its peak to its end. Juniper's words were croaky, husky and tired, the most serious I'd heard her speak in a while.

'But you did all this, because you cared,' she finally finished.

I didn't notice my tears at first, but she did. Juniper's hands touched my cheeks, dragging her fingertips down my new scars. I was shivering, I wanted to speak but I couldn't.

I couldn't tell her how happy I was to hear these words, but also tell her how upset I was by my actions.

I wanted to apologise again, but I'd overdone that.

'You jumped headfirst, because you cared,' she paused, breathing in gently. 'I'm still mad at you, upset that you kept that lie bottled up...'

I leaned back, so I could watch her mouth move, her eyes, any part of her gorgeous face. Her eyes wandered over my own face, fingers behind my jaw.

'But I know you only did it, because you cared,' she said. 'You only wanted to help.'

I felt obliged to say something, but she'd stolen my ability to speak. I only stared at her.

Juniper chewed her bottom lip, maybe she expected an answer from me, but all I could do was open and close my mouth in a desperate attempt to speak.

'Next time, come to me about things like this,' she continued. 'Don't hide, don't play hero, like I said...'

Juniper softly pulled me down to her height, and I fumbled, sitting against Nat's hospital bed. I was instantly drawn to Juniper's eyes, just like always. She was calm, but I knew she was still healing, we all were.

She was touching my face, every wound that lingered. And I was once again soothed by her touch, my heavy heart was lifted, if only for a moment.

She leaned down, pressed her lips to my forehead and sighed again.

'I don't need a hero; I need a girlfriend,' she repeated.

I lowered my head again, holding her waist gently, I wasn't sure I had the right to touch her. So they hovered, until she grooved into my grasp.

I could only lean forward and hug her stomach with my head, muffle a short groan. I felt stupid, really, really stupid.

I breathed in, leaned up and looked her in the eye, where she eagerly awaited my words.

'T-that night, where we...' I swallowed. 'Both times, I didn't mean to keep the lie... I just–'

She touched my lips again with her fingers, shushing me.

'I know, Red,' she mumbled. 'I know it must have been hard.'

I was getting sympathy now, and I couldn't handle it, I shook my head and hugged her tightly.

'Don't,' I whimpered. 'Don't feel bad for me, I've done nothing but stuff up.'

Her hands were on my head, stroking.

'I've hurt so many people.'

'You've hurt yourself, too.'

'I know, but...'

'Hmm?'

I looked up once more, Juniper's head was angled, waiting for me to finish. I grimaced, swallowed and tensed my neck.

'Are you trying to say that both nights weren't acts of love?'

'Of course not!'

I shook her a little, rose to my feet and grabbed her arms. 'Every moment was because I care for you, I felt nothing but comfort and relaxation.'

I paused, shook my head and held her face in my hands. This time, Juniper's eyes twitched, she was taken back by my touch.

'I wanted nothing but you...' I mumbled. 'I couldn't stand the beating reminder of my big mistake, just jolting in my head.'

I examined every freckle on her face, stroked every loose strand of hair from her eyes. I was tearing up, but I still kept a sturdy face.

'I just kept telling myself I was helping; I was doing the right thing... I was going to save Nat.' She watched me speak, and I exhaled shakily. 'But I never wanted to make you feel used... ever...'

Juniper relaxed in my hands, and I watched her do so.

'I wanted nothing else but to share that experience, with you.' I stammered. 'Because I love you, I've never felt that before, with anyone else-'

I was cut off by a kiss, a rough but sweetened kiss. Juniper had wrapped her hands around my neck, dragged me lower to her height and taken my breath away.

I shut my eyes quickly, held her face gently and allowed it, it was all I'd wanted for days.

And here I was, receiving it.

I felt my eyebrows furrow, my want for her rising. It was emotional, so emotional that I had to break off and take a shaky breath. She leaned in for another kiss, but I was frozen.

I felt as though I didn't derserve it.

'I'm sorry,' I sobbed. 'I'm so sorry.'

Juniper grabbed me into her arms, rubbed the back of my neck, hushed me.

I felt silly, like a child being scolded and then sympathised with.

I wondered how long it would take me to get over this, get over my stupid choice.

'I love you,' Juniper said sternly. 'You know this.'

'I–I know.'

'And although you made mistakes, I know you were only trying to do the right thing...'

'I don't deserve this...'

'Stop that, Red.'

'I hurt you, why did I hurt you, I'm a fucking idiot... shit.'

'Hey!' Juniper grabbed my face roughly, bringing my attention her way. 'Enough!'

I swallowed, and she shook me once.

'You stop that!' her tone was serious. 'You don't stand here, and self loathe any longer, you made a mistake, I forgive you.'

'B–but.'

'No buts, Red!' Juniper pushed me gently. 'You wanted to help, you may have royally fucked up, but you did help.'

I blinked, breathing in harshly. Juniper nodded her head to her sister and raised her eyebrows.

'You got Nat's surgery,' she said.

Christopher came to mind when she said that. His death and his falling, he was used and abused, and now his parents had paid for Nat's surgery.

Which I had no issues with, the only issue that lingered on my mind, was Christopher was framed, and that asshole was still out there.

I knew right now, wasn't the right time to talk about it.

But I would, I would open up more and I wouldn't lie to Juniper Bridges.

She'd forgiven me, yes, it may take time for her to completely forgive me, but we'd made up, even just a little.

'She'll walk again,' Juniper said, her voice was shaky too. 'She won't have to suffer anymore.'

I was watching her break down now.

'She won't have to sit there and cry, she won't have to...'

I took her close, held her and propped my head against hers. Juniper sobbed, and I never let go.

My emotions were in hyper drive, but I did feel something I hadn't in a while.

Relief.

Relief that we were okay, that Juniper still loved me and she saw the real reasoning behind my stupid acts.

After all, that's all I wanted to do, was help.

I glanced to my left, and caught eyes with Nick. He watched from the doorway, his arms crossed and face sympathetic.

I buried my face in Juniper's long hair, listened to her sobs and muffled words.

I was content with being so close to her, I loved this girl.

My love for her was to an extent I thought I could never reach.

I never wanted her to cry, ever again.

But with my court date set, my future looked hazy.

I was afraid she may be crying more than ever.

Chapter Twenty-Eight

RAYNE

The mind is always active.

It never stops working, even when you fall asleep and drift off into a world that never was. It worked like a computer of sorts, and I always wondered why we as humans couldn't control the way our brain worked. We have limited power over the way it functioned, the way it wired out movement, our fears and stimulants.

Maybe headaches were the cause of too much thinking, too much movement, too much pressure and heaviness. And maybe there was an off-button that we just couldn't figure out, somewhere in our body, on our body and around our body that turns off our ability to think, to stress, feel.

In the past week, that's all had I wished to do. Turn off my mind so I didn't have to continue to think about the mistakes I made, atone to them, the wishful thinking of being able to rewind time and never step foot in that territory again.

But wishful thinking gets you nowhere, it wasn't working for me at all.

My hospital trip was a wave of emotions, I stepped foot in there nervous, full of angst and terror, and I stepped out of there with a similar feeling.

Juniper had kissed me, and for a moment I felt like nothing else mattered.

It was frightening, how one simple touch could turn my mind off, maybe that was the only way it worked for me.

But I couldn't rely on Juniper to make my awful thoughts simply vanish at the touch of her lips against mine, no, I had to act upon that myself and fix whatever was going through my head on my own.

At least, that's what I thought.

Atoning for my mistakes was time consuming, especially because everything was still happening, nothing had stopped yet, the train was still ripping through the valleys of unwanted self-loathing and pressurised guilt.

But I realised one thing, it was slowing down.

Until Monday, I was still captain of that train.

After Juniper had calmed down, though it only took her a mere two minutes. She took me by the face, told me she needed time alone, and set me on my way.

It was hard to leave her, all I wanted to do was sit with her and continue to linger in that mutual understanding the two of us shared. The feeling of her understanding me, understanding why I did what I well, did.

Was relief beyond words.

But I had to respect her space, I wasn't used to that. Though I spent most of my time alone before Juniper, I hated the idea of being secluded, especially with my own mind.

I enjoyed someone else's presence around me, to numb the awful feeling of creeping anxiety that slowly made its way up, without consent.

So I made my way back with Nick, who didn't utter a word to me. Funny, I didn't want to talk to him at all, so I guess he was respecting my space.

I didn't understand it completely, but I was learning to.

When I was left alone in my apartment, I stood for a solid few minutes, letting the emotions calm, the ringing in my ears subside.

I was having trouble slowing down, I couldn't find a stop button. Nick had muttered something to me before he left, but I didn't catch it at all.

He couldn't get through to me.

It was a slow day, the time still wavered over five o'clock. I sat on my couch, bringing in the sounds of my next-door neighbours arguing, and finally the city of Boston in the distance picked up its pace. I could hear the cars honking, the rev of engines and the yells of hoons. The church bells around the corner began to ring, I paced the rhythm with the pacing of my heartbeat.

Slow, but steady.

I took a breath, my hands on my lap, the ceiling was the only comfort I could seek. Staring at it, following the string of light that bounced to and from my view. My mind was racing, lots of thoughts, lots of images, but it was almost like a mushy blur.

I pressed my fingertips together, and figured that wasn't enough distraction for my bustling mind. I grabbed the TV remote, shoved my finger down on the power button, and hoped the voices of scripted characters would sooth me to a calm slumber.

I hoped one channel would have a sixties film on, something I used to watch with my grandfather. The apartment didn't have cable, so everything was boring, which was the best stuff to fall asleep to.

I flicked to and from channels, but paused when I caught a familiar face flash towards me. I should have kept changing channels, I should have shoved my nail deeper into the arrow button, I should have closed my eyes.

The news anchor droned, but I could only focus on Christopher's photo. It must have been an aged photo, from high school. But he still looked as innocent and anxious as he seemed just a few days ago.

I couldn't catch the trauma before it hit me again, the images that left my headache worsening. I fumbled with the remote, dropped it against the tough carpet and cussed loudly, trying to drown out the name.

Christopher.

Christopher.

Christopher.

I couldn't help it, I felt like his death was my fault, I was the reason he got into trouble. Maybe if I didn't join, I could have helped him, maybe if I didn't join that stupid group, he'd be alive.

I felt a struggled moan leave my lips, as I hit the change channel button on the remote with so much force I felt the rubber indent break.

The TV flickered to an old movie, something I recognized as 'Miracle on 34th Street.'

At first I wondered why it was on so early into the year, a Christmas film?

But then I breathed a sigh of relief, the channel was changed, there was no more frightening reminder of a death I convinced was on my hands.

I sniffed, grabbed the whisky bottle on the coffee table, and examined the label, turning it side to side.

Guilt.

I never resorted to alcohol, but here I was.

I sniffled and I sculled a large sip, swallowing the awful taste. If I wasn't as tired, I would have bothered to buy a Zoom Cola, to wash down the strong taste.

I leaned back into my awful couch, letting the tough ruggedness of it touch my neck. Over my heavy breathing, the alcohol hit my head fast.

Now, hear me out, I wasn't a lightweight.

But I was glad to feel that dizzy feeling take me by surprise, leave my senses tingling and slowing down.

I closed my eyes, concentrated on the muffled voices from the television, and drifted off to the relaxing music of 'Miracle on 34th Street.'

§

There was a big storm, in my dream.

I walked the streets of my neighbourhood back in Tampa, let the familiar smells linger around me. I could smell my bedroom, the grass outside my house, the neighbours rose bush, all mixed up in the muggy scent of fresh storm rain.

These nostalgic smells only left a sick feeling in my stomach.

I didn't find any pleasure being here, even if it were a dream, it felt too real.

With a crackle of lightning, I was somewhere else.

To my right was the gym that Cole and I sparred in, to my left was the convenience store that I was arrested in.

I felt the panic rise now, as I saw the same police officers catch a glimpse of me standing on the drifting road. I swallowed, and they barred their teeth like wolves.

Their faces contorted, becoming malicious and wild. I felt my chest tighten, did they always look so vicious?

It hit me that this was indeed a dream, when they became sickly mammals, rushing after me with snarled noses.

I tried to run, but my movement was halted, when I caught a glimpse of a boy just a few feet ahead of me.

In the darkness, shrouded by the moonlight that Illuminated his coat, I noticed the red baseball pattern first. His shoulders were hunched, his body shaky and cold.

Christopher stood, he didn't care to move.

I saw his eyes, bloodshot and tired, his lips pursed and wobbly. In his hand, he held the same gun.

I shook my head, I didn't want to see this, I couldn't experience this again.

With all my strength, I tried to move, tried to call out to him, warn him of the others heading my way.

At first I thought the beasts were coming for me, but in just moments I realised they were heading for him.

I panicked, pushed forward, but felt a familiar tightness around my wrists and legs. I breathed in sharply, glanced to my body and wailed in anguish. The ropes were ripping into my skin, blood oozing from my struggle.

The rain wouldn't help, I couldn't slip free, I couldn't help Christopher as these vicious beasts ran towards him, their paws pounding into the muggy road.

Christopher caught eyes with me, as he lifted the gun.

I shook my head, feeling ill as this scene was being recreated in front of me.

He was so close, why couldn't I just rip free and save him, grab the gun and shoot the beasts?

The rain hardened, even more so then it already was. I couldn't see through the splitting water, it was so rough against my shoulders and face that it practically stung.

I opened my mouth, tried to scream, I could feel the words rumble in my chest, but they were having trouble escaping the cage that kept them secure.

Christopher smiled, a short perk of his lips as he lifted the gun to his temple again. The beasts were seconds away, and I couldn't focus on the both of them.

His mouth opened, and he mouthed something I couldn't catch, before he was trampled, the gun set off and my scream for plea finally left my lips.

§

A heavy knock woke me up, three to be exact.

My eyes were split open, my breath returned to my heaved chest and I felt the last of my fuzziness tingle before my senses came back.

I swallowed loudly, examined my surroundings and flinched to hear the thunder boom from outside. It was hard to breathe, but I did my absolute best to regain myself as I shakily rose. The TV was still on, now it was just infomercials, I must have been snoozing for a good three hours.

Another knock.

I sniffled and rubbed my eyes quickly, examined my hands and watched them tremble. The dream hadn't left my mind, it was still rushing to and from, Christopher was still staring at me, the beasts were still barking, alongside the neighbour's chihuahua next door.

Yet another knock.

I was getting frustrated, so I rose and stumbled towards the door, unlocking it with shaky fingers. it was almost like my energy had been zapped as I pushed the handle down, dragging backwards. I didn't even bother to think who it could be, but I was surprised to find Juniper.

She peeked to me under her hood of her red coat, it was drenched in rain but everything underneath was dry. Around her shoulder hung my guitar, id missed it, honestly.

And in her other hand she held a duffel bag.

It was quite big.

I swallowed and listened to the water pitter patter behind her, and lost my words again.

She seemed to notice my shaky persona, even more so then earlier this afternoon.

'Hey, Red,' she muttered, sympathetically.

I combed my hands through my hair and stepped back, letting her in, my heart was leaping, but I wasn't sure what from.

Her appearance, or the dream, it could have even been the use of my nickname.

Or maybe all three.

Juniper gave me a sideways glance as she made her way in, dragging her shoes against my welcome mat. I closed the door behind her, and listened to her move. I wasn't quite sure what to say or do. I didn't expect to see her twice in one day, but a small part of me hoped she'd show up again before my trial on Monday.

'I thought you'd be hungry, so I picked you up some stuff,' she spoke softly, turning to me. 'And I thought you'd miss this.'

She pulled my guitar off her shoulder, though the black case was wet, the guitar itself was most definitely dry.

It was also very nice to know she didn't smash it to pieces, after my blatant disobedience.

Juniper cleared her throat as she handed it my way, and I grabbed hold of it rather sloppily. I hadn't touched it in what felt like years, even though it had only been a few days.

The past week felt like that.

As Juniper took her wet coat off and folded it, I touched the spine of my guitar.

'Thank you,' I muttered slowly, my voice was croaky.

'Did something happen?' she asked over me. 'You look...'

I glanced up when she stepped closer to me, touching my chin with her fingertips. 'Shaken up.'

'I'm fine,' I shook from her grasp and slid out of the awkwardness, placing my guitar somewhere dry. She'd come at a pretty awful time, after that appalling dream. Christopher's smile was still there, flashing to and from a bloody pair of parted lips.

I felt my chest tighten, and I paused to catch myself against the wall. Oh god, how long would it be until he could find peace in my dreams?

How long would I deal with this?

'Rayne?' Juniper asked softly, she was behind me, not far off. 'What,'

'Bad dream,' I shuddered, interrupting her. 'Bad dream, sorry.'

Again, I rushed from her touch, the awful voice of guilt and self-loathing reminding me I didn't deserve it. I could feel her eyes on me as I hit my kitchen, placing my hands against the countertop. I couldn't bend, but I arched my shoulders forward and sniffled gently.

Juniper cleared her throat, I could hear the roughness.

'Well, I bought you some dinner,' she repeated, popping her duffel bag against the couch armrest. I could hear the familiar sound of plastic rustling, and the warm smell of something delicious.

I hadn't eaten all day, and she knew that somehow.

Juniper saw the alcohol, she stopped in her tracks, blinked and sighed gently. She was muttering to herself as she took the packaged food out of her bag. I think she was disappointed, but maybe she understood.

I watched her walk this way, placing three plastic containers of Thai food in front of me. I wanted to eat, but I felt like everything I consumed would make me throw up.

God, this was awful.

It had been a total of five minutes, and I was still struggling to even process the big things happening around me.

'You look like you need something…' Juniper paused when I grabbed at my heart, rubbing the soreness, the aching. On the corner of my eye, I saw her eyebrows furrow with concern.

Go away, I thought, hushing the anxiety to back off. Go away, go away.

I covered my face with my spare hand, breathing in sharply. I wasn't used to this type of pain, this type of mourning and despair, death wasn't leaving my doorstep.

Familiar hands took my waist, pulling me into an embrace. I was turned, weak as I was, I was coaxed into Juniper's arms, I slumped.

I'd longed for this, ever since I left her at the hospital, I needed this.

'You look like you need something warm,' she muttered into my ear, her fingertips pressing into the spots at the bottom of my spine.

I shivered under her touch, but let her hold me.

Until I was pressed against another, did I realise how shook up I really was.

My body was trembling, chin pressed into the crook of Juniper's neck, eyes watering. But God she made the thought vanish, if only for a moment. Christopher was giving me a break, the memory of him had been pushed back.

Juniper was here, I felt the tension in her, but she and I were softening.

And we were together, again, at last.

Alone, secluded, with the heavy sound of Boston crying outside, the warmth in my world had returned.

I finally let my hands touch her, even if they clung to the bottom of her shirt desperately, she reacted and brought me even closer.

Although I believed I didn't deserve this, I remembered her determination in the hospital just hours prior, the words she spoke, the understanding I so badly ached for.

Now it was time to continue healing.

But who knows how long that would take.

I held her for a fair few moments, she swayed me, side to side with utmost comfort. Although it made me feel like a child, I wanted this.

I could feel the warmth, her skin was hot and soothing, my fingertips slipped to and from her elbows to her waist, until she brought the last remaining distance between us to a close.

'Let's get you into something more comfortable yeah?' she said. 'I'll help you.'

'Juniper, why are you here?' I asked, the words fell from my mouth. I didn't mean to sound rude, but it came out quite rushed.

She broke away, her eyes locking onto mine.

With every blink, I felt like slumbering, still groggy from my past sleep, I felt like I hadn't slept at all.

Juniper Bridges looked a little hurt by my words, but she smiled shortly and pressed her forehead to my collar.

'Because,' she began. 'I don't like the idea of you being this way.'

I swallowed, my throat sore and rough.

'You need me, more than ever,' she muttered. 'Okay?'

I felt my heart thump when her hands touched my face, being careful with every brush of her fingers. I flinched, furrowed my eyebrows and waited for her to continue. Staring at her in the eyes at this close proximity left me emotional.

'And I need you,' she admitted, her voice croaky. 'I want to be here, so you don't drown in your own sorrow and terrible cheap whisky.'

She pointed to the couch, and flicked her finger.

I felt ashamed, but kept my eyes on hers.

Juniper hunched her shoulders, grabbed mine and stroked them gently. 'I'm here.'

It hit home, hearing that. And I tried to keep a strong face, but I think from the way Juniper's eyebrows furrowed sympathetically, I'd given her my biggest puppy dog look yet.

Having her here would help, it would be the first time we were alone, with no interruptions. I wasn't sure Nick would be happy knowing she were here with me, a suspected criminal, but I honestly think she didn't care.

I didn't care either.

'And anyway,' she said. 'I brought my laptop and all the necessities for a reporter in training.'

I felt like smiling, but I just couldn't.

Juniper scratched her neck, and cleared her throat. 'Unfortunately, I do have a paper to write.'

'Another one, huh?' I finally spoke.

She paused, looked at me and let her hand drop, just so she could hold mine. I was expecting a witty comment, but instead she brought my body close to hers again. She examined my face, and I tried my hardest to cower away, but she wouldn't allow that.

She brushed her fingers through my hair, tucked it behind my ear and fixated on my eyes.

'Everything's going to be okay, Rayne,' she assured. 'Everything's going to be okay.'

I felt the tears well up in my eyes again, and wondered how I got here.

How I got to stand in my kitchenette with my girlfriend, about to sob my eyes out.

Nick had told me the same thing, but I didn't have the want to cry. But here was Juniper, saying the exact same thing, though it was coaxing, it still left me absolutely vulnerable.

I opened my mouth to speak, and she hummed to me, hoping I'd say something. But I could only lean forward and touch my forehead with hers, hold her waist and bring her closer.

We stood in silence, I watched her eyes close before I closed my own.

We shared something, something I'd missed. I felt the tension rise, if only for a moment.

I wanted to tell her I loved her, but I could only stand in silence, with the overwhelming feeling of sympathy and care bouncing to and from the two of us.

'Forget about Monday,' Juniper said. 'Just forget Monday exists, Red.'

I wanted to scoff and shake my head, tell her that was ridiculously hard to do.

I couldn't.

Monday was daunting, it was so close, two days away. Just the thought of it made me sick, I was too weak.

'Hey,' Juniper grabbed my attention again. 'Hey, look at me.'

I opened my eyes, saw the seriousness in hers and swallowed. She took hold of my face again, stroking the new scars that danced along my skin.

'Forget, Monday,' she whispered gently. 'Look at me, and forget Monday. Just focus on me and think of something else.'

I was having trouble digesting her words, my stomach was lurching and every pump of my heart was irritating me.

'Okay,' I mumbled. 'Okay...'

It was going to be terribly hard, but Juniper looked determined, that's all I needed for a reminder.

Juniper smiled to me, and it was infectious, I felt the sides of my lips twitch.

'Alright, see?' she chuckled gently. 'Stop thinking about the negative, Red.'

'I'll try,' I replied.

'I know you will,' Juniper answered. 'C'mon.'

She pulled me into my room down my messy hall. I held her hand tightly, examining her back. I wondered how a human being could make any circumstance better, an awful storm become a beautiful melody.

A tortured woman like myself, become a puddle of comfortable human cells.

Only Juniper Bridges could do that to me.

She brought me into my own room, and rummaged through my drawers to find something. I stood awkwardly for someone in their own house.

'You don't mind if I stay here, right?' she asked. 'I mean; I probably should have asked.'

'You're always welcome,' I replied. 'Don't be silly.'

Juniper seemed to brighten every time I spoke. She and I had only exchanged broken and ached words since.

But here we were, trying our absolute hardest to make everything normal again, even when a court date was sneaking up behind.

'Alright, here!' she said, pulling out sweatpants and a sweater for me. I smiled shortly when she turned with her arms stretched.

'I'm too good to you,' she winked. 'You know that?'

It felt brilliant to smile, I'd missed it.

'I know you are,' I replied, amused. 'You're wonderful.'

Juniper giggled, and I watched her. But my face fell, my eyes eased and I felt that unwanted sadness hit me again.

And Juniper sensed it.

'You're... wonderful,' I repeated, almost as if I was realising it all over again.

She shrugged her shoulders, sat against my bed and cleared her throat once more. I wasn't so sure what came over me, but I just wanted to be close to her.

'Juniper,' I said, aware. 'Are you alright.'

'This isn't about me, Red,' she interrupted, rising quickly to take hold of the bottom of my shirt. 'This isn't about me at all.'

I wanted to protest, but she had already begun to undress me. I swallowed when she shushed my attempted reply, and tugged my clothing upwards.

I could have done it myself, yeah it might have hurt all the bruises and pulled muscles, but I was old enough to do it on my own.

'You don't have to dress me, Juniper,' I mumbled. 'You don't have to do this.'

'Oh, stop,' she chuckled nervously, throwing my shirt into my open drawer. She turned to smile again, but it faded very quickly when my bare torso was in her view.

I heard the thunder rumble from outside, the wind picked up and blew leaves into my grotty windows. Boston seemed to pick up on the sadness that erupted from

Juniper.

I saw her neck tense, her bottom lip tremble as her fingertips touched every bruise and cut on my skin. She had cleaned me up the day I had received these marks, but now she was engulfed in a completely different emotion.

Complete and utter sadness.

I flinched at her touch, she touched my abdomen, my ribs and my collarbone, until finally her palms flattened and rubbed my neck, back and forth.

I could feel my heart hammer, but it was a different type of feeling.

Seeing her so distraught only left me distraught.

Though the feel of her nails dragging alongside new scars left a bundle of butterflies fluttering about inside me, I couldn't even imagine what was going through her mind.

I knew if Juniper was this scruffy and cut up, I'd be a walking waterfall; I'd want to cry every time I saw her, knowing she'd been hurt and I wasn't there to help.

But these scars on my body were most definitely my fault, my stupid actions.

I knew I deserved them.

Juniper continued to examine me, her bottom lip wobbled so she pursed them to look strong. I held her waist, and my touch left her shivering.

'Jesus...' she sniffled. 'S-orry.'

I shook my head, muttering that she had no need to be sorry. She grabbed me close again, kissing my neck quickly.

'Don't be sorry, this wasn't your fault,' I assured her now, the roles had changed. 'I'm okay.'

'You're not okay,' she replied. 'God, you're not okay at all!'

'Juniper...' I said softly.

But she wasn't finished, she finally started to cry. I froze then, clenching my teeth.

'I'm sorry, I wasn't able to,'

'Don't even say it,' I snapped. 'Don't.'

Juniper pursed her lips and sniffled, shaking her head quickly. I grabbed the sweater from her hands, and though it hurt to do, I slipped it over my tense torso.

'What were you just saying a moment ago?' I asked. 'No more thinking about the negative, right?'

She glanced aside, with her arms crossed and a strong face. I sighed a little and held her shoulders.

'I'm sorry,' I said. 'I'm sorry I look like this right now, it'll be like this for a while, and I just,'

'It's not that, Red!' she whimpered, grabbing my hands off her shoulders.

I was taken back by her words. I wanted to touch her eyelids and wipe those tears away, there was no need for more.

'The thought of them hurting you...'

'Stop it,' I mumbled.

'God, you must have gone through so much, and...'

I was getting irritated now, the images flashing to and from my perspective once more. Juniper was sympathising, but it wasn't needed, I didn't think she realised until I yelled.

'Stop!' I sobbed, grabbing the sides of my head. 'Stop it, please Juniper!'

I leaned back, dropping to my bed. I was shivering again, and I couldn't stop the images. I covered my face, hoping to push back the pain.

I tried focusing on the rain outside, the squeak of my bed and bark from next doors dog that I woke up with my cry.

My shoulders were hunched, legs trembling.

'I'm so sorry, Red...' Juniper croaked, her voice was higher than usual. 'I'm sorry, I didn't mean to...'

I nodded, and roughly rubbed my eyes with the base of my palms.

'It's fine,' I muttered. 'It's fine.'

Was it though? I wanted to question that exact thing, when would it be 'fine?'

Juniper sat beside me, and grabbed hold of my left arm, so she could hug me close. I let her do so, I knew I was a sap for any sort of comfort, especially in times like this.

'I'm sorry, baby,' she whispered, stroking my collar. 'I'm sorry.'

We sat there, together in silence.

With my face covered, I watched nothing but darkness dance in my perspective. That pitch blackness scared me, but with Juniper next to me, fear was having trouble harming me.

I was blessed to have her here, but I was afraid for us. Afraid of what would rip us apart next, what would strike us down.

Could the world just give us a break, to be happy?

§

I ate in silence as Juniper tapped away on her laptop just next to me. I was surprised I could actually down my food without the urge to bring it back up again. After our fiasco in the bedroom, Juniper left me to myself, she respected the minimal space I needed.

She kissed me across the cheek, told me she'd be in the next room, and shut the door softly so I could breathe.

I was ashamed, that I was still being affected by all this.

But who could blame me, nobody.

So, here I sat in my dingy apartment, with the girl of my dreams sitting beside me on my awful couch. The clock struck nine PM, the rain hadn't stopped at all, it was terrible that even the newsman was surprised. I was dressed and comfortable, chewing my coconut rice with a grimace. It felt nice, though it was a small amount, I felt stress free.

Juniper was concentrating, I peeked a few times at her screen, and she had an alarming amount of news articles popped up.

I'd asked her previously what she was writing about, and she'd replied with a topic I wasn't even aware of. I wasn't aware of anything but my own issues since my mishap with the Jackals. I always made sure my wrist was covered, I wasn't ready for the reminder just yet.

It was hard, pretending everything was alright, but I just had to.

By half past nine, I'd finished eating, surprised by how much I consumed. I was exhausted, but I couldn't bring myself to sleep. I glanced to the whisky on my bedside table again, and cleared my throat.

'Did you want a drink?' I asked.

Juniper turned to me, her eyebrow quirked. 'Really, Red?'

I smiled shortly, shrugging my shoulders. 'It's not that bad.'

'Looks absolutely awful,' she replied.

I was amused by her snootiness, so I grabbed my glass and poured her a small amount. She whimpered back when I pointed it her way, urging her to try.

'C'mon, at least try.'

'Red, I have a paper due on Sunday!'

'But you gotta try it.'

'Red...'

'Juniper, you just gotta, taste the awful whiskey, please.'

She sighed, grabbed the glass and grouched at me. But when she saw me smile, she rolled her eyes and took a sip.

I watched her eyebrows arch inwards, and she groaned as she swallowed. I knew exactly what she'd say.

'Awful!' she cussed after she swallowed. 'Oh my god, that's awful!'

I laughed and sculled the rest of it, which she responded with a gasp.

'Rayne!' Juniper snapped.

'What?' I laughed weakly. 'It's good, helps me forget the shitstorm we're in.'

Juniper gently smacked my legs. 'Don't you dare make the same mistake I did.'

She was referring to the very first time I set foot in her apartment, the drunken disorderly girlfriend of mine throwing punches and drowning in her own tears. I watched her give me a stern look, before she returned to her laptop, smacking her lips disapprovingly of the taste that lingered there.

'I won't,' I promised. 'But it does help, a little.'

'I guess so, but it shouldn't.'

'You're not happy with me drinking, not only a little?'

'Nope.'

I sat still, chuckled and placed the whisky down. The little moment of amusement was over, and I was pretty sad about that. I think Juniper knew too, that we wouldn't be able to act like nothing was wrong, we could try, but I doubted the two of us.

I'm sure she was sitting there, doing her absolute best to type an article, but all that was on the back of her mind was me, and how I was in trouble.

As for me, I was thinking of the same things.

I sighed, leaned back and watched the television with tired eyes, every blink left my head heavier and heavier.

'Ugh,' Juniper groaned.

I turned my head to ask what was up, but she had already crawled over my lap to grab the whole bottle of whisky. I watched with an amused grin as she sculled a large portion of it, bringing the bottle up high into the air.

She let it pop off her lips, and let out an anguished moan of disgust. But I was already laughing, something I hadn't done in a while.

She turned to me and cussed, pushing the bottle into my hands.

'Shut up!' she chuckled. 'I needed it.'

'Oh, but you were so upset at me for drinking!' I replied. 'What happened?'

Juniper shrugged her own shoulders and eased her eyes at her computer screen, hiccupping a little. 'I can't say no to free booze.'

I knew she was kidding, but she made me laugh, and I owed her the world for that. I took a large gulp of whisky too; the taste didn't bother me as much as it did Juniper. She huffed and rolled her eyes playfully, as I winked and continued to drink.

'Still cocky, even after all that,' she teased, harmfully.

I broke off the bottle and sighed quickly, leaning back even more into my dingy couch.

'It's just hard to stop thinking, y'know?' I muttered. 'I'm trying; I promise you that.'

'I know.'

'But, I'm scared.'

Juniper placed her laptop upon the coffee table, and brought her legs up onto the couch. She leaned back, lifted her right arm and examined me twiddle my fingers in thorough thought.

My eyes were still set on the television, but I was looking right through it. My mind was gearing up again, a little messier with the help of the whisky, but it was still revving towards misery. I touched my forehead with my hand and grumbled.

'Talk to me,' Juniper said. 'I'm here, you know that.'

I nodded, I'd been meaning to talk to her about everything, all of this, but it was harder to get out than to sit for hours piecing it together.

I pursed my lips, leaned forward and scooted a little closer to her. I had sunken so low into my couch that she welcomed me with a hand upon my head.

'Ever since I was young, I've always been afraid of being a bad person...' I began. 'Even when I hung out with the bad kids and stole, I couldn't help but feel guilty.'

'Which proves you were aware of bad choices,' Juniper chimed in.

I looked at her, examined her eyes and twisted my lip in response. She was itching my scalp, brushing my hair between her fingers.

'No, but...' I croaked. 'I would sit back and fear who I was, fear that I'd make someone's life a misery, my parents sat there and told me I was doing so much harm, and over time, I just started believing it.'

I paused, touched my knees and blinked slowly. Every time I breathed in, my nose would ache, every time.

I turned my head to Juniper again, and examined her gorgeous face. She cocked her head in response, her hand dangling above my head, holding strands of my hair. The bags under her eyes were just faint now, but I could tell she was tired to the extent I was too.

Her freckles were just as cute as ever, lips pale and skin smooth. I urged to kiss her.

'Am...' I froze, shuddered at the thought and continued. 'Am I a bad person?'

Juniper brought herself even closer, she crossed her legs and let the hand above my head fall over my shoulders. I let her touch my face with her free hand, she had a tendency to trace the new scars I had. It made me feel comfortable, but it also made me worry, fear that I looked like an absolute monster. But when I saw her eyes, they seemed as sincere as ever.

'If anything...' Juniper hummed. 'What happened this week just proves you're a good person.'

I watched her lips move, her voice trail to and from my ears.

'You did something completely dangerous for someone else,' she itched behind my ear and pulled. 'And although I'm not happy about it, you've done so much...'

I swallowed, the emotional ball rising in my chest.

'You've been brave...' Juniper continued to stroke my face as she spoke. 'Strong, and loyal.'

'I lied.'

'You lied, yes, but you were honest about your lies.'

I wanted to fight back, but she pressed her lips to my temple and shushed me.

'There's no need to talk about that again, we've already discussed that,' she told me. 'You're going to be honest with me from now on, we've established that already.'

'Yeah.'

'So, let me continue,' she mumbled, touching and fixing the loose bandage over my nose. I wanted to hold her, but I was content with being stroked and pet like a puppy dog.

The feeling of being worth something was addictive.

'You did it because you cared, and although a day ago I scolded you about it,' Juniper paused again, chuckled and sighed. 'I still couldn't stop myself from thinking how much I owe you, you took so many risks for my happiness.'

I swallowed as she grabbed both my cheeks, bringing our view close.

'You're a good person, Rayne Holmes,' she said. 'Inside and out, no matter how much your mind tells you otherwise...'

Her words left me speechless, but I felt the uneasy feeling of tears. She smiled again, stroking the bruises on my face.

'You are the most perfect being in my eyes, Red,' she finished. 'Don't you forget that.'

I smiled when she kissed my nose, a short weak stretch of my lips, but it was enough. Those words lifted me, over all planes of self-loathing and hatred, hearing that I was worth it from someone else, only made me think the same.

It was a start.

'This isn't just the booze talking,' Juniper added, giggling when I grouched in return. 'I mean it.'

'Thank you,' I said, but my tone was serious, very serious. I grabbed her face too, until we both mimicked each other's touch.

Juniper coaxed herself into my hands, making my heart flip. I wanted to kiss her, right there, but I also had another idea I'd been wanting to experience with Juniper Bridges since the day I met her.

'Juniper...' I mumbled seriously, hands shaky.

She swallowed and leant closer, her nose brushing against mine. 'Red?'

'I wanna listen to Ella Fitzgerald,' I blurted.

Juniper quirked an eyebrow, her eyes opened, head brought back. I tried to keep a stern serious look, for the jokes sake, but I couldn't.

I chuckled and stood up, held her hands and smiled.

'I wanna dance with you.'

'Ugh Red, we've discussed this whole dancing thing too!' Juniper fought back, still flustered from our close contact. 'Jesus, way to ruin the vibe.'

I let her hands go and grabbed her laptop, which she tried taking back. I shushed her and felt the dizziness hit my head, but as I started pressing around her laptop, I realised I hadn't used a new model in a while.

I paused, lifted my hands from the keyboard and blinked when Juniper wrapped her arms around my chest.

'Oh no...' she muttered into my ear. 'Someone doesn't know how to use modern day technology.'

I smelt the whisky on her lips and leaned back into her.

'Oh c'mon, help me out.'

'Why should I? after that?' she tickled under my chin. 'We have a nice little meaningful conversation, and you ruin it with something silly like that.'

'Silly?' I pouted.

'So, silly,' she teased.

I gave her the biggest pair of puppy dog eyes I could, she returned a roll of her own. It was hard to believe we were sitting here laughing and acting like the world wasn't ending around us.

But I had to keep going, for her sake, for my own sake.

For once, I could thank alcohol.

'What song?' she asked, grabbing her laptop to her lap.

I rose with a clap of my hands, twisting to point at her. 'I've got a crush on you.'

'I know, but what's the song name?' Juniper mumbled, winking playfully.

I smirked and leaned over her. 'That is, the name of the song.'

She went red in the face and started typing, ignoring my grin.

When the music started, I clapped my hands and cheered gently. 'Augh, a voice of an angel.'

Juniper gave me a look, and I returned the exact same one to tease.

'Come here,' I mumbled, holding my hand out. 'Please?'

'No way.'

'Juniper.'

'Nope, I don't dance.'

'C'mon, it's really easy.' I said, grabbing her hands to lift her up. I felt my back ache when I did so, my shoulder tug, but I ignored that too.

Juniper groaned when I messily pulled her into my arms, lifting her a little bit.

'Don't, I just drank shit whisky, you don't want to do that!' she laughed.

I smiled and let her down, bringing her arms around my neck.

'So, I learned this in high school,' I explained, glancing at our feet. 'You have your arms here.'

Juniper had a smirk on her lips, but she let me speak.

'And my hands go,' I paused and slid my hands down her back, squeezing below. 'Here.'

'Rayne!' she squeaked, smacking my chest softly.

I laughed loudly and brought them above her waist again. 'Sorry! They go here, they go here.'

Juniper rolled her eyes with a giggle, as soon as I started to sway the both of us.

'I used to dance with my grandfather.'

'Major turn on!' Juniper mocked.

'Shh, it was great, I can dance really well now,' I fumbled, stepping on Juniper's feet. 'I think.'

Juniper was laughing, it was music to my ears, and it honestly made me join in. I'd missed this emotion, happiness, comfort, carefree sensations.

I brought her close and hummed alongside Ella's beautiful voice, remembering my grandfather doing the same. We used to dance all night back in Florida, and he'd always surprise me with a great dance move, that left me in stitches laughing.

I told Juniper this as we swayed, and she listened to every story I had to tell. The song was only three minutes long, but I made sure to get sentimental halfway through.

We stopped laughing, and I took her head in the crook of my neck, where she responded by tightening her grip around my neck.

I breathed in her scent, even though it ached my nose to do so. I was so glad I could still smell her gorgeous perfume, the smell of paper and binders, the sweet tinge of candy.

I'd missed this, and she was so light in my arms.

'I love you,' I mumbled, kissing her across the cheek. 'I love you so much.'

Juniper's fingers were brushing the back of my neck, she shushed me, swayed with me and let me kiss her head with undying emotion.

'I love you more,' she replied. 'Even after all this, you're still the same Red in my eyes.'

I leaned back, giving her my most genuine look, and she nodded, itching the back of my right ear.

'Always,' she said sweetly.

Juniper Bridges was something special, and yes the anxiety was reminding me that I could have lost her, but she was right here, we were together.

I didn't lose her, and I wouldn't.

Ever.

I kissed her lips, my hands nestled into the bend in her back. Juniper responded by arching her shoulders, holding my neck and kissing me eagerly back.

The song was just coming to an end, but Juniper and I were just starting up.

We were both emotional, lust and passion had taken us by surprise. But there was something different, this was intimate, even more so than last time.

Through our kiss, even though it physically hurt to do so, I picked her up by the thighs and made my way to the couch again.

She breathed in when I laid her down against the rugged cushions. Her legs wrapped around my waist, her touch was rough on my lips, but soft around my body.

I let her palms brush above my neck, fingertips dragging down the length of it. I took a breath, as my nose wasn't working the best, and she waited patiently for me to regain that air.

Every touch was heaven to me, all the pain was being pushed back by passion, with force.

Juniper held behind my head as I painted her neck with kisses, every bite and press of my lips left her gasping in anticipation, pleasure.

I knew my anxiety was baring its teeth, the guilt from my past mistakes, but when I felt her hands around me, I was brought back to reality.

She was a reminder of my goodness.

We broke free from one another, but kept our faces close. She was taken by lust, her eyes were half lidded, her want for me rising.

I could feel the arousal in my abdomen, but it wasn't the only emotion that lingered around the two of us.

There was love.

A lot of it.

So much that my heart ached.

She held my head, let me coax into her touch like a mewling cat. The fingers of her right hand brushing over my bottom lip. I let her kiss each and every scar on my face, every ache and sore.

She didn't mind the tough rugged feel of scarred skin, she still pressed her beautiful lips against them all.

With a tug, I lifted her to my lap first, she straddled me, kissed me deeply and let my hands roam up the back of her shirt.

Every bump of my fingers against her spine left her shaking, every kiss had a hitched breath, a moan. I examined her lift her head, and listened to the beating of my heart. Again, I lifted her, and she twirled her legs around my waist to keep steady.

We kissed as we moved, slowly so I didn't drop her, closer to my bedroom.

The storm outside hardened, but it didn't matter to me.

I owed Juniper my love, I wanted to give her everything, my all.

And if a night of love making could fill that wounded empty space for just a few moments, it was worth it.

Chapter Twenty-Nine

JUNIPER

I've had mixed thoughts for days now, and its tiring. That endless race against your own mind, as it continuously tries to make you fall deeper into a never-ending cycle of never-ending thoughts. I find it hard to find my way out of its clutch, as it squeezes every last drop of sanity from my already bustling mind. It's understandable given my circumstances, our circumstances. For days now Rayne and I have been teetering over the edge of what will be. I thought that my sister's illness would be the extent of my mental exhaustion, as I worried day in and day out about how she was and what she was doing at that exact moment in time. I thought I had hit the peak.

Boy was I wrong.

I found it awfully hard to fall asleep when my mind is so active, as the game plays on. Since that eventful night, a night I wish I could easily forget, exhaustion follows me everywhere, but I can't seem to ever find my way to slumber. I toss and turn, stare at my ceiling, and fight the urge to cry and throw a tantrum at how awful life could be. Nat was alright, she was healing and pretty soon may be walking again, with enough support from the whole family, doctors, and the money we received from Christopher's family.

But there was the issue, Christopher.

I thought after the person responsible would be accounted for, my nightmare would be over, I'd never have to worry again, life would release me from the clutches of uncertain anxiety and worry. But, I was still lingering.

It could be that my girlfriend was going to court, that she was unfortunately framed for a deed she didn't do, for being part of a group I knew she'd never join for any other reason than to help me and Nat. but there was something else, something I wish I didn't have to think twice about.

I didn't like thinking about it, but I was believing Rayne, I couldn't rest easy about Nat's retribution, because I know Christopher wasn't the one who did it.

Why did I think this? Because I just couldn't add it all up, it made no sense. And of course, the anxiety told me that Rayne could have been making up all of Christopher' innocence, but her story didn't add up either.

I trusted Rayne, I even trusted Christopher too.

That's why this made no sense, the whole situation made absolutely no sense at all. I could see the strain between Nick's eyebrows when he thought too hard about it. I could see the pain in my father's face when the idea that Christopher may have been framed rose into conversations between him and the police. I felt that awful feeling in my chest when I began to believe it myself, as much as I tried to keep it from myself, the person who hit my sister was still out there, and now they'd caused even more issues to keep themselves safe.

Christopher wasn't the type of person to do what he did, not only was there lack of evidence, there was just a beating feeling in my chest that told me this was all very fishy.

Seeing his mother like that, his brother and father, seeing them all break internally and externally. Nobody at that funeral thought he was guilty, even I, the sister of the victim herself.

I told myself after the individual was caught, I'd stop searching, calm down and continue living the way I wanted to.

But something told me the fight was still going on, and we weren't safe at all.

Especially Rayne.

My promise to Samantha still ran through my mind, alongside the voices of hundreds, with my conscience kicking and screaming.

As much as I'd like to close the case and end all my worries, I couldn't.

So here I lay, naked, sheathed by Rayne's bed sheets with the loud thunder grumbling from outside. My sore back felt lighter on her makeshift bed, but my mind was aching from the thoughts that ran through it. The room was dull, dark and only the moonlight from her window whisked a tiny portion of brightness along our bodies. Like the nights before this one, I couldn't sleep.

I sniffled and shifted my body closer to Rayne's, who was sprawled out on her back, her deep breaths were soothing, yet I could still feel the tension between us. I found myself staring at her sleeping face, examining every inch of that tattered and scarred beauty.

God, I could only imagine what was going through her head. I'd never experienced the pain she endured, in that cold and dark seat, with monsters who called themselves human beings surrounded her. We didn't speak of that night much, yes the topic was lifted from the shadows here and then, but talking about it was a no-go game.

I didn't want to remind her of the pain she went through, she was suffering enough.

I brought my right hand forward, touching her chin gently with my fingertips. Through her sleep, she mewed into my grip and sighed, her head arching my way, I couldn't help but smile a little.

Three hours ago felt like the first day we met.

With a little help by whiskey, we were able to laugh, relax and dance. I was able to forget about the storm brewing between us, within ourselves.

I couldn't stay mad at her, not after all she did. Because she did everything for me, for my family. Of course, it would take a little time to get over the fact she lied, and held all this from me, but she was aware of her own fibs and issues.

Rayne Holmes meant no harm at all.

All I wanted for her was happiness, and the chilling reminder that all of that could be taken away in just a few days, was daunting. It seemed Rayne and I never caught a break, and when we did, something was just around the corner.

No, Juniper, you need to stop focusing on the negative. Something could come up, something could surprise the both of us and we could be a happy couple with no issues at all.

We could go to baseball games, or sit and watch a movie, cuddle and make jokes. The gripping happiness that I so desperately wanted, seemed so far away.

I wish it weren't.

During sex, nothing else mattered between us but each other. The endorphins were sinking through my veins, through the press of our bodies, the electricity kept my mind from venturing forth into the hazy dimension of self-doubt and worry.

I kissed her, and only her, she existed in my world, and nothing else in that moment. We weren't rough, the both of us shared something else earlier that night.

We were careful. Like we could have shattered if one of us stepped over a boundary, we were weak and tired.

But we were weak and tired together, and together we were strong.

I let my fingers drop from Rayne's chin, and brought it to my forehead. I needed to remind myself I was here, press my nails into my temple to feel the rushing pulse.

As much as I loved the rush of sex, and as much as I'd love to escape the thoughts doing so, it wasn't the answer to a peaceful mind.

But, being here with Rayne was.

I tried to close my eyes, but instead they fluttered and battered towards the ceiling. There was a process for me before I slept; it normally took me at least twenty minutes to finally drift but when I was overly stressed, like now, it took hours.

Ugh, I just wanted this low feeling to subside, I wanted Monday to happen and drift away. I wanted Rayne happy, I wanted everyone to be happy. But it was a process as well, happiness wasn't easy to take hold of.

Was I happy?

My eyes were open now, especially after I asked myself that terrifying question. My lips parted, so I could take a deep breath.

To my left was a girl that made me feel so much, so many things I thought I forgot about myself. I loved her to absolute bits, even in the short time of knowing one another. I trusted her, and that's why I knew this whole fiasco with the Jackals was terrifying for her the most. When Nat was sick, I wasn't happy, but now she was fine.

So what was this awful feeling looming over? Was it the frightening feeling of knowing that man was still out there? Pebbles wasn't the man people thought he was?

I ran my hand over my bare chest, to touch my beating heart. It was thumping, not in a way I loved, but in a way I loathed. It was a tight feeling, a squeeze of my organs. He was still out there, he had to be.

I tried to shut my eyes and force myself to sleep, but my anxiety wasn't the one thing keeping me up, Rayne too, was having trouble doing the same.

Chapter Thirty

JUNIPER

I woke at 3:16am on Monday.

She'd been fussing, twitching her leg here and there, mumbling under her breath. I wonder what she dreamt of; it was troubling her. I leaned up on my elbows and peered at Rayne, brushing the hair from her face. The contact calmed her, but only for a moment. She was distressed, her eyebrows furrowed, mumbling, I heard his name, twice.

'Christopher.'

God, I couldn't imagine watching someone commit suicide right in front of my eyes, let alone see two other deaths at the same time. Ever since this whole mess started, I'd tried to wonder how my girlfriend was feeling, but I just couldn't.

Not after all she saw and felt, smelled and tasted.

Again, I stroked her face, shushing her as soothingly as I could, bringing her head to the crook of my neck.

'It's okay, Red,' I said softly, 'Shh...'

Despite my coos, she struggled from my grip and clung at the blanket over her body. And with one raspy breath, she woke with a startle.

Rayne was leaning on her elbows now, the breath kicked from her chest. I grabbed her waist, lifting myself up to observe.

'Hey, hey!' I said gently, palming her cheeks with my hands. 'Rayne, what's wrong?'

She swallowed loudly and glanced towards me, her eyes moist, fresh with tears.

'Christopher.'

I felt the pang in my chest, and sadly grimaced. She huffed back and forth, glancing to her lap and the walls around us.

I didn't know what to say.

I still couldn't wrap my mind around the past week.

Christopher was gone, my sister was saved, but something still felt so terribly off.

I cleared my throat and brought Rayne down to the pillows again, letting her lay her head in the crook of my neck once more.

'I know, baby,' I replied, I couldn't think of anything else. 'I know.'

Did I?

She was out faster than she awoke, her left arm snaked around my body, clinging to me like I was the last person on earth.

I held her, closer than I ever had before, and succumbed to sleep, next to the person I loved most.

§

Detective Rodgers was at Rayne's door at ten AM the morning after, with a cleaned suit in his scarred hands. I stood in the kitchenette as my girlfriend welcomed him in, when she turned, I could see her face contort with worry; he was a reminder that her time as a free girl may be up.

I surprised the detective as he walked in, a short smile on his lips.

'Ah,' he chuckled. 'Miss Bridges.'

'Sir,' I awkwardly mumbled, tapping the plate of cold toast in front of me.

He checked the time and closed the door behind him, breathing in heavily. 'Good morning!'

I smiled sheepishly, watching as Rayne walked by, showered and ready for the day ahead of her.

'I take it you will be joining us today, for the court meeting?' Nick asked, holding his hat by his side. 'A miserable day for it.'

He pointed outside, where it had been raining all morning, Rayne and I slept in, clinging to one another for warmth. I wished we never had to get up, and ignore today as if it were to never happen.

I noticed Nick was waiting for a reply, but I was so tired and distracted I wasn't sure what to say, so instead I mumbled in response, nodding and keeping to myself.

I could hear Rayne fumbling from her room, and so I took that moment to ease myself from the uncomfortable situation in the living room. Nick and I hadn't really spoken one on one since the fall of everything had happened.

I wasn't ready to talk to him so heartily yet.

'Excuse me,' I murmured, rushing into Rayne's room, closing the door quickly behind me.

When I turned, as expected, Rayne was having trouble buttoning up her white shirt, her bruised fingers fumbling, she'd managed to get her slim pants on, but the marks and cuts on her torso were fighting.

'I got you, I got you...' I said, stepping forward and taking her hands away.

Rayne sighed, standing still as I buttoned it up for her, every flick of my fingers slow. 'Thanks.'

I mumbled a short 'Uh-huh.'

It wasn't awkwardness between us, or unwanted contact, we were both together, but I felt so far away.

Rayne stepped closer and touched the top of my head with her lips, her hand hovering by my side, I broke the space between us and wedged myself into her grip, hugging her gently around the waist.

'I'm nervous,' Rayne croaked, her hands by her sides. 'I'm not ready for this.'

'I know.'

'What if I go to jail?'

'You won't.'

'How do you know that?'

'I...' I paused and swallowed, holding her tighter. 'I don't know.'

Which was true, this situation was a grade-A fuck up, and Rayne was in a lot of trouble, as much as I wish I could rush up to the judge and tell him or her that her actions were all for good, I wasn't so sure I would help.

I breathed in and stepped back a little, not too far.

Rayne was grouching, her shirt all buttoned up, suit blazer on the bed. She looked lost, eyes peering to the ground, hands trembling.

'Rayne,' I started, holding those hands of hers. 'You can do this, you have Nick, us.'

'I know,' she replied, clenching her teeth. 'I know...'

I examined her face, still bruised but not as bad as it was before, she was healing fast.

'You have me,' I reassured, breaking the space between us again.

I leaned up to kiss her, but she denied the touch and turned her head to the side, I could feel her saddened breath against my ear.

I wasn't hurt by it, maybe it was a silly move on my behalf, not everything could be healed with a kiss.

Instead I hugged her, tightly.

I'd never wanted to be anywhere but with Rayne Holmes, in that room, safe for what seemed like only a moment.

I'd told Dad I was hearing the court date, told him I was going to be with Rayne as much as I could to help her through it all.

He was a bit antsy about her, of course he was, he had no idea who she was before she was pulled out of a warehouse bleeding and crying. Of course, she looked guilty in his eyes.

Nat was making a smooth recovery, it was nice not having that unwanted feeling lingering off the tip of my heart, if she was going to make it or not.

I had everything going well for me and my family right now, so why was I still so miserable?

Nick opened the car door for me, and his officers opened the other side for Rayne, grabbing at her arm tightly.

'Hey, can you be a bit more gentle?' I asked sourly, but they didn't listen to me. 'Jesus.'

There was a crowd of Boston settlers around the court building, snoops I say, even though some of those were reporters, I couldn't stand my own kind today.

The flicker of cameras left me uneasy, and as I reached to take Rayne's hand, I was pulled back by Nick.

'You aren't allowed to follow her in, Miss Bridges,' he said softly, patting my shoulder. 'Best to let the officers do their thing.'

I wanted to protest and fight him, let me stand by my girlfriend's goddamn side.

But I was frozen next to him, and could only watch her tall structure be guided into the gothic building.

I pursed my lips, ignoring the questions buzzing around my head as I walked with Nick, ignoring the recorders and devices being stuck in my face.

Ugh, was I really going to get involved in a career like this?

As we reached the door, a familiar face jumped through, brushing off the dust from his pants.

Reedy smiled to me and tensed his neck. 'Thought you might need a friend, I knew you'd be coming today.'

I glanced to Nick, who was focusing on the scene around us.

Robert almost appeared out of nowhere, but I wasn't even curious enough to ask, I just wanted inside the building and I wanted to find out Rayne's fate.

It all sounded so surreal and morbid.

The three of us were ushered inside as well, and thankfully the crowd was quiet and still once the doors were shut.

I walked silently into the belly of the beast, the court was gigantic, just like the ones in the movies and television series.

The real deal.

Nick guided me towards the front row seats, a great view of an old white judge, with the whole judge get up, even the fancy hair do.

Rayne was standing still beside her lawyer, someone Nick had found in the system. He was tall and slim, a bit lanky.

He looked weak.

God if only I could take his place, maybe I could talk some sense into the judge, protect Rayne, get her out of this mess.

I was the sister of the girl in trouble, surely, I had more of a say than any other.

Nick took his place beside Rayne, and she gave him an uncomfortable glance. He returned a short smile, a nod.

And so it began.

And ended faster than I imagined.

When the judge lifted his mallet, declaring Rayne guilty or not guilty, he stumbled with his papers and breathed in.

I was watching this man with wide eyes, hoping he would say the words I wanted to hear, Rayne had her head low, Nick, his head held high.

'Detective Rodgers,' the judges booming voice left me shaking. 'You were able to get in contact with Rayne Holmes parents, correct?'

Rayne's head shot up, and looked Nick's way, eyes wide.

I felt it too, my heart tensed, her parents?

The people she ran from in the first place? The people I had heard such terrible stories about?

Nick cleared his throat and nodded, 'That is correct, your honour.'

The judge breathed in and lifted the papers to his eyes, reading aloud all of Rayne's crimes she had committed, the verses from multiple testimonies, things that made her sound guiltier than ever.

Finally he spoke, but what left his mouth had Rayne shaking more than ever.

'Have the young woman stay with her parents, with complete police access to her every location, for eight months until later court dates are made.'

There was a lot of chatter among the crowd, among the police officers, everyone.

I breathed in tightly, and swallowed when Rayne turned to find my eyes. She hadn't even looked Nick's way.

The judge whacked the mallet, shutting us all up.

I was sure Reedy could hear my heartbeat from beside, he hadn't spoken a word.

I looked to Nick, and he shortly smiled at the judge.

It was bittersweet, it meant that Rayne was safe, not put in jail or juvey, or some terrible cell. But I knew exactly what was going on through her head in that exact moment,

Home was hell for her.

There was more speaking, more ushering, and finally the mallet silenced.

I pushed by the crowd to find my place beside Rayne, but she was turned to Nick, eyes wide, she seemed betrayed.

'I'm sorry kiddo,' Nick said, sincerely honest. 'It's all I could do to save your hide.'

'But,' she stuttered, looking towards me, and then Nick again. 'But I can't go back.'

'You have to,' Nick replied, he rubbed his neck and sighed. 'I needed to buy you time.'

I wasn't sure if I should have thanked Nick Rodgers on that day, or curse his name. I was completely stuck, unsure what to do.

Rayne was safe.

But she looked more broken than ever.

She looked my way once more, and my heart sped vigorously.

All this time, I never expected to say goodbye.

We'd met here in Boston, we'd shared our first words, our first kiss, the pleasure of intimacy, the warmth of love.

And now she had to leave all of it behind.

Chapter Thirty-One

JUNIPER

Rayne wasn't happy, even after the court hearing was over, and we made our way back to the police car and back towards the station, she said not a word.

Who could blame her, she was being forced home, under watchful eye of the Florida police department every day. This was going to be hell for her.

Nick tried to make conversation with Rayne as he drove, but she was acting like a sour teenager, much to his dislike.

It wasn't until the other police officer left the car, when Rayne finally opened her mouth to speak.

'So this was your plan all along?' she asked, cold. 'Send me back to the people I escaped in the first place?'

'It was either that or be locked away, what would you rather, Rayne?' Nick returned, 'I had no choice in the matter, I wanted only the best for you.'

'The best for me?' Rayne scoffed, raising her arms up. 'Those people practically banished me, no wonder I was homeless for weeks before I had enough money to find a place to stay.'

I stayed quiet, not a word came my way. I sat in the back seat and ignored the vibrating inside my pocket, Dad was probably wondering where and what had happened, but I was frozen on the spot.

'What did they say when you explained all of, well, this?' Rayne asked another question and I saw Nick's face tense. 'What did they say?'

'They were worried for you.'

'That's bullshit.'

'It's the truth,' Nick interrupted, his voice rougher than usual. 'Your mother said she missed you, your father worried about your safety.'

'I don't believe you.'

'I heard the sadness in your mother's tone, she was almost in tears!' Nick was sounding like a stern parent himself, made me wonder if this was a conversation he'd had before. 'Now if you're going to sit here and act like an ungrateful child, I won't stand by it.'

He began to unbuckle is belt, the engine was off and cooling, and he was only getting riled up. 'Now let's go.'

He pushed his door open and left, slamming the door behind him. It was very unlike Nick to do, but Rayne had really brought out another side of him, one that left me a little uncomfortable to say the least. As he passed my door he opened it, Rayne was still unable to leave the car on her own, I could see her face contort sourly.

In that few seconds of silence, I still didn't speak a word, only listened to the smallish sniffles that left my girlfriend's state.

She'd hit another low today, and she wasn't ready at all.

When we stepped foot into the station, I was asked to stick back in the waiting room, something I wasn't so keen on, but understood given the circumstances.

Rayne gave me a small nod before she was followed off with Nick, and I watched her back from where I stood, hoping she and Nick would speak a little calmer wherever they were off to.

Once the door was closed behind them, I finally took my phone from my pocket to examine three missed calls, all in the duration of that entire car ride.

I sighed and dialled my father's number, he picked up after two rings.

'Juniper, there you are!' he spoke rushed, 'I was trying everything to get a hold of you.'

'I know, I'm sorry,' I replied, sitting near the emptiest corner of the room. 'I was in the hearing.'

'Oh,' he mumbled, I heard the sourness in his tone, I didn't like it one bit. 'And how did that go.'

'She's on bail,' I replied, itching the tip of my knee. 'She has to... go back though.'

'Go back where?'

I paused and finally let it hit me, sniffling a little and kicking my foot against rough carpet.

'Florida, her home.'

Dad was silent for a brief moment, but cleared his throat and sighed. 'I see.'

'Don't sound too happy about it Dad.' I grimaced.

'Juniper, don't say that.'

It fell silent between the two of us, I focused on another father with his daughter, who was crossed armed and pouting, she held a few forms in her hands, and from where I sat I could see something to do with losing her licence.

I remember being in the police department once as a teenager, and that was for breaking into my high school at night to find goss on one of the teachers, back then my friends were a group of wannabee reporters in training, and funnily enough I was the only one who fulfilled the dream and studied to become one.

'Are you going to come home tonight?' he asked. 'Nat wants to see you.'

Oh, Nat.

I sighed and shrugged my shoulders, somewhat hoping my father could sense I did so.

'I'll see what happens with Rayne, I'm not sure how long she has before she has to, you know.'

'I know, just let me know alright?'

I nodded and brought my phone closer to my ear, sniffling again. 'I will.'

We hung up shortly, something told me Dad was happy about Rayne leaving, maybe he thought she was a bad influence on me, it wasn't true.

Rayne was such an uplifting person, yeah sure she got into trouble, we all do, it's part of life isn't it? We get on someone's bad side, we pay the price, we get sent back home.

I swallowed and put my phone away, crossing my arms and sighing.

Home.

She was really going to go back, after everything we'd been through together, our meetings and our adventures, the people we both met, everything.

All had to come to an end.

But hey, what was I expecting? What could have been the other options in all this? I walked into that court hearing with two thoughts,

She was going to jail, or, she was going home.

Something told me Rayne believed she was going to walk free this afternoon, unfortunately I had a darker look on it all.

I waited for an hour before the doors to which she entered, opened again.

She looked exhausted, maybe even spent a few more moments crying, something showed in her face that she was after a good night's sleep.

But she had the answer I was waiting for, and hey look at that, she didn't have a cop on her back leading her everywhere.

Nick stood beside her though, I kept forgetting he was the leader of all these... what I'd call 'pigs.'

I stood up a bit giddily, and rushed towards the two, but this time I was welcomed by Rayne, with a rough hug.

I squeaked on impact, awkwardly smiling towards Nick who fixed up his collar and shirt as we embraced.

'So what's the story? When do you have to, you know...' I mumbled into Rayne's ear, she grimaced and nodded towards Nick, who cleared his throat and returned a short smile.

'She's got four days before she heads back,' he explained. 'I did all I could.'

There was a feeling of utter distraught, my heart dropped.

'Four days?' I asked, my voice wasn't clear so I swallowed. 'Four days.'

Nick sighed and lifted his hand, it was heavy against my shoulder. 'I tried my best, Miss Bridges.'

I didn't reply, just nodded and pursed my lips, I was looking right at him, but it was only seconds when I realised I was looking through him.

I looked towards Rayne, who had her eyes set on the floor, she hadn't looked up yet.

Just like I, she had a thousand thoughts running through that mind of hers, and something told me returning to mom and dad wasn't on her to do list.

Nick reminded me that Rayne's suit needed to be back tomorrow as well, and finally, let us be alone.

I watched him walk towards the back, nod to his officers and close his door behind him.

And I grabbed onto Rayne harsher than I ever had.

I started my plan, to act like nothing was wrong.

'Ugh!' I groaned, squeezing her tightly. 'I thought I'd never have you to myself again.'

'Well you do,' she sighed, pocketing her hands after I let go. 'For just a few days'

'Nope,' I put two fingers to her lips, head up high almost scolding her like a child. 'We're not even going to discuss that.'

'But,'

'No buts,' I interrupted, grabbing her hand and pulling her towards the entrance. 'Not a word.'

'Juniper,' she tried stopping, but I pulled with all my might.

She wasn't escaping my grip for a long time.

As we stepped outside, I realised one thing: no car.

I paused, Rayne paused.

'Oh,' I sighed. 'I didn't,'

'You forgot about that part didn't you.'

I turned to face her, with big puppy dog eyes. 'Rayne.'

She tried her hardest to ignore them, keeping her sour mood.

And I counted a minute before she grumbled and checked her watch, shrugging her shoulders.

'I really doubt Arty will pick us up, not after what happened with me and her.'

'I doubt that too,' I replied quite fast, pulling her down the street. 'You two need to sort that out by the way,'

'Hey, she was the one who attacked me, and she pushed you! I wasn't going to let her get away with that!'

'One push was nothing,' I replied, crossing my arms. 'She was just upset,'

'Right,' Rayne sourly said, touching the bandage across her nose. 'Upset...'

I sighed and grabbed my phone, searching through the apps, we could have just asked a police officer for a lift home, but I doubted Rayne wanted to be once again in the back of a police car.

Uber it was.

I wonder how long we could act like everything was fine for?

Our Uber driver was thankfully one of those men who didn't say a word, just had their radio on, head forward and eyes on the road. Rayne was afraid of the public eye, she mumbled to me before we set foot in the car, she had to be in the back seat she said, made her feel better.

Poor thing.

I dismissed the thought of her leaving more than once on our journey back to her apartment, it was bubbling to the top, wanting to drain out of me and drag all my emotions along with it, but I wasn't going to let it, not today at least.

Not now.

He parked rather messily beside another car in the parking lot and I jumped out quickly, Rayne followed slowly.

She was very torn; not one word was spoken on the way back, she just watched Boston's streets with sorrowful eyes.

These were the streets she'd grown to love over the years, after she'd escaped Florida. She was about to find her way back there and unfortunately, it was without me.

I knew that, whenever she looked my way her eyes eased with unimaginable pain, we'd been through a hell load of torment these past few days, and this was just the cherry on top.

Oh god, just the thought of saying goodbye left me shaking in my shoes.

Stop, Juniper, don't even let that thought come through.

I breathed in tightly and held Rayne's hand as we walked upstairs, she was dangling her keys and twirling them around her finger, I glanced to her foot and noticed the bulge around her ankle, that too was a reminder of all this mess.

It'd just started to rain as we stepped foot inside, Rayne grumbled something as she closed the door behind her, and I tried my best to hear it.

When she turned, she opened her mouth to speak, and without even thinking, I grabbed her by the shoulders and kissed her deeply.

I know, I know. The night before we'd made love three times before collapsing naked into one another's arms, but I had to distract her, I had to distract myself too.

She caught me quickly and I let her take a breath, knowing quite well her nose was still an issue.

'Juniper, what–'

'Shush,' I mumbled, grabbing her suit blazer and slipping it from her shoulders. 'I want to,'

'Oh?' she asked, flirtatiously, letting me fumble around with her white shirt. I unbuttoned the whole thing and kissed at her neck now, ugh, but I could still feel the thought rushing in the back of my mind, every little worker inside my brain was painting a big ass mural that screamed: 'Girlfriend is leaving forever.'

I groaned and pulled her shirt off, she caught me again as I threw myself into her, letting her kiss my lips.

C'mon Juniper, I thought. I can do this, I can ignore it, for the both of us.

I waited to hear her dismiss my advances, maybe this was a stupid idea seeing as just a few hours ago she found out crucial news, but as soon as Rayne grabbed at my backside and squeezed roughly, I knew her mind had gone elsewhere.

Just what was intended.

Don't get me wrong, this wasn't for my own selfish intentions.

Sex was a good distraction, and after finding out dire news about moving back to a state she'd done all she could to escape? It's probably what she needed.

Plus, she did look fucking amazing in a suit.

I pulled back from her and let her mouth hover above my upper lip, she smirked gently, and I returned a sly smile.

'Why are you acting all–'

'No questions!' I moaned playfully, pulling her back into her bedroom. 'Just, you know...'

I took my shirt off and laid back against her bed, giving her my most flirtatious look.

'Fuck me.'

She stood still for a moment, and finally swallowed, a little giddy if you ask me.

'Oh,' she whimpered, looking down to my eager self. 'Okay.'

I rolled my eyes as she unbuckled her belt. 'Okay? Is that all you have to say?'

She knew I was kidding, but she still gave me a puppy dog look of sorrow. 'I'm sorry!'

'Stop that,' I grumbled, laying back and waiting for her to come down upon me. 'You know I'm only joking.'

She'd successfully taken her pants off, and stood in her boyfriend style underwear, the ones that defined her hips and her butt, my favourite kind actually.

She straddled me first and whisked my hair from my neck, burrowing her lips upon my skin and kissing sheepishly.

I bit my bottom lip, legs aimlessly curling around her waist, giggling.

Our foreplay lasted for a good few minutes, but every single time I felt the urge to dig deeper, I was welcomed with another unwanted thought.

And it seemed I wasn't the only one.

She'd kissed my neck, lips, ear and jaw, taken my bra off and kissed my breasts, nipples and collarbone. I could feel my abdomen fight back, the rush of my blood flowing through me. It was when she was fumbling with my jeans, when we both as if on que, dropped our efforts and went cold turkey.

I laid back with a sigh, and she dropped her head into the crook of my neck, groaning in annoyance.

'I can't,' she said simply. 'I just, can't.'

'I know,' I replied, glancing aside to her drawers and bathroom door. 'I can't either.'

We lay in silence. After a minute passed, I began stroking her bare back, itching the back of her neck, soothing her.

I knew exactly what was going on through her head.

'I'm sorry, babe,' she said against my skin, 'Too much is happening.'

I hushed her.

'You don't have to explain yourself…' I replied, 'I know, trust me, I do.'

'I can't believe today,' she finally said. 'I really have to go back.'

The way she said it was horribly upsetting to hear. I thought I'd heard all of Rayne's emotions, but there was something about her going back to her hometown that brought out a whole new one to experience. When I'd met her, she was a busker, I didn't know one thing about her past, but the more we spoke, the more she opened up. She would tell me about her father, and how cruel he was, and how degrading her mother was, to her only child.

It was a huge difference from my childhood, where my parents were around together for most of it, until mom left after having Nat.

After escaping it all, now she had to go running back.

Rayne lifted herself from my embrace and smiled shortly, grabbing at her sports bra and looping it back on. I lay across her bed and watched, not wanting to move at all.

I saw her my necklace secured around her neck, same as I left it there the day we said our short goodbye. Now that I think about it, I'd caught Rayne touching it throughout the night and days we spent together, even throughout court this morning, she clung to it whenever she felt or looked tense.

She sat at the end of her bed, bruised shoulders hunched.

So I took it upon myself to try and cheer my girlfriend up, with whatever strength I had left.

I could feel myself falling, too.

I leaned up, crawled her way and wrapped my arms around her upper body, kissing her ear quickly.

'I know,' I said.

'Do you?' she replied.

'Do I know we only have a few more–'

'days together, yeah,' she interrupted, sighing loudly. She rubbed her neck, but stopped when I took it upon myself to do so with my own fingers.

'I'd much rather you home than jail, Red.'

'I'd much rather jail than home, Juniper.'

I felt my ears redden, and swiftly I patted her against the chest a little roughly.

'Don't say that!' I snapped, and just as she touched my thighs, I leaned back further from her touch. I was getting a little fed up with her wanting something other than freedom in her hometown, well, not complete freedom, but it beat jail and jail food, didn't it?

'Rayne, you're not going to jail, shouldn't you be happy about that?' I asked, 'You're going home, yeah. But Nick got you freedom instead of confinement, I'd be relieved in your shoes.'

'Yeah,' she scoffed, rising up to grab her shirt. 'But that's the thing, you're not in my shoes. You don't know what home is like, I haven't told you everything.'

'You've told me enough for me to know it's not, well...' I paused and crossed my arms against my bare chest, 'Perfect.'

'Not in the slightes,.' she grimaced, she took her shirt and began folding it, wincing when she tensed her arms. 'I can't believe that was even an option really.'

'What were you expecting, full bail?' I chuckled and shook my hand, 'Yeah, right.'

It took me a moment to realise what I'd done was quite rude, and quickly I took my mouth and turned to face Rayne.

She was grimacing, hard.

'I'm sorry,' I pleaded, patting my hands against my legs. 'I just meant,'

'Save it,' she replied. 'I get it.'

It fell silent in her room, I listened to the rain above, hitting the tinder roof. She changed quietly, but there was an odd tension in the room that made me feel pretty uncomfortable, maybe I'd overstayed my welcome.

But then I'd be wasting time without her, and our days were short now, very short.

'Do you want me to go?' I asked, checking the time on my mickey mouse watch, it was Nat's but she never wore it once.

Rayne sighed again, turned and shook her head. 'No, baby.'

I pouted at her use of words, ugh, all I wanted to do was hold her right now.

'I'm just, on edge,' she replied, fiddling with her shirt. 'It's a lot to take in.'

'So, lets not think about it right now,' I answered back.

'You keep saying that, like its easy.'

'I know it's not easy, I just think it's the right thing to do, well, now.'

We both paused, and Rayne quickly nodded, sitting back down against her bed end. 'You're right, you always are.'

'That's not true,' I joked, grabbing my bra from beside me. 'I've been wrong many times, like how I argued fruity pebbles were better than cheerios.'

I realised what I'd said was stupid, and felt my cheeks redden. 'Or, whatever.'

Rayne chuckled, it was music to my ears, honestly.

I'd almost forgotten what it sounded like.

'Come shower with me, Juniper,' she muttered.

I glanced up, halfway through putting my bra back on, 'really?'

'Yes, really,' she smiled, grabbing my hands. I sighed and let her pull me up into a short embrace. 'I was just about to get ready for work, you know I still have a job to go to.'

'Makes one of us,' she replied.

'Don't say things like that.'

'I know, I know,' she rolled her eyes playfully, I think she was trying her very best to ignore the fact her world was turning upside down. 'I'm sorry.'

I leaned back in her arms, hands around her neck, examining her face again, the scars were deep, her nose was still broken, but god she was beautiful.

'Mm, you're still charming, even with all your bangs and bruises,' I smirked, dragging my finger along the bridge of her nose. She winced and moved her head aside, mouthing ouch.

'I think it adds personality, don't you think?' she joked back, lifting her eyebrows my way.

'Oh, does it just,' I replied, stepping forward and lifting myself on my tip toes.

She welcomed me with a kiss, a deep and romantic kiss that said many words without being spoken. Through it, emotions. Sadness, guilt, fear and lust.

I could write a whole book about this one kiss, and how heart-breaking it felt.

When we broke apart she stretched, wincing again in pain.

'Easy,' I warned, brushing my fingertips against her tough abdomen.

'Yeah, that's also why I wanted to ask you about the shower...' she laughed nervously.

It took me a moment, but when it hit me I raised my eyebrows and snorted.

'You honestly need me to scrub your back or something?' I laughed. 'No way!'

Rayne followed me around the room as I denied her want, giggling when she took me tightly into her arms and squeezed. 'Please!'

'Nope!'

'Do you want me to smell bad?'

'You always do.'

'What!?'

'Yep!'

I turned to face her again, and she quickly lifted her arm to smell herself. Oh gosh, she really was gullible.

'God, of course I'll help you, as long as I get to see you naked.'

'No, I was going to shower with my clothes on...' she grimaced, pressing her forehead to mine. 'Dummy.'

'Hey, watch it,' I hissed. 'Or you can clean your own back.'

So, we showered.

For about an hour.

Half an hour was the two of us standing under the hot water, Rayne's arms around me, swaying me along. We said a few sweet words, small kisses, jokes and flirtatious comments.

But it was one moment where she held my waist and touched the brim of my nose with her lips, mumbling how much she loved me, that threw me off guard.

I started to cry, but she didn't notice.

She was rambling on about music again, how if she had to go back home, she'd probably set up at another station and make her money the same way she did here.

I scrubbed her shoulder gently, it was still cut up and bruised, it'd been stitched up and all, but she still winced in pain when I touched it.

I bit my bottom lip, I didn't want her knowing I was crying, the shower was so loud and her speaking could cover any breath of hitched air I needed to take, to drop a few sneaky teardrops, they'd mix with water anyway.

After she finished her speech about how muggy Florida was, she realised she'd been speaking pretty confidently about the whole situation, and it quickly took her by surprise.

'I'm sorry,' she said, bringing my body between her legs. 'I just,'

'Don't stress about it, Rayne,' I mumbled back, voice cracking. 'You can talk about it.'

'I don't want to, or even think about it to be honest,' she sighed, pulling her wet hair behind her ears. 'But it's a bit hard not to.'

'I know.'

It fell silent between the two of us again, I took a few moments to wash my own hair, force the rainwater from my brown locks. She watched me, leaning back against the shower wall, covering her wrist. Oh, that wrist of hers, with that tattoo reminding the both of us of a grim day.

I hoped she'd get it covered when she could.

I peeked behind Rayne to check the time on my watch laying on the bathroom counter, I had work in an hour and I don't think the boys would want me late, not after I took time off to sort out all this stuff going on.

I stepped back and examined Rayne, checking for spots she couldn't reach with her bruised arms and all. 'I have to get out and get ready babe.' I mumbled, I could already see the desperation in her, 'I'll just be out there.'

'No way,' she pouted, holding me close to her naked body. 'Just stay with me, don't worry about work.'

'Don't worry about work, are you crazy,' I chuckled, palming her cheeks with my hands. 'I'll be roasted alive if I don't show up.'

'Roasted like coffee beans?' she asked, wiggling her eyebrows.

I paused, held her face still and then let go. 'I'm out.'

She tried her absolute hardest to keep me under the waters rush, but with a few stern words and a kiss to the lips, she let me go.

And boy did it feel uncomfortable leaving her arms.

I closed the shower door behind her, drying my body with her towel, we'd share it, no big deal, we shared kisses, a towel wouldn't hurt.

You know, I was just getting used to all of this.

The showering, the sleeping and waking next to one another, breakfast... dinner.

It was all normal couple shit that people longed for, for what I longed for.

It was all starting to fall into place.

But of course, something had to come and ruin it all, something big and ugly called the police force, and laws, and–ugh.

I cleaned my hair as I grumbled to myself, wiping down the wetness.

The last time we showered together, we spoke about how much leaving one another hurt us, and here we were once again, feeling the exact same emotions as we did prior, knowing one of us was leaving once again.

This time, it was real.

I shivered and grabbed the hair dryer, swallowing as I plugged it in and began wafting my fingers through my hair.

Don't think about it Juniper, please.

I begged myself.

It'll only bring you more sadness, if that's even possible.

I swallowed back tears once again, and watched my reflection as I dried, focusing on the shower in the mirror, waiting for Rayne to pop out and grab the towel I left for her.

I was going to savour this moment, not dread ever having it again in the future.

And so it hit me faster than the thought made its way into my mind.

I was running on pure adrenalin right now.

Rayne must have been too, because not one of us had broken down yet, not to the extent I was expecting.

In five minutes she stopped the showerhead from running, and stepped out dripping all over the bathroom floor.

She sighed, grabbed the towel and wiped down her arms first, her tattoo still looked sharp, even after all the years she had it.

It was such a lovely tattoo, I didn't even give myself the chance to stop and check it out more than once, examine every line every dotwork and shape.

So many wasted opportunities.

I was noticing them all now.

'Need me to grab your clothes?' she asked me, wiping down her body next.

I smiled and shrugged my shoulders, keeping the towel above my chest as I continued drying my hair. 'Up to you.'

She smiled and stepped towards me quickly, kissing me across the cheek. It was small things like this that left my heart racing, but every time I had that content feeling flow over me, the unwanted feeling of doubt soon followed.

She left the bathroom, rummaged through my duffel bag and picked out a pair of black jeans. I turned the hair dryer off and listened to her mumble to herself;

'These?' she asked, lifting them so I could see.

'Yep,' I replied softy, squeezing the last amount of wetness from the ends of my hair.

She rummaged again, grabbing a pair of underwear and winking my way; 'Don't need these do you?'

I smirked and rolled my eyes playfully, 'Ha, ha! You want customers checking out my ass in tight jeans without knickers, doll?'

Her face changed quickly, and she pouted. 'On second thoughts.'

I giggled as she grabbed my bundle of clothes, stepping in to the bathroom once more to deliver.

'Your necessities,' she said, holding me around the stomach.

I blushed as her chest pressed against my bare skin, brushing my hair was hard when she was being awfully flirtatious.

'What about you naked?' I asked, looking at her in the mirror, 'You going to get dressed or just hang around bare bones in your apartment all day?'

'The day is nearly over, so,' she replied, shrugging. 'Doesn't bother me.'

'Bothers me if Nick comes around...'

'You make a good point,' she grimaced. 'That wouldn't be good.'

'No,' I returned, grabbing my bra from the pile of clothes. 'Not good at all.'

I returned to getting changed, as she wiped her hair down and wrapped a clean bandage around her wrist.

She really hated that mark.

'You want to catch dinner after work?' sheasked, smiling towards me. 'I mean, what time do you finish tonight?'

'Nine,' I replied, pulling my shirt over my head. 'Not too sure the boys want me to stay back or not.'

'I can come pick you up,' she offered, 'I don't mind waiting.'

I thought for a moment, wondering how they would react seeing her out already, I wondered how anybody would react really.

Her face had been plastered all over Boston's news, if only for a moment, people still recognised her. I wondered if she was even going to be safe, with or without that thing around her ankle.

'Are you sure?' I asked, nervously. 'I don't want you getting into anymore—'

'Trouble?' she asked, shaking her head. 'I won't, not anymore.'

'You say that, Red,' I sighed, 'But trouble could find you this time.'

'Hey now,' she leaned over the counter and glanced my way, grimacing. 'I wasn't looking for trouble, you know that.'

'I know...' I sighed and realised I was letting my doubt flow through, everything I was saying was being misread, but if I was her, I'd be thinking the same. 'Forget I said that.'

We both fell silent, I could feel the chill from her open bathroom window, it was already starting to snow outside; another snowy winter night in Boston was ahead of us, reminding me exactly how we met.

I pulled my underwear on and mumbled to myself, Rayne passed me my jeans and smiled shortly, more like another grimace in my opinion.

I hoped I wasn't hurting her with my words, really.

After I slid the material up my legs, I buttoned up and watched her drag her body around slowly, putting piece by piece of clothing back upon her body.

She was upset, I know she was.

'Red,' I called, she mumbled back.

I chewed my bottom lip, she grabbed a grey hooded jumper and slipped it over her shirt, staying in her boxers.

I breathed in and turned again, shrugging my shoulders.

There it was,

That neutral sadness we both felt, easing its way into the room like a big bad monster.

It was unavoidable.

We were breaking.

§

Vadim and Yefim welcomed me with open arms when I finally returned to work that afternoon, they went on about how they hadn't seen me in weeks when it had only been a few days. Next was the news about Christopher, and finally the news about my sister.

They were so loud customers could hear, and as I tried moving to the back room, they just wouldn't let me.

'I know you're happy to see me boys,' I chuckled nervously. 'But please, keep it on the down low.'

'And your tall girlfriend!' Vadim cried, hands up high. 'She was bad all along.'

'She isn't.' I cussed, opening the back-room door and grabbing an apron from the rack. 'Don't say that please,'

'But you saw the news, right Yefim?' Vadim asked loudly, patting his brother against the chest. 'The tall girl was guilty, guilty as they come.'

I was bubbling as they spoke about the whole thing, my anger was seeping, or maybe my uncontrollable emotions, whatever it was, I was about to snap, and I wasn't sure I'd have my job if I did.

So instead of sitting there listening to the same news I'd heard over and over again, I left them to their rabble and escaped to the front of store, to serve my usual's who hadn't seen me in a few days.

To them it probably felt like years as well.

It's true, it felt like weeks to me to be honest.

It's funny how much it feels like you've lost yourself after a terrible situation, after the emotional rollercoaster I was shoved on, I almost forgot what it was like to feel normal.

Or did I ever feel that way in the first place?

I remember our date before Rayne left, that was the last I'd felt normal for a long time. Sitting down, eating a lovely dinner, dancing and singing at the top of our lungs, kissing under the moonlight next to Boston's riverbank.

Those moments felt real and normal.

But now, after the realisation of what Rayne had done, what Christopher had been said to have done, everything was catching up to me.

Maybe I should have taken a few weeks off, all this emotional trauma was going to leave some scars, I knew it.

So the night went slow for me, of course as it started to snow outside, not many people left their warm houses for a warm beverage they could make themselves. I had the usual few people lingering at around seven PM, one man always brought his laptop in, ordered decaf, then sat and wrote for hours. Another woman did her shopping every night at six on the dot, and always came in with bundles of bags, wanting a hot caramel latte to sooth her pain.

As Vadim left, I felt a sense of relief, Yefim was the second in charge who didn't really talk much at this time of night.

He would stay in the back room, work the machines when peak hour began, but tonight? I really doubted having three customers at once.

It was at eight-thirty when one of my usuals walked in, not one I loved to see, no, one I loathed to see. He was a middle aged man, always clad in work clothes, drunk, holding the Boston newspaper in one hand, his wallet in the other.

He would always click his fingers if I wasn't present at the service desk, something all baristas fucking loathed, or anyone in customer service really.

So when I stood to face him, he always had something sarcastic to say, and tonight it was;

'Finally caught your attention did I?'

'I'm sorry sir, what can I get you?'

'Some good service, maybe?'

I paused and swallowed, my eyes closed for longer than a second. Oh, he was barking up the wrong tree tonight.

'Like I said,' I smiled sheepishly, forced. 'What can I get you tonight?'

'A tall mocha, extra sugar, and the chocolate on top, I want the chocolate on top.'

'A tall mocha, extra sugar, chocolate on top...' I pressed the order in as he grumbled. 'Anything else?'

'I know you,' he suddenly said.

Here we go.

'You're the girl I saw on TV,' he pointed right at me, a customer behind him took his eyes off his smart phone and listened in.

I was becoming the main attraction for the night.

I cleared my throat and continued my work, trying my best to ignore his words.

'Yeah you were the one with the girl, the Jackal one, who got all beat up nasty.'

'I don't know what you're talking about, sir.'

'Yeah you do, I know you do.'

I swallowed and continued to tap in his order, my fingers fumbling.

I didn't need this right now, not at all, no way.

I didn't need some middle aged fucker coming in and reminding me of a moment I wished wasn't true, I didn't need a reminder of all the pain and suffering Rayne experienced that morning we found her.

'Tell me what it was like, being next to a criminal, or maybe you're a criminal too,' he scoffed, throwing his money down towards me. I felt my ears redden, I really wished Yefim was out of his office right now, so he could kick this drunk ass adult out of our store. 'Hey girly?'

'Hey man, cut it out,' the guy behind him spoke up, but only to be told to shut up and mind his own business.

Bless his kind soul, he tried his best.

But this was part of my job, I was going to come across people like this in my career, and right now I was facing some of the worst.

Drunk, idiotic morons, who watch too much cable and listen to every word a news reporter says. Even if it was lies and slander.

'Sir, if you'd just wait over there for your order.'

'Fuck the order!' he roared, I jumped in my shoes. Breathing in to catch myself once again. 'I want to know why you're hanging out with Fire Jackal scum.'

Oh, god don't call her that.

She was far from it.

'Sir.'

'Don't sir me, I want answers.'

'How about you find those answers somewhere else, asshole?'

I flinched from another's voice, but quickly noticed it was Reedy, he pushed the elder back from where I stood, and stood firmly above him. 'Get out.'

'And who the fuck are you, to tell me what to do?' he asked back.

'Just get out man, you're not wanted here.'

'How dare you,'

'Get. Out.'

I watched the scene unfold before me, more drama I just couldn't handle to hear or see.

Reedy was tense, he held the money this animal had handed me, and shoved it back into his chest, along with his newspaper and wallet.

And with one final huff, he turned, pushed the other customer aside and walked out with a yell of frustration.

And in just moments, the hustle and bustle of my café workplace was back to normal.

Reedy sighed and turned to face me, I only took the next persons order and thanked him softly for trying his best back there, the customer returned a sweet response and waited for his coffee on the side-lines.

'You alright?' Robert asked. 'That guy is such a jerk, my dad deals with him at the mechanics too.'

'I'm alright,' I replied, moving aside to the machines, I sighed as I started brewing, giving Reedy the side eye.

'Thank you,' I mumbled, shivering. 'I just wasn't in the mood.'

'No, I understand completely,' he replied, leaning over the counter to talk to me. 'I hope you're alright, Juniper.'

I shrugged my shoulders, 'It's not about me anymore, Rob.'

'Who's it about?' he asked, rubbing his arms. 'Nat's doing well, right?'

He had a sense of urgency in his tone, but all I'd heard from Dad and the docs was nothing but positive news.

It was a relief to know.

'She's doing really great, actually,' I said. 'It's...'

He waited for my words, and I couldn't bring myself to say them.

I grabbed a cup and slipped it under the nozzle of the coffee machine, watching the dark blend bubble into its hollow opening.

'It's Rayne,' I said finally. 'She's gotta go back.'

'Ah,' he replied. 'Right.'

He was there after all, heard the judge say it and all.

Thought it went silent between us, his presence left me feeling less lonely then usual.

'So,' I mumbled, cupping the coffee and handing it warmly towards its owner. 'I'm stuck.'

'You won't be for long.' Reedy muttered, smiling sheepishly at me. 'She won't be gone for too long, right?'

I shrugged my shoulders as I cleaned the nozzle, wiping it down roughly, I could feel the burn against my skin, but it didn't bother me at all anymore.

I was used to it.

'I'm actually not sure…' I returned, crossing my arms and leaning back against the tabletop.

Reedy sighed and crossed his arms as well, pondering on his thoughts it seemed.

'I don't really know what to say, Juniper,' he grimaced. 'I don't know how I can help, the court hearing and all went the way it did, and Rayne's going to have to go back and all, but maybe she can try and sort it out with the cops back home, maybe they'll make her stay shorter, they'll put her on bail or something.'

'Hopefully,' I replied, 'I really, really hope so.'

There weren't any customers after Reedy, so we spoke for a little longer. He asked more details about Nat, and I told him how the surgery went, how she could be walking sooner than we expected. He looked so pleased to hear that, and it actually brightened up my mood just thinking about it. I imagined her running, and that left my heart beating faster than usual.

My baby sis, finally able to jump for joy again.

It was bliss.

A shady figured stepped foot into the store, one I noticed quite easily by her height. She was in the same hoodie I left her in, but also her red jacket, puffed high over her shoulders.

She was hiding.

She stepped towards the till and cleared her throat gently, but Reedy missed the point and slapped her hard against the back.

'Rayne!' he laughed, patting again. 'How are you man?'

'How do you think, Reedy?' she replied, her scarf covering her mouth. 'Hiding from the public eye.'

'Sounds like fun,' he replied jokingly, but the joke went right over Rayne's head. 'Ah, I'll leave you to it, but protect Juniper over here, had an asshole of a customer just twenty minutes ago.'

'What?' she asked, glancing to me. I smiled nervously and waved it off, 'It was nothing.'

'Oh he's a real jerk,' Reedy sugar-coated. 'Big fat bald man, always has his paper in one hand, drunk mostly.'

'Did he hurt you?' she asked, bringing the scarf down from her lips.

I rolled my eyes at the both of them.

'You know I could have handled it,' I returned. 'He's not that scary.'

'Are you kidding?' Reedy laughed, patting the counter table with his gloved hands. 'He's a monster!'

The three of us spoke about it for a moment longer, Rayne was content on hearing exactly what happened, and Reedy was content on telling the whole story, over exaggerated of course, as always.

All that was missing was a tall lanky male, standing beside his friend and chipping in whenever he could.

I felt my smile fade a little, and as Rayne and Reedy spoke, I zoned out completely.

Christopher was going to be missed.

More than ever.

§

The time was ticking, and soon Rayne would be on a plane home to Florida. I sat with her in her apartment, as she folded clothes into a duffel bag and sighed. Every piece of clothing she put away, she grumbled and said something under her breath. I was working on my laptop, glancing in my peripheral whenever she did so, and with one final grumble I took her hand and squeezed it.

'Love, you're grumbling,' I said, smiling shortly to her, Rayne looked at me with those big puppy dog eyes, and grimaced. 'Come here.'

I opened my arms, and she fell into them, another breath of air releasing from her nostrils. I stroked her hair and comforted her, but that looming cloud above us continuously reminded us that she was leaving tomorrow morning. I swallowed deeply, keep the feelings down Juni, you can do this. I traced her jawline with my fingertip and watched her mew into my touch, she was my everything, and now she was going to be gone, just like that.

We had only met a month ago, but she was my all, my everything. And I knew she felt the same about me, it was evident in the way she looked at me, felt me, kissed me. Love was so bittersweet, no?

'I just don't want to go,' she said.

'I know,' I replied.

'I want to stay here,' she grumbled.

'I know.'

'I don't even know how long its going to be for.' She was frustrated, she kept tossing and turning, anxiously. 'And that makes me feel... uncomfortable.'

I glanced around her apartment, everything was packed, what she owned was in boxes, ready to be boarded onto a plane and gone without a trace. She and Detective Rodgers had already spoken to the landlord, who was more than ecstatic that she was leaving, she was a mean old bat. I looked past the Chinese takeout she'd barely touched and in to the bedroom, the room we had made love in multiple times. I sighed, and listened to her go on before I felt my emotions slip. I started to cry.

It took Rayne approximately twelve seconds before she realised, jumped up and grabbed me into an embrace, hushing me gently. 'I'm sorry.'

'You don't have to be...' I said back, hicking. 'You are just... my everything and now you're leaving...'

'But we'll text every day, I'll go to court there, maybe they'll even let me go,' she said, holding my face between her hands. 'I'll be back before you know it.'

It was a full three-sixty from what she was saying earlier, but I knew she was putting a brave face on for me in the moment. I wanted her to show her true emotions, not battle against them because her girlfriend was crying in the same room. Before I could speak, she said something that left a sour taste in my mouth.

'And when I get home, I'm finding out who Pebbles really is, because Christopher didn't die for nothing,' she snapped, leaning back into the couch. 'No way.'

I went a little stale, and she caught my second glances, then slowly muttered; 'What?'

'Nothing... it's just.' I paused and shrugged, sighing. 'Are you...'

Rayne glared at me, knowing what was coming out of my mouth next. 'Am I sure it wasn't Christopher?'

I nodded sheepishly, avoiding her eyes.

'Yeah,' she muttered back, determined. 'I know it wasn't him.'

I wanted to fight this, knowing Nat was going to be okay, knowing the case was closed, the papers were spread with Christopher's face all over it, my sister in there too, everything was finished, done, no more searching.

'I'm sorry, I know that's not something you want to hear,' Rayne said back to me, looking me in the eyes. 'But I know what I heard, I know what I saw...'

She looked towards the television, but her eyes glazed, and I quickly shot up to grab her attention, anything away from what she experienced that night. We discussed it here and there, but she would quickly shut down, and rub her new tattoo with a rough grip, she was ashamed, guilted by the thought of abandoning herself and doing something so reckless, but I knew it was out of love, she just got so caught up in all of what had happened. I knew it was going to take time for her to heal, Detective Rodgers even introduced the idea of therapy when she was back in Florida, Rayne was hesitant, but with a little bit of soothing by myself, she'd agreed to the idea.

She was going to go home to a place she dreaded, be on a good behavioural bond, and work her way out of being held captive in a state she loathed, I didn't fancy her situation, at all.

'Rayne, it's okay,' I said, ruffling up her mullet. 'You're going to be alright. *We're* going to be alright.'

She looked into my eyes again and I melted under those brown orbs, she was still so battered and bruised over what had happened only nights ago, but she fell into my embrace again, sighing. 'Thank you, Juniper.'

And so we slept on her rough bed that night, in each other's arms, final hours ticked by, and I stayed wide awake, watching the red numbers, we had no strength or enough heartache to delve into each other's bodies, we simply just lay there, in silence, until I broke that silence and I kissed her on the head gingerly, she smiled.

'I love you to the moon and back, Rayne,' I whispered, closing my eyes.

'I love you too, Juniper,' she replied.

We said our final night time vows, and shared a chuckle about the plans we had when Rayne would return to Boston. As she lay there and spoke animatedly about her ideas, I felt my lips purse. I never thought I would meet the girl of my dreams in such absurd circumstances, as she spoke all I could do was reminisce on was the way we met; how we were brought together through such traumatic experiences, how strong we had become. All my life, I wished for a partner who would be so understanding, a normal relationship as some would say, but this relationship was not normal, there were negative and positive aspects of the way we matched, but I had to try my absolute best to focus on the positive part. For my life was only beginning with Rayne Holmes, our stories only starting to be written, our destinies tied together in such a difficult way. I was eager to have her return home to Boston, Massachusetts.

If she ever did.

To be continued.

www.ingramcontent.com/pod-product-compliance
Lightning Source LLC
Chambersburg PA
CBHW070153120726
47909CB00001B/98